# PORTER'S RUN

KEN GALLENDER

KEN GALLENDER
PORTER'S RUN

This is a work of fiction. Names, characters, incidents and places are products of the author's imagination. They are used fictitiously and are not to be construed as real. Any resemblance to actual events, locales, organizations, or person, living or dead, is entirely coincidental.



www.jerniganswar.com



Thanks go to Betty Dunaway Gallender whose devotion and collaboration help make this and subsequent books possible.

Special thanks go to Marie Downs for her extensive help in editing and making this book possible. Marie has been an invaluable contributor in this creation and her encouragement has been appreciated.

Thanks also go to my good friend Bill Downs for insights into directions the storyline took.

ISBN-13: 978-1500553968
ISBN-10: 1500553964

Library of Congress Control Number: 2014913270
CreateSpace Independent Publishing Platform
North Charleston, South Carolina

# BIOGRAPHY

Ken Gallender has always been able to spin a yarn. As all good Southerners do, Ken likes to "visit" with people putting them at their ease with his personality and subtle wit. Ken lives in Gulfport, MS, with his wife, dog, three grand dogs and two grand cats. He is an avid outdoorsman having spent countless days on his Grandfather's farm in the Louisiana Delta, walking turn rows, hunting and fishing. His great love for his family and country has guided his entire life. Ken's motto has always been "Family Comes First, Take Care of Family." His greatest fear is having his country descend into chaos at the hands of witless voters and corrupt politicians willing to take advantage of them.

# CHAPTER 1

Sergeant Porter Jones was tending his two mules when Private Chevalier found him.

"Sarge, your grandfather, I mean Captain Jones, wants you in the radio shack on the double."

"Sure, what's up?"

"He didn't say; he just sent a half dozen of us to look for you, so it must be important."

Porter double timed it to the radio shack. It really wasn't a shack; it was the old radio room at the former city police station.

When he got there, he found his grandfather with a devastated look on his face. "Porter, I've got some bad news. I just got off the radio with Charlie Cross. One of his boys rode up this morning with a sick girl who had wandered across the river. It was about an hour before I reached them to warn them about the plague. Charlie's whole family has been exposed with the exception of Sandy and Ally. The girls had ridden down to the lodge on John's old mule to check on it. Charlie was able to wave them off before they got back to the house."

"I'll pack up and head back."

"Porter, we are under standing orders to stay in place for six weeks; you can't go anywhere."

Porter answered, "I don't see how y'all are going to stop me."

Cooney Jones had seen that look before and knew that there wasn't a man on Earth who could stop him from leaving. "At least let me notify our commander that you will be heading out."

As Porter watched, his grandfather got on the radio to Dix Jernigan. When Dix answered, Cooney said, "Major, we have a situation."

"What's up now, Captain Jones?"

"I just got word from one of my guys in West Texas. My grandson, Sergeant Porter Jones, has a girlfriend out there; they've been staying with Charlie Cross and his family. They may have a plague victim in their house. Porter's girlfriend and her little sister have not been exposed and are holed up in a hunting lodge about five miles down the road. Porter needs to go save them, and I would like to get your permission for him to go. Otherwise, he will just go AWOL and go anyway."

Dix interrupted him, "Is that the tough, skinny, son of a bitch that cut off my little toe?"

Cooney answered, "That's him."

"I ought to have you put him in irons to keep him from going, but if it were my wife, there is nothing on Earth that would keep me from heading out. Can you explain to him in great detail what he's got to do to keep from getting exposed and spreading the plague or dying?"

Cooney replied, "I think so, I appreciate you not locking him up."

Dix was cursing under his breath, "Do you understand why I don't like being in command? I haven't been back in charge for an entire day, and I'm already contradicting my own orders.

There are some battles you just can't win. Bottling him up isn't an option, I just hope he doesn't get his ass infected or killed. I kind of got attached to him after he patched me up. Thinking back, I don't know what was worse, getting shot and blown up, or being dragged back to town on those bouncing bamboo poles, behind a mule with bad gas. Tell him I expect his first male offspring to be named after me; otherwise, I'm locking him up for the next six weeks. I also want him to serve as our eyes in the field. There is only one way we are going to find out what's going on out there. Send a radio with him, so we can get back some sort of reports. It's going to take him weeks to get back on horseback. Let me know when he gets away; outfit him the best you can; he will probably have to live off the land."

Cooney laughed. "Thanks, I owe you one chief." Cooney looked over at Porter. "You heard the man, you can go, but you have to realize that you are going into a land of death. The Chinese and communists will be the least of your worries. You will not only be going to rescue the girls, but you will be our eyes and ears on the ground. I'm sending a radio with you; you'll have to check in every few days and let us know what you are seeing. I suggest you spend the rest of the day getting your gear together. Figure on about two months in the saddle. Let me know how much food you have and how much you'll need."

Porter, in his typical subdued manner, said, "I'll be ready as soon as I can cook up some hard tack or tortillas. I'll need some corn meal to make some corn chips and some beans if we have any. I've got plenty of ammo for my AK47 and pistol, but I can use some .308 if you have any extra."

"Make me a list of what you can't scrounge up, Porter. I can't promise anything, but I'll try to fill it. You may have to make do with Chinese rations; we have a ton of those."

Porter brightened up. "Those would be great; they're sealed and taste pretty good."

The battle that had taken place against the Chinese invaders and their communist allies had taken a toll on the patriots' men and equipment. A great deal of what they had was captured from the enemy. The societal collapse that preceded the invasion had pretty much emptied the cities, and there wasn't anyone alive who hadn't lost some or most of their family and friends. Dix Jernigan had lost his entire family and wound up fighting a one man battle against the communists; against all odds, he survived. He joined forces with the new Constitution army and helped form militias who held the invading Chinese army at bay.

Dix walked out on the deck of the catamaran and looked down the lake. The weather was warming up, and with it would come the delightful swarms of mosquitoes. He was still hurting and weak. The bullet wound through his leg was healed but hurt like the devil when he tried to walk on it. He plopped down in a cloth camp chair and pondered his predicament. For the time being, he wasn't being shot at or trying to shoot anyone. He had plenty of food and water, and there was nothing to do, but sit and think; that was bad. It was times like this that he missed his family horribly. The two half grown Catahoula pups lounging on the back of the boat perked up their ears when they heard a paddle bump the side of old man Beagle Boyer's boat. Beagle was about four-hundred yards down the lake slowly paddling his way back to the houseboats.

Rachael Johnson called from her houseboat, "Breakfast will be ready in about thirty minutes." Rachel's boat was the biggest of the three and was securely anchored in the middle. Dix's catamaran was tied up on the east side, and Beagle's houseboat was on the opposite side; the three formed a floating island out in the middle of the lake, so that no one could just walk up to the boats and knock. The last thing they needed was someone sick with the plague to pay them a visit. The bad part was someone could shoot at them from the bank, and they would have nowhere to retreat. They would be sitting ducks. There were still thieves, communists and displaced Chinese troops roaming the countryside looking for what they could steal. They would be getting very desperate, spreading the plague and killing whoever got in the way. The next project would have to be fortifying their boats to make them harder targets.

Since it was late April, the water was warming up. Two eyes and a snout appeared in the water about fifty yards in front of the catamaran. The tip of the big gator's tail broke the surface as the big lizard slowly cruised at an angle toward the boat. Dix reached for the old Springfield rifle and put the crosshairs between the two eyes and squeezed. The old rifle bounced and pieces of the gator's head plopped across the water. The carcass floated at the surface long enough for Beagle to paddle the aluminum boat over to it. He got a rope on it and paddled over to the catamaran.

"I've been hoping to get that one. I think he's the one that got my dog Barney last year, so I've been gunning for him. We'll have some boots and belt leather off this one. I'll show Rachel how to cook gator."

Dix laughed. "We'll tie him up to my big fishing boat, take him to shore and pull him up on the bank with the four wheeler where we can skin and clean him."

Rachel called from her boat, "Breakfast first, you boys come get it while it's hot." They sat down at the table. Rachel had cooked some pan fried corn cakes, scrambled powdered eggs, and some pork chops from a pig Beagle had shot the week before. The rest of the pig was smoking inside of an old upright freezer that was now a makeshift smoke house. When Dix got back on his feet again, the plans were to build a real smoke house. Things were quiet on the lake, too quiet. This made Dix Jernigan nervous.

# CHAPTER 2

Captain Cooney Jones helped his grandson prepare for the journey. The evening before the journey was to begin they studied a map of the proposed route. The only dangerous river crossing was the Red River where it snaked its way down through the middle of Louisiana. On the trip a couple of months earlier, Porter and Daniels Devils crossed with the help of a local who carried their gear across in a boat. Roger Daniels, leader of the Devils, was there at the map table. He was missing most of his ring finger on his right hand and had a new part in his hair just above the ear--mementos of the last battle with the Chinese. Every bridge with the exception of the Mississippi River Bridge at Natchez had been blown. Some were repairable; others would have to be replaced if civilization ever recovered. The wart hogs had pretty much destroyed everything on the Red River with the exception of the bridge at Natchitoches.

Daniels leaned over the map and pointed out all the blown bridges. "Our guys damaged the on ramp of the Natchitoches Bridge so that no vehicular traffic could cross. We had two snipers that pretty much locked it down. I think we can repair it enough that you and your mules can get across easily."

Porter grinned. "I was a little worried about swimming it with the mules again, that last time across had me a little worried."

Cooney smiled across at Porter. "I didn't think anything worried you, son."

"Well, usually I get worried when I've had a little time to think about it. When it's taking place, I've found there's not a lot of time to worry. Things happen too fast."

Cooney agreed, "That's pretty much the way it goes. When the bullets start flying, whatever you planned pretty much goes out the window. Feed and water your animals good tonight; tomorrow will be a long day."

About that time Doc Brown showed up. Doc Brown, a retired general practitioner, was now the only doctor, vet, surgeon, dentist and barber around. Doc had been a big city doctor working at a University Hospital for most of his life. He had moved back home to the Louisiana Delta to live the life of a country doctor before the collapse hit. He had a couple of young ladies in training who would be taking over his duties one day. Doc Brown spent an hour explaining to Porter what the plague was and how it was spread. Porter realized he could have no contact of any kind with anybody or anything they may have been handling. That meant no scavenging unless he was wearing rubber gloves and had some way of disinfecting anything he found.

That night he ate a good country meal. A couple of the local widow ladies cooked a good old fashioned supper for him. The hot cornbread and red beans and rice were great. Where they found sausage was anyone's guess. Pecan pie and a glass of milk polished it off. Someone had managed to save a milk cow in all the carnage--life goes on.

The next morning Porter was up before dawn. He sacked up the hard tack, biscuits and corn bread while eating a handful of the Chinese cookies for breakfast. Cooney came clomping into the barn carrying eight boxes of .308 bullets. The radio man was right behind him with a portable ham radio, a spool of wire and a small solar battery charger. Porter soon had the mules saddled and the packs loaded. He took a canvas tarp that would also serve as his tent cover and had it secured across the pack on Ruth. He led the mules out of the barn. Ruth, dutifully, fell in behind Ole Dollar.

Cooney asked, "Don't you have to tie her to the saddle ring?"

"No, she came untied one day and just loyally followed. I really haven't bothered tying her since. She knows her job. She and Ole Dollar pretty much read my mind. I think slipping them a biscuit with some syrup every now and then helps. They enjoy the Chinese cookies as much as I do."

Cooney pulled the crutches out from under his arms and gripped them in one hand. With his free hand he grabbed his grandson and gave him a tremendous hug, as tears burst from his eyes. He whispered, "I wish I could go with you but this damned broke leg would only get us both killed."

Porter couldn't speak; he just nodded, because some feelings can only be expressed with a look.

About that time Daniels and a couple of the surviving members of Daniels Devils came driving up in a truck pulling a large stock trailer. "We can shave a couple of days off your trip and drive you as far as the Red River Bridge."

Porter was all smiles. He hadn't anticipated this stroke of luck. That would save two days of wear and tear on him and the animals. They were under strict orders to not come in contact with anyone. If the plague was to be contained, there could be no personal contact between people. If Daniels or his men made contact, they were to remain away from base for six full weeks. The trip was uneventful. Porter rode in the back of the truck where he could keep an eye on his mules. They passed several bodies on the side of the road. There was no way of knowing if they were dead from disease or fighting. They picked their way around disabled vehicles and debris and finally got to the bridge. Since this was all open farm country, he was glad he wasn't riding the mules. He would have been exposed to sniper fire from any direction and would never be able to pinpoint where the shots came from. They unloaded the mules, and after hearty handshakes, Porter headed across the bridge. Daniels and his men quickly took down the temporary repairs and left the bridge once again impassable.

The bridge seemed a hundred miles long as Porter and the mules made their way across. Ole Dollar's head bobbed up and down, and he shook it once when some flies found his nose and ears. Porter had the AK47 slung across his chest. His faithful Kbar knife was on his belt, and his pistol was in his shoulder holster. A small .38 pocket pistol was in his vest pocket, and a British commando knife was in a sheath strapped to his ankle. These last two were added in case he became separated from his gear. He didn't like traveling down the road; he much preferred traveling cross country by compass. On the road he could be seen for miles. He hoped that the war and now the plague had forced the bad guys into hiding. There was also a strong likelihood that he would run into Chinese troops. The hair on the back of his neck stood on edge as he continued down the road. He was in the habit of traveling an hour or so and then stopping to let the animals rest. Around lunch as he was approaching a small bridge, a lone man walked out and stood in the middle of the road blocking their path. Porter quickly looked around and realized he was boxed in. His left hand had been resting in his vest pocket, and he secured his grip around the handle of the revolver.

The man in the road called out, "Boy we got you surrounded; you can chunk down your weapons and walk away or die. The choice is yours."

The others came out of hiding. Porter could see that one of them was sick and simply said, "Don't come any closer. I am Sergeant Porter Jones with the Constitution army. I can and will kill you."

The one on the bridge started walking forward. "Is that supposed to scare us? We don't recognize no damn Constitution army. I said get your a...."

He never finished his sentence. Porter shot through his vest pocket hitting the man almost center chest with the .38 bullet from the revolver he was holding. He didn't wait to see what effect the bullet made but rolled off Ole Dollar with his AK47 blazing. The three men and one woman who were covering him fired wild. Old Dollar and Ruth bolted across the bridge as Porter hosed the highwaymen with the AK on full automatic. Three of them went down, and the fourth jumped into the ditch on the other side of the road. Porter exchanged the magazine in his AK for a fresh one from the pouch that rode on his back. Blood was running down the side of his head from a scalp wound.

Porter called out, "You want to play this out, or do you want to come out of that ditch empty handed?"

The man answered, "I'm hit."

"I figured that; can you move? If I come over there, it's not going to be good for you."

The man crawled out of the ditch. He moved to a sitting position cradling his left arm.

The man was hit in the arm, and a bullet had passed through the skin on his neck. He was bleeding, but Porter knew that any contact would mean death from the plague. "What can I expect if I continue down this road?"

The man looked at Porter. "Aren't you going to help me?"

"Answer my question. What will I run into down this road?"

"There is another group about ten miles down the road at the next bridge. We stop people coming in both directions and get what we need."

Porter glanced down the road and looked back the man. "How long since y'all started getting sick?"

"It started about a week ago; aren't you going to help me?"

"It might not seem like it, but I am going to help you."

Porter shot him through the head with the AK and reloaded his pocket revolver. He walked down the road, across the bridge and found Ole Dollar and Ruth grazing on the side of the road. He felt around and discovered a small hole in his scalp. It must have been a ricochet or piece of gravel from a ricochet. He rubbed some antibiotic cream in the hole and left it open to dry out and heal. He checked out the two mules; they were none the worse for wear. A bullet had hit the pack, but it only passed through the frame above Ruth's back. He could mend his tarp once he stopped for the night. He reloaded his spent magazine, replaced it in his magazine pouch and then pulled out his map to determine his exact location. The last thing he wanted was another shootout, so he needed to determine a route that would let him avoid the next bridge. He elected to go cross country. He found a gap in a fence and took a compass heading that would take him in the right direction. This would lead him through overgrown fields and past homesteads. He would have to stop and cut fences with his bolt cutters. It would take longer but his odds of ambush would fall to near zero. He was lucky the highway men hadn't shot him rather than just trying to rob him. He tried not to ponder if they were good or bad for not killing him on sight. If they had asked for help, he would have probably given them some food, but it really didn't matter one way or the other. They were infected and would have been dead in a matter of days or weeks.

Porter climbed back into the saddle and headed down a turn row, crossed a shallow ditch and slowly made his way across a huge cornfield that sat unharvested. Most of the corn, having been picked by people and scavenged by animals, was gone. He stopped and removed the bridle from Ole Dollar, and let him and Ruth eat some of the corn that they found still in the shucks out in the middle of the field. He was careful to not let them overeat. They finished the day moving slowly from field to field, and that night made camp in a small corpse of woods next to a bayou. He set up the radio and was soon talking to his grandfather.

Cooney Jones asked, "How are you making it son, any trouble?"

"Nothing I couldn't handle. I figure I made about twenty miles. Since I am traveling cross country, the going is slow."

"Have you run across anyone with the plague?"

"Just one group; they were all sick. I didn't get close enough to get infected. So that you will know, they were within ten miles of the Red River Bridge. I would post a team there to stop anyone trying to cross at that point."

"That's a good idea. I'll get someone on it immediately. Call back in a couple of days. Good luck, son."

Porter rolled up his antenna wire and turned off the radio. He built a small fire and hung up his hammock with the mosquito netting. He didn't bother with the tarp as there was no indication of rain. The mosquitoes weren't bad yet, but they would be a nuisance once it got a little warmer. The cool evenings would keep them somewhat at bay for a while. The hobbled mules, which were close by, were still full from eating the corn. The bayou full of water was near, so they wouldn't wander far, if at all. Porter sat gazing into the small fire. Off in the distance, he heard some gunfire, and his thoughts drifted back to his home in Los Angeles. He could still see in his mind's eye his little brother lying dead across his mother's still body. He checked his father's watch on his arm and dozed. Tomorrow would have to take care of itself, because for now, he was tired.

# CHAPTER 3

Dix was disturbed from his slumber by the crackling of his radio.

He keyed the mic, "This is Jernigan, what's up?"

Cooney answered, "I got our first report from Porter. Looks like he ran across some plague victims on the west side of the Red River. I have a team guarding the bridge and the pipeline bridge next to it."

"Did that boy run into any trouble yet?"

"He said it wasn't anything he couldn't handle. What that means in Porter speak is: All hell broke loose, but he prevailed."

"How is everything on your side of the river?"

"I haven't heard anything out of Butch Erwin since he dropped me off. Have him radio me for an update."

"No need," Butch chimed in on the radio, "I've been monitoring the frequency. There's been some boat traffic on the Mississippi River. None of it has stopped at Natchez or Vidalia. I think it's Chinese. Evidently, they are trying to contain the plague within their ranks. Their offensive activity has almost completely ceased. They are sure to have some outlying patrols or bases that were not stricken."

"Keep me posted; as far as I'm concerned, the battle is far from over. Cooney, check with Doc Brown and find out how we can spread the disease to their bases. I don't mind practicing a little germ warfare if we have the opportunity."

Cooney was quiet for a moment. "I remember stories of the Indians being given smallpox infected blankets in order to kill off villages; maybe we could infect tobacco, or whiskey bottles."

Dix chimed back in, "Have Doc set up several of the empty houses around town where we can direct potential victims. We need a place to isolate them, and it could very well be a place to collect contaminated clothing, bedding, etc. Maybe we could cushion a case of whiskey with contaminated bedding cut into strips that we can leave for them to find or deposit in their camps. Do we have any way of making a hazmat suit so we won't get infected baiting our trap? Cooney, get Doc Brown working on it. In the meantime Butch, I want someone with a radio watching the river. Do we still have any Warthogs operational from the airport at Natchez?"

Butch thought a minute. "They have two fully operational and two more if we can get parts delivered."

"The next time you spot a boat load of them heading up or down the river, do you think we can order a strike? Cooney, get word to Colonel Miller and find out what they want us to do. I say we keep killing and shooting at them until they are all dead or packed up and gone. We will never be able to take the fight to them, but we can make sure they never come back. Meanwhile, they have had to go to ground and ride out this epidemic just like we have. We need to locate them."

Butch piped in, "The boats are about seventy-five feet long. Large enough to be ocean going, but small enough to go around the mess you left in the river at New Orleans. There is no set time of day that they come through."

"Try to find out how many there are. There may be only two or three. See if they are loaded heading north or south. They could be hauling out what they have been stealing."

Dix sat back in his chair and mused to himself, "I hate giving orders and orchestrating this stuff. I would rather be in my boat or out on my four wheeler tending to business."

Rachel walked across the plank to the catamaran from her houseboat with a mug of coffee.

"I figured you were ready for some coffee. I can see you've got yourself all worked up again."

"How do you figure that?"

"Well for one thing you're muttering to yourself and shaking your head no."

"Am I that transparent?"

"I see through you like a glass full of water. You're not happy unless you're doing something. The last time I saw you happy was when you got back from cleaning up Natchez. We've got to figure out a way to keep you from getting killed while organizing the resistance."

"I'm not planning on getting killed."

"Oh sure, tell that to your little toe."

At that moment the Catahoulas, while looking down the lake, started barking. Off in the distance a small boat was slowly making its way down the lake.

Dix reached for the Springfield rifle and turned to Rachel. "Holler at Beagle and tell him we got company."

Dix put the scope on the boat and the man operating it. A grizzled man with a substantial beard was running the boat. The beard was braided and tied neatly out of the way. He wore a straw cowboy hat with the edges turned up, and a ponytail hung out from under it. There were tattoos on his forearms. A rifle was leaning up on the boat rail within his reach.

When he was within fifty yards, he killed the motor and called out, "I'm looking for Dix Jernigan."

Dix was somewhat perplexed. "Who's looking for him?"

Dix turned and whispered to Rachel, "Where's Beagle, tell him to get his gun, look around behind us and make sure this isn't a distraction. Get your gun and keep it handy."

The man stood up; he was wearing what appeared to be a Colt 1911 in a holster at his waist. The camo outfit he was wearing was almost faded to a dull olive drab. "I'm Euniper White from Florida. Everyone calls me Fox. My friends call me Fox after the revolutionary war hero nicknamed the Swamp Fox. I've been fighting the damn communists and Chinese for the last six months. I spent some time with a private in the Constitution army named Jacobs. He was on a boat transporting some troops across the Pearl River. I camped with them on a sandbar one night."

Dix said, "If you know Jacobs, then you must realize that I will not hesitate to ventilate you between sips of coffee."

"That's why I am standing here where you can easily kill me."

"Tell me about Jacobs. How's his leg healing up?"

"His leg was just fine, but his shoulder was still bothering him."

" At least I know that you knew Jacobs. Paddle on up, but stay in your boat. Have you heard about the plague?"

"What plague are you talking about? I've been hiding out and camping back in the swamp and backwater for a month. Jacobs told me where to find you if I made it this far."

"Well Fox, until you can go another couple of weeks with no symptoms, I can't invite you aboard. The plague is a super bad version of smallpox. If you get it, you won't survive. There are some empty camps up the lake that should be a little more comfortable than that boat. Beagle, which one can he use?"

From out of sight on the top of Rachel's boat he answered, "There are two more houseboats that are in decent shape. I say let him stay in the blue one; it still has a working gas stove. He'll have to work on the water and batteries."

Dix glanced back at Fox. "If I had missed you, Beagle wouldn't have. How's your food?"

"I'm good on food; I'll try to catch some fish tomorrow."

"There's no need unless you just want to go fishing. We have a fish cage with a dozen or so river cat ready to clean. If I were you, I would untie the house boat, take it out in the lake and anchor it up. In the event you don't have the plague, you don't want somebody knocking on your door that does."

"What happens if I have the plague?"

"That problem will take care of itself unless you want me to speed up the process."

Fox quit grinning once he realized that Dix wasn't kidding. "Jacobs said you would do whatever it took without hesitation and without remorse."

"I think he summed me up pretty well. What is it you want from me?"

"I want to do the same thing you've been doing. They pretty much wiped out my family and everyone I know. I need a base to operate from and someone to point me in the right direction. I have an old six horse Mercury that will go a long way on a gallon of gas and a rifle I can hit with."

Dix looked down at Fox. "I have one question, 'What do you have to live for?'"

Fox pondered the question for a minute. "Not one damned thing; I've lost every person and thing that mattered to those bastards."

"I think we can use you. Do you want to join the Constitution army? There is no pay and you are in the army until you die, and I can't even guarantee you will eat regularly."

"Sign me up; where's my uniform?"

"You're in it. Get your camp moved and get comfortable. I'll have plenty to keep us busy in a few days."

"Who is my commanding officer?"

"I'm Major Dix Jernigan; we answer to Colonel Miller. You're Private White. You'll answer to Captain Butch Erwin in Ferriday and Captain Cooney Jones over in Jonesville, and none of us get paid. If you don't have the plague, you are going to be busy."

Captain Butch Erwin was sitting on the levee on the Vidalia side of the river. A loaded boat was heading north fighting the river's current. Its powerful engines were straining as the vessel made its way up stream. Through his rifle scope he could see that the men on board were all in uniform, and a few were packing AK47 assault rifles. After cranking up the magnification on his scope to 12 power, he could see the men clearly. They were Chinese troops heading north. He keyed the mic and reported while writing down the boat's colors, symbols and numbers.

# CHAPTER 4

Porter woke before daylight and ate a breakfast of cold biscuits. Ole Dollar and Ruth never left the campsite during the night. He saddled up, skirted the bayou for several miles and turned west when they found a farm road that crossed the bayou. The huge cypress trees lining the banks and standing in the water were probably growing when Columbus landed centuries earlier. The road crossing the bayou was put in by the local farmer to access the fields on the opposite side. A large culvert was dropped in the middle with dirt dumped in the bayou forming a road. It was wide enough for a large tractor with implements. There was a distinct trail in the dirt road where men and animals had been crossing. The grass and weeds in the road were at least knee deep with the path worn down to dust in the middle. Ole Dollar and Ruth plodded along with a little puff of dust produced under each hoof as it sat down on the path. Porter looked close but saw no human footprints. The next field he entered was a cotton field. The stalks were still there with rotting cotton hanging in their boles. A few of the boles were starting to sprout as the cotton seeds were coming to life. They climbed out of the bottom where the bayou ran and stopped on the crest of the hill. The field was at least 300 acres. It was bordered by fence rows of small trees and brush. He could see a road in the distance and the telephone poles that followed it. A hawk was sailing far overhead, oblivious to the human tragedy that was unfolding in the countryside below. Porter pulled out his binoculars and carefully surveyed the countryside and the road. On the far side of the road sat a farm house. It had a chimney and a stove pipe hanging out of a window but there was no smoke or sign of habitation. He didn't have to goose Ole Dollar; all he had to do was say, "Let's go." They slowly crossed the field with Ruth dutifully following. Crossing the road they came to an opened gate and proceeded down the drive towards the farm house. Since the driveway was heading west, Porter took the chance and headed down it. When he got to the house, he realized that it was occupied. Its owner was sitting under the carport in a lawn chair.

The old man looked up and said, "Stay back; I'm sick. I don't know what I've got, but it's killed everyone in my family."

"Thanks for the warning. I'm Porter Jones with the Constitution army. I'm traveling to Texas and reporting what I find on the way. Are there any Chinese that you know of or bandits I need to look out for?"

"The bandits are running the roads. The Chinese quit advancing and have retreated; to where I have no idea. I think they have the same sickness I've got." The man's eyes were sunk deep in his head and his skin was ashen. There were several pustules on his face, and Porter could see wet spots on his shirt where the ones on his body were leaking. A shiver went up his spine as he watched the man try to move. Porter told him that he had small pox and that they thought it was a biological weapon that got out of hand.

"I can't help you; I can toss you some water or something, but I can't come any closer."

"No need, son. This should be over pretty soon. See that big old oak tree there in the yard?"

"Yes, sir."

"There is a cache of food, gear and weapons that I won't be using buried directly under the tire swing. Because it's been there for about a year, it is not contaminated. It's yours if you need it."

"Thanks."

They sat gazing at each other a moment. The man slowly relaxed, slid to the ground and took his last breath as Porter watched. After seeing the shape the man was in, he no longer carried any remorse for finishing off the bandit, back at the bridge. He pulled out his map and determined his location. He rode out to the mailbox and jotted down the number so he could find the house should he need to come back. He thought about digging up the cache but decided not to take the chance. He was well stocked with food for now, and he wouldn't be adding or swapping weapons. Thinking this may be a good place to retreat to in an emergency, he filed it away in his mind and moved on. The driveway had a fork leading around the house and out to a farm building in the back. Porter passed several fresh graves in a pecan orchard and continued into the cotton fields beyond. The old man at one time had had a really nice farm. The mules plodded along until they came to a ditch. They followed it until they came to a place to cross and continued on. The rest of the day was uneventful. When he stopped for the evening, he was on the banks of Toledo Bend Reservoir. He remembered his dad telling him about a fishing trip with his Grandpa Cooney up here. He wished he and his dad could have gone fishing, but his mother and grandmother would have pitched a fit. They would have nothing to do with hunting, fishing or camping. They felt that it was the past time of rednecks and backwoods people. He thought *what would they think now?*

The reservoir was lined with camps; all were abandoned. He resisted the urge to sleep indoors, because there was no way of knowing if there was contagion from sick people and besides it would be difficult for someone to sneak up on him if he were outside. He gathered up wood and debris from the lake bank and soon had a fire going. He propped up some plywood to block the fire from being seen across the water. There was plenty of grass, so he let Old Dollar and Ruth loose in the fenced yard. He carried up a couple of buckets of water from the lake and popped open a can of beans that he had scrounged up before he left Jonesville. There was no need to heat the beans because they were still warm from the sun shining on Ruth's pack. He looked at the map in the waning hours of daylight. He would have to head south following the shore line until he could cross at the levee. The levee would be a dangerous place. He would be out in the open, and it was a natural choke point. Unless he was willing to cross the Sabine River, the levee road was it. He set up his radio and soon had his grandfather on the line.

"How you making it, son?" Cooney called.

"I'm doing fine; found some more plague victims, but they are all dead. I stayed at least twenty feet away and didn't leave the saddle. Do we have any Constitution troops manning or near the Toledo Bend levee road? I'm crossing the Sabine River there tomorrow. I was wondering what to expect."

"I'll have an answer for you soon." Cooney left the frequency. Porter finished his beans and poked at the fire while he waited. About ten minutes later the radio crackled, and Cooney said, "Porter, you there?"

"Yes, sir, I can hear you."

"You're in luck. We have a guard stopping all traffic on the Louisiana side. You will need to tell them who you are. They'll be expecting you; remember no personal contact. Whoever's in charge will probably want to question you. Remember no handshaking or exchanging anything. Stay outdoors in the sunshine if possible and take no chances."

"Have you heard anything from Charlie Cross?"

"Sorry, not a word. I told them you're on your way when I spoke to them after you left. They're not sure if the girl has the plague. She's running a fever and has a rash. I don't know what they are doing, but I'm certain that Charlie is not sitting still waiting for the end to come. He'll fight till he's dead."

"I'm not sure what time I'll get there. I'm leaving as soon as it's light enough to see. I'm camped in the backyard of a camp on Toledo Bend. It's not the ideal spot; I can't check out the houses. There's a lot of grass for the mules and plenty of water. I figure the mules will cut up some if anyone tries to sneak up."

"Be careful; douse your fire early and look for any fires or lights in any of the houses within shooting range."

"I'll have the guys radio you back when I pass tomorrow, Porter out."

"Goodnight, son."

Porter retrieved a fresh bucket of water and warmed it next to the fire. He disrobed and gave himself a good scrub and doused the fire with the leftover water. He set up his hammock between two oak trees growing about twenty feet from the water. He looked out in the darkness. The only light he could see was a fire off in the distance across the reservoir. He couldn't judge the distance; it could have been a boat on fire. He tried to look through his binoculars but couldn't tell what he was looking at. A light fog was forming on the water. It was just as well, the fire was as good as a million miles away for all it mattered.

Sometime in the night he woke. He wasn't sure what woke him, maybe it was a bird or fish splashing. Ruth and Dollar got to their feet; both had been lying down. Then he heard the barking, and a pack of wild dogs appeared on the other side of the fence. They were safe for the moment. He unzipped the mosquito netting from the roof canvas of his hammock. Using his flashlight, he shined the beam towards the dogs. Nervously, Ole Dollar and Ruth retreated to the opposite side of the yard behind him. A pack of at least a dozen or more dogs were all lined up at the fence. Over half were pit bulls. The rest were a mixture of other breeds, former pets, all large. A big pit hit the fence with his square chest but bounced back. A large shepherd mix almost made it over the top of the six foot fence. It wasn't until they started digging did Porter become really concerned. He grabbed a half brick from around a flower bed, hurled it at the fence and yelled. That only seemed to enrage them. One of the pits snapped and bit the chain link fence and tried to pull it down.

Porter thought *if I don't do something now, they will be trailing me tomorrow. I can shoot better standing than from horseback tomorrow.* He flipped the AK on full auto and ran a full thirty round magazine full of ammo through the pack. When it was over, there were at least eight dead dogs within sight of the flashlight. All the others were gone. The big pit still had the fence in his death grip. He had expended two of his eighteen magazines. He replaced them from his pack and checked the time. It was two a.m.; he wouldn't get much sleep tonight, and he dared not head out before daylight. He had made a lot of noise. Everyone within miles would know he was here. They would also know he was armed to the teeth. He gave Ruth and Dollar each a square of corn bread to calm them a little; they knew they had been on the menu. He climbed back in the hammock and lamented expending another magazine. At this rate of fire he would be knife fighting before he got halfway back to the ranch. As he lay dosing, he was glad that this happened in a controlled setting rather than out on the trail. The closer he got to the ranch the safer he would be. He had several hundred miles of formerly high population areas to travel though. Somewhere off in the distance he could hear dogs howling, and he thought *last year this time I was afraid of the dark and to camp overnight.*

# CHAPTER 5

The dogs started barking when Captain Butch Erwin drove over the levee, hopped in an old green aluminum boat and paddled out to Dix's catamaran. He stopped about twenty feet away.

Dix looked up and grinned. "It must be something important; are you out of tobacco already?"

Butch laughed. "Tobacco stash is still good. I didn't want to get on the radio in case they had some way of listening. I got a good look at one of the boats. It looks like they are Chinese heading north. Not sure if they have something up their sleeve, or if they are evacuating healthy troops to an encampment somewhere. I've got a man sitting on the river making note of the comings and goings."

"Do you think we can follow at a distance without getting killed? I want to paint my white boat camo and use it as a chase boat. Do you think you can find me some green, tan, and brown paint? Also, I have you a new recruit. He's moving a houseboat from up the lake at this moment. His name is Fox White. I can't pronounce his given name. I have him quarantined for two weeks. He looks healthy, and he says he has been hiding for the past month. Jacobs sent him up here. If Jacobs is still alive, verify our new recruit."

Butch nodded. "We should be able to follow the boats with no trouble. We can hang back about a half mile. I doubt they would even see us. No problem with the paint. I have enough of what's left in my shop to cover it. I'll get it over here tomorrow. I should also have verification from Jacobs if he's still alive."

"There are some fish in the box if you need any. Beagle has a gator in the smoke box that will be ready in a few days. We killed a big one yesterday."

"Thanks, I'll grab three or four fish for supper."

"Hopefully, your men will have us a count on the number of boats and what their schedule is in a few days. Also, do we have a Barrett .50 cal in our arsenal? If we had one, we could probably stop one of the boats if we can scrounge up some armor piercing ammo. I would think a .50 cal or two through their engines may slow them up. But before we do that, I would like to find out where they are going."

"I'll be back tomorrow with the paint, brushes, rollers and word from Jacobs."

"Let me know if you find any sick people. The last thing we need is for any of us to get sick and die. I wonder if there are enough Americans left to re-populate the country."

Butch laughed. "We still have a number of young ladies; we are short quite a few young men, but I'm certain they'll figure something out."

"We just have to keep everyone apart long enough to let this plague burn out. Are we using encrypted radios to communicate? If so, give Captain Miller an update on our plans. Let me know about the Barrett .50 cal. I figure two more weeks of lying around, and I'll be able to get back in the field. Don't get the plague; that's an order!"

"The radios are supposed to be encrypted, but I don't know enough about the electronics to feel comfortable; CB radios maxed out my communication skills."

Dix watched him paddle across to the boat landing where Beagle had the fish box floating.

Rachel, who had been listening from the deck on her house-boat, smiled. "I heard what you said about re populating America. My clock is ticking over here if you can take a hint."

Turning red, Dix said, "Jesus Christ woman, I have a big enough burden on me with just keeping us alive and killing communists. I am just one man, and I'm missing body parts."

"I don't think losing a little toe is going to interfere with re-populating the continent."

"If you can hold off six or eight months, we'll revisit the topic. Too much has happened and too much is fixing to take place to put romance or children in the mix."

"Ok, Sampson, I'll give you a year. If you haven't whipped them by then, we are going to find a place to hide. There will be plenty of wilderness to choose from by then."

Dix nodded and ducked back in the cabin of the catamaran. The exchange left him muttering to himself, shaking his head no, and thinking *why me Lord, why me.*

He was still sore and healing from the last battle. The broken ribs were still tender and even though his loose tooth had firmed up in the socket, it was still sore when he tried to eat and touch it with his tongue. From his captain's chair at the helm, he could sit and look across the lake and see the levee. Fox White came into view pulling his houseboat with his old stump thumper boat. The little fiberglass boat with the six horse mercury looked tiny compared to the big houseboat. There was a bundle of concrete blocks sitting on the front deck of the house boat; next to them was a coil of rope. Once they were in position, about fifty feet from Dix's flotilla, Fox stopped and shoved the pile of blocks in the lake and left about twenty feet of slack on the rope. He had another bundle hanging on the opposite corner that he cut loose to anchor that side. Satisfied with the results, he tied off the stump thumper to the hand rail and plopped down in a lawn chair on the deck of his houseboat.

Dix walked out on the catamaran deck and called out, "How you feeling today, any symptoms yet?"

Fox looked up. "No, save your ammo; no need to finish me off yet."

Fox walked back into his houseboat and laid his old Marlin 30-30 out on the table. He rubbed it with an oil cloth before taking the dust cover off the old Bushnell scope. He checked the lens and sighted down the lake. This old rifle had taken countless deer over the years. It had been handed down to him from his father many years earlier. The leather sling was dark and worn from having been carried and handled for so long. Loops on it held ten cartridges. He had ten on the sling, seven in the gun and twenty more in an old green Remington box that was well worn from riding in his coat pocket. He had started out with about five-hundred rounds six or eight months earlier. He would have to find some more ammo soon, or he would have to start shooting the AK47 and ammo he had picked up from dead Chinese soldiers. He wasn't comfortable with the AK. He had shot the old Marlin his whole life and could shave a possum with it at a hundred yards.

Butch Erwin made it back the next day with the paint for Dix's fishing boat. "I hate to see you mess up that beautiful boat with all this camo paint."

Dix looked over at the boat tied to the catamaran. "Me too, but it will be the same boat. It'll run the same and serve the same purpose. The days of pretty boats are over for quite a while as far as I can see. Any word from Jacobs about Fox?"

"We got him on the radio, this morning. He is lying up recovering from another bullet wound. This one is in his leg. He said that our new recruit, Fox, saved their tails down on the Pearl River near the Gulf. A Chinese patrol boat had them cold, before Fox opened up from a hidden spot in the willows with that old 30-30. They lost a couple of their guys but would have lost everything if he hadn't showed up."

"Sounds like he might be a good man to have around in a fight."

Dix yelled out, "Hey Fox poke your head out; I got someone you need to meet."

Fox came out of the houseboat with his rifle in his hand. "What's up, Chief?"

"I want you to meet Captain Butch Erwin. Once we are sure you aren't going to contaminate anybody, you'll be spending some time with him. Hide your tobacco; it's liable to disappear."

"No worries about the tobacco, I ran out six or eight months ago."

Butch called out, "Glad to meet you. Is there anything you need?"

"Yep, I'm about out of 30-30 cartridges."

"Do you have anything to trade? I'm sure I can round some up. It just helps if I have something to trade."

"Sure, I have about a hundred hand grenades and an extra case of cartridges for an AK."

Dix reminded them, "No trading any items for twelve more days. Go ahead and line up the trade; just hold off until this plague burns itself out. It only takes one mistake to kill us all. How many boats so far, Butch?"

"It looks like we have six so far. Four boats have passed going north, and we haven't seen them return. But two different boats were heading south. Based on their estimated speed, we should be able to figure out where they're going. Captain Miller wants us to find out where they're going before we start sinking them.

We have a Barrett .50 cal and ammo on its way. They found some armor piercing rounds that weren't destroyed over at Fort Polk."

"That's some of the best news I've heard all day. How far apart are those boats? I'm afraid once we knock out one; the others will quit running."

"They have to come by here if they're heading north. Even if they stop running, it will be the same effect as our sinking them."

"That's a good point, Butch. The other thing they might do is drop off a couple of their best men to try and silence the gun. It's hard to be stealthy with one of those. Once you pull the trigger everyone within five miles will hear you, and they'll know we're within sight of the river. We'll have to have good men hidden up and down the levees to make sure we aren't ambushed."

"All we have left are good men. All the mediocre guys were killed off over the last six months."

"As soon as the first boat that we identified gets back down here let me know. I want to know how long it takes them to pass Natchez, drop a load and return. See if you can mark two spots, at least three-hundred yards apart on the opposite shore that we can see as they pass. By timing how fast they pass the marks we can compute their speed."

"Will do, Major," Butch saluted and waved off.

"You know I really hate all that military crap."

Dix spent the next three days painting his fishing boat. He pulled it out of the water onto an old boat trailer that had been abandoned at one of the camps. He was able to camo the entire boat with the exception of two strips on the very bottom where it rested on the trailer runners.

The next two days were spent hooking up the solar panels that were on the top of Rachel's house boat. Now all three boats had charged batteries and lights. The work had helped get Dix back on his feet.

He finally took a seat and called across to Fox who was still working on his house boat, "You still feeling good? Only one more week before I put you in the field."

"I can't wait. I like sleeping indoors; but I am ready to do something productive."

"Don't worry; we're going to be very busy real soon."

Dix, Rachel and Beagle had a good dinner on Rachel's boat. Rachel had a glass of wine from a local winery that Dix had liberated from the Natchez police. He and Beagle enjoyed a shot of bourbon.

Rachel could see that something was bothering Dix. "Can't you relax; something's eating at you?"

Dix poured himself another drink. "I feel like a sitting duck out here on these boats. A couple of men with rifles could do a number on us from the levee."

Beagle, who never said much, spoke up, "Unless the Chinese come sneaking in, there aren't a whole lot of people left to shoot at us."

"You're probably right. I've become so accustomed to looking over my shoulder; it is next to impossible for me to relax. I always sleep with one eye open. Make sure that y'all never come busting in on me or surprise me. Be very careful waking me up, I sleep with a pistol in my hand."

Rachel reached around her back and pulled out a Beretta that was tucked behind her belt. "We all do."

They gave each other knowing looks and Dix said, "I am going to stress that to Fox too. What's he doing for dinner?"

Beagle nodded toward Fox's boat. "He scrounged up a barbecue grill and has some of that gator cooking; it smells pretty dang good. I think he can teach me a thing or two about cooking it." With that Beagle got up and stretched. "This old cooter is hitting the sack; see y'all in the morning."

Dix grinned. "Lock your doors."

Beagle left and crossed over the planks to his boat. He could feel the boats rock as he crossed from one boat to the other.

Rachel gathered up the dishes, and Dix helped her wash and put them away.

Dix yawned. "Rachel, I am ready to hit the sack. Make sure you lock and latch the doors and keep that pistol close. I want the dogs to sleep in here between the entrance doors and the stairs down to your bedroom. That way you can sleep better; you know nothing on earth can get in or around them without them raising a ruckus."

"You know if you stayed over, I wouldn't be afraid at all," Rachel whispered as she put her arms around his neck, gave him a hug and a kiss that landed on the corner of his mouth.

"You're probably right; in fact, I know you are right, but I'm not quite finished. I was transformed from being a man into an animal that I never knew existed. It's going to take a little while longer before I can be a man again. It won't be long. I just want to kick the Chinese back into the ocean. Do you think you can hold off a little longer? If I live through what I have in mind, I believe we can deliver a death blow to the enemy in this part of the country."

"Ok, tough guy, I'm giving you one year. I know you can't fight with me home, barefoot and pregnant. With that she gave him a kiss that made him weak in the knees. "You know where you can find me when the time comes. ONE YEAR." She left him standing speechless as she disappeared down the steps to her room.

After letting in the dogs, he closed and locked the door; then crossed back over to his houseboat. A full moon was shining. He could see Fox's grill smoking and the aroma of the cooking gator smelled good.

"Fox, how you making it over there; you settled in yet?"

"I'm trying; but it ain't easy. Something has the hair on the back of my neck standing up."

"You hear or see anything?"

"No, Dix, it's just an uneasiness I can't explain."

"I've got it too. My dad always referred to it as the Zizzy Witch trying to tell you something. He said he had it during WWII and that his dad had it too. I'm sure it's just nonsense, probably because we are a little bit touched in the head."

Fox opened the lid on the cooker, forked out a piece of gator and some garlic wrapped in foil. The smell made its way across the water. "You know that Zizzy Witch you talk about has saved my hairy rear at least a half dozen times. I think we need to be on high alert the next few days. I am tempted to get in my stump thumper and hide in the willows to see if it goes away."

"Just so you know, I sleep fully clothed and ready to fight. Do not ever surprise me; I won't be taking time to do much thinking."

"Same here, old man, you get some rest. I'm going to lock down after eatin this gator."

Dix climbed into his bunk. The two shots of bourbon and the day of working on the boats had done their job, and he was soon asleep. He slept soundly for the next few hours, but then began to toss and turn. His ribs hurt; he couldn't get comfortable. It was times like these that his mind drifted back to his previous life.

The moon was bright outside; the light streamed through his porthole windows and the glass doors leading out onto the deck. He felt the boat rock ever so gently as though someone had climbed aboard. His first thought was that a big gar or a gator had bumped the boat. Then he felt it again. It was just the faintest little rock; the bumping could even be a log that had floated in the current created by the Mississippi River a couple of miles away. The lake was at one time the old river channel and still had outlets on either end that led out into the river.

No one could see where he lay, but he could see the shadows on the floor as the moon light streamed through the glass doors. Then he saw the shadow move and then another. He raised his hands over his head and found the Beretta 12 gauge shotgun on the rack where it rested. He quietly eased the safety off and slipped out of his bunk. He slid his feet into his shoes and silently tipped across the floor to where he could see around the corner. There were two men on the deck. One squatted in front of the door fiddling with the lock. It didn't take the man but a moment to get it opened. Dix didn't want to destroy the door by killing the bastards. At that moment, he heard the Catahoulas barking next door, and then Fox's rifle firing. Dix didn't hear the other shots because he blasted the two intruders back through the doorway. The short barreled shotgun belched flame across the room as the rounds of three inch buckshot devastated the men. They were both knocked off their feet and died on the spot. One of them emptied his automatic weapon in the air; his dying hand gripping the trigger in his death throws. He could hear the dogs barking, and then Beagle's AK47 came to life. Water splashed.

Dix crossed over to Rachel's and called out, "Rachel, are you ok?"

"I'm ok; they didn't get in."

"Stay put. Beagle, how about you?"

"I got mine. One on my boat and the three who were at Rachel's door. I've got an empty boat over here."

"Fox, how about you?"

"I got both of mine. My boat is shot up pretty bad, and there is a guy tied up in a skiff over here."

"Watch him. I've got to do some checking."

All was quiet; there was no noise to be heard on the lake. Dix checked the time, 4:30 a.m. The attack was timed for the time of day when the human body is programmed to be in its deepest sleep. If the dogs hadn't barked and the broken ribs hadn't been bothering him, they could have very well been killed in their sleep.

"I want everyone to just stay where they are. No lights; it will be daylight in an hour or so. Fox, find out who is in the boat. Don't come in contact with him and stay away from the bodies; they could be sick. We'll clean up our boats with some liquid bleach and some soap when we can see. Kick your shoes off before you go back in. Rachel, you stay in with the dogs."

"Don't worry; I'm not coming out."

Dix got on the radio to Butch Erwin. "Butch, we came under attack just now. I think it was some sort of commando raid. We killed all of them and nobody got hurt. The dogs warned us in time. I don't know if they came in from the river or over the levee, and I've got what appears to be a hostage tied up in a boat."

"I'll have the guys run a sweep of the levee. They probably came in from the north end of the river. I've got guys watching the river near the south end. We'll be there within thirty minutes. Stay put."

Dix sat fuming. *I knew things were too quiet.*

# CHAPTER 6

Porter was packed up before dawn ready to pull out as soon as it was light enough to see. The mules could see to walk just fine; but he couldn't see to shoot. He didn't know where the remaining dogs were, and he would be traveling through areas where there had once been a lot of dogs. It was only logical that dog packs would start filling the ecological niche of wolves. He would need to be mindful of that in his journey. He made good time, only running across a few scattered people who all appeared healthy. He told them about the plague and how to avoid it. These people were all living on the lake and eating what they caught; as a consequence, they were not trying to rob and kill travelers. He traveled through the Toledo Bend State Park. It was difficult to stay out of sight as all the roads and fences funneled him towards the spillway; so he kept his hand on the AK47 as he rode towards the checkpoint in the distance. When he was passing the engineering office on his right, he noted that it had been secured as an army post. Sandbags lined the building's walls and formed a wall around the sidewalk heading up to the door. Several soldiers stepped out and watched as he proceeded down the road to the checkpoint where he was stopped by the guards manning the road block.

Porter looked down at the two men and stated, "I'm Sergeant Porter Jones. You should be expecting me."

The shorter of the two looked up at him. "You don't look old enough to be out of the boy scouts; how do you figure you're a sergeant?"

Porter, accustomed to the reaction he was getting, smiled. "It wasn't my decision; Major Dix Jernigan made me a sergeant."

"I'm Corporal Sam Conway. We were told to expect you. Sergeant, if you'll follow me, Captain Lancaster would like to see you."

"Corporal, I don't mind talking to Captain Lancaster, but I am under orders not to get within spitting distance of anyone on this trip. That means I will only talk with the Captain or anyone else if we are outside. I will not be shaking hands or trading items. I've seen what this plague does to a man. I have no intention of catching or transmitting it."

"No problem, Sarge. Climb on down, and Private Johnson will take your stock."

"Corporal, I don't mean to be disrespectful; but you need to understand: None of you will touch my animals or equipment, and I will not touch anything of yours. There can be no contact whatsoever. And I will be staying out in the open air as well."

"The Captain isn't going to be happy; he likes to sit behind the big desk."

"Lead the way, Corporal; I'll follow you." Porter climbed off Old Dollar and led him as he walked behind the Corporal. The Corporal had a chaw of tobacco in his mouth and spit as they were walking. He led Dollar and Ruth around the spot being careful not to step in it.

The Corporal gave him a funny look. "Aren't you carrying this safety thing a little too far?"

"If you had seen what I've seen, you wouldn't think so."

When they got to the building, Corporal Conway went in while Porter waited out by the road with his mules and gear.

A short time later a red faced man came storming out and appeared as though he was about to burst from his anger. "What do you mean you will not come into my office? I'm going to have you locked in our brig until you develop some respect, young man. Corporal, take his guns."

Before he could take a step, Porter had the AK47 aimed at the officer's chest.

The Captain said, "You haven't the nerve to...." He was cut short by the audible click of the safety coming off.

In typical fashion, Porter stated, "Captain, I'm sorry you are all upset; but it's obvious you haven't been briefed about the plague as I have."

At that moment he heard Old Dollar make a sound that was not a whinny but more of a low moan. Porter had heard him make that noise before when a stranger or different horse came too close. "Captain, I know someone is slipping up behind me; call them off now, or you and the Corporal are going to get shot. My finger is on the trigger, and I won't hesitate to kill you."

The Captain looked over Porter's shoulder and commanded, "Stand down."

Without taking his gun or eyes off the Captain and Corporal, Porter cautioned, "Walk around here where I can see you. Walk slow. I don't want to kill you." Private Johnson walked around still carrying his rifle.

Porter repeated, "I don't want to kill anyone; so Johnson, if you will lean your rifle against that tree and step away from it, I would appreciate it."

The Captain bellowed, "Do it, Johnson. Conway, drop your pistol belt too."

"Thank you sir, now I am going to brief you on the plague." Porter spent the next thirty minutes explaining what the plague was; how it was spread and what he had personally witnessed.

"Now that you've been briefed, am I going to have to shoot you or can you get Captain Cooney Jones, Colonel Miller or Major Jernigan on the radio and give them my report?"

"I understand, Sergeant."

With that Porter lowered his weapon but never let his hands leave the trigger or apply the safety.

The captain inquired, "Sergeant, would you have shot me?"

"Yes, sir. I have something very important to do; you or nobody here is going to stop me."

"How old are you kid?"

"I'll be fifteen in few more months."

"Have you ever killed a man?"

"Yes, sir, and no, I don't know how many. I quit counting a while back."

"Can you wait here until I get off the radio?"

"Yes, sir."

Captain Lancaster got on the radio with Cooney Jones and gave him Porter's report. "Captain Jones, I've got to know something. I just spent the last thirty minutes with an AK47 pointed at my chest by Sergeant Porter Jones who briefed us about the plague and what he was doing. Was I in danger of getting killed?"

"Lancaster, Porter doesn't bluff. He would have killed you without blinking an eye. He is a man of few words; but he means what he says. He is respectful, honest and deadly. I don't have time to explain what he has been through and accomplished. If we live long enough, we may be answering to him one day. One other thing, get the address, if he has it, of the plague victim he ran across yesterday. We may have to retrieve the body. Do not under any circumstances try to retrieve the body yourself. We have men who will be equipped to attempt the recovery."

"Understood. I'll get the address or directions to the plague victim and send him on his way."

Lancaster walked out of the radio room and out to where Porter was waiting. "Ok, Porter, I need the address or directions to the plague victim you ran across yesterday so Captain Jones can retrieve the bodies." Porter read the address to Lancaster while he wrote it down.

Lancaster looked up. "You can head out. Sorry for giving you a hard time; I've had hell trying to keep some sort of order around here. Most of these guys are real good at slipping around killing people in the field. They are not soldiers; they are just plain survivors. I get the ones who don't have families. The other guys are home taking care of their families. This is the closest thing to family some of these guys have right now."

"Thanks, Captain. I'll stop and give a radio report every few days. What can I expect once I cross into Texas?"

"We have some guys scattered out over there. They are scouting areas around their homes. We've had no reports of the plague. You will need to travel southwest for at least a hundred and fifty miles. You want to make a wide swing around Fort Hood since the radiation is still hot. Because it started showing up in the Toledo Bend water, we don't drink it or eat the fish out of it."

Porter looked sick. "I bathed and watered my stock in it last night."

Lancaster called Conway. "Bring out the Geiger counter and let's check Porter and his stock." Looking back at Porter he said, "There are people catching fish and living on the water, and none of them have died yet. We've had a lot of rain; so, I am sure it has been diluted and washed downstream."

Conway walked out with the Geiger counter and did a sweep of Porter and the mules. There was a slight reading on one of

Porter's boots, but not enough to warrant losing or washing the shoe. "Looks like you lucked out again, kid."

Porter nodded. "Thanks guys, I hope I get to see you again one day." He climbed into the saddle and headed across the spillway towards Texas.

Lancaster waved. "You're entering no man's land, kid. I can't help you over there; you're on your own."

Porter started across the spillway and entered Texas. He turned south, headed down the river and found a spot where he could let the mules eat and rest. He unsaddled and took the pack off Ruth to give her back a rest. She had been carrying the pack all day, and he knew she was tired. He took a chance letting them drink from the river. He gave them two full hours of grazing and resting before saddling back up to head out. He traveled another three hours before turning away from the river in a southwesterly direction. He traveled until they came to a pond in the back of a rancher's pasture. He could see the ranch house in the distance. He hobbled the horses and made his camp at the base of the pond levee where he was completely hidden from view. There was no place to set up his hammock; so, tonight he would sleep on the ground, but after the events of the day, he was tired and sleep came easily. The mules were hobbled but didn't go far. They were also tired. His last thoughts were of Sandy, Ally and the Crosses.

## CHAPTER 7

Dix sat fuming in the dark. He didn't mind fighting and killing; it was second nature to him after the last year. This was probably an assassination attempt. That was why they came in the night, and this was why there was a hostage tied and gagged in the boat. Yes, the time had come to take the battle back to the enemy. Dix was happiest killing bad guys, and he had recovered enough to get back to doing what he did best. Captain Butch Erwin and his men finished their sweep a little after daylight. Dix found some blue dishwashing gloves under the sink. He stepped over the blood and around the dead Chinese commandos. They were in black fatigues and were armed with Sig MP5, .40 caliber submachine guns. It was the type used by the American DHS, FBI and any number of other Federal agencies. These Chinese had been outfitted by some of our communist Americans. Dix went over to the boat, and with his gloved hand pulled the bag off the captive's head. Duct tape was over his mouth, and his hands were duct taped together behind his back. The man was just about beaten to death. His mouth and teeth were a horrible mess. It took him a moment to recognize the man. His name was Chip Rawson, and he was one of the men rescued from the Natchez jail when the town of Natchez was liberated.

Dix said, "Chip, I'm going to reach around and cut your hands free; do not touch me or come in contact with me in any way. We are taking extreme caution when it comes to the plague, do you understand?" Chip could only nod his head.

Dix cut him loose and looked up at Fox. "Do you have any water?"

"Sure."

"Just pass it too me. I hate having to practice extreme contagion measures, but it's not going to help if we all get sick and die."

Fox passed over a bottle of water, and Dix handed it to Chip. Chip leaned his head back and poured the water past his chewed up lips and teeth. He closed his eyes and composed himself. "Major Jernigan, I had to spill my guts; they have my wife and kids in my house. I started talking when they started cutting on my wife. If these guys don't check back soon, they will kill them."

"You didn't do anything wrong. You have nothing to be ashamed of; I would have done the same thing to buy my family some time."

Butch paddled up to the boats, and Dix brought him up to speed. "Chip, give him your address. We'll have a team there in ten minutes." Dix waited while Butch got on the radio and gave his orders.

Dix then told Butch, "These guys didn't travel far on the river in these boats. Take my big boat, go out the south outlet and head upriver as fast as you can roll. Let's see if we can spot and kill the sons of bitches."

Butch said, "I'll take your boat, and four men and head out."

Dix nodded. "Good hunting."

Dix got on the radio with Captain Cooney Jones. "Jones, we had a commando raid over here this morning. We killed the commandos and are pursuing their comrades. I need you to send Doc over here. We have a guy hurt real bad and a big mess to clean up."

Chip Rawson just sat sobbing. He knew that his family was probably dead. Dix remembered the feeling he had had after his family was killed. "Chip, there isn't anything anyone can say or do to ease your pain right now, but I can tell you what helped me."

Chip looked up through swollen eyes as blood oozed from his nose and lips. Dix continued, "I figured I had two choices: I could put a gun to my head and join them, or I could make the ones who did this pay and pay and pay. You can let this be the end, or you can do something about it. You might get killed right away, or you may get lucky like me and really put the hurt on them. Either way, you will not have died for nothing."

Dix could see Chip's back straighten a little. "I'm going to have Fox paddle you over to the landing. Doc is on his way; he's going to check you out. Is anyone in your family sick from the plague or are you aware of anyone being sick?"

"We were all ok so far as I know. We have stayed to ourselves. I think they picked us because ours was the last house on the street and we're closest to the river. They were inside and on us before we knew they were even there. I'm sorry I told them where to find you."

"I told you, Chip; I don't blame you. I would have done the same thing. Fox, don't get contaminated. I'll clean up the mess over here; I have the only pair of gloves."

Walking out through his shot-up front door, Fox appeared with a pair of leather gloves on. "I filled them with dish washing soap. That should kill any virus that would penetrate the leather."

Dix nodded in agreement. "Great idea. I'll get these bodies cleaned up and secure their weapons. Beagle and I will wash off all the blood with the hose and follow up with bleach. You'll need to clean your shoes with bleach when you get back."

Dix and Beagle spent the next two hours cleaning up the boats. After they had dumped the bodies, they hosed off the decks and followed up with a spray of diluted chlorine bleach. They then sprayed their shoes, as well as the doors and railings. All of the invaders were Chinese soldiers except one; they had with them an American who had a US dog tag around his neck. After carefully going through their pockets, Dix disposed of them over the sides of the boats. The current in the lake slowly carried them toward the river where they would join countless others on their way to the Gulf. He unloaded their weapons and gear. They had state of the art equipment that had come out of a US government armory. Dix clicked their radios off and decided he would pass them on to Colonel Miller or Cooney so that the radio men could look at them. While they were finishing up, Fox paddled over. Dix looked up. "How's our hostage?"

"He dropped dead while Doc was looking at him. Doc said it was probably a brain hemorrhage from the beating." Dix's lips were white from the anger he held within as he looked down the lake at the bodies floating away.

"Get your shoes sprayed with bleach. Then we're going to spray down the assault team's boats and motors. We may get to put them to use." Now that Fox had seen Dix in action, he knew that he had come to the right place to fight.

Dix got on the radio and reached Butch. "Have you run across anything yet?"

"We just passed the north cut. There's a boat hauling tail north about three quarters of a mile ahead of us."

"Follow it and see if it puts in somewhere. Remember, you only have about thirty gallons of fuel. I want to find out where they came from. Any word on Chip's family?"

"They were dead. The wife and daughter had been raped."

"Chip's dead too; he didn't survive the beating."

Butch asked, "Are you sure you don't want me to catch them?"

"There will come a day when they will want to sue for peace. I will not stop fighting until they are resting in peace. I want the Americans who are helping them also. One of the bodies was an American. He had US dog tags, and they were using Sig MP5's in .40 caliber. It's an absolute miracle we weren't all killed. My two cur dogs alerted us in the nick of time."

Butch radioed back. "It looks like I found their base. It's one of those big boats that's been cruising by."

"Stay back and watch. They are probably launching raids from those boats and resupplying their men on the ground. Have you determined how many boats there are?"

"Yeah, there are seven of them, and they can't be going much further than the Mississippi Delta."

Dix thought about it a minute. "That's because the bridge at Greenville is sitting down in the river and has it blocked. They may have some marine engineers trying to open the river. I don't want you to do anything but observe and report."

Dix got on the radio to Captain Cooney Jones and Colonel Miller. "Colonel, I need permission to mount an offensive. I've got seven Chinese boats operating on the river. I need to start sinking them. Can you order an airstrike from the Warthogs? The best we can tell the boats are scattered from New Orleans to around Greenville, MS, and the Chinese are using them to resupply and as a base for commando raids."

Miller came back on. "Jernigan, I know you are itching for a fight, but we've been kicking around your idea of using germ warfare and would like to try that. Do you think you could get close enough to one of those boats to get the plague virus on board?"

"I think so. We just need to deliver it in a package they will accept."

"Do you think we can acquire a sample of the virus?"

Cooney Jones interrupted, "Doc just retrieved a corpse, clothes and bed sheets from a family of victims. We have a body and their clothes, frozen and under guard, in body bags in a refrigerated truck."

Miller asked, "How did you arrange that?"

Cooney Jones answered, "Sergeant Porter Jones found them and reported them to me."

"Is that your grandson that I've heard about?"

"Yes, sir."

Dix broke in, "Do you have any experts on staff that can help Doc come up with a delivery system for the virus?"

Miller quickly spoke up, "Jernigan, y'all are the experts; come up with something and keep me posted. That is your top priority. I know you want to kick their asses, and I want them kicked as bad as you, but this is our chance to kill almost all of them. You can shoot the leftovers."

Dix said, "I'll call you back with the plan. Cooney, I want Doc to come examine my new man Fox. I need to get him in the field. I think he has some of the skills we need, and I don't want to worry if he has the plague or not."

"Doc just got back. I'll let him get some breakfast, make his rounds and then send him over."

He called across to Fox who was sitting on the front porch of his house boat, "I've got Doc coming over to check you out; I am going to need your help right away."

Dix got on the radio with Butch, "What's the big boat doing now?"

"It picked up the small assault boat and is continuing north."

"Don't follow them. I want to meet with you and Cooney tonight."

"What about the quarantine?"

"We'll meet on the levee, and we'll have to refrain from hugging and kissing like we normally greet each other."

"Damn boss, I was kinda looking forward to a big ole kiss from Cooney!"

"When you get back here, we'll radio Cooney; Doc should be here by then."

Rachel called down, "I know you are preparing to clean those weapons. I want you and Beagle to eat first. I've got breakfast ready, and can I let the dogs out?"

"Let 'em out. We're all cleaned up out here. Beagle, you ready to eat?"

"I'm starved; all this shootin and killin has got my appetite worked up."

As Beagle came across the plank from his boat, Dix inquired, "Beagle, how come you were able to start shooting so quickly?"

"I was up on top of the house boat looking at the stars; my arthritis was killing me. I couldn't sleep, and I didn't want to wake anyone up, so I just climbed up on top. When I felt the boat move, I started looking to see if it was a big gator trying to get up on my porch. That's when I saw them working on the door to get in. When the dogs barked, I shot the ones I could see. If you ever get the nerve to go visit Rachel some night, you better clue me in ahead of time."

"What makes you think I'm going to be visiting Rachel in the middle of the night?"

"I've got eyes. You ain't dead yet and that is one boat load of a woman. I'll give you one thing. You shore picked out a good one to rescue." Dix closed his eyes, bit his lip and headed to breakfast.

# CHAPTER 8

Porter slept undisturbed and awoke to a light rain. He rolled up his sleeping bag before it got wet and stowed it under his tent tarp. He put on an oil skin slicker given to him by his grandfather, Cooney Jones. He took the hobbles off the mules, saddled and loaded the packs on Ruth. He ate another cold breakfast and led them up to the pond to drink. Once they drank their fill, he checked his compass and continued southwest. He estimated that he could cover twenty to thirty miles a day. He would need to travel for ten days to the southwest before he could turn west. He only had about a week's worth of biscuits, hard tack and cornbread left, so hunting for game would soon become a priority. He still had plenty of rice and beans, but he had resisted cooking over a fire until now. Tonight he would have to start cooking.

The next two days were uneventful. He crossed roads, fields and went through neighborhoods. He ran across several communities where everyone had been killed by the plague. No one tried to kill or rob him; however, occasionally, he would see people. He warned them about the plague and how to keep from getting it.

He was somewhere north of Silsbee, TX, and was travelling toward a bridge shown on his map. When he got there, he found, to his dismay, that it had been road-blocked. The men manning it did not appear threatening, and none of them were pointing their guns at him. Porter stopped about fifty feet away and had his hand on the grip of the AK47 with the safety off.

A big guy stepped out around the barricade and said, "We are the South Texas Militia, and we have the entire area quarantined. No one comes or goes until this plague has run its course."

Porter relaxed a little. "You're showing good sense; it's not something you want to play with. I'm Sergeant Porter Jones with the Constitution army. I'm traveling and reporting to headquarters about what's going on. I need to travel south and west for about another week."

"I don't care if you're General George Washington; you aren't coming through here."

"I understand. How far are your boundaries? I don't have the luxury of waiting around. Is anyone here with the Constitution army?"

"We work with them. We have Sergeant Benson who is in the area."

Porter was looking at his maps. It would be a three day ride in either direction to get around their boundaries, and if he ran into any other delays, he would never make it to the ranch.

He looked up at the man. "Do you mind getting him for me?"

"We'll radio him for you and see when he can get here."

"Thank you, sir. I have one other question, 'Where are the Chinese and communists in this area?'"

"All of them we could find are dead. The others headed south when the plague hit. We think they are in or around the Port of Houston."

"Is there any way we can verify that? The best we can tell they're the ones that brought the plague," Porter continued. "We think it's a biological weapon that got away from them."

"You're just a kid; how come you know so much about it?"

Porter grinned. "You aren't the first person who's underestimated me, and I hope you aren't the last. I have been fighting for my life almost nonstop for the last year, and I've been on the offensive for the past six months or so." Porter realized that his youth and innocence had led to the bad guys underestimating him time and time again. It was an advantage that he would outgrow if he lived long enough.

Porter took the opportunity to let the mules rest. He led them down to the water and took off their saddle and packs. He hobbled them and lay back in the grass while they waited for the Sergeant to call in or show up. The mules took full advantage of the lush grass and fresh water.

"Hey kid, Benson will be here before dark. I don't see how his coming is going to matter one way or the other. I ain't gonna let you pass."

"I want to report to him what we know and take his report. I will set up my radio and pass on the information."

While he waited, Porter set up his radio and the solar charger so that the batteries could recharge. Down in the water, he spotted a large snapping turtle that would poke his nose up about every twenty minutes.

Porter called up, "Do you mind if I shoot my rifle one time? I see my supper down here."

The man looked and didn't see anything. "I don't care kid; do you know how to handle that thing?"

"I think I can handle it where no one will get hurt."

"Be careful, you can kill someone with that thing."

Porter grinned to himself as he unslung the rifle and aimed between his knees. Right on schedule, the old turtle poked his nose up, and Porter fired. The turtle never knew what hit him. Porter kicked off his boots, waded into the water and rolled the huge turtle out. It probably weighed fifty pounds and was quite a chore to handle. Once he had him on the bank, he put his boots back on and retrieved a hatchet from Ruth's pack. He flipped the beast on its back and chopped the carapace between its legs on each side.

The man looked down. "You planning on eating that critter?"

"Yes Sir, I am going to stew it and with a little luck will enjoy it along with some beans and rice.

Porter decided that this would be as good a place as any to camp for the night. He dragged up some drift wood and soon had a fire going and a pot of water boiling. He added some wild onions he had found on the road bank and salt and pepper to the meat he had trimmed from the carcass. About twenty minutes before eating, he threw in a cup of rice. Finally, he had the best meal he had eaten since leaving Jonesville.

The four men, manning the roadblock, were soon leaning over the bridge rail looking down on Porter and his feast.

Porter looked up. "I don't think a virus could live in this hot pot of turtle stew. Bring your bowls and set them down, and I'll dip you some up. As long as we don't touch or spit on each other, we'll be ok."

The men came down with their bowls, and Porter ladled each a helping.

He told them, "Y'all need to take your food and eat it at the roadblock. The more we sit around, the greater the chances of us cross contaminating each other."

The man said, "My name is Pepper, Joe Pepper. I like you, kid."

"I like you guys too."

About that time Sergeant Benson came riding up on a motorcycle.

Joe Pepper yelled, "I see you finally got here, Benson."

Benson asked, "What's this about a Constitution army scout? Where is he?"

Pepper pointed at Porter. "He's down here. Benson, meet Porter Jones."

Porter was sitting cross legged by the stew pot. "Sarge, I've still got some stew if you want a bowl."

"Don't mind if I do, kid." Benson was about sixty years old with hard miles etched into his face and hands.

Porter filled his bowl. "When you're finished, I want to make a report to headquarters, and then we need to figure out a way for me to get out of my predicament."

"From the looks of things, you don't have much of a predicament."

Porter answered, "First thing first, let's get headquarters on the radio, give them an update and get their orders."

They soon had Cooney Jones on the radio, and after thirty minutes, Cooney had all the updated information.

Cooney's final order was, "Benson, you and Pepper figure out a way to get Porter across your territory. He can't waste weeks going around. Escort him across if necessary or put him and his stock in a trailer and drive him across."

Benson looked at Pepper. "You heard the man; we can escort him. We don't have enough fuel to drive him across with a truck and trailer. Porter, when do you want to start?"

"First thing in the morning will be fine."

"What would you have done, if we refused?"

"I would have just gone up or downstream and traveled across anyway."

"We would have stopped you."

Porter gave them a serious, matter of fact look. "You wouldn't have survived. My crossing was never an issue. The issue was whether or not I could cross without having to hurt anyone."

"You can't be serious. You expect us to believe that a big kid like you could take us on? Do you realize that some of us have killed a dozen men?"

Benson was standing next to a pile of sandbags that fortified the road. In one fluid motion Porter pulled his Kbar knife and threw. The knife stuck up in the sandbag about a foot from Benson's head. Benson pulled out the knife and chunked it back handle first. Porter scooped it out of the air and returned it to its sheath.

"Sorry, kid. Thanks for not killing us."

"You guys need to be more careful. I would keep someone in reserve at all times with a gun on whoever shows up. I think the only reason y'all are alive is that you Texans have already killed most of the bad folks."

Benson got on his motorcycle and looked at Porter. "I'll be back with my horse in the morning. I don't live far from here. You gonna be ok here tonight?"

"Sure, I've got food, grass and water. I'll be geared up and ready when you get here."

The next morning when Benson arrived before daylight, Porter was packed up and ready. He led the mules up to the road and climbed on Ole Dollar.

Porter followed Benson. "Are we safe traveling in the open like this? I always travel cross country whenever possible."

"We're ok until you cross out of our area. We don't have anyone that I know of in West Texas. It is truly a no man's land. How's your food holding out?"

"I'll be living off the land in about two weeks; I'll be hunting as I go."

Benson turned around in his saddle and looked over his shoulder. "I have some unopened cases of MRE's in storage. No one has touched them for months. I'll let you open them yourself and you can take all you can pack."

"Thanks, Sarge. That will take some of the pressure off."

They swung off the main road, and Benson watched as Porter opened the boxes and loaded up Ruth's pack and the saddle bags on Ole Dollar's saddle. He figured that this would last almost to the ranch if he made good time.

They made it to the next checkpoint where Benson pointed to Porter's map with a stick.

"You are going to have to travel at least a day past Austin before you turn northwest. That whole area around Austin was a center of fighting because it was the last Chinese stronghold before they retreated to Houston. We had quite a few communist Americans working in the government there; although most of them disappeared, you never know who or what you will run into. Our group is concentrated mostly in the countryside. You may want to travel at night when you're in the Austin area."

Porter looked up from the map. "We weren't bothered too much on the trip across. There were nine of us when we came through here. We were a little more intimidating than just a man riding alone."

Benson reached up, grabbed the saddle horn, and just as he swung his leg over the saddle, he was knocked off the horse. Gun fire had erupted from down the road where at least half a dozen men were storming the barricade. Porter didn't have time to think. Dollar and Ruth were instantly running in the opposite direction back down the road they had just traveled. As usual Porter was armed to the teeth. He had his AK47, six extra magazines and his pistols. He got a glimpse of one of the attackers and dispatched him with a shot to his head. He dove headfirst into the ditch right on top of two more of the attackers. Without thinking, he just squeezed the trigger and continued his roll. The one to his left caught a bullet in the chest. Porter's Kbar plunged deep into the other man's belly. Porter pulled hard on the knife and felt the man relax as the internal bleeding drained the life from him. He crawled down the ditch in the direction of no man's land. The gun fire was to his rear and across the road. Porter was mad. This constant fighting and killing had to stop, or he would never get to the ranch. Now he was exposed to a man's blood. He hoped to God that he didn't have the plague. He crawled on his belly across the road, across a ditch and up into a small patch of woods. He circled around to where he could see the attackers from the rear. Two had been killed by the men at the roadblock; there were three left. One of them was holding his rifle up and shooting wild; while the other two were trying to flank the men at the barricade. Three shots silenced them forever. Looking down at his clothes, Porter saw that he was soaked in the dead man's blood.

He called out to the men at the roadblock, "This is Porter; I got 'em."

After making certain that his fellow defenders wouldn't shoot, he walked down to the road and over to where Benson lay, not moving. He had taken a bullet through the neck; there was nothing to be done. Porter watched him take his last breath, a low moan left Benson's lips as it was expelled. Porter looked around at the carnage, of the three men guarding the roadblock: one was dead, one was wounded and could die and one was uninjured.

Porter asked, "What's your name?"

"My name is Havard."

"I'm Sergeant Porter Jones; do you have a radio?"

"Yes."

"Then get Pepper on it and tell him what happened. I can't help your friend, because his injury is past what I can nurse. He's gonna need a real doctor. Call Pepper while I go and catch my stock.

Porter mounted Benson's horse, trotted him down the road and found Old Dollar and Ruth after traveling about a mile. He tied Benson's horse to a fence, went over the mules and was relieved that they had once again escaped injury. He split open a couple of the MRE's, got out the candy and gave each of them a treat. They were calm now.

Benson's horse seemed ok, so he held on to his lead and rode back to the roadblock.

"Did you get in touch with Pepper?"

"They are on their way."

He looked over and saw that the wounded man was dead. "Sorry about your friend."

Havard just shook his head. Porter gathered up the defenders' weapons; a couple of them had AK47's. He gathered up some full magazines to replace what he had expended. At least he had recovered his ammo and was restocked with food. He undressed, took a bath in the ditch and washed out his bloody clothes. He lathered them up with soap before rinsing them. He wrung them out and laid them across Ruth's pack so they could dry. He took special care to clean under his nails. He then donned his other set of fresh clothes. If the man had the plague, he now had it. Porter knew what to do if he had it. If infected, he would have symptoms in a couple of weeks. That would give him enough time to infiltrate the Chinese base at Houston. He unrolled his antenna, set up his radio and reached Cooney.

Cooney answered, "What's wrong?"

Porter explained the situation to Cooney, and he said, "Stick around till they get the roadblock manned again. You saved the quarantine zone. Continue to the ranch as soon as you can travel. If you start having symptoms, I want you to radio in so that we can verify them with Doc. Only then can you proceed to Houston. Good luck son, I love you."

"I love you too, Grandpa."

Pepper arrived with several men in a pickup truck. Porter stuck around until they had their dead loaded in the back of the truck. Pepper's men wore gloves and masks and quickly had the attackers burning in a pile on the no man's land side of the road block.

Turning to Havard, Pepper asked, "What happened?" Havard told him blow by blow from his prospective.

"Havard, how many did you kill?"

Havard's eyes darted from Pepper to Porter and back again. "I don't know if I killed or hit anyone. I was shooting in the direction of the sound. I never actually saw one of them until it was over."

He looked at Porter. "Tell me your story."

Porter recited the sequence of events to Pepper.

Pepper looked around at Havard. "Is what he said true?"

"Pepper, everyone else was dead or wounded. I was pinned down; he was the only one who could have done it."

Pepper shook his head in disbelief. "Porter, how did you do what you did?"

Porter looked at Pepper. "I didn't have much choice; it was either fight or die. I was lucky I didn't catch a bullet. I was able to get the last three only because I crawled down that ditch and came up behind them. I shot all three of them in the back."

"How many men have you killed?"

"I'm not sure. I've been through an awful lot in the last six or eight months. I just need to get back to my family; but if I start developing symptoms, I am going to need your help getting to Houston and into the Chinese base."

"Are you serious?"

"Yes sir, I can take the disease to them and wipe out their base. I'll radio Captain Jones, and you can coordinate my transportation should I be unable to travel on my own. Also, I would relocate this checkpoint down the road away from this timber. These guys were able to sneak right up on you. And you should dig a shooting pit within rifle range and have someone who can hit sitting in it. That way you have a hidden sniper to supplement your position."

"We'll do it. Can you stay here with us until our replacements arrive?"

"Sure, I owe Benson that much." Porter unsaddled Ole Dollar and Ruth and hobbled them on the opposite side of the road away from the bloody grass and ditch water. He pulled the saddle off Benson's horse and hobbled him with a piece of rope. They couldn't go far. Porter broke out an MRE and ate in silence as they waited. He used his binoculars to glass the road ahead. The only thing he saw was the heat dancing off the pavement.

He asked Pepper, "Do you know who those men were?"

"They are part of the group that operates near Austin. They have a little kingdom set up over there. They think that civilization is over so they are ruling it like a feudal kingdom. You'll probably have to contend with them before you get through. That's why I recommend you travel at night. It will be difficult to travel cross country unless you can find the trails you took coming over."

"I know approximately where I am. I could never exactly retrace our steps. The GPS we were using is long gone. Pepper, there is something you need to know. I am not some hero; I just don't hesitate to act. I am one of those people that haven't taken a good sound hit yet. I've been shot and lived through it. I would be dead except for the generosity of strangers. Just like some people can throw a basketball, I can throw a knife and hit what I'm shooting at. I have managed to get ambushed twice in the last two weeks; three times if you count a pack of wild dogs. I just want to get to my girlfriend before it's too late."

Pepper nodded, stood up and peered down the road. "It looks like our relief is almost here."

Porter saw several men on horseback coming. He proceeded to saddle up his stock as Pepper watched. Pepper noted that Porter never once took off his rifle. Instead he positioned it around his back with the butt resting on his left shoulder.

The men arrived just as Porter swung into the saddle. He recognized one of them from the first road block. He waved and headed out. His only thought was Sandy, Ally and the Crosses. Once again he was looking down the road between Ole Dollar's ears; Ruth dutifully followed. He looked at the smoldering pile of bodies and wood as he passed, and in typical Porter fashion, he never looked back. He never killed anyone that didn't need it; his conscience was clear.

# CHAPTER 9

Rachel had breakfast laid out on the table. "I broke out one of our last boxes of biscuit mix. I figured after last night you guys needed some calories. Enjoy it. I can make about three more breakfasts like this. Then we start seeing how many different ways I can cook corn bread and catfish." The biscuits were served with cane syrup, canned bacon, grits and scrambled powdered eggs.

Dix looked up while sopping his biscuit in the syrup. "Beagle, I need you to do two things this week."

"What's that, Dix?"

"I want to rig some sort of early warning system so no one can slip on these boats at night."

Rachel pointed to the door where Ben and Frank were looking in. "We got an early warning system, and it worked great."

"I suppose you are right. Try to keep all the gators culled from around here. I don't want a gator getting one of the dogs off the decks. I also want you to look and see if there are any wild hogs on the island behind us."

Beagle pointed. "I can tell you right now that there are a slew of them back there. I see them all the time while I'm running my lines."

"Do you think you could start killing one every now and then; and another thing, do you think we could take one of the abandoned camps and turn it into a smoke house? All we need is one room, and if it catches on fire, all we lose is an old camp that's going to rot down anyway."

Beagle nodded his head. "That's a good idea! All I need to do is rig up a smoke pot on some concrete blocks in the middle of a room. I can take out all the furniture and put some meat hanging poles up. I never messed with other people's camp houses because they weren't mine. I don't reckon anybody will be coming back any time soon, if ever. I'll have one converted before dark, and a pig hanging in the next couple of days."

Dix finished his coffee and headed for the door. "I'm going to take those weapons, magazines and ammo and disinfect them."

Rachel looked puzzled. "You can't wash them, can you?"

"I could wash them, but I figure to pass a flame from my propane torch over the surfaces. I'll also give them a good coating of spray oil that should encapsulate what I miss. If you hear an explosion, you'll know that I flame washed the ammo too long."

It took him a couple of hours to get the guns disinfected and test fired. He had eight submachine guns and fifty-six 30 round magazines--three of them were empty.

He wasted two magazines showing Rachel how to shoot the gun. It was small enough she could carry it on her back when she was outside and would give her tremendous firepower in the confines of the boat.

Doc arrived, and Fox paddled over to the boat launch at the levee for his physical. Dix could see the gloves and mask on Doc as he gave Fox the once over.

Doc and Fox paddled over to the catamaran; Doc called out as they paddled up, "If he were exposed he would have a fever by now and probably a rash, I think he's ok."

"How well were you able to check out Chip before he died?"

"He didn't have a fever. I checked after he fell over dead; he was beaten too badly to see if he had a rash."

"What did you do with the body?"

"When we found out his family was dead, we thought it best just to bury him up the road in the cemetery next to the little Baptist church. We scratched his name and the date on a piece of thin aluminum and left it there should there ever come a day someone would want to retrieve the body or mark the grave."

"That will be unlikely, Doc. We're fast running out of people. I want you to stick around until Butch and Cooney get back. We're going to develop a weapon's system that we can use to deliver the plague to those boats. We want them getting sick and then spreading it among their ranks." Dix noticed that Doc carried a pistol in a shoulder holster, but no rifle. "Why no rifle, Doc?"

"They're too big and heavy. I can't handle a rifle and my equipment too."

Dix held up one of the small submachine guns. "I want you to have one of these and some magazines. You need a little more firepower than just that pistol; this should keep someone off you in a pinch."

Butch motored up in Dix's fishing boat. From a distance you couldn't tell what it was. The camo paint job was very effective in breaking up the outline. With the addition of some limbs and camo netting, it would be difficult to spot unless you were practically standing on it. Dix, Doc and Fox stepped in the boat and rode with Butch over to the landing. He passed Doc the MP5 and a magazine pouch with six loaded magazines.

"Doc, be careful, the magazine in the gun is full; all you have to do is pull back the charging handle."

Dix looked around at Butch. "Can you use one of these?"

"I'd like to give one to my wife. She's too small to handle the AK47 very well, and she keeps laying it down."

"When you drop me off at the boat, grab one."

They looked up to see Captain Cooney Jones crossing over the levee in an ATV. His crutches were in the gun rack behind him and a rifle was slung across his chest.

"Sorry, I'm late guys. I had a little trouble getting my ride across the river."

Dix pointed at Fox. "Cooney, meet Fox White. He's staying in that old blue houseboat over there. He's the man that came to Jacob's rescue and is from the North Florida area. He traveled here in that old fiberglass boat with the little Mercury on it that he affectionately calls the 'stump thumper.' He doesn't know it yet, but he's going to help me deliver the plague to our friends on the long boats."

Fox looked a little nervous. "Can't I just shoot them?"

Dix interrupted, "Don't worry, Fox, I think there will be plenty to shoot, but right now we need some ideas on how we are going to weaponize this virus. Doc, I know you have given this some thought. I want to hear what your thoughts are."

Doc said, "As a matter of fact, I do have a few ideas. I worked my way through graduate school before getting into med school. One of my jobs was working on vaccines. In order to make vaccines we had to culture the viruses in the lab. At that time we used monkeys, but I think we can use people. If you could get me a prisoner, I could make a lot of virus until he died. We would have to strap him down where he couldn't move, and we would have to have very strict measures in place to keep him from spreading it to the staff."

Dix thought a minute. "What if we had a volunteer; someone who has the plague and knows that we need the virus? Butch, you and Cooney get the word out right away and see what we can turn up."

Cooney nodded. "That might be a viable solution."

Dix looked back at Doc. "What about the body and clothes that y'all have in the refrigerated truck?"

"If I had a real lab and equipment, I could isolate the virus, grow it in an animal or live chicken eggs; but I would need a temperature and humidity controlled room to attempt that."

Butch piped up, "What about the egg room at the turtle hatcheries?"

Dix asked, "Turtle hatcheries?"

"Yes, you heard me, turtle hatcheries. We had a thriving business here in the Parish, hatching and raising turtles to ship to China as pets. They harvested the eggs, disinfected them, put them in incubators and hatched off millions of baby turtles to ship to China."

Dix grinned. "Are any of them operational?"

"All we have to do is get power and water to them. I don't see where it would be a problem. A couple of those ole boys that used to run the hatcheries are under your command."

Cooney spoke up, "I know where I can get ten hens and three roosters; if we can find some more hens then I can deliver more fresh eggs."

Doc looked concerned. "We need to get about fifty or seventy five birds to make sure we have the eggs."

Dix grinned. "Don't worry Doc, when people realize that we are fighting the Chinese with eggs, they'll come up with what you need."

The wheels in Doc's head were turning. "I need some guys to hit the science labs at the high schools, water treatment plants and at the Junior College. Tell them I want everything they can get out of there, including the tables and sinks. Find me a plumber, a carpenter and an electrician if we have any left. I'll need gloves, surgical gowns and masks; check the hardware stores for the kind that are used when you spray chemicals."

Dix sat thoughtful for a few minutes. "How will we know if we are successful in reproducing the virus?"

Doc looked over his glasses. "We'll need a volunteer, or we will have to take a leap of faith."

Fox quickly piped up, "I volunteer to shoot the crap out of every Chinese I see. I ain't volunteering to catch the plague."

Dix looked around at the group and grinned. "Get that thought out of your head; you don't have to volunteer. I'll just order everyone to catch you, tie you up and we'll do it against your will."

Everyone burst out laughing as Fox stared at Dix. "By God, I wouldn't put it past you from what I've heard."

Dix told Fox, "If you and I are going to figure out a way to deliver the product, we need the product first. Doc, coordinate everything with Butch and Cooney. Unless we come under an offensive attack, that will be our top priority. I would start with the corpse you have and the victim's clothes. If you find a victim who would be a good candidate, call me if they won't volunteer. I don't want to, but we may have to force the issue."

Cooney looked concerned. "You mean...."

Dix interrupted him, "Yep, if they won't cooperate, we will take them against their will. We'll explain that they'll receive the best medical care available, and we will do everything in our power to save them. We'll be trying to save them with every resource we have. We'll also be harvesting the virus from them, and if we happen to save them in the process, we will have developed a treatment protocol for future victims."

Doc replied, "Sounds like a plan."

Cooney looked at Dix. "I often wondered why Colonel Miller insisted on putting you in charge. Now I know. You have the ability to look at things from different directions. You're a little careless on the battlefield, but that's because you had to learn from scratch. That reminds me, you need to harden your boats with some sandbags or something. Someone with a light machine gun could do a number on you where you're floating."

Dix looked across the water. "That's been bothering me since I anchored them out there and especially since we had a shootout last night. Speaking of shootout, could you use one of these light submachine guns? I've got several more with ammo."

Cooney shook his head. "I'm not going to learn how to handle a new weapon. I can hit real good with what I'm carrying; if I think of someone who needs one, I'll let you know."

Dix climbed over into his boat with Fox and Butch. "I want a report tomorrow, and I would like to see our first sick egg by the day after that." They motored over to the catamaran, and Dix stepped off. He handed Butch the gun and a pouch of full magazines.

"Fox, take Butch back to his truck and give him some hand grenades and AK ammo, so he can get you some ammo for your rifle."

Butch broke in, "I've got ten boxes in my truck I picked up last night from a friend."

Dix watched as Fox took Butch back to the truck. Butch, Doc and Cooney disappeared over the levee in their vehicles.

Fox returned with the boat. "Ok, Major, what's on the agenda today?"

"First--I'm not wild about all this army talk. I don't want any saluting. Second--I want to harden these boats in some manner. We can't go overboard with sandbags, or we're liable to sink the boats."

Fox pointed up the lake where there were still another half dozen houseboats sitting unoccupied.

"Why don't we pull all those empty houseboats down here and anchor them between us and the bank. We can position them so that we can run our boats in behind them. It will be like having our own yacht club. We can put sandbags in them and at least we can make sure there's not a direct line of sight from the levee to where we sleep and eat. It won't stop them from trying to blast us out of the water, but it would give us time to respond or run. We can put some small boats out back so we can escape to the island if needed."

Dix nodded in agreement. "I think we are safer out in the lake, and those extra boats will give us a big physical boundary. Fox, I knew you would come in handy; let's get started."

## CHAPTER 10

The next two days were quiet for Porter. Several times he couldn't avoid roads and developments; in these areas he traveled late at night. He came under gun fire one evening; fortunately, they missed and after galloping the mules hard for a half a mile, he was out of the area. He turned them off the road and behind a warehouse. He thought about going back to silence the shooter, but decided he had been lucky. He stuck around long enough to make certain he hadn't been followed.

He was able to follow a set of train tracks out of the industrial area, and after several miles he was back in a more rural setting. The mules took their time and in their sure footed way safely negotiated the cross ties and rails. The rails turned south so Porter left them at a rural crossing. He was entering a more arid region of Texas, leaving behind the lush green fields and light timber that he came through on the eastern side of the state. The sun came up in spectacular fashion in deep reds and rust. There were clouds on the horizon, but nothing menacing. Ole Dollar lifted his nose and shook his ears. He could smell water; it had been a while since they had drunk, so Porter let him have his head. Soon they came to a beautiful river of blue green water. Ever vigil, Porter crossed the river on a small rural bridge. Bridges were always a place of concern because they were the favored spots for an ambush. Looking back over his shoulder, he saw no one or nothing. It was early in the morning, and the water was inviting. He turned north on the river and stopped to rest, drink and eat. The previous night had been stressful, so this quiet river was a great spot to stop and recharge their tired bodies. The spot he found was below a bluff so no one riding or walking by would readily see them. On the other side of the river was a large stand of trees, so unless someone was already there waiting, it would be unlikely he would be surprised. Because there was abundant grass around the river, Porter unsaddled the mules and hobbled them so they couldn't go far. He stripped down and took a good bath in the cold water.

He thought *damn, this river must be spring fed to be so cold this time of year, but it sure feels good to get the dirt off.*

He washed out his clothes and hung them on a rope between two trees. He now had on the clothes he had worn when he had the fight near Silsbee. He checked his weapons and added a drop or two of oil to the mechanisms, as they were dirty from the trail. He wanted them fresh and working should the need arise. Since it was too early for plague symptoms, other than being tired, he felt fine. He reached up and ran his finger around the scar where he had been shot in the shoulder. It felt hard and rubbery--that battle seemed like a long time ago. He thought back to when he buried his parents and little brother in their back yard. His dad's watch was still running; he wondered what he would do when it stopped. The MRE he opened tasted good, and the mules liked the grass and water. His last piece of cornbread was molding, so he chunked it in the water and watched as a swarm of minnows swirled around it. Here there were also cypress trees growing. Their fronds looked a little different from those in Louisiana. The mules were still feeding, and after their busy night he wanted them well nourished. He leaned back against Ruth's pack and was soon asleep. The spring weather was perfect, and he was tired.

He stirred, opened his eyes and almost jumped out of his skin. An old gray haired man was sitting by the river smoking a pipe.

The man's face was dark and wrinkled from years spent outdoors. His old cowboy hat was curled on the sides with a broad sweat band, and he was wearing blue jeans and a canvas shirt. He was holding a lever action rifle and had a large revolver in a shoulder holster. The rifle was cradled in the old man's arms and was pointing away. Porter had his hand on his rifle but hesitated using it.

The old man took the pipe out of his mouth and spit. "Don't panic, kid, I could have killed you thirty minutes ago; it looks like you and your stock are wore out. Even your mules are sacked out." Porter looked over his shoulder. Both of the mules were asleep under a small tree.

Porter looked back at the man. "I'm Porter Jones, what can I do for you?"

"I am camping about a hundred and fifty yards up the river. I heard you when you unsaddled your stock. You look like a traveler and not a robber."

"I'm just passing through. I am heading into West Texas. I've been fighting with the Constitution army in Louisiana. There's something I need to tell you. I may have been exposed to the plague, so you need to stay clear of me and my gear."

The old man shook his head. "Thanks for the warning. I've been trying to stay hid out with what little I got left. I don't see how we are going to survive. What do you know about this plague? I heard about it from some fellows who were traveling by canoe a couple of weeks back."

Porter explained. "We think the Chinese have been impacted as they have more or less ceased their offensive. They may have been abandoned by the Chinese mainland. The reports we've gotten are that the plague got away from whoever launched it."

The old man pondered. "If that's so, any Chinese left will be desperate."

"We think they may have contained it among their remaining troops. If it turns out I have the plague, my plans are to abandon my attempt to get to my family and instead infiltrate their base in Houston and spread the disease. What happened to you and your people?"

The old man looked down. "My wife and I were retired and living upriver about fifty miles from here. She was ill and died when the health czar's new benefit cost analysis guidelines determined that she was too old to qualify for kidney dialysis. When the dollar collapsed in value, I simply ran out of money to pay for it privately. I had to watch her die. My daughter is married and living in Alaska with her husband and kids; my son was in the army. Last I heard, he was in Korea. I haven't been able to get in touch with them in over a year. I was diagnosed with lung cancer, and I was too old to be considered for any treatment other than pain pills."

"What's your name old timer?"

"My name is Lester Graves."

"If you don't mind my asking, how old are you?"

"I was eighty-two last month; I don't expect I'll have to worry about seeing eighty-three. I'm not really worried about getting the plague; my number is pretty much up."

"Mr. Lester, have you been around anybody in the last few weeks?"

"Don't worry kid; I have been camping up stream by myself for the last six weeks. I've only seen one couple, and I didn't get within twenty feet of them."

"Why did you leave your house?"

"Looters hit our neighborhood. My neighbors were killed when they tried to get to the hospital. Their car was taken, and they were left dead in the street. I dusted off my deer rifle and packed up all the food. I put together all my hunting and camping gear along with what I could find at their house. Everyone out here claims they have a ranch, so they had a barn and a horse on this three acre mini ranch. They used her to carry their camping gear when they went hiking and camping in the national forest. So rather than try to ride it out at home, I loaded her up and have been living on the trail."

"Mr. Lester, how's your food holding out and what about the cancer?"

"Other than coughing up blood every now and then, I've felt normal. I had a knot pop up in my groin, so I know the cancer is running loose. I still have thirty pounds of rice and twenty pounds of beans. I get a squirrel to throw in the pot every now and then. So I figure about the time I run out of food, my time will be running out. I figure I could eat a bullet or find me some bad guys and die taking them out. There ain't no shortage of bad guys preying on the helpless."

"Mr. Lester, I can't argue with your decision; at least you will die for something. That's pretty much the way I look at. If you have time to stick around, I've got to radio in and report to headquarters."

"I've got nothing but time, Porter."

Porter strung out his wire and soon had Cooney on the radio.

Cooney asked, "How you makin' it, son?"

"I'm making my turn north to head toward the ranch; I'm not showing any symptoms, but it is still too early for them to start. I am camping on the banks of a cold clear river, and I'm sitting here with an old guy who is camping nearby. He doesn't have the plague and isn't concerned about getting sick. He already has cancer real bad. He says it's not an issue; he just wants to get some bad guys before he goes."

"Porter, what's his name and about how old is he?"

"His name is Lester Graves, and he said he is eighty-two."

"Porter, put him on the radio; I need to talk to him."

Porter turned and motioned. "Mr. Lester, Captain Cooney Jones, my grandfather, wants to talk to you."

Lester got up and walked over to the microphone and headset.

"Mr. Lester, you need to put the head phones on and press the button on the mic to talk."

He shook his head at Porter. "Son, I was a radio man back during the Korean War; I know how to use a shortwave. Just stand back, and let me talk. Captain Jones, this is Lester Graves, what can I do for you?"

"Mr. Graves, I need to ask you something. Porter tells me you have cancer, how bad?"

"Captain Jones, I've got it bad. I figure sometime in the next thirty to forty-five days I'll have to eat a bullet if I don't get myself killed."

"This radio is encrypted so feel free to talk. Porter Jones is my grandson and a Sergeant in the Constitution army. I need to know on what side of the fence you're on before I discuss this further."

"What do you mean?"

"I need to know if you are an American or if you are a communist."

"Listen Jones, if you call me a communist again, I'm going to try to live long enough to come kick your ass!"

"I'm sorry, Mr. Graves. I didn't mean to insult you; but when I ask you what I am going to ask, you will understand."

"I'm listenin."

"Do you think you would be willing to volunteer for a suicide mission that could help us defeat the Chinese?"

"Hell yes, I ain't got nothing else to do. I'd like to get even with them bastards for what they've done to us; what can I do?"

Cooney spent the next thirty minutes explaining to him about the virus project. His final words were, "Do not tell Porter. I don't think they have anyone in the field out where you are, but if

Porter were captured and drugged, I don't want them to be able to get any more information than what he already knows. Also, if y'all get in a fire fight let Porter do the heavy lifting; it is very important that you live until I can get you back here."

Lester looked around at Porter. "He's just a kid; are you sure he can fight like that?"

In a serious voice Cooney replied, "How many men have you killed Mr. Graves?"

"I shot a couple in Korea when we were attacked one night."

"I know of ten men Porter has killed in just the last three weeks. He has been fighting and killing bad guys for the past year. He's been through more in the last year than ten men have in their lifetime. He is respectful, honest and deadly; try not to surprise him. He may act before he has time to think."

"Hell, I could have got myself kilt. I thought I was being cute sneaking up and sitting near him when he was napping."

"Can you tell me exactly where you are? I am going to try and arrange a pickup; put Porter back on." The old man explained where they were in relation to local towns and about where they were on the river. He gestured for Porter to come back to the radio.

"He wants to talk to you, Porter."

Porter put the headset on and keyed the mic, "Yes, sir?"

"Porter, your trip is going to be delayed a couple of days. How long would it take Pepper and a company of men to get there and retrieve Mr. Graves for a mission?"

"If the company was big enough and they had fuel for vehicles, less than a day. By horseback two days if they didn't have to stop and fight."

"I am arranging to have Mr. Graves picked up. I'm not sure how, but it is imperative that you keep him alive until we can get him transferred. He's going on a mission. If we can pull it off, the war will be over and the only thing we will have to do is a little clean up. I can't give you the exact details, but it is crucial that we get him back here in one piece. Charge your batteries and call me back in two hours. Cooney, out."

"Mr. Lester, I've got orders to keep you alive until they retrieve you."

Lester looked at him funny. "Porter, your granddad says for me not to accidently surprise you."

"He must have told you...never mind, you know better than that; if I were going to kill you, we wouldn't be having this conversation. Is there a place at your campsite where I can set up my radio and hobble the mules?"

"Sure kid, it's more secluded than this; get your gear loaded up and follow me."

Porter moved all his gear and the mules up stream and let the mules join Lester's mare. He set up his solar battery charger and ate some squirrel and bean stew with Lester while waiting the two hours so he could call back. He strung out his radio antenna and got Cooney back on the radio.

"Porter, I need you to see if there is a place nearby that we can land a helicopter."

"Hold on, I'll ask Mr. Lester. He knows this place better than I do."

Porter looked over at Mr. Lester. "Is there a place close by where they can land a helicopter?"

Lester nodded. "There's a pasture about two-hundred and fifty yards due west of here. There's a windmill feeding a water tank and plenty of room to land."

Porter relayed the information. "Will y'all be coming in during the day or night?"

"Looks like we may be there first thing in the morning. Can you hang something high in the water tower so we know we are at the right spot? We have you pretty well located on the map; that will just let us zero in on you quicker."

"That won't be a problem. I'll go look at it now and find something to put on it. I'll call you as soon as I get back."

"Mr. Lester, I need you to show me that windmill. Do you feel up to walking that far or do I need to put a saddle on Old Dollar so you can ride?"

"Hell, I ain't dead yet kid; I can walk that far."

Mr. Lester headed out with Porter walking behind. "Mr. Lester, you're going to have to let me lead the way. I have to keep you alive. You are very important, or they wouldn't be sending a helicopter!"

"Sorry kid, look up through that gap in the trees you can see it from here."

"Why would they have a windmill pumping water this close to the river?"

"You'll see."

When they got there they were standing next to a large fence.

"This was one of them fancy game ranches where people paid a lot of money to hunt exotic game."

Porter looked in both directions. "Is there a gate?"

"Not around here."

"Let's get back to camp. I've got some bolt cutters. I'll have a section cut out in just a few minutes."

They returned to camp, and Porter made sure Mr. Lester was resting by the fire.

"I'm going to cut a section of the electric wire off that fence and pull up one of my shirts as a flag."

Mr. Lester dug around in his pack. "Don't use a shirt; I have something better." He pulled out a good sized Texas State Flag.

"That's perfect, Mr. Lester."

Porter spent the next hour opening the fence and getting the wire hung so he could pull up the flag. He stood for a moment admiring his work. The flag was slowly flapping in the breeze with the sun setting behind it.

When he got back to camp, he radioed Cooney, "Look for a Texas State Flag on the water tower below the blades."

"Porter, they will be coming in there just about daylight. A helicopter landing could create a lot of attention; so as soon as they lift off, you need to high tail it out of there with your mules and equipment. Make sure you have Lester packed up and waiting at the tower before daylight. Good work, son; if this works, we will have dealt a death blow to the bad guys."

As Porter packed up the radio and all his equipment, the old man asked, "Porter, I notice that you always repack all your equipment after you use it, why is that?"

"I never know when I will have to leave in a hurry. I can't afford to lose anything. Tonight let's pack the things that you want to take with you. You can't take all this stuff."

He looked over at his mare. "We've been through a lot; I've known her a lot of years. I used to feed her apples and carrots through the fence."

"Don't worry, Mr. Lester. She will help me make better time. I can move non-stop with her helping. I will be able to divide the load between all three animals; we can go a lot further before I have to stop and let them rest. When we get to the ranch, there will be plenty for her to eat and fresh water to drink."

They put all of the old man's essentials in a big duffel bag with a strap. He packed some photos of his wife, children and grandchildren along with some clothes and other personal items. Porter stuffed in two MRE's on top in case he needed a snack on the way. Lester started to leave his rifle and pistol, but Porter insisted that he carry those with him.

"Mr. Lester, you never know what lies between here and headquarters."

Porter insisted that the old man get some sleep. There would be no sleep for Porter. He prepared the animals' packs, leaving most of the old man's gear at the camp. He divided the remaining load between Ruth and the mare, had them saddled and ready about forty five minutes before sunrise. He tied them securely and hobbled them. He couldn't have them spooking and running off with his gear.

He and the old man walked up to the fence where Porter created the opening the evening before. While waiting, Porter enlarged the opening and pulled the wire back so that he and the stock could easily get through. Right on time the helicopter came into view. They heard it before they saw it. It circled once and landed just west of the tower.

The old man looked at Porter. "You take care, son. Thanks for letting me get my licks in before I go."

"Mr. Lester, it was nice getting to know you; give 'em hell."

The helicopter wasn't even out of sight before Porter was back to the stock and had them moving toward the opening in the fence. They passed through and stopped at the water trough just long enough to let the animals get one more chance to drink. He tied the mare's lead to a ring on Ole Dollar's saddle, and they headed out. He would decide by the end of the day if the extra horse was helping or hindering his progress. Ole Dollar's and Ruth's loads were about fifty to seventy five pounds lighter than they were accustomed. He kept the absolute essentials in Ruth's packs. He didn't know the new horse's temperament, and he wasn't about to trust her with the radio and his extra food. She got to carry his hammock and non essential gear. He looked up at the Texas flag flapping in the wind as he passed the windmill tower and continued on his trek north and west.

## CHAPTER 11

Other than a quick stop to refuel near Alexandria, LA, they made it to the former turtle hatchery that was now a vaccine lab. The hatchery was not an ideal setting for a lab, but it had the advantage of being somewhat isolated, a climate controlled building and had working incubators. A large walk in cooler was set up as an isolation room. Although very crude, the entire building was foam insulated. The plumbers, electricians and carpenters had transformed it into a virus factory. All the sink drains went into a cistern with chlorine bleach so that no pathogens could leave the building in the waste water. HEPA air filters were set up throughout the lab and would run nonstop day and night. The floor drains in the building had the covers loosened and swimming pool chlorine tablets were dropped in and would be replenished daily. Doc and his volunteers were the only people allowed in or out. Masks and face shields were to be worn at all times, as well as, surgical gowns and gloves. The body of the plague victim and the family's clothes had been transferred to a large chest freezer in the lab. The top had a magnetic gasket lid. In addition, a run of tape around the top spanned the gap between the lid and the body of the freezer. The large walk in cooler was set up like a hospital room, complete with oxygen bottles. Two fans were pulling air out of the room and venting it out a stack on the roof. Doc insisted on a quarantine area of three-hundred yards in every direction.

Lester Graves walked through the door behind Cooney Jones.

"Doc, I want you to meet Mr. Lester Graves. Lester, this is Dr. Brown; we just call him Doc."

"Lester, I'm sorry we have to meet under these conditions. Has Cooney explained to you what we intend to do with you?"

"Yes, sir, I understand. I figure this is my way of getting even with them for doing what they did to us."

Cooney explained, "We know how to keep the plague from spreading among our people. We haven't had a breakout since we shut down all the traveling and personal interaction. So we figure if we can infect the remaining Chinese troops, our battle for North America will be won."

Doc said, "Lester, I have a room set up for you. We even have a TV with a huge assortment of movies; but if you prefer to read, these guys will scrounge up any kind of reading material you like. As soon as you're undressed and in a gown let me know, I need to give you a going over to see where you are health wise. They told me about the lung cancer. What I am going to do to you goes against every fiber of my being."

Lester looked up at him. "Doc, this communist takeover took everything I love and hold dear from me. I have no idea what has happened to my children and grandchildren. They killed my wife and destroyed everything I accumulated in my entire life; all I have left is the will to fight and this is the only way I can do that. What you're doing ain't any different than handing me a rifle and asking me to lead the charge. I want you to let me lead the charge."

"Ok, Lester, let's do it. I'm going to do several things: I am going to inoculate you with the virus, monitor you constantly to determine the progression of the disease and will then take blood samples and specimens to use in creating our cultures. The other thing we are going to do is try to save you. If we can develop a treatment protocol, we may be able to save some of our people when they become infected."

Doc did a complete physical workup of the old man and documented the findings in his chart. He felt the golf ball size lump in his groin and listened to his breathing. Other than lung congestion and the lump, all his vitals were typical of an eighty-two year old man. He ran the blood work himself with equipment salvaged from the local abandoned hospitals. The blood work was typical for an old man with lung cancer. Doc then donned his face shield, mask and surgical gown and opened the freezer. He unzipped the body bag and looked at the face of the deceased plague victim. He took a large needle and scrapped the frozen pustule on the man's cheek. Once he was certain that he had a good sample of virus infected tissue, he placed it in a stainless steel pan and closed up the body bag and resealed the freezer. He walked to Lester's bed with one of his volunteer assistants behind him holding the stainless steel pan containing the needle.

The old man looked up. "So, this is it."

Doc looked through his mask. "This is it; are you ready?"

Lester grinned. "Let the attack begin!"

Doc, using the contaminated needle, gently punctured the skin on the old man's left arm and scrapped the needle back and forth in the wound. "Now we wait."

Dix was sitting out on the deck of the catamaran nursing a sore back and aching ribs. He and Fox had completed the moving of the abandoned houseboats, so that they formed somewhat of a barricade. It would not eliminate the threat from an attack, for that matter nothing would, but they would provide some protection.

Fox was busy repairing his shot-up window and door when Dix called over, "From the looks of that door, I don't see how they missed you."

"I was lying flat on my belly shooting up. There were bullets dancing all around me. From the way I feel, I'm not sure they didn't hit me a time or two." Fox grinned. "I had no idea that dragging and anchoring boats could be so exhausting. I hurt all over."

The radio crackled and Dix answered, "Cooney, how is our patient?"

"How did you know it was me?"

"Butch doesn't like using the radio; so unless it's important, he just shows up."

"Our patient is resting comfortably. He has been inoculated, and we're just waiting for the virus to take hold. We have some eggs already infected from samples taken from the corpse. In twenty four hours Doc is going to open one up and see how it compares to a normal egg."

"Good, we are right on schedule. I have some sick eggs, and I've got my defenses beefed up; so all we have to do is figure out a way to bait the trap. Keep me posted."

Rachel came over and planted a kiss on Dix's cheek. Fox looked up grinning.

Dix looked at Rachael. "See what you're starting, first I've got Beagle poking fun at me and now you got him started."

Rachel just grinned and kissed him again. "Let me know when you guys are ready for me to start cooking."

"I hate for you to feel like you need to do all the cooking."

She frowned. "The only thing Beagle can cook is fried catfish; Fox can put gator on the grill, and you will eat anything you can swallow. To make a long story short, I have no desire to choke on y'all's cooking!" Rachel smirked. "I'm the only one who can cook around here. Beagle better kill us a pig. I'm cooking turtle soup tonight. I found a recipe in a Cajun cook book in the galley. Beagle caught one on his trot line and cleaned it for me."

"Just call us when you're ready for us to eat."

She gave him another lip-smack and headed back to her boat.

Dix looked back at Fox. "Not a word. That's an order."

Fox laughed. "I thought you didn't like all that military crap."

"I don't, but I'll drag it out when I have to."

Dix keyed the mic, "Butch, are you listenin?"

"I'm here, what's up?"

"Did you hear what Cooney said?"

"Yes, have you and Fox come up with anything yet?"

"We are working on different delivery ideas right now. How many cartons of cigarettes can you come up with?"

Butch paused a minute. "I don't know if I can stand to give up my cigarettes. What do you have in mind?"

"You didn't answer my question; how many cartons of cigarettes can you come up with?"

"I have five cases of cigarettes."

"Bring 'em here; I have an idea."

Butch sighed. "I was afraid that was what you were going to say."

Butch arrived in time for lunch with his five cases of cigarettes and a dour look on his face.

"Don't look so sad; I know you have cigars, pipes and chewing tobacco. We are bound to be able to come up with some tobacco seeds one of these days."

While they were eating around the bar in Rachel's kitchen, Dix asked, "Have we established any kind of schedule on the Chinese boats?"

"There is one coming by here every other day; the times vary."

Dix had a look of satisfaction on his face. "What if we dropped a pack of cigarettes seeded with the virus on each boat until they quit running. If my calculations are correct, we have about six-hundred packs of cigarettes we can drop. When they pass under the bridge, all we have to do is drop it on their deck. You and I both know soldiers; there will be someone who will snag the pack and sell or smoke them. If we inject a little of Doc's virus up in the filter area, they will put it in their own mouth. We can also drop a tainted egg or two each time. If we can do it at night, that's all the better. If that doesn't work, we can take Fox's little boat, ease up to them at night, and toss a pack on board. Do you guys have any better ideas?"

Butch grinned. "Damn, that's a good idea. I might know where I can put my hands on another case or two."

Dix punched him on the shoulder. "I figured you were holding out a little. We can't toss a bunch of cigarettes because they'll know it's a trap. Just one pack will be enough to fool them into thinking that someone on board dropped a pack. My other question is 'Do you think we need to create a diversion like dropping some grenades so that a pack of cigarettes just shows up in the middle of the chaos?' If one comes through at night we can just drop it quietly, but we wouldn't know if it made it on the boat or not. I'm thinking we drop a couple of eggs and a pack of cigarettes. I'm not sure if just dropping eggs would work. Let's get Cooney on the radio."

Dix put the radio on speaker so they could all listen. When he reached Cooney, he told him the plan. Cooney agreed.

"I'll run it by Doc. He can tell us how to proceed, but it sounds like one hell of a plan."

Dix piped in, "It was your idea to use the tobacco and whiskey. I like the idea of padding some whiskey bottles in infected padding. I don't know of any army where soldiers don't like to drink. I just don't want to get any of us killed delivering the package."

Fox was nodding in agreement. "I don't care for that getting killed part."

Dix turned to Butch. "You know that Barrett .50 cal you've located. If we had someone popping away at them from the bluff, we could get the attention away from the bridge. I know they are expecting to be shot at from the bridge; that's why dropping the cigarettes anytime other than night time will give away our plans. They probably have night vision scopes and will spot anyone on the bridge."

Fox spoke up, "The only sure way of doing this is for me to hide up or down the river in my stump thumper. I saw the boats on my way up here. My little boat will outrun them when they are going upstream. All I need to do is ease up from behind at night and gently toss a pack on board."

Turning to Butch, Dix asked, "What if we put one of these boats floating downstream with a sea bag in it? In the bag there would be some folded clothes, whiskey, cigarettes, and toiletries. We could even have the bow line snagged so it was bobbing in the edge of the river. It would look like the traveler just fell overboard. We would have to guard it to make sure none of our civilians spot it and try to retrieve it."

Dix finally had a plan. "For the first drop we will need to have an explosion just up the river. I think a hand grenade and five gallons of gas ought to do the trick. We can set one off on the levee. While they are all looking at the explosion, we'll just drop a pack from the bridge. Remember guys, all we have to do is get one of them sick. It will be spreading like wildfire before they know it."

Butch and Dix took his truck over to the virus factory where they met with Doc Brown.

Doc scolded them. "Gentlemen, I am going to ask you not to come by here again. This is a very crude facility. I am trying to create twenty-first century biological weapons at a turtle farm; it's not unlike doing brain surgery in a barn using a hatchet and broom straws. I have established a three-hundred yard quarantine area. Nobody in or out, so we need to go down to the end of the road."

Dix turned to Butch. "Do we have enough men to cordon off the area?"

"I'll get on it. We'll put up a fence of barbwire and posts to mark no man's land."

"Doc, is that satisfactory for you?"

"Yes, it's only me and my three volunteers here, and we're not leaving."

"Did Cooney tell you about my plans of using the packs of cigarettes?"

Doc nodded in agreement. "It is an excellent idea to contaminate the filter tips. I'm not as certain about dropping egg bombs. I don't see where it would hurt, especially if they got some of the contents on them before it dried."

They stopped at the end of the driveway and looked back. Dix asked, "How long before we have a product, Doc?"

"Give me three to five days. I don't have any way of testing it, but I am certain I will have a virus soon."

Leaving the factory, Dix said, "Butch, I want to be lying on that bridge when the next boat passes. Can you get me some eyes up and downstream to give me some notice when one is coming? Get me someone up on the river about fifteen miles north of town and about ten miles south. That will give me plenty of notice to get up on the bridge. You radio me and come pick me up when they see them coming."

"Sure thing, I'll reposition my men as soon as I drop you off."

"If you need Fox, come get him."

"Also, see if you can get me a barrel of ground wheat, I'm starting to get a little tired of corn bread at every meal; take some catfish for yourself and to trade, I'm sure Beagle has a cage full. There's an empty barrel by the launch you can use to put the wheat in."

"Sure thing, Major."

"Get out of here and take that army stuff with you."

Butch left. Dix hopped in his boat and ran across to the houseboats. Rachel's pot of turtle soup was ready to pour over a bowl of rice.

They finished eating, and Dix looked at Fox. "Here's my plan. When we get the call I'll wake you, so that we're on the bridge when the next boat comes through. We're going to be on our bellies in the middle of the bridge. I want to see how hard it's going to be running around on the bridge. We're got to keep our heads down because I'm sure they have spotters and heavy weapons. I'm certain they feel vulnerable going under bridges; I know I do."

Fox nodded in agreement. "I'm ready when you are."

Dix couldn't get away without a kiss. As was customary, he stayed to help Rachel clean up. Beagle and Fox left and went to their boats. When Rachel kissed him this time, he kissed back, but resisted the urge to go to her room. She gave him a final hug, let the dogs in and locked the door behind him. The call came sooner than expected. Dix had just settled into his bunk for the night when the radio crackled.

It was Butch. "Dix, we got one heading up the river. It'll be here within the hour."

"Pick me up at the launch. I'll wake Fox." Dix opened the door and called to Fox, "Fox, roll out; Butch is fixing to pick us up; we've got a boat coming up the river!"

They motored over to the launch and only had to wait a minute before Butch drove over the levee and down to the launch. Soon all three were heading up the bridge hill at a fast walk. All three were armed to the teeth. Dix was packing Jake's AR15 and had his Browning High Power in a shoulder holster. Fox had his old 30-30 and the old 1911 forty-five pistol. Butch was packing the AK47 that Dix had given him several months earlier. A brisk wind was blowing up on the bridge. Dix realized that this could be a problem when trying to drop a lightweight pack of cigarettes onto a boat ten stories below.

In the moonlight they could see the vessel approaching. When it was about a half a mile out, they lay flat on the bridge where they could peer just above the walkway. They were certain there were spotters on board with night vision scopes scrutinizing the bridge. As they waited for the boat to get closer, Dix hoped that the heat from the bridge would mask their thermal signature. At the half mile mark they determined that the boat would go under the east side of the bridge. Moving to the north lane, they ran in a low crouch to the east end of the bridge. Since the roadway had drains for water to run off, each man took a drain and looked at the river rushing below. It was dark and foreboding; the moonlight shining on the water sparkled in the small waves and whirlpools. They were almost startled when the boat appeared beneath them. The diesel exhaust reached them as the air currents carried up to the bridge road bed and beyond. As Dix started counting, the boat took a full twenty seconds to pass under the bridge. Dix and the guys were itching to open up on them with their rifles, as they could see men lounging around the boat's pilot house and out on the walkway behind it. They looked at each other and grinned when they realized that half the men were smoking.

Butch suggested, "I think we need to take Dix's boat down under the bridge and see if we can hit it with a pack of cigarettes. If we can come anywhere close, the pack will easily land on the big boat."

Dix nodded in agreement. "I can't wait. We need to practice dropping them through the drain while wearing gloves. I want to simulate the actual conditions. I want everything, but the virus when we do the dry run."

The trip back to the boats was practically festive. Victory was within their grasp.

"Do you think we can make a sling shot out of some inner tubes or surgical rubber that we can use to shoot the cigarettes to the deck?"

Fox chimed in, "If we do that, we're going to need a diversion, and we need to pull out those grates so we can have a clear shot. We can build racks with triggers so that we can fire down through the holes without exposing ourselves."

Dix laughed. "A good old boy from South Georgia ought to be able figure out a way. Tomorrow, that will be your job, Fox. Butch, do we have any welders still alive?"

"I've got a good one; in fact, he was making some IED's using propane and oxygen when we were working on the Chinese retreating from Jonesville."

Dix looked over his shoulder at Fox in the back seat. "Do you have a design in mind?"

Fox grinned. "I already know how to do it; I just have to be careful not to overpower it. We don't want to tear up the pack of cigarettes."

"First things first. We have five days before Doc has us some sick eggs and some weaponized cigarettes. As soon as it's light, I want to be heading out to the bridge in my boat and sitting under it. We'll take a carton of cigarettes; with one of you guys on the bridge, we'll see how close we can come just dropping it through the hole. If we can get within ten feet of the boat, we can just drop a pack. Our diversion needs to make a lot of smoke and noise. Fox, we're going to need those hand grenades. If we can't hit my boat, then we will have to make your sling shot."

The rest of the trip was spent telling war stories. Butch still had his family intact. Dix had lost everything. Fox lost his parents, brother and his brother's family. Fox had a son who was working in the North Dakota oil fields; but he had lost contact with him a year ago when he left with his girlfriend heading to her family's farm.

Dix clenched his fist. "We're gonna drive them into the sea and with them the criminal American communists who started this." They all nodded in agreement and headed home.

The next morning Dix and Fox were up early gassing the boat and getting geared up to meet Butch at the launch. Butch and Dix each took a small two way radio handset, so they could communicate from the bridge deck to the boat on the water. Spotters up and down the river would warn them if any of the big boats were coming so they could hide from view. Fox and Dix took the boat down the lake and out of the outlet into the river slowing as they entered the river to make sure there were no boats and no surprises. It was clear. Spotting a small figure standing on the bridge, Dix looked though his binoculars; it was Butch. They ran the boat south with the current under the bridge. As soon as they were past the bridge, they turned the boat so that they were heading north against the current. Holding it in position under the bridge, Dix called Butch on the radio, "We are ready when you are."

"As soon as you come into view, under the middle grate, I'll drop."

Dix ran the boat up to a spot directly beneath the storm drain. The pack of cigarettes dropped; then two eggs behind it. The cigarettes pack fell about fifteen feet behind the boat; the eggs hit dead center. They tried ten times, and the cigarettes fell within the area of a hundred foot long boat all but two of the times. The eggs hit every time.

Dix called on the radio to Butch, "I recovered the cigarettes with my landing net. They barely got wet. I'll let you smoke these."

Butch radioed back, "As soon as they dry, they'll smoke fine, thanks."

Dix waved and hit the mic again. "Meet me at the launch. We need to plan the diversions."

Planning the battle had Dix's heart racing; his recuperation was almost complete. The only thing really bothering him was his missing little toe. He couldn't understand how something that wasn't there could hurt so badly. When he was in the hospital, Doc explained that it was ghost pain coming from the severed nerves.

He ran the boat dead slow in the river. There was always debris in the river, so unless a person was chasing or escaping, there was no need to take a chance on damaging the motor or boat. He could smell the earthy aroma of the river as they motored toward the inlet to the Old River Lake. Purple Martins skimmed across the water dipping their bills to drink.

Just as they entered the lake, the sound of a single rifle shot rang out. Dix punched the throttle on the boat, and Fox got up in the front with his rifle. They were running down the lake full throttle fearful that there was trouble at the houseboats. They ran down the lake only to find Beagle waving them down from the island. Dix killed the throttle.

"What are you shooting at?"

Beagle grinned a semi toothless grin. "I got us about a three-hundred pound hog for the smoke house."

Fox gave him a thumbs up, and Dix yelled, "Fresh bacon!"

He nosed the boat up on the bank, and Beagle hoped in. He was muddy up to his knees with a little blood mixed in.

"Beagle, do you think you and Fox can handle the hog while I meet with Butch?"

"Sure thing. We can pull it behind the boat until we get to the launch. We can lift it up into a tree using the winch on the four wheeler, and have it dressed and in the smoke house in no time."

They dropped Dix off at the catamaran where he stopped long enough to check on Rachel. Ben and Frank were barking and raising the devil until they realized it was Dix. The boat dipped a little when he stepped on board. Fox and Beagle disappeared back down the lake to retrieve the hog.

Rachel came out and gave Dix a big hug and kiss. "Looks like you had a big day so far."

Dix held her hand to steady her as she walked the wide cypress plank across to the catamaran. When they reached the catamaran, Dix pulled her hand to his cheek and kissed her wrist. "The reason I didn't want to start this was because it affects my performance as a fighter. When Beagle shot the hog, my heart jumped into my throat because I thought something was happening here again."

She fell into his arms. "Well it's too late to undo it all now. How do you think I feel wondering if you'll make it back? I hope after this next battle you'll realize that you've done your part. You are the ramrod who calls the shots; this would have pretty much fallen apart if you had gotten yourself killed."

Just then Butch drove over the levee. Dix turned to Rachel. "Gotta go, we got some planning to do."

"Wait, I made you a sack of biscuits with syrup."

"Thanks, I'm starved." He grabbed the biscuits and stole a kiss as he hopped in one of the empty boats and cranked the outboard. He ran across to the launch where Butch was unloading the barrel of wheat. Dix climbed out of the boat almost slipping on the slimy boat launch concrete and taking a dip in the lake.

Butch laughed. "Careful old man or you'll break a hip."

"I've got at least one more battle to orchestrate; I've got to be careful."

Butch nodded towards the houseboats out in the lake. "You've got a battle waiting for you on that boat."

"Not you too."

"We've just about got them licked; and the way I see it Dix, we've got to keep on living. I've got my family and like it or not you've got yours. It was your idea to rescue the lady and take care of her."

"Are you saying it's like feeding a stray cat?"

"That's one way of putting it, but you didn't just feed a stray cat. You and she found each other and y'all need each other. Let's get this great battle fought; and if we live, we can set about doing what we want: surviving and living."

"Enough of that, we've got to concentrate on executing this next fight. Let's set up an ambush on the levee where four or five of us open up on the Chinese and pepper the boat with gun fire. We'll open fire when they are under the bridge, and all we have to do is drop a pack of cigarettes and a couple of eggs. We'll need a spotter to make sure the pack lands on the boat. If he sees it hit the water, he'll radio to immediately drop another. Once it lands; we simply retreat and wait for the next boat. If it's at night, we just drop a pack and hope it hits. We'll set off a five gallon can of gas with a grenade for the next daytime boat and set up the Barrett .50 cal after that."

Butch nodded in agreement. "I already have sites prepared. I knew we would have to start shooting at those boats sooner or later."

Fox and Beagle arrived with the hog in tow. The four of them quickly had the animal strung up, and Beagle had a pot of water boiling so he could scald the pig and scrape off the hair.

Dix pointed to Fox's boat. "Fox, we're going to need the rest of those hand grenades. My guess is they are going to make a run for the sea once the plague hits them. I want to set up a going away present for them. I'd like to rig up a way to drop a handful of grenades on a boat as they pass under the bridge. Why don't we suspend them by their pin rings under the grate and rig a wire so that we can be off the bridge when we pull the pins.

That way we can bomb them with the falling grenades as a going away present."

Butch grinned. "I like it."

"Fox and Beagle, y'all take care of the pig and fire up the smokehouse. Butch, bring Cooney and Doc up to speed and make sure Doc has what he needs. Tell him that it's important for the cigarettes to appear not to have been tampered with. He needs to use a small needle and a safe way for us to transport our weapon. We'll need rubber gloves and disinfectant that we can use after we deploy the virus. I don't want this to be a suicide mission."

Butch nodded in agreement. "We don't want this backfiring on us."

Dix got in his boat, motored back to the catamaran where he plopped down in his chair and put his sore foot up. He saw Rachael through her window. Then he glanced up to see a drone flying in from the island side of the houseboats.

## CHAPTER 12

The mules were feeling a little frisky this morning. The cool air and a day of rest had them feeling their oats, and they were anxious to get down the trail. The path they were on looked like a cow trail, but it could have just as easily been made by horses or any other large animal. They were making their way more or less parallel to the river. The trail led up to a small rise, and Porter was amazed to see a herd of American buffalo quietly grazing. He was surprised to see them, since they were so close to Austin and its high population. He guessed the fenced enclosure had kept out some of the crowds. There were also some red deer, and what he assumed were African antelope. He came to a cattle guard with a gate next to it. Cutting the locks on the gate he continued on. He came to an abandoned lodge with vehicles parked around it. They looked like they had not been run in some weeks having a good layer of windblown Texas dirt coating the windshields. Porter started to turn around and open the gate, but figured the open fence at the river would be enough to free the animals if they decided to leave. At least they could get to water when the windmill water pump gave out one day. He resisted the temptation to prowl around. He wasn't sure if he had the plague or not and wasn't willing to chance the exposure in case he didn't. His one goal was to keep traveling. He traveled all day stretching out the rest time to every three hours. The mules and mare didn't seem to mind the lighter loads they were carrying. Still avoiding roads when possible, he crossed several ranches.

After traveling several days, he left the area with all the mini ranches and was in an area with larger tracks of land. Most seemed abandoned, but he found one with a family on it. A pair of dogs came running out, but stopped short when Ole Dollar almost connected with a sudden kick. The owner rode out on a four wheel ATV and had a gun on Porter. The man looked healthy enough and challenged Porter. "You need to get off my property before I start shooting."

Porter grinned at him. "I'll do that; I don't want any trouble. I'm traveling cross country to West Texas to get to my family. I'm sorry I had to trespass. I'm Sergeant Porter Jones with the Constitution army. Has anyone warned you about the plague?"

"What plague? I haven't seen anyone for weeks. I've got my family here on my Dad's ranch. There are twelve of us. Don't try anything; I've got a man with a rifle on you."

"That's a good idea. Otherwise what you are doing would be suicide."

"Suicide? What do you mean suicide?"

"I mean, a man riding up to a stranger in these parts shouldn't get within range of his weapons if he doesn't know who he's dealing with. You should have stopped about one-hundred and fifty yards out and been around some cover."

"You don't look so tough, kid."

"Mister, I don't mean to be disrespectful, but that kind of attitude can get you hurt. You need to assume that everyone is out to hurt you until you find out who they are."

Old Dollar's ears folded back on his head, and he made that little noise resembling a moan warning Porter that someone was coming up from the rear.

"Mister, there's two ways we can do this. I can start shooting and kill you and whoever is sneaking up behind me, or you can call them off and give me some directions. In case you're wondering, I have a cocked pistol pointing at your chest."

The man grew pale when he realized that Porter's hand was in his vest pocket and the pocket was aimed at him.

"Mister, I'm getting real nervous, even if he shoots; this gun will go off; and you can't use any of my stuff because I may have been exposed to the plague. You're dead either way."

The man looked past Porter and motioned with his head. "Caleb, come on around. We need to hear what he has to say."

Caleb was a young man not much older than Porter. Porter noticed that both Caleb and the man were wearing red arm bands. Evidently, they could tell friend from foe from a distance with the arm bands. Porter never took the gun off the man on the ATV.

"Let me start over. I'm Porter Jones, Sergeant in the Constitution army. I'm on my way to West Texas to get to my family. The best I can figure I have five or six-hundred miles to go, and I'm scouting and reporting what I find to headquarters."

The man seemed a little more relaxed and lowered his gun. Porter's hand never left his pocket and his aim never wavered. "Do you mind if I continue to travel across your land to the northwest?"

"No, but I don't want you cutting my fences. You can follow the horse and cow trail to the back until you hit a fence. If you turn right at the fence, you will come to the gate after about a half mile."

"Mister, do you mind if I ask your name?"

"I'm Hugh Harvey; this is my brother Caleb. This is my dad's ranch where we grew up. My parents are up at the ranch. I have my wife and kids, as well as, my sister and her family. We all rendezvoused here after the collapse."

"You need to hear about the plague." Porter spent twenty minutes explaining to him about the plague and how to avoid getting it. "I'm not here to trade, visit or spend the night; I'm just passing through. Is there a river or creek where I can water my stock and let them feed and rest tonight?"

"Sure, when you pass through the gate, keep heading northwest. You'll come to a road. If you cross it, you'll hit a huge grass field. On the back side you will see a long line of trees. That is where a small creek runs. Look for a big oak tree; you can't miss it. You can camp, and there is plenty of grass. As soon as summer hits, it will dry up, but for now there should be plenty for the stock."

"Thanks, Hugh, how far are we talking about?"

"Only five or six miles. You'll get there in time to set up camp."

"Have you guys seen any of the communist Chinese around here? Or are there any communist Americans operating here?"

"The Chinese cleared out a while back. Everyone says they high-tailed it for Houston. The real communists, the ones who dreamed the dream, joined the communist Chinese, and most of them realized too late that the Chinese didn't want or need them. The useful idiots voted the party line because it meant they would get a government check and all the other free stuff. They would have identified with the Martian party so long as they got free stuff. When the grocery stores shelves emptied, they went crazy. They were the first to start fighting and looting, and it was a blood bath for weeks."

Porter stated, "We've run across a few Americans with the Chinese units acting as advisors and helping them conduct interrogations. If there is a colony of them around, I would like to know about it."

Hugh looked up. "They disappeared. We assumed they went to Houston. The rumors were that the Chinese just executed them. They went from pretending to be UN peacekeepers to conquerors. We were just lucky all this came to a head before they could confiscate our guns."

Porter thought *my mother and grandmother sent money to some of those politicians in California.* "I can't keep using up daylight; I've got to get home. Thanks for letting me cross your ranch."

Hugh pointed to Porter's vest pocket that was still pointed at him. "Do you really have a gun on me?"

Porter took his free hand and held the vest pocket and pulled it off the gun, revealing a .38 caliber pistol with a three inch barrel.

"I didn't live this long being trustful or by bluffing. As soon as you put your guns in the rack, I'll be on my way."

"You bet, kid, you taught me a lesson today."

They put away their guns and drove back toward the house. Porter goosed Ole Dollar, and they disappeared at a fast gallop across the pasture and out of sight. He only slowed when he came to the gate and exited the property. Porter let the animals walk, and he didn't pause for them to rest but once. He knew that once he got to the creek they could rest and graze. The vast grass field was exactly as described, and the little creek was babbling away. There was even an oak tree of fairytale proportions standing next to it; its roots drawing moisture from the little creek. Porter hobbled the stock and let them graze. He set up the radio. He could only reach Cooney at night now. He had travelled beyond the range where he could communicate during the day. It was only when the interference from the sun disappeared over the horizon that his radio would work.

"Cooney here, how's it going, son?"

"I'm thinking I'm about five-hundred miles out and I've been making good time. I haven't run across any Chinese or communists. The last people I spoke to this afternoon thought that the Chinese are in Houston, and they also told me that there are rumors that the Chinese executed most of the American communists. They said that the Chinese got rid of their American communist benefactors as soon as they were no longer needed."

"Served them right. I still haven't heard from the Cross family. Have you experienced any symptoms?"

"Not yet. I've been feeling tired, but I think that's normal for the way I am traveling and fighting."

"Porter, you're a good man. I'm proud of you. Watch your back and respect your gut feelings. If something seems wrong, it probably is. Check back in a few days. Take care."

"I'll radio back in a few days."

Porter set up his hammock between two saplings, put in his sleeping bag and made it up to look as though he were sleeping inside. He built a good fire and ate an MRE. He then took his AK47, crossed the creek and hid in the edge of a thicket out of sight, but where he could see the camp. The stock was grazing off to his right next to the creek. He couldn't remember being more tired than he was now, so he dozed and periodically woke when he heard a sound in the night. It wasn't a strange sound, but a familiar one that roused him. Ole Dollar made his little disturbed sound. It was not a whinny but could have been if he came on out with it. It was sort of like a moan that resonated a bit. Hugh and his brother Caleb appeared in the edge of the firelight across the fire from the hammock. Hugh raised his rifle and shot the hammock three times. Porter waited just a bit to make sure there was no one with or following them. When they got almost to the hammock, Porter shot twice. Hugh did a sort of pirouette and collapsed where he stood; Caleb tried to run, but collapsed. Porter took his time and popped each one through the head. There was no sleeping now. He was careful not to touch the bodies or step in the blood. He took down his hammock. It would have to be repaired, but he would take care of that when it was daylight, and he could see. For once he wished he had the Rokon motorcycle. He could have been back by now if he could have located gas. He packed up his camp and had the animals loaded before dawn. The little creek was running from the direction he was heading so he climbed on Ole Dollar and rode parallel to the creek proceeding out of the area at a walk. If he hadn't suspected these guys to be crooks, he would be dead, and he knew that others would be coming to check on them. Porter thought *they sure knew a lot about the communists; maybe they were some that got away from the Chinese.*

As usual, Porter did not concern himself about killing Hugh and Caleb. They were bad guys. They preyed on the innocent and helpless. They underestimated him; it was as simple as that. He didn't ask for the trouble; he simply played the hand they dealt him.

A year ago he was going to school and eating meat behind his mother's back. He was afraid to go camping, and felt sorry for his dad's having to put up with his mother and his grandmother. His past life seemed like a million years ago.

His thoughts quickly returned to the here and now when he heard the dogs baying in the distance. The sun was just peeking through the trees behind him. He kicked the animals up to a lope and started looking for a defensive position. He didn't know if the dogs were on his trail or if they were chasing game. He wasn't going to wait to find out. He came to a spot where he could cross the creek and go up a hill. The trail looked like a well-used cow path, so up it he went. It flattened out on top so he tied up the stock on the far side of the clearing. He went back to the top of the hill and took a position behind a tree where he could see his back trail. The baying gradually grew louder as he waited. He took a sip from his camel back canteen and mentally steeled himself for the task before him. As he sank down on one knee, the leaves crunched, and he dug the toe of his boot into the soil behind him. He could see about a quarter of a mile up the creek from where he crouched. This reminded him of his time back at the Cross ranch hiding in his blind out on the range. The dogs soon came into view. They were the same ones that greeted him back at the Harvey's ranch. Behind them on horseback came a gray haired man and three other men on horseback. All four of them wore red armbands and each had rifles. They were about a hundred yards behind the dogs with their horses running at a steady lope.

Porter was way past the point of worrying about what he had to do. He thought to himself *if they want to commit suicide it's their choice, I'm sure they're not coming to apologize for Hugh's and Caleb's trying to murder me, and I'm not going to give them a warning.*

As soon as the big dogs crossed the creek, he opened up with the AK47. The gray haired man took the first round and rolled backwards off his horse. The others tried to rein in, but it was too late. They were all down along with two of the horses. His last two shots killed the dogs that were running away with their tails between their legs. One of the men was trying to take shelter behind one of the dying horses. Porter shot through the dying horse hitting the man again. A dead horse was lying on another man who was still flaying about and cursing. A bullet through his chest stilled him. Porter replaced the magazine in his AK47 and waited. He could see the three men who were lying around the horses. The two unhurt horses disappeared at a full gallop in the direction from which they came. He couldn't see the gray haired man, but he was certain that he had taken a round as Porter's first shot had hit him when he reined his horse back before crossing the creek. If the man were still alive, he would be hit badly, so Porter patiently waited, hidden and silent. He wished he still had a couple of those Chinese hand grenades. This would be a good time to chunk one down the hill. He sat completely silent and did not move a muscle. A shot rang out in his direction, but it was wild. He resisted the urged to shoot back. The old man was probably trying to draw him out. Patience was the name of the game. He then saw a hand come up with a pistol. Six quick shots in his direction did not connect. When he saw the pistol pointed roughly at him, he leaned behind the tree and immediately got back on target when it was clear the gun was empty. The AK47 was not accurate enough to take a shot at the man's hand, so he waited. The pistol disappeared behind the dirt bank in the creek. The old man was lying in the creek. Porter just sat quietly and thought about the red arm bands and the flowing gray hair of the man leading the pack on his trail. He saw the pistol appear again. The grey haired man poked his head up and looked around before disappearing behind the bank. A moment later, using the bank, he tried to get up. A crimson stain was high on the left side of his shirt. He staggered to his feet and turned to head back to the dead men and horses. Porter placed a round between his shoulder blades knocking him forward on his face and then placed another shot for good measure. Porter walked back to the horses and replaced the used magazines with fresh ones from Ruth's pack. He turned the horses and rode back down across the creek and past the dead. He glanced at the sightless eyes. He felt bad about killing the horses; they were the victims here. The dogs were mean and bloodthirsty, just like the men; they were all out for blood. He knew a few mean horses. There was a couple he knew back at the Cross's that would bite you if you weren't paying attention. One old horse was bad about kicking. He kicked at one of Charlie Cross's grandkids and wound up in the smoke house as dog food. Porter had lost the ability to regret killing bad guys. Anytime he felt a tinge of guilt, he simply had to remember how his parents and little brother were murdered. He also remembered how the Chinese and the communist American beat one of the Cross boys almost to death. Porter thought as he left the battle scene *the world will eventually run out of bad guys.*

There were no more bad guys or wild dogs for the next few days. He was entering the dry country, and soon the ranches and people were few and far between. The task now was to travel from water hole to water hole. When he found pasture and water, he would have to let the stock eat, drink and rest.

# CHAPTER 13

Dix watched as the drone slowly passed overhead. He reached in the door of the catamaran and pulled out the 12 gauge shotgun loaded with buckshot. He stepped out from under his Bimini canopy and with one motion started shooting at the drone. He saw pieces coming off of it before it crashed on top of Beagle's house boat. Dix reloaded the shotgun and placed it back in the catamaran. He grabbed his bug out bag, his rifle and yelled to Rachel, "Grab your gun and your bug out bag; get in the boat with the dogs." Without questioning him, she grabbed her gear. Dix raced up to the top of Beagle's boat and retrieved the remains of the drone. The battery compartment had burst open, so Dix removed the battery in case it was still broadcasting a signal. He threw it in the boat and radioed Butch. "I'm bringing Rachel to shore; we can expect incoming ordinance or men any second." Butch got on the radio and had men notified to be ready to come on the double. As usual, Fox, Beagle and Dix were already loaded up and ready with full battle gear.

The radio crackled. "Cooney here, I've been listening, Dix. What's happening?"

"I just knocked a drone out of the sky directly over our houseboats. It's a short range battery powered unit. Make sure that you have enough men to guard Doc. That is your top priority. I'm taking my boat out the north inlet, and I am sending Fox out the south. Beagle will stay with Rachel on shore, and Butch will be with me. I think they are in the river towards the north end of the island. We'll keep you posted."

Cooney paused. "What do you want me to do if you get incapacitated?"

"Get with Fox and attack as soon as Doc has the gifts wrapped. Run it by Colonel Miller of course, but you know what has to be done."

Dix turned to Rachel and Beagle. "I want you guys to find a place to hide. Take the dogs and the four wheeler. I think they are going to either mortar the area or send in another team to clean us out."

Beagle hooked up the trailer behind the four wheeler. The dogs and gear went in the trailer with Beagle and Rachel on the bike.

Rachel leaned out and gave Dix a hug and kiss. "Be careful and give 'em hell."

Fox said, "Drop me off at the stump thumper. I'll take it out the south end and meet you up the river unless I run into them, and then I will radio. I can get in close to shore with my boat and beach it by myself. If I find anything or where they've put in on the island, I'll radio."

Butch and Dix dropped Fox off long enough for him to transfer to his old boat. They watched as the little Mercury started on the second pull and raced away down the lake. They spun out just as a half dozen mortar rounds landed in and around the boats. Dix was really angry as they raced up toward the outlet that would lead them out into the river around the north side of the island. They spotted the mortar men on a sandbar and immediately came under fire when they attempted to beach the boat. A sniper had them pinned down from the woods on the island.

Butch shouted, "We're trapped."

Dix grabbed him by the collar. "Follow me."

He pulled Butch into the river water and pushed backward pulling the boat towards them and into the river current. Bullets were hitting the boat. A bullet hole appeared next to Dix's arm as he held onto the boat and let the current carry them downstream. They were a good five-hundred yards downstream before the hail of gunfire ceased. They swam around to the outboard and used it to climb back over the stern into the boat. There were random holes all over the boat, but the motor wasn't hit. Firing up the motor, they headed upstream to make certain they were out of range. They cut across the river where they could use binoculars to see what was taking place. They got on the radio with Fox who was by now in the river and heading north.

He reported, "I can see them. I'm putting in and approaching on foot."

"Be careful, they have snipers on this end."

"No sweat. I figured as much, so I stayed real close to shore. In fact I just saw movement about three-hundred yards up the bank. I've got to get closer before I can shoot."

"Remember, we are fixing to kill all these sons a bitches, so don't do anything careless."

"Be quiet, Dix, and let me have some fun."

Dix looked around at Butch. "Crap, why didn't you say you were hit?"

Butch looked down. "I'm hit?" Blood was pouring from his leg. Dix grabbed a roll of duct tape and wrapped the wound up tight.

"Damn, I didn't even feel it. I got too excited and distracted when those people were trying to kill me. Now it's starting to hurt."

"Lie down in the bottom of the boat and let me make sure I've got the bleeding stopped." Dix double checked to make sure he had the blood flow stemmed. "I wish I had the Springfield with us. I could engage them from the far bank."

In the distance they heard Fox's 30-30 bark. Dix fired up the motor and ran back toward the north inlet. Butch rolled to a sitting position and had his AK47 ready for action.

Dix looked at Butch. "I'm going back down the north inlet and cross to the north side of the island from there. You stay put in the boat. Radio Cooney and tell him where you are and what I am doing."

In the distance he could hear the explosions from the mortar rounds and the echo of Fox's old 30-30. Dix nosed the boat up to the bank where there were willow trees growing in the water and up the bank. He wedged the boat among them and grabbed his ammo pack. He was carrying Jake's AR15 as he disappeared over the front of the boat. Knee deep in mud, he trudged up the bank onto the island. Dix shook each foot to kick off the heavy gumbo mud caked on his boots and legs. Once in the woods, he cursed the dry leaves as he crunched his way towards the river side of the island. He slowed when he reached a point where he could see some daylight through the trees. He couldn't be far from where the sniper was shooting at them when they were in the river. The soil and leaves were giving way to sand, so the walking was a bit quieter. Cautiously, he eased toward the opening. He put the rifle on his back and got down on his hands and knees. As he approached the sandbar, he crawled on his stomach the last twenty feet. Wax myrtles lined the sandbar providing excellent cover. Their branches bent over and touched the sand creating an opening beneath the canopy where he was well hidden from the sandbar. He moved quietly beneath the branches as he worked his way toward the firing mortars. He kept his eyes peeled, as he crept toward the mortar fire. A second drone came buzzing overhead and landed near the mortar men. At that moment, two men with rifles came bursting out of the myrtle bushes fifty or sixty yards in front of him and headed toward the other men. They were pulling out. He heard Fox's 30-30 bellow and saw one of the men go down. They all turned and started firing toward Fox. This was Dix's cue to open up. He hit the two that were nearest him and then started firing at the mortars. They were forced to abandon the mortars and retreat to their boat. They sprayed the wood line with fire, forcing Dix to take refuge behind a bank of sand and willows. He heard Fox's 30-30 firing again. The men in the boat were maintaining a steady stream of fire from their machine gun. Although the fire was less focused, the slugs were chewing up the trees overhead. Limbs and debris were raining down as the slugs tore through the canopy. When the gun fire subsided, Dix looked over the sand bank and saw the boat heading north about three-hundred yards away. He aimed a little high and emptied the magazine on the retreating boat. He saw one of the men go down, and the cowling on one of the two outboard motors flew apart. The boat slowed, but didn't stop.

Fox came walking up with a bad cut under his right jaw. "Sorry, I'm late; I had to talk to one by hand."

"Crap, Fox, they almost cut your throat; that's going to leave a mark."

Fox grinned. "You didn't come away unscathed either."

"What do you mean?"

Fox pointed at Dix's side. A bullet had passed between his arm and his chest. An expanding ring of crimson revealed the location where the bullet narrowly missed his chest cavity but had cut the skin open and burned the skin on his arm.

"Fox, I'm too old for this crap, but I sure enjoy taking 'em down; don't you?"

"I sure do, Major."

They walked past the two snipers that Dix had cut down. One was still breathing, so Dix triple tapped both of them, and they trudged on through the sand. Then they came to the abandoned mortars. The area was littered with three dead Chinese.

An American lay dead with the controls for the drone around his neck. The drone was lying in the sand behind him where it landed. Two trails of blood led to the slide marks where the boat was beached on the sandbar.

Fox pointed back over his shoulder. "There are two more back toward the south end. Both of them died from one of the worst cases of lead poisoning that I've ever seen."

"Where's your radio, Fox?"

"It's in the boat. You stay here old man; I'll get the boat and come get you."

Dix watched as Fox walked away. Fox's ponytail was cut off at an odd angle and matched the beginning of the slash on his neck. Dix thought *it must have been an interesting fight.* He unhooked the drone controls off the dead American. The American was dressed in what appeared to be US army camo. A metal box containing the drone's accessories and instruction manuals was resting next to it. Since it would take Fox a few minutes to get back with the stump thumper, Dix sat down in the sand and took stock of the mortars. There was one unopened case of mortar rounds and four launchers. There were seven unused mortar rounds in an open case. Dix wondered what sort of range the mortars had. In the distance he saw the escaping Chinese. He turned one of the mortar tubes around and just made a wild guess as to where it needed to be set. He grabbed one of the mortars out of the opened box and held it over the opening. He hoped it wouldn't explode in the tube. If it did, he would never know what hit him. He closed his eyes and dropped it down the tube. The mortar round rocketed out of the tube and exploded about ten seconds later in the river somewhere in front of the boat. He quickly dropped in another round, and it took off following the previous path. The boat closed the distance to where the first mortar round hit, and the two almost arrived at the same moment. The boat wasn't hit, but the explosion ruptured the ear drums of all the men in the boat. Dix thought *I think I have another diversion we can use.* Fox came puttering up in the stump thumper, and they loaded up the drone, controls, mortar launch tubes and the unused mortar rounds.

"I'll have Butch send some guys around to gather up the remaining guns and ammo. Let's head around the north end; I left Butch shot up in my boat."

"How bad is he hit?"

"He'll probably walk with a limp like me for a while; he took one though his thigh."

They motored around through the north inlet. It was choked with willows so that the limbs hung down almost touching the water as well as touching overhead. The part Dix hated about going through them was the funny looking brown spiders that invariably fell in the boat and ended up on his clothes and gear. He had always been told they had a nasty bite, but he never had been bitten in all the years of hunting, fishing and squashing them in the boats.

They soon pulled up to Dix's boat. Butch had dozed off and was snoozing leaning against the console. He roused when the stump thumper bumped the boat.

"Did you get 'em?"

Dix climbed over the side. "We got most of them, and the others are sitting in soiled underwear. You need to send some guys wearing gloves to gather up the weapons and ammo. Has that leg started aching yet?"

I can wiggle my foot, but it only aches when I move. I think it's still in shock."

Dix got on the radio. "Cooney, any action on your end?"

Cooney came back on. "Nothing on this end. Were you able to intercept them?"

"Yes, we were able to take out about half of them and wound up with some good equipment. Butch is hit badly. I need Doc and or his trainees with plenty of sutures. Butch may need surgery. Fox and I just need a couple of hundred stitches."

"We're on our way. I don't know if we can bring Doc or not, but we'll bring the two young ladies he is training."

"Good, meet us at the boat launch."

When they got back in the lake, they saw that several of the houseboats were blown to bits. All the boats were scattered, and Beagle was gathering up what was left. Rachel was stacking concrete blocks and bricks to create anchors.

Dix pulled up to the launch and asked, "Why aren't you and Beagle somewhere safe like I ordered?"

Rachel cried, "All of you are wounded; oh no, does it hurt?" She reached for his bloody shirt and fainted when she realized that it was glued to his body with coagulated blood.

Dix grabbed her and eased her to the ground. "I don't have time for this."

Beagle came motoring up with a rag around his bloody scalp. "I've got all of them that are still floating rounded up. The catamaran is tied up to a tree about a mile down the lake."

"Beagle, I thought I told you to take Rachel to safety."

"I did. Then I came back and cut the anchor lines and the lines tying them all together. I figured we might save a few if they were floating free. I'm afraid Fox is going to have to move into my spare bedroom because his boat and three of the extra ones got blown up. I got Fox's stuff out of his before it sunk."

Rachel came to. "What happened? Oh my god, you're shot up again."

Dix gently pushed her head down between her knees and made her stay down until her head cleared.

"Sit quiet a minute. Cooney is bringing some the medics to patch us up."

Dix looked around to see Butch grinning and shaking his head. Dix glared. "What are you grinning about? Are you about to bleed to death again?"

Cooney came over the levee with an ambulance and the two medics in the back. He hopped out. "Doc can't leave. They are in a critical phase; he wanted these ladies to look at Butch. If they can't handle it, we'll go get him." They put Butch on a stretcher and got him in the ambulance where they had light and equipment. They took off the duct tape and soon had the bleeder stitched closed. There was no Novocain, so he had to grin and bear it. They washed out the wound and used antibiotic cream before covering it up and wrapping it. He would be chair bound for a few days. The rifle bullet had missed the femoral artery and the bone. He could still wiggle his toes, so the nerves were spared. If infection didn't kill him, he would probably make a full recovery. They pulled him out of the ambulance and took Fox and Dix in to suture their wounds. They had clippers and shaved Fox's beard and head, so they could get the extra hair away from his slash.

When they got to Dix, one of them said, "You don't remember me, do you?"

"I'm afraid I don't, where did we meet?"

"Porter brought you in shot and banged up pretty bad. You passed out quickly when we started probing that wound in your side. I'm surprised you made it. First man I ever knew who had his appendix removed by shrapnel. We stitched up all the holes, flushed you out with salt water and gave you a dose of Penicillin from the feed store. You healed up and haired over just fine. I wish Porter hadn't tried feeding you on the way back though; you were a mess."

Dix looked up at the young lady. "He also cut off my toe, and to think I promoted him to Sergeant for almost finishing me off. I've got to remind myself to check up on him. I hope he ain't trying to doctor on anybody else."

"I haven't seen him around in weeks. I'm sorry, but we don't have anything for the pain. I'm going to flush out the wound, douse it with some moonshine, and stitch it closed. I can get you a stick to bite on if you think you need it."

Dix grunted when she poured on the alcohol. "Go ahead; it can't hurt much worse than it does now." His prediction was wrong. While she stitched, he watched Beagle tow up the catamaran and anchor it. Rachel started a fire under the crawfish pot full of water.

She looked up. "We've got to eat, so I'm going to learn how to scald and scrape a hog."

Dix thought *damn, I hate stitches.*

## CHAPTER 14

Porter jerked his face out of the cold water and mud, coughed and blew the sand and mud from his nose. His vision was blurry in his left eye, and it took every ounce of his strength to crawl up out of the stream and onto the bank. He was caked in a combination of mud, clay and sand. His teeth were gritty from the mouth full of dirty water he had to spit out. His head hurt and throbbed. He pushed a foot into the mud and with one last lunge made it completely out of the water. He rose up on his elbows, and tried to look around but the bright sky made his eyes hurt, so he looked down and watched as a steady stream of blood dripped off his chin and formed a little puddle. He collapsed back to the ground not waking again until sometime in the night. He ran his hands through his hair and found a goose egg knot on the back of his head. The night was cold. He had mostly dried off, but was still dirty with caked mud and clay. He could only shiver until it was light enough to see.

When morning came, Porter rolled to a sitting position. His left eye was still a bit blurry and light sensitive. He found himself keeping it closed. If he turned his head too quickly, it made him dizzy and caused his head to throb. He looked around for his weapons and found that everything was gone except the British commando knife tucked away in his boot. The mules and all his gear were gone. A large dead dog lay on the bank on the opposite shore with a bullet hole in its side. Another lay dead halfway up the bank on the side he was on. His last memory was spotting the creek and heading down a well-worn cow path toward the water. It was obvious that he had been robbed. They were stupid not to have triple tapped him. They may have just left him for dead. He pulled out the knife and admired its two razor sharp edges. He transferred the sheath to his back pocket where he could reach the knife quickly and surveyed the area for sign. He saw where the stock came out of the creek followed by boot prints of a lone individual. He saw where the robber followed the mules and horse trying to catch them. There was nothing to do, but follow. He walked for a half hour or so, noticing that the animals appeared to stop from time to time and that the stride of the person following would increase as he ran to catch the animals. It was amidst one of these sprints that he found the .38 revolver. One of the bullets had been fired. In his haste to chase the stock, the pistol must have fallen from the perpetrator's vest pocket. He soon came to a grassy area by the creek where the mules had stopped to eat and where the human tracks ended. There he found the mare with her pack removed and the contents scattered. The mare had a broken leg. She must have broken it when they crossed the creek and the robbery took place. Porter left her alone and looked to see what he could find of his gear. There was no food, but the radio and charger were still there. The canvas used to cover it was there also. He found his day pack still full of his extra clothes, some paracord, a small plastic compass, and a small med kit with a magnifying glass. Whoever robbed him just took what they needed or didn't already have. He wished he had found the extra rifle and ammo. He fashioned a makeshift belt from the paracord and soon had his knife on the belt and the pistol in his back pocket. He needed to see if he could spot the mules and rider so he wrapped up the radio, hid it and left the mare. He didn't want to leave her in misery, but didn't want to shoot her if they were within hearing of the assailant. Walking at a fast clip, he followed the trail north along the creek. The tracks followed the creek, and after a couple of miles he stopped and turned back. He walked back to the grassy area, pulled the .38 from his pocket and fired a bullet into the mare's brain. She died instantly, and for the first time since climbing out of the mountains behind his home in Los Angeles, Porter cried.

His grief was short lived as he steeled himself by thinking of the men who killed his parents and baby brother. He quickly skinned the mare using the commando knife. He had to take his time as she was old and the skin did not come off easily. It took several hours to gut and dismember her. He built a fire from wood he found along the creek and soon had meat cooking. It was getting dark, so he took out the radio and called Cooney.

Cooney answered, "How's it going, son? I was expecting to hear from you last night."

"Sorry, but it took me a couple of days to recover the radio. It may take me a week or so before I can check back. Any word from the Cross ranch?"

"What happened? Did you lose some gear; and no, I haven't heard a word from the ranch. How far from it are you?"

"I got robbed a couple of days ago, and I just recovered a little of my gear. If I get my mules and gear back, I think I can be there in a week to ten days. If not, it will take me several weeks or longer. I think I can catch up with the robber in a couple of days, if I can travel at night. From the direction he is heading, I shouldn't be delayed very long."

"You sound confident that you can catch him."

"It looks like it's just one guy, and he isn't very smart, or he would have finished me when he had the chance."

"Be careful. Mr. Lester is on his mission. It's probably going to get pretty busy back here. Radio me or leave me a message when you can."

Porter spent the rest of the evening working on his gear. He formed the canvas into a backpack using paracord and strips of horse hide. He felt bad eating the horse, but he knew this was all the food there would be until he recovered his gear. He fashioned a poncho from the hide turning the hair side in to keep from getting bloody. By morning he had eaten all the meat he could possible hold. He had a horse hide bag full of meat he had dried over the fire. The final addition to his gear was a water bladder fashioned from the stomach of the mare. He took it down to the creek, turned it wrong side out and washed it as clean as possible. Paracord tied up the ends and created a sling. He was hopeful that he would only need it a couple of days, if at all. As long as he followed the creek, there would be no need to fill it; but, if the trail veered away, he would have a generous supply. By morning his head only hurt when he put his horse hide hat on, and his vision had cleared up. As soon as it was light enough to see the ground, he headed out at a brisk walk. He found the first campsite before dark and continued on. The moon was bright, and his eyes became accustomed to the dark. Although the traveling was slow, he kept going. He paused to rest sometime before dawn when he lost the trail. He slept soundly for a couple of hours and was awakened by birds in the trees along the creek. He only had to back track a couple of hundred yards before picking up the trail again. By midmorning he found the second night's camp. One more hard day and night should bring him close to his mules. Early the next morning just before daylight, he got a whiff of smoke. He cautiously continued on somewhat slower anxious to arrive at the campsite before the thief arose.

The horse meat was tough as he chewed on and swallowed one of the last pieces in his bag. His cocked pistol was in his hand as he peered at the prone figure in his hammock. Old Dollar and Ruth were tied to a tree. The thief didn't know enough to hobble them but at least they were unsaddled so their backs could rest. Porter remembered how Hugh had tried to murder him in the bag so he hid and waited. It seemed like a good idea to make certain that there was indeed someone in the hammock. It wasn't long before the thief stirred. The thief unzipped the bag, and two long thin legs emerged. The thief stood up and let her long dark hair fall loose onto Porter's tee shirt which she was wearing. Porter suddenly realized he wasn't breathing; he now had a problem. If it had been a man, Porter was pretty sure what would be taking place. This was different and would explain why he was alive and the old mare hadn't been put down.

Porter made sure she was not near a gun before he spoke, "Don't go moving around a whole lot; I've got you covered."

She almost jumped out of her skin. "Please don't hurt me. You can take my stuff; just don't hurt me."

Porter walked out and could see the terror in her eyes. He then realized that he must have appeared menacing with the bloody horse hide poncho and hat.

"Where are your pistol, rifle and clothes?"

"The pistol is in the hammock, one of the rifles is leaning on the tree, and the other is over there in the pack from the mule. My clothes are drying on a line down by the creek where I rinsed them out."

Porter verified the location of the weapons, including his Kbar knife, before letting her walk down to get her clothes. She was beautiful and near his age, and was **the last thing** on Earth he expected to find with his gear and wearing his tee shirt.

"Stand over there by the fire so I can keep an eye on you." He took off the bloody horse hide poncho, hat and stomach canteen. He put on his Beretta 9mm pistol. Checked his AK47 and slung it over his shoulder.

Pointing toward the creek, she said, "Your vest and that old Chinese coat are drying with my clothes."

He pointed with his rifle. "You first. Let's see if your clothes are dry." She slipped her feet into her untied boots and headed down the hill.

His only thought was *dang she looks good in nothing but a tee shirt and boots.* Porter had about decided that unless she came out with a weapon he would let her live.

He turned his head just enough to be polite, but not so far as to let her leave his peripheral vision. His vest was dry, so he put it on. The Chinese coat would take some time. He took down the paracord line and carried the coat on his arm as she led the way back up the hill to the campsite.

"Why didn't you finish me off back at the creek crossing?"

"You were already dead; I couldn't just shoot you to make sure you were dead."

"That's what I would have done if I had tried to kill somebody."

"I didn't try to kill you. You got thrown when those wild dogs tried to catch the mules. You shot one with that little pistol when it tried to pull you off that old mule. The mules bolted across the creek, and you got thrown when that old mule started spinning and kicking the other dog. You got bucked way up in the air and came down on your head on a rock in the creek. I pulled you up to the bank, but you were dead. I couldn't see you breathing. I waited a while, but the mules and your gear were getting away. I grabbed your rifle, ammo, shoulder holster, knife and belt and took off after them. They didn't run far, so I came back and checked, and you still looked dead, so I just went after them. The old mare was just limping along. I didn't have the heart to kill her."

"Ok, your story seems plausible. I did see two dead dogs and my pistol had been fired. Where were you when all this was taking place?"

"I was in a tree about ten yards upstream. Those danged dogs had me treed since daylight."

"Why are you out here all alone with no gear?"

"My backpack and rifle were stolen, and I escaped with my life several days back. Some men with red bands on their arms jumped me. I got away because they wanted me alive, and I could run faster than they could. When they got tired of chasing me, they shot up in the air a few times, but I never looked back.

I came to this creek and have been following it ever since. I have been eating small fish, frogs, turtles and lizards. I thought I died and gone to heaven when I caught up to the mules."

Porter was mentally kicking himself as he walked over to the packs. It was useless, he knew he wasn't going to shoot her or leave her out here alone. She was either going to try and kill him or not. He found an extra ball cap he had squirreled away in his gear. He grabbed some fresh clothes, a towel, and soap. He handed her the other AK47.

"Do you know how to use this?"

She looked surprised and said, "Yes, it's like the one I had stolen. Where are you going?"

"I'm going to take a bath and put on some clean clothes, and then I'm going to get some sleep. I've never been killed before, and it has about tuckered me out. Don't try to run off with the stock. I'll just catch up in a few days. It would be best to just shoot me and make sure I'm dead."

He untied and hobbled the mules so they could pick at the grass along the creek. Pointing to the thicket he had been hiding in, he said, "Take that rifle and go hide out of sight in that thicket over there, but where you can see the camp. If someone shows up before I get back, throw a rock down the hill to warn me; otherwise, I'll be back in a few. I'm Porter Jones. What's your name?"

"Katherine Hesston. My friends call me Katy."

"Great, just try not to shoot me, Katy."

She grinned a mischievous grin. "You'd better run."

Porter grinned and headed down for his bath and returned a short time later. Katy was still standing guard in the thicket. When he got back, they finished the horsemeat and threw the skin bag in the pile with the poncho and hat. In the next two hours he learned that she was the only person left alive in her family. She had just turned fifteen and was returning home from a church fall festival the previous winter when the looting and rioting started in her neighborhood. She ran to her grandfather's house and hid out in the shelter built by her grandfather back in the 60's. The shelter was the family rendezvous point in case of an emergency. She was the only one who made it. Her dad was an outdoorsman and had taught her and her brothers how to shoot. Her rifle and food were stored in the shelter. She had ventured out after a month to see if anyone was at home. She found her family's bodies in the garage where they had been executed. Their arms were still zip tied behind their backs, so she took some family photos and personal items back to the shelter and did not try to move their remains. She remained in the shelter until she ran out of food and water.

Porter told his story. "You're going to have to stick with me until I get back to the ranch. Did you come into personal contact with those men who robbed you?"

"No, they caught me with my pack off and my rifle leaning on a tree. I had made a bathroom stop. They just held the gun on me until I figured out what they wanted to do; then I just ran."

"Smart move. I've got to get some rest." He turned to head towards the thicket with the Chinese coat.

Katy pointed. "The hammock is over there, where are you going?"

"I'm sleeping hidden in the thicket. Keep an eye on the mules; don't let them wander too far. You can entice them back with a couple of those Chinese cookies. Keep that loaded rifle on you at all times. I sleep pretty light so just call out or throw something if you see or hear anything; even if it is just a gut feeling."

Porter woke up when Katy clamped her hand over his mouth and said, "Quiet!"

## CHAPTER 15

A week had passed, Dix sat grimacing as Rachel clipped and plucked out his stitches. Fox sat across the table with a terrible look on his face. He knew that he would be in the chair next. Just as she finished, the radio came alive.

Cooney Jones asked, "Are you slackers still sitting around making Rachel wait on you hand and foot?"

Dix grinned. "You mean our being victims of torture. She's yanking out stitches and enjoying every minute of it; what's up?"

"Santa says the first six packages are ready to deliver."

"Great. Get with Butch; make sure we have men in place to let us know when a boat is coming up or down river. I need someone who is trained to handle and deliver the gifts. They don't have to make the delivery, but they need to be able to teach us how to handle it and avoid getting infected. I want you to keep Santa and his elves safe and busy. Protecting the North Pole is crucial if we are going to have a good Christmas. Get back with me this afternoon. I want to start deliveries today, if possible. How is Mr. Lester?"

"He is as you might expect. He has a high fever."

Dix paused a moment. "God have mercy on our souls."

Dix looked around at Beagle, Rachel and Fox. "We've been hit two times here. They know we're here, and I expect them to make another attempt. It could be an attack helicopter next time. My Zizzy Witch is telling me that we need to move to a different location. I'm calling Butch and asking him to find us a new spot to fortify."

Dix grabbed the mic, got on the radio and Butch answered, "What's up, Chief?"

Dix keyed the mic again. "Butch, we're moving off the river. I think they will be trying to hit us here again."

"I've already thought about that. If you cross the levee and head up on Lake Concordia, there are some empty camps we've located. I'll have one of the guys meet you in a bit to take you there. You won't be located far from where you are, so you can still get to the river fast when the time comes.

How's your leg healing, Butch?"

"It still hurts like hell, and it's still draining, but it's not infected. I am walking a little; however, it will be a while before I can hit the line again."

"You keep organizing things. I need to know when the boats are coming, and I need a truck to get all our stuff moved. We'll have everything moved to the landing shortly. We'll also be moving the solar cells, batteries, water tanks and pumps."

"Don't worry, Dix, we'll help get the lights and water working in the camps. One of the camps is already covered with solar cells; my guys will get you powered up before dark. The water well is already working."

"How many camps are we talking about, Butch?"

"We have two furnished cabins, each with two bedrooms. One has a big kitchen and den. The owners abandoned them over a year ago, and no one knows where they are. That means the owners probably are not coming back."

Dix looked around to see Rachel grinning, and he felt himself turning red.

Cooney broke in, "Dix, Santa has the product in the fridge; I have a guy ready to bring it. Delivery is simple and so are the preparations. We can have it in your hands within twenty minutes."

"Great. Butch, do you have people in place to give us plenty of notice?"

Butch came back on. "I have guys placed to give us at least an hour's notice. We should have a boat coming through this afternoon."

"Fox and I will deploy at the launch point right now. We'll have radios with us. Rachel and Beagle will supervise the move. Be on standby, Cooney. I can't wait to start dishing out some hurt. Butch, I'm going to need four or five guys with AK47's to fire on them from the levee. I want lots of lead peppering that boat. I don't want any firing until my command. Is everyone ready?"

They all chimed in, "Hell, yes!"

Dix and Fox geared up and got in Dix's boat. They were both loaded for bear. Fox had the old 30-30 and his .45 auto 1911. Dix had Jake's AR15 and the Browning HP 9mm. As they were cranking up, Rachel handed them a sack of sandwiches and a jug of tea. She bent over and gave Dix a big hug and kiss, and for the first time Dix didn't turn red. They crossed the lake to the landing and threw all their stuff in a jeep.

Dix turned to Fox. "Fox, I've got a problem. I don't need to have family waiting in the wings. I have been very effective fighting because I didn't have anything left to lose. Getting killed would have been a release from my agony."

Fox gave him a knowing look. "Those bastards took everything from me too. I figured I would keep shooting at them until I bought the farm, or I ran out of bad guys."

Dix reflected. "If we are successful, this will make our track record, so far, insignificant."

They pulled up to the base of the new bridge and parked under it. They didn't want to be spotted by a drone. The old bridge had been blocked by several 18 wheelers that crashed and burned during an attack over a year before. Both were dozing when the call came about two hours later.

Butch called, "We have one coming upstream. Cooney has been notified."

Dix grinned. "Have Cooney meet us under the end of the bridge. We're ready to deploy. Have your men get in position to ambush them. I don't want anyone taking any chances, so if they open up with machine guns or other ordinances, I want our guys to cut and run. We don't need any heroes today."

"Understood, Major."

Cooney arrived with a technician who was one of Doc's assistants. He was carrying a small plastic ice chest and two pairs of long sleeve coveralls, two full face shields and two pairs of rubber gloves.

Cooney ordered, "Suit up guys, while Louie tells you what you need to do after you deploy."

Louie explained, "It is imperative that you do not touch anything here with your bare hands. You know how to deploy them. Just drop the pack of cigarettes when the boat goes under. If you miss, we will wait for the next boat to deploy. We'll be watching with binoculars from the bluff to see if we can verify a successful deployment. After deployment I want you come straight back here. Do not touch anything or take off any of the gear. I will spray you down with a pump up sprayer filled with chlorine. We'll bag everything and take it back for disinfecting. If you break this protocol, I can and will shoot you and burn your bodies. Do you have any questions?"

Dix looked over at Fox. "I think we need to be careful."

Louie emphasized, "Put the radio in this plastic bag **before** you open the ice chest and don't take it out afterwards."

They hopped in the truck with Cooney and Louie and were dropped off in the middle of the bridge. Cooney and Louie continued to the bluff side of the river while Dix and Fox lay on the bridge deck and looked down stream. After thirty minutes, the boat came into view. It was slowly fighting the current and would come under the east side of the bridge. They stayed low. The bridge was hot, and they were sweating in their coveralls. They lined up at the drains and waited. Just as the boat reached the bridge, Dix gave the order to the men to open fire. They heard the men firing from the levee. They looked through the grates as the men on the boat deck scrambled for cover. They could hear the impact of the bullets. The radio went into the bag and was sealed. Dix opened the ice chest and dropped the pack of cigarettes through the grate. The Chinese sprayed the levee with machine gun fire. Dix could see the pack of cigarettes resting on the deck near one of the hatches. Fox was not contaminated and was upwind from Dix. As soon as the boat was out of view, they walked down the bridge with Fox staying well back. When they returned, Louie hosed Dix down and took his gloves, facemask and coveralls and double bagged them. He also double bagged the ice chest. He sprayed the radio bag before opening it and returning the radio to Dix.

Dix said, "I can verify that the pack was on the deck."

Cooney said, "I can verify that I saw one of the men pick it up."

"Y'all head back to the lab. We'll wait until tomorrow to deploy again unless one comes through tonight. If they see one pack dropped, they will lock down the boats. We want to make certain that at least one of them is infected. This is one plan we can't screw up."

Dix got on the radio. "Butch, did any of our guys get hurt?"

"No one was hurt. Were we successful?"

"Yep, our venture was successful!"

"Rachel and Beagle are getting settled in. They have the boats unloaded, and I have the electrician and plumber finishing the lights and water."

"Great job, Butch. If we can make a few more successful drops, we should start seeing some results in a couple of weeks."

Dix and Fox drove back talking about their families and their lives before the war. They drove around cars and debris and eventually found their way up to the camps on Lake Concordia. As they pulled into the driveway between the camp houses, Ben and Frank came running up barking at the jeep.

Dix told Fox, "I always wanted to have a house at the lake, but could never afford it."

Fox nodded in agreement. "I grew up on a lake in North Florida. My folks always wanted a nice house in town. When they died, I moved into their house. The stump thumper was my dad's old boat. I'm divorced, my son is grown, and all my brothers and sisters are dead or missing. I've lost everything including the old house. I managed to fight off the bad guys until I was overrun. I escaped in the stump thumper with my rifle, pistol and what I had stored in my sea bag. I've been hunting a fight ever since."

Dix had a grim look on his face as he relived the loss of his family in his mind's eye.

He got on the radio with Colonel Miller. "Colonel, the final battle has commenced. We need to notify all our people that the Chinese and their American comrades are the walking dead."

Miller answered with a chuckle. "Good work, Major. As soon as we confirm that the seeds have taken root, the word will go out. I want you to continue with the campaign until we can hit three or four more boats. Then you need to follow one of those boats to see where they are going."

Dix walked to the back door of the camp and entered. Rachel greeted him with a smile.

"Supper's ready. Beagle is running his nets and checking the fire in the smoke house. How goes the battle?"

"The first battle of this campaign was a success. After we successfully hit three or four more boats, Fox and I will be making a run up the river to look for their base."

"You have that same look you had when you rescued me."

"What look is that, Rachel? I didn't realize I had a look."

"Oh, you have a look. It's hard to describe. You look resolved. I'll leave you alone so you can think."

Fox came in, and the three ate their meal in silence. The enormity of what they had started was weighing on them.

Dix looked at Fox. "Tomorrow, while we are waiting for the next boat, we need to gather what we'll need to follow one of those boats. We're going to have to stay back far enough that they won't see us. They'll have snipers on the bank looking for someone like us to be following. We need someone who can run that drone we captured. We need to check its range and see what kind of run time it has."

Dix got on the radio. "Butch, are you where you can talk?"

The radio crackled, "Dix, where do you think I'm going to be? I've been shot."

"Let me tell you what I need. I am going to need some gas and oil for my boat. I am going to need about fifty gallons of gas and a couple of gallons of two cycle oil. I also need someone who can run that drone we captured. We are going to tail one of those boats within the week."

"I have the fuel and oil. I'll have to canvas the men and see who I have that can run the drone."

"I need to be able to charge the drone batteries on the boat, and I would like to have another motor on the boat in case my main engine gets knocked out."

"Major, I'll get someone started on it tomorrow. Our guys aren't accustomed to this new kind of warfare. A lot of them just want to go hit the enemy where they are camped. The men had a ball shooting at that boat this afternoon."

"Tell them as this campaign matures, the Chinese will be breaking out. The Chinese leaders won't be able to contain what's going to take place within their ranks. It will be worse than any Zombie movie they have ever seen. The ones that are healthy enough to run will run in the hopes they aren't infected. That will be when they are most dangerous. We will have hell on Earth within two weeks. We will need to seal the highways heading south, and we will need to stop all small boat traffic heading south. I need all the men ready to deploy. Get with Cooney and see who he can spare."

"Will do, Major."

"I suppose I am stuck with y'all calling me Major?"

Butch laughed. "It'll be cool when you're an old man hanging around. All the kids will be awestruck because the old Major shows up. You've been a hero ever since you busted us out of the Ferriday jail."

"I'm having second thoughts about it now. I'm going to bed. Wake me up if another boat shows up."

Rachel came out of the bathroom. "I have a surprise for you; I already have the water drawn."

Dix had the first soaking bath in recent memory. He didn't realize how stove up his old bones were until the hot water did its work. He resisted having a whiskey drink in case he had to meet another boat tonight. His new bed was bigger than his bunk in the catamaran, and he slept soundly. He didn't have the bad dreams that normally plagued his nights. Tonight his dead wife and children came to his dreams once again. He awoke from the dream and was sad. The dream wasn't terrible, but he still missed and regretted the turn of events. He felt guilty about being alive.

Rachel came in with coffee and a beautiful smile. After drinking coffee and having some pancakes at breakfast, he felt better.

"Enjoy the coffee. We're going to be out in a couple of weeks."

Dix took a sip. "I'll keep my eyes open for some while I'm out. Also, ask Beagle to start acquiring some when people come to trade for fish."

The radio crackled and Butch said, "It's show time."

"Call Cooney and tell him. He knows where to meet us. Have the guys blow up a can of gas on the levee on my order."

Rachel hugged his neck and gave him a kiss. "Be careful big guy."

## CHAPTER 16

Porter slowly rolled to a sitting position and looked to where Katy was pointing. It was not dark yet, and he could see the red arm bands on the two men. They were following the mule tracks along the creek. He switched off the safety on his rifle and asked, "Are those the two who jumped you?"

"Yes."

"Just ease over behind me and quietly lie down."

When the Red Banders reached the camp, but before they entered, Porter spoke, "Don't move guys, and don't think about it. I will kill you before you can blink."

They froze in their tracks and looked over at Porter who was looking at them across his rifle.

The nearest one said, "Hey kid, are you lost? We'll be glad to help you out."

Porter never relaxed his aim. "I'm not lost, and I don't need your help. Thanks for your concern. What are you guys looking for?"

"I'm looking for my baby sister. She's lost, and we picked up her trail a while back."

"I haven't seen her. Can I ask you a question, 'What are those arm bands for?'"

"Sure, kid. We are the local police who work for the government in Austin."

The man started to reach for his hat and at the same time moved his other hand toward his hip.

Porter simply said, "You move your hands one more inch, and you're going to have a bullet through the chest." The man paused when he realized that Porter wasn't bluffing.

"Why the red arm bands?"

"That's so we can recognize each other at a distance."

"Who's your leader and where is headquarters?"

"Headquarters is back in Austin. Our leader is T. Ransom. He was appointed governor by President Whitmore, and we are trying to restore order to the state."

Porter knew enough about current events to know that President Whitmore was the communist President that invited the Chinese into the country. He was head of the communist party.

Porter inquired, "Have any of you run across anyone with the plague?"

"What plague you talking about, kid?"

Porter looked and saw that the one following was sweating and looked a little pale. Porter also saw the beginnings of a rash on his neck and arms. "I'm talking about the one your friend has and what you will have in a very short while. There's only one thing that will save you. You've got to get back to your people and get on a glucose IV. Once the pustules start you'll get dehydrated and die. But if you hurry, you can save yourself."

The man looked back at his friend and then back at Porter. "How do you know he has the plague?"

"Look at him. He has a rash already starting. A week or so back he probably came across someone dead or sick and touched their stuff."

The man looked back at his friend. "Is what he said true?"

The sick man looked back and forth between them. "I didn't know what they had, I just robbed them; they didn't put up a fight. The woman didn't even put up a fight when I....."

The first man turned back to Porter who was still looking at them down the barrel of his rifle. "Kid, how do you know so much about this plague?"

"I am traveling cross country to check on my family. I ran across a doctor who told me about it and what to look for." Lying he continued, "He said the only way to cure it was with a glucose drip or with a vaccine the Chinese have that'll clear it right up. If you can get to their camp, all their medics have it in their kits. You guys don't have much time left."

"Kid, can we leave?"

"Sure, just drop your rifles, holsters and knives; you first. I know you aren't far from your horses or vehicles. As soon as you're disarmed, you can head back and get some treatment."

The first man dropped his rifle and took off his belt letting his pistol drop to the ground as well. The second man followed suit. "Can we go now, kid?"

"Sure thing, from the looks of your friend, you need to hurry and find one of those Chinese medics."

They turned and headed back the way they came. Porter told Katy, "Don't touch their guns; they are both walking dead men. You and I both may be infected. Me from a knife fight, and you from pulling me to the bank and sleeping in my hammock. We'll know in a few days if I start getting sick."

Katy stared at him. "Are you serious? Shouldn't we be looking for a Chinese medic, and why didn't you just shoot them? You know what they are."

"I lied about the Chinese vaccine and glucose IV. When I realized they were infected, I wanted them to go back to their people and start the rumor that the Chinese had the cure. That way they will spread the virus among their group as well as take it to the Chinese in Houston. If I get sick, I am going to try to get to Houston and into the Chinese barracks and mess hall where I can spread it before I die."

He gathered up the two mules, saddled them and got ready to move out.

Katy asked, "It's getting dark, why are we packing up?"

"I'm not waiting around for them to go get their backup guns at their vehicle or off their horses and come back. Chances are they won't, but I'm not going to stick around to find out. The sickest one won't be on his feet much longer. If we can get a day's travel on them, we won't be seeing them again. If we take our time, we can travel all night following the creek, and then we can head west towards the ranch. We should be able to make it there in a week or so if nothing happens."

Old Dollar and Ruth had had good grazing all day and plenty of water. Porter filled the horse stomach canteen with water and hung it over Ruth's pack. Katy rode behind Porter on Dollar. Travel would be slower as the mules each had a heavier load. They would have to make more frequent stops.

Sometime before dawn, they stopped to let the mules rest. Porter unsaddled them, pulled out his radio, put up the antenna and called his grandfather Cooney.

The radio crackled, and Cooney answered after a few minutes, "You are rising mighty early this morning, any problems?"

"I'm not rising early. I haven't been to bed; it's been a little busy out here. If any of our guys run across men with red arm bands, tell them that they are American communists." Porter proceeded to bring Cooney up to date on what had transpired.

Cooney said, "That was a smart move telling them that the Chinese have a cure. I'll pass the word so our guys can use a similar ploy. It's our modern version of catapulting a plague victim over the castle walls."

"I also have a girl that is traveling with me. She pulled me out of the water a couple of days back and kept me from drowning."

Shaking his head in disbelief, Cooney answered, "Y'all be careful, and check back when you can." Cooney thought *in all my years I never knew anyone who could wind up with more young ladies tailing him than Porter. All he needs is a suit of armor and big sword.*

Porter rolled up his antenna wire and put away the radio. With two mouths to feed, his food supply was going to dry up fast. Together they ate a cold breakfast by splitting one of the remaining MRE's. Porter hobbled the mules and let them feed along the creek.

"Katy, you haven't slept in a while; I want you to sleep while I stand guard."

"Where do you want me to sleep? I don't see a good place to hide."

"See if you can get comfortable leaning against the mule pack. I'm going to head out into the scrub and sit where I can watch you and the mules. I'll let you sleep for a few hours. We can relax a little once we get away from the creek. There won't be a lot of houses and farms where we're going."

While standing guard, Porter took the opportunity to touch up the hone on his knife blades. He had a small oiled sharpening stone in his shirt pocket that he used to touch up the blades. He soon had both knives sharp enough to shave the hair on his arm. His shoulder still felt stiff from the gunshot wound he received on the ranch months ago. It was fully healed, but gave him fits when he slept on it wrong. He could only imagine the discomfort it would bring if he lived long enough to be an old man. Starting today, he would have to start foraging for food as they traveled. He turned over a rock and spotted a large scorpion. He resisted the urge to squash it and instead used the sharp pointed blade of his commando knife to pin it and the Kbar to cut off the stinger. He impaled it on a sharp stick. In the next thirty minutes he had six sticks with wiggling scorpions impaled and ready to be cooked over a fire.

Katy awoke to find Porter sitting by the fire. "What smells so good? I'm starved."

Porter bit off a claw and crunched it grinning. "Sort of reminds me of grilled shrimp."

She crinkled up her nose when he handed her a skewer full of toasted scorpions. "It's got to be better than raw fish, frogs and lizards."

A loud crunch came from her mouth. "Yum. It's a shame we don't have any honey mustard."

They both laughed and finished the meal. Picking his teeth with the skewer, Porter uttered, "There's plenty more where those came from. There seems to be one under every rock. We need to be careful if we take off our boots."

"You're not kidding."

Porter gathered the mules and saddled them. He made sure the horse stomach canteen was full. He would water the mules from it if they couldn't find water soon. They came to a road and rode down it until they found an intersection with signs. Porter unfolded the well-worn Texas map from his pocket. What had taken his entire hand to span the distance on the map, now only took the width of his thumb. He was almost on the same track that he and Daniels Devils had taken coming to Louisiana all those months ago. Water was at most a day's ride, and with a little luck he would hit the trail they used coming off the ranch. Porter told Katy his story about his trek from California on the little motorcycle, about finding Sandy and Ally, and how they arrived at the Cross ranch. He left off the details of killing the Chinese. People were a little squeamish when they found out how many men had fallen before his guns and knife. He told how he joined the Constitution army at the ranch, and how they traveled to Louisiana through this very area. About halfway through the day, he stopped and dug a small depression in the sand and clay soil about as large as half a bowling ball. He took the canvas pack he had made days earlier and used it to line the hole. He poured half the contents of the horse stomach water bag into the hole and let Old Dollar drink. He led him away and told Katy to hang on to him. He brought Ruth over and repeated the process. The mules needed more water, but that would hold them until they reached the next little river. They spent the rest of the day heading west.

Porter told Katy, "We aren't far from water because Old Dollar smells it. See his ears and notice how he has picked up the pace a bit."

"I felt him pick up the pace; it's a little hard on my rear back here."

"Only about three more days if we don't run into trouble."

The trail they were on crossed an abandoned ranch, and they soon came to and crossed the shallow river at the spot where Porter and Daniels Devils crossed earlier in the year. They set up camp and hobbled the mules. Porter caught a mess of scorpions to roast and killed a big turtle in the river. He boiled his last pot of rice with the turtle, and they had a feast. He slept soundly that night with Katy on guard for most of it. Porter awoke to Old Dollar making his disturbed sound. Katy was leaning against a tree where she had fallen asleep.

The old Indian was standing next to Porter, and said in a low voice, "Don't worry, kid, if I was going to kill you, you would've been dead."

Porter didn't jump. He knew that what the Indian said was true. "I think there's some turtle and rice left in the pot if you're hungry."

He looked up; the old man had dark weathered skin deep with wrinkles from years in the sun. His old cowboy hat had a sweat ring around the base and the edges were turned up. His old blue jeans were patched, his cowboy boots were scuffed, and the heels were well worn on the outside edges. He was carrying an old lever action Winchester, and he had a big knife on his belt with a leather lace hanging from the end of the sheath.

The old man said, "Thanks, but I've already eaten. I hope you aren't over paying your guard."

"I'm not getting my money's worth, am I?"

Porter eased out of his blanket and walked over to Katy and got his hand on her rifle. He didn't want to startle her and have her shoot up the camp.

She awoke with a start. "What's wrong?"

"We've got company. I didn't want you to jump awake and start shooting."

"I didn't mean to fall asleep, I'm sorry."

"Don't sweat it, I think he's a good guy, or we'd be dead."

The old Indian just smiled from across the fire.

"What can we do for you?"

The old man sat down cross legged and poked at the fire with a stick. "This is my ranch you've been crossing. I spotted you when you crossed the river. I recognized Old Dollar; that was one of Charlie Cross's hunting mules. I guided for Charlie over the years when he had more business than he could handle."

Porter looked worried. "You talk like he ain't around no more."

The old Indian continued to poke the fire. "He's dead along with his family; the plague got them."

Porter's throat started to knot up, and he felt himself hyperventilating. "What about the two girls staying at the hunting lodge?"

## CHAPTER 17

The next few days were a blur. They were able to deploy three more confirmed packs. One night boat also got three eggs. The next boats would be getting packets derived from viruses harvested directly from the old man who was dying. Mr. Lester was getting worse, and the disease seemed to be progressing fast. The rest of the boats would only be hit at night. The Chinese grew weary of running the gauntlet of men shooting at them when they passed. They started timing their runs at night which was perfect for delivery of the virus laden packs of cigarettes and eggs.

On the seventh day, Rachel walked into Dix's room. Dix was still in bed. "Don't you knock?"

"Sorry, I know you are leaving today, and I wanted to fix you a good breakfast. I've got a surprise; Beagle sliced up some bacon from the smoke house. Cooney brought us some extra eggs that weren't needed at the germ warfare lab. I finally figured out how to make biscuits from the whole wheat, and I found some grits in the kitchen when we moved in."

Dix grinned. "Sounds like you are preparing my last meal."

Rachel laughed. "Oh, no, if I thought you weren't coming back, I would be naked right now."

Dix could only stutter, "Iiiiiiiii'lllll be out in a minute."

Rachel winked and headed back to the kitchen. The breakfast was the best he could remember. After he gave Rachel a real good hug and kiss, he headed over to Fox's and Beagle's camp. They were finishing up their breakfast; Rachel had fixed them a tray earlier. "Fox, it's time."

Fox grabbed his rifle; like Dix, he always wore his pistol. "All my gear is in the jeep." Dix grabbed his pack and had his 30-06 Springfield 1903 rifle in addition to the AR15.

Fox said, "I heard about that rifle. Can you hit as well as they say you can with that thing?"

Dix patted the old rifle. "If I can see the target, I can come pretty close."

"How many kills have you made with it?"

"Fox, I honestly don't know. I quit keeping score when I was home in Gulfport. I just went to work killing human roaches. I'm hoping to kill a few more this trip. The other day when I came under fire, they were out of range of this AR; so I'm bringing the 30-06 just in case." Dix placed it in a padded case and put it in the back of the jeep with a can of ammo. They were met at the boat by Hunter Morgan, their new drone pilot. They had a week's worth of food and enough ammo to fight their way back home. They soon had the fuel and all their gear loaded.

Dix looked at the back of the boat. Next to the main outboard motor was a 25hp backup outboard. It wouldn't move the boat fast, but it would bring them home in a pinch. The mosquitoes had come out, so they were slapping them as they loaded the boat. A quick spray down with repellant soon had them stinking. The faint stinging sensation from the Deet made their skin feel hot. The spray on their lips made them numb.

Fox reached into his pack and came out with three cans of cola. "They're hot guys, but I think we need to toast this mission."

They bumped the three cans together and cranked the engine. The tanks were full, and they had ten, five gallon cans of gas. With their gear they had a full load.

Dix paused a minute and looked at Fox. "Fox, what do you say we take the stump thumper with us? It's small; and if we need to go up a small stream to hide or move inland, it will be what we need. It runs on the same gas and oil that this boat uses."

Fox nodded in agreement. "It's also low in the water and would look like a log at a distance. That's why my dad painted it brown when he used it to duck hunt."

They tied the bow line of the stump thumper to the back of Dix's boat. Dix pushed the throttle forward and looked back at the levee. Rachel was standing at the top and waved. He gave her a wave and shoved the throttle open to get the boat to plane, and they were soon running down the lake. He passed the catamaran and houseboats still anchored in the middle of the lake. He ran out the south outlet into the river. He got on the radio with Butch. "I'm in the river. Have your guys spotted anything this morning?"

"Nothing today. How far are you going to run?"

"I'm going to run twenty miles or so upstream and find a place to hide until one comes by. Then we'll follow as far back as we can, so they won't see us until we see where they're putting in. We'll keep our eyes open for a returning boat and hide until it passes."

"Major, we'll radio as soon as we spot one."

Dix was once again in the waters of the Mississippi River. Water from as far away as the Milk River in Canada was flowing down this river to the Gulf of Mexico. Dix always looked forward to seeing the purple martins skimming the surface with their beaks dipped in the water drinking. He ran the boat at a good clip, but not wide open. When they spotted places to hide the boat, they made note of the GPS coordinates. Private Hunter Morgan was a techie geek and quickly had the boat's GPS unit figured out. Dix had owned the boat for years but was never able to figure out how to use the GPS. Morgan was the computer hacker responsible for making the communist's and the Chinese's lives miserable. Before the lights went out, he hacked the Ferriday city hall's computers and erased all the tax bills. He made numerous IED devices in everything from soda cans to spare tires. He even stole some of the Chinese's AK47s and booby trapped them, so that when they were fired, they would blow up.

It was a beautiful day for a boat ride on the river. Dix turned the helm of the boat over to Fox. According to the GPS they were traveling twenty miles an hour. After an hour and a half they found a cut off in the river where they could hide the boat. They motored in and hid in the shade of some willows. The breeze off the river kept the mosquitoes at bay. The sun set, and they quietly talked about hunting and fishing trips. They all avoided talking about their dead family and friends.

Cooney got on the radio with Dix. "Major, I wanted to let you know that I heard from Porter. He is still alive and traveling toward the ranch. He said that there is a group of American communists around Austin. They are wearing red arm bands. He said that the last two he ran across were sick. He told them that the Chinese medics all carried a vaccine in their kits that would cure the plague."

"I knew I liked that kid; don't let him doctor on you though; you'll come up missing body parts. I realize he's just a kid, but we need to make him President one day. The kid's got grit."

"Yes, sir, he does. It's a shame he never got to be a teenager. He jumped straight from boy to manhood."

"We're hidden about thirty miles north waiting on tonight's boat. As soon as it passes, we're going to tail them all night. If we see a red armband on a communist American, we know what to do."

Dix looked around and told the guys, "Fox, you stand guard. Morgan and I are going to take a nap. Wake up Morgan in a couple of hours, and then you get some sleep. Morgan, you can get me up two hours after that. It should be dark by then, and the next boat north should be on its way."

Fox clapped him on the shoulder. "Get some rest, Chief; we'll wake you later."

Dix lay down in the bottom of the boat and let his head rest on a life vest. Moments later he was asleep. He had developed the ability to sleep anywhere at almost any time. He slept great this time because he had two seasoned fighters with him. Neither would fall asleep on their watch.

The radio woke Dix. Captain Butch Erwin's voice crackled from it, "Major, we've got one below Natchez heading your way. It will get to Natchez right after dark, and should be up there by you about two hours later. They don't make good time running against the current."

"Thanks, Captain."

"Oh, so you're going to start talking like a soldier now." Butch laughed.

"Just giving you a taste of your own medicine," Dix kidded back.

They were too excited to sleep after the news. Dix looked at Fox and Morgan. "We need to make sure we are out of sight of the radar. They will be running it when they come up the river tonight."

Fox thought about it. "There are only two ways to avoid radar. We either have to stay within twenty feet of the stern so that the radar is going over us, or stay so far back that we can't see them. We should have thought and got us a radar unit and mounted it about twenty feet above the boat."

Dix pondered a moment. "We'll know if they spot us, because they will launch a boat or start shooting at us from the big boat. The only way we can stay out of range of the .50 caliber machine guns is to be around a turn of the river. I say we ride their wake behind the boat until daylight. At that point we head to shore and get lost in the shore clutter."

Morgan broke into the conversation. "Why don't we follow them in the stump thumper? It's made of fiberglass; it's as small as a log so the radar signature will be next to nothing if they see it at all. It will be nothing like this boat. All we have to do is follow behind the thumper in this one from about a half a mile or so. We have extra radios."

Dix looked back at him. "We do?"

"Sure, I always bring redundant equipment. I have two extra radios along with a bunch of other stuff."

"What kind of other stuff?"

"Hand grenades, smoke bombs, and wire…."

Dix stopped him. "**Enough**, it's too much for me to think about. Just let me know what you have as we need it. Fox, take a couple of cans of gas and put them in the stump thumper along with some oil for your motor. I want you to take a radio, and follow the big boat. We'll be well behind you."

Dix looked back and forth between them for a moment. "No, we're going to do this differently. Fox is going to get tired trying to run that boat all night from the tiller controls on that motor. I'm going in the stump thumper with you, Fox. Morgan will stay back with our extra gear and follow. It's going to take two people in the stump thumper; one to watch and direct from the front and shoot if needed and one to run the boat. If we get in trouble, we can call Morgan and high tail it back to this boat. This boat can outrun anything they've got that I've seen."

They loaded the stump thumper and waited for the big boat. Dix took the Springfield because any shots taken from the river would probably be in excess of three-hundred yards.

They heard the big boat before they saw it. The moon was barely up and cast its light across the water. The little waves and whirlpools created an occasional sparkle as they reflected the beams off the water. The big boat was like a huge dark shadow when it appeared out in the river before them. They could feel the vibrations of the engines from deep inside the boat. A light in the pilot house was the only thing visible. A door opened, and a man came out smoking a cigarette. It flared as he took a final deep puff. He thumped it and a red glow left his hand and hit the water about twenty feet in front of Dix's boat. An audible hiss came to them as the river water extinguished the ember. In the pitch black darkness Dix stated, "In another week they will be getting sick; right now they are starting to spread it among themselves. It's show time boys."

The old Mercury outboard on the stump thumper cranked on the second pull. Dix and Fox eased out into the current with Fox running the little outboard. They could see the light from the pilot house, as they followed the boat in the current. Fox pushed a boat cushion floatation device over to Dix. "I don't think this boat will float if we turn over. You're going to need this out here in the river so keep it close."

Dix could barely see him in the dark. "What about you?"

"I'm sitting on mine."

Dix carefully moved up to the center seat and kept his eyes on the big boat. Sometimes they saw men walking around, and occasionally a hatch would open and close. Several times men came to the rail and threw up over the side. One didn't make it, and some lights came on while the deck was rinsed off. Dix wondered if that was one of the symptoms. As they ran on into the night, they passed a boat going south. They warned Morgan by radio.

He responded, "I am well camouflaged. I am going to just kill the throttle and drift like a tree top in the current. If they put a light on me, I'll shoot it out and come upstream full throttle."

Dix looked back toward Fox and keyed the mic, "Sounds like a plan."

Fox fumbled around in his pack and came out with an old .22 rifle. He dug around in his shirt pocket and came out with some .22 short ammo for the little single shot.

"I've had this rifle ever since I was a kid. When you put in a .22 short, you can't hear it shoot. It is practically silent. I can punch out a light with it or shoot me a commie in the head. I used it to clean out one of their camps one night. I just shot each of them in the temple from the shadows. Only one called out before he died; the others thought he was having a dream and laughed."

They slowly followed the big boat all night. As the sky started to lighten, they eased up on the throttle and let the stump thumper distance itself from the big boat. Soon the sun would rise. The night had been chilly, but the day was warming up fast. They had been an insignificant speck in the huge river shielded from the logs and whirlpools when they were close to the big boat, but now they were subject to the full fury of the river. They were about a mile behind the boat and were all but invisible to anyone looking back. They could barely make out the big boat. Morgan was about a half a mile behind them.

Dix got on the radio. "Where are we right now?"

Morgan called back, "We are near Port Gibson."

"Let's keep going. If we see another of the big boats heading south, we're going to have to turn tail and hide. So keep looking for places we can hide the boat. I know the Big Black River is not far from here because I went up it months ago on a mission."

**"Look!"** Fox pointed.

In the distance a big boat was heading downstream. Dix got on the radio, "Morgan, a boat is coming; we need to hide!"

"Come on down. I spotted a hole we can get in about a mile back."

Fox turned the stump thumper downstream and opened it up. The little Mercury outboard purred as it raced to Dix's boat, where they tied up and climbed aboard. Soon they were going up a small bayou and out of sight. It was quiet and cool, and fortunately the mosquitoes weren't there. Since the water was cold, it must have been a spring fed creek coming from the bluffs along the river. It wasn't long before the southbound boat crossed the entrance to the little bayou. Because they were well hidden, all they had to do was wait for it to get a couple of miles downstream, and then they could catch up with the one they were following. They pulled out into the river with Dix's boat pulling the thumper. Morgan was on the bow with binoculars and waved as soon as he caught a glimpse of the big boat. They killed the throttles and transferred to the thumper. Once again the little motor cranked on the second pull. Dix and Fox ran upstream until they spotted the big boat in the distance. Fox slowed the boat not wanting to overtake them. Dix looked back and saw that Morgan had retaken his position about a half a mile back.

"I hope they didn't notice us on the radar when we approached just now; I'm hoping they aren't watching it since it is daylight."

Fox grinned. "You spoke too soon. It looks like they have stopped and are launching a boat."

Dix looked through the binoculars and realized that they were indeed launching a boat.

He keyed the mic, "Morgan, get up here! They are launching a boat."

They turned and headed south and were met by Morgan. They scrambled aboard Dix's boat and tied off the thumper to a rear davit. Dix shoved the throttles wide open and headed south. Soon they were back at the little bayou and went in. They got out of the boat and took positions on the bank and waited. The men in the launch would be looking for them to either be running down the river or hiding in a place like this. The Chinese ran by the opening to the bayou, turned and made a big circle. One of them was looking through binoculars. The boat was well camouflaged; and in the shadows of the bayou, almost impossible to see. The Chinese boat looked to have a pilot and seven men. It ran down stream and pulled to shore. They were going to come on foot.

Dix said, "I've got a shot; anybody else got one?"

Fox whispered, "I can see them."

Morgan said, "I don't see a thing."

"Stay put, kid."

Dix put a round from the Springfield through the boat pilot and then shot the next one through the big outboard on the back. Fox's rifle bellowed as he fired and ejected spent hulls. Dix kept his eyes open for targets. He saw a glimpse of a man's hand as a grenade was tossed from the other side of the boat. Both Dix and Fox dove and were covered in a spray of mud, sand and water. Dix came up and started shooting through the Chinese boat. With the engine and pilot dead, the current of the river pulled the rear of the boat down steam and away from the shore. When it did, it left the four remaining men clinging to the side and exposed to fire. Fox's rifle bellowed over and over again until no one was left clinging to the boat. Dix searched for targets in his scope.

"Fox, how many do you see? I don't see any more of them."

"None, unless one is lying down in the boat. I think they were all trying to use the boat as cover."

Morgan tossed a grenade to Dix. "How's your throwing arm?"

"It's terrible. Catch, Fox."

Fox caught the grenade, pulled the pen and lobbed it into the boat. At that moment automatic gunfire coming from up the bank had bullets dancing around them. The boat bounced up from the water as the grenade blew out the bottom. It floated off, half submerged on its journey to the Gulf. Fox, Morgan and Dix all opened up on the two soldiers who made it up the bank. The log they were behind offered little cover from the rifle slugs that tore through them. A final lobbed hand grenade sealed their fate.

Dix climbed back in the boat. "Guys, our secret is out; they'll be looking for us. I think we ought to head south; find us a quiet place to hide and rest. None of us have had any sleep in quite a while."

Fox and Morgan climbed back in the boat. A piece of rock or fragment from the grenade had opened Dix's head over his left eye. Morgan cleaned it and placed a Band-Aid over the small puncture. Dix fired up the boat and, pulling the stump thumper, headed south. They passed the half submerged boat and resisted the urge to see if there was anything to salvage. If their plague attack had been successful, everything in the boat including the boat itself could be infectious.

Dix got on the radio with Butch. "They spotted us tailing them and sent a boat to intercept us so we are beating a hasty retreat and will hide until we can get some sleep. We'll follow another boat as soon as we rest."

"Were you able to outrun the boat they sent after you?"

"They were having a little engine trouble the last I saw of them. It sounded to me like they had a little lead fouling."

"I figured that; call me back when you are ready to resume the mission."

"Will do."

They ran down to a spot that Morgan noted and were soon nestled among several abandoned barges and tugs. All were flooded and sitting on the bottom in the shallows. They motored between them and were hidden from view of the river and the bank. Dix took the first watch while Fox and Morgan sacked out in the bottom of the boat. Dix checked his weapons and watched as storm clouds began to gather. It would be miserable on the river. He didn't relish being on the open water during a storm, but it would provide excellent cover. Dix put up the canvas Bimini top in anticipation of the rain, and soon the plops of water were hitting the boat. Fox and Morgan were trying to sleep leaning against the seat as they huddled against the storm under the Bimini top. Dix fished some plastic rain ponchos out of the front compartment for them. The ponchos kept most of the rain off, but the rain made it a miserable night. The water beaded up and ran down the stock and barrel of the well-oiled Springfield. Fox was asleep with his old 30-30 cradled in his arms. Dix noticed that Morgan had a tight grip on his rifle as well. Hunter Morgan was a young man in his twenties; he was not unlike Dix's dead son Jake.

As the rain dripped off the Bimini top, Dix thought back to when he was a young man living in the South. He recalled going fishing in these same waters he was fighting in. His parents were alive then, and life was easy. He recalled meeting his wife and the birth of his children. He remembered cutting Christmas trees and the holidays when he was surrounded by family and friends. Then he thought about the communist elections and the crazy unregulated government spending. He recalled when they had to turn their money in for the new money. He remembered when they started putting the microchips under the skin on the back of people's hands. They told everyone that it was for medical emergencies and that it would help save the children. They named it the Child Safety Act and mandated that all newborns be chipped at birth. The next phase was to be implemented the following year at driver license renewal time for the adults, but it never quite got to that point. They looted all the retirement accounts and 401K accounts first. They rolled them all into the social security system so the government could manage and keep them safe. It wasn't fair that some people had more money in their accounts than other people, so the retirement accounts were redistributed. Everyone pretty much bought the story that was being told, hook, line and sinker. It was late in the communist president's second term that the price of food skyrocketed. Soon after that, food became scarce, and the millions of people who depended on food subsidies went crazy. About three weeks later, martial law was declared, and two weeks after that they decided to confiscate guns, precious metals, and extra food. At that point people realized that the government was not there to save them, but to rob them. The President invited the UN to bring in troops to restore order. The Chinese troops were the largest contingent, and it didn't take long before they turned into a conquering army. As a result, three men were sitting in a boat, in a thunderstorm with everything they ever owned or loved destroyed. Between the desperate starving populations, looters, communist Americans and the Chinese, this once great country digressed into a desperate struggle. It was a struggle they were destined to lose until the plague was unleashed from a biological warfare lab. As bad as the plague was, it was the one thing that stopped the Chinese. Their offensive was stopped when their supply chain died. They were abandoned in this hemisphere. Dix didn't know how many were left, but each one they killed was one less roach in the kitchen as far as Dix was concerned. This mission was to try and determine exactly what they were up to. The Chinese were ferrying men and materials up the river. Dix knew that the Chinese were in Houston and in New Orleans and that the Chinese were heading up the river. In one more week they would know if the plague infected cigarettes and the infected eggs had done the trick. Dix was startled awake when the bilge pump on the boat kicked on. He didn't realize that he had dozed off. Fox and Morgan were still sleeping, and it was getting dark.

He kicked Morgan and whispered, "Take over the watch; I am falling asleep."

He took Morgan's place and fell asleep leaning up against the seat post.

## CHAPTER 18

Porter's heart was about to jump from his chest as he waited for the Old Indian's next words. He looked at Porter. "Sandy and Ally are safe at my house. My wife and daughters are taking good care of them. You must be Porter. They said you would be coming."

"I almost didn't make it several times."

"Y'all need to stay with me; you can't stay over at your place."

"What do you mean my place?"

"Charlie left the place to you and the girls, but you can't go back until enough time has elapsed for plague pathogens to die off."

"What about their bodies and the animals?"

"The cattle are all free roaming right now. The best horses and Sandy's mule are at my place. The other horses are on the range; they won't go far from the water towers. There's grass right now from the rains. Charlie and the boys managed to bury almost everyone. Charlie took his old backhoe and dug enough graves when it started. I could only watch from a distance, because Charlie would not let me get within twenty feet. I don't know who buried who since all the graves are covered, and there is only one open grave. The backhoe is still sitting where they left it. One of his boys is lying dead on a cot next to the wood stove."

Porter choked back the tears. "I'll bury him by them one day; I can't believe it. What is your name, sir?"

"I'm Burt Watson. Charlie called me Indian Joe along with everyone else. But don't worry about all that Native American crap. I'm an Indian just like my mother, dad and all my brothers and sisters. Charlie made a will before he died. He sterilized it along with a letter for you and left it on a stump, and called me. He left everything to you and the girls. He said that he considered you one of his sons."

Porter took a deep breath. "Mr. Joe, I may have been exposed to the plague. This is Katy. She saved me from drowning. I got in a knife fight about two weeks ago; so if the guy I killed had the plague, I've got it."

Katy sat crying after hearing about the Cross family and seeing Porter's face.

She spoke up, "His mule threw him, and he landed on a rock. He was bleeding from the back of his head. I pulled him up into the shallows, but he looked dead. I caught up the mules, and I used his gear and slept in his bedding."

Porter nodded. "How far am I from the Cross ranch? We can stay at the lodge until we are sure we aren't infected."

Indian Joe looked at them. "You are a good three days ride by mule. I usually drive over there to look around. I put some signs up warning people of the plague. It takes me a couple of hours by truck or ATV to get over there. I have a cabin I can let you stay in. I used to have hunters come out to hunt my place, and it is where I put them up. It's already stocked with some food and clean bedding. You'll stay there until we see if you're going to die."

"I appreciate you letting us stay. I hope I don't die and mess up your cabin."

Indian Joe laughed. "I'll come get you in the morning. Y'all should be pretty safe here till morning." He whistled and a big brown horse came walking in from the darkness. "I trained him from a colt to come when I whistled. I slip him a treat every now and then when he comes."

Porter pulled out the hammock, and set it up for Katy. Old Dollar was within sight of the fire, and Porter knew that he would sound the alarm if anyone or anything came up. He shook out his blankets in case of a scorpion and crawled back in to finish the night. Sleep did not come easy; the thoughts of the Cross family being dead had him tossing and filled his dreams with misery.

He was up before the sun; his dad's watch showed 4:30 a.m. He reheated the rice and turtle. When Katy got up, they polished off the meal. He saddled the animals, and they were ready when Indian Joe crossed the little river and met them.

"I've got the cabin open and airing out. The beds are ready and there's even electric lights and water. There's a bathroom with hot water. You have to light the gas water heater and turn it off when you're finish. We have natural gas from an old oil well on the property that was abandoned years ago. Part of my lease deal was for them to run a gas line to the lodge and house and leave it when they left. There's a washing machine and a clothes line. I'll get the ladies to round up Katy another outfit or two.

It took them a couple of hours to ride back to Indian Joe's ranch. When they got there, the sun was high in the sky. They unsaddled the horses and carried the gear into a small stable near the cabin. The cabin was small, but it had several double beds down one wall. There were some old leather chairs and a big couch covered in cow hide. Antlers were hung on the wall, and a gun rack was by the door. The kitchen had a big bar and two stoves. One was gas; the other wood. A big wood heater sat in one corner. The house had electric lights from solar panels on the roof. The water came from a rain cistern with an electric pump connected to the solar panels. Like every ranch in the region, a windmill pump filled a large water tank near Indian Joe's home.

Indian Joe told Porter, "Y'all get settled in; I'll bring the girls down later."

"Thanks, be sure to warn them that we may be sick. I need to go another week to make absolutely sure if I am or not. Oh, another thing, don't get close to the guys with the red arm bands. I ran across some who were infected."

Indian Joe raised his rifle. "I've been shooting them. I hate those communist bastards. They stole from us when they were in the government, and they are trying to steal from us now. Before the collapse they wanted to tax the water that ran off my roof and into my cisterns. Taxing rain! They would have taxed the air we breathed if they could've figured out a way to measure it."

He hopped on the big brown horse and disappeared up the dirt road. Red dust blew up behind the horse as his hoofs kicked it up.

Porter lit the gas hot water heater and hit the shower for a deep scrub. He shaved and put on the clothes he had washed in the river. His only footwear was the boots Charlie put him in many months before. Katy hit the shower next while hers and Porter's clothes were washing. Porter had them all hung up and drying when Katy came out in one of his tee shirts and a pair of jeans she found in an old bureau. Porter punched some holes in an old belt with his knife and soon had her outfitted until her clothes were dry. He put his shoulder holster on, slid the ammo pouch over his head and slung the AK47 on his back before walking outside. He couldn't wait to see Sandy and Ally, so he walked out to the fence to wait for them. As promised, Indian Joe came driving up in his electric golf cart with the girls. They were about ten feet away, but he could see the tears and smiles when they saw him.

"I told you I'd be back."

Sandy asked, "How long before I can hug you?"

"To be sure, I need one more week with no symptoms."

Ally, who had been unusually quiet, held out a box. "We made you some cookies; we knew you have been missing our cooking."

Porter grinned. "Thanks, I haven't had a decent meal since I left."

Katy walked out to meet everyone. "Y'all are the only thing he has talked about since we met. I'm Katy Hesston from Austin."

Porter pointed to the girls. "This is Sandy and this is Ally Bailey. We've come a long way together."

Ally was looking at Katy. "She sure is pretty. Are you going to marry Porter like me and Sandy?"

Everyone turned to look at her including Indian Joe.

Porter turned red and stammered, "Wait a minute."

Indian Joe came to the rescue. "Well are ya, Porter?"

At that everyone started laughing. They all sat around and talked about what had taken place in the last few months. They left after a couple of hours, and Katy and Porter went back to the cabin. Porter retrieved the radio and set up the antenna. He would report the good and bad news to Cooney Jones.

They cooked some of the beans, rice and cornbread that they found in the cabin. They shared the cookies that Sandy and Ally had brought and sat silent for a long time.

At last Katy spoke up, "You know, Porter, that's a decision you are going to have to make. From what I have seen there have been a lot more young men killed than young women. How many women have you killed so far, Porter?"

"Just one. If you were a man, I would have killed you when you crawled out of the hammock."

"Well, Porter, you are going to have to make a decision. Its obvious Sandy and Ally are your ladies. I know Ally is just a little kid, but like it or not she is yours. What about me; what are you going to do about me? You could have gotten rid of me by just giving me some food and a gun, why didn't you?"

"I've been asking myself that question since I let you live. If you had wanted to leave, I would have let you, but there is no way on Earth I could have abandoned you. I don't know; I guess it's some sort of a guy thing."

"I think it's a primordial instinct. I found myself jealous of Sandy and a little of Ally. I'm sure they felt a twinge of it themselves. You were red as a beet after Ally blurted out the obvious."

"I don't want to think about it; I'm not going to think about it. The Chinese are still here, and you and I have both met the communist Americans. I am still a Sergeant in the Constitution army; and until they are eliminated, I will be fighting."

The shadows were long as the sun was getting ready to set. The red Western sky created a beautifully spectacular scene before him. He thought of his murdered parents and little brother. He thought of his house and room and wondered if all his stuff was still where he left it. He hoped the wild dogs had eaten the bodies of the murderers he left dead. It had been months since he saw Big John. He wondered if he were still alive and staying in his shelter hidden beneath the old shop. Katy stayed in the cabin while Porter made the necessary connections for the antenna. Old Dollar and Ruth were content munching on a bale of hay in the corral; they had earned a quiet rest after all the miles they had been ridden.

The sun was setting when he fished the antenna wire though the window so it would reach the radio. Porter sat down at the table in the cabin and attached the antenna wire to the back of the radio. He made the call to Cooney and waited.

The radio crackled and a voice on the other end answered, "Porter, this is Chevalier in Jonesville. I just sent a runner to get your grandfather; I mean the Captain. I'm surprised you ain't got yourself killed by now."

Porter grinned as he answered, "Well, it isn't because I haven't had the opportunity."

"From what we hear, you have seen a lot."

"I've seen a lot more than I thought I would. I figured we would be out of American communists by now, but they keep popping up."

Cooney came in and took the radio. "Porter, how close are you to the ranch?"

"I am almost to the ranch. I am staying at Burt Watson's hunting cabin. He and his wife have been looking after Sandy and Ally."

"Old Indian Joe? I can't believe he is still around. I hunted with him a time or two over the years. Get him to tell you about the time we shot that big old mule deer that fell into a canyon on the south end of his place. It took us all day and half a night to get to him and pack him out. I take it Charlie and his family didn't make it, or the girls wouldn't be at Indian Joe's."

"No, they are all dead and buried except for one of the boys. Doc is going to have to tell me how long before I can go in the house and move his body."

"Porter, at this point, we don't know. I would stay clear of the place. If you have to go in, make sure you are wearing a respirator not a paint mask. You also need to wear gloves and a face shield if you can find one. I would stay away until we have more answers."

"I figure I have one more week before I know if I am contagious or not. I have Katy down here at the cabin with me. The way I have it figured if I have it, then she has it too. So, as it sits now, all the girls are safe unless I come down with symptoms in a week."

"Porter, we have determined that one of the first symptoms is a fever. We think, but are not certain, that the fever is followed by nausea. So if you start puking, you might be infected. If you develop a rash, then it is pretty much over, except for the really bad suffering. Let me know if you start developing symptoms, and we will decide what to do at that point. I can't help you with the young ladies. That's a whole different problem you'll have to solve."

"Gee, thanks, looks like they are turning into my real problem."

"Porter, I am going to confer with Major Jernigan and Colonel Miller and apprise them of your situation. Now that you know the girls are safe, we may want you back in the field, so for now just relax, but stay alert and ready to move if necessary."

"Yes, sir, I love you, Grandpa."

"Love you too, son, Cooney out."

Porter plugged the radio into an electric outlet. The solar cells charged batteries that fed an inverter that provided the cabin with power for radios and small appliances. Everything else was fed by the natural gas well. He and Katy finished off the beans, rice and the last few cookies. While Katy folded her clothes, Porter walked out on the front porch and sat in the rocker. The moon was bright and all was quiet. Suddenly, the silence was broken by gunfire coming from the direction of Indian Joe's ranch house. Several guns were firing. Katy ran to the door and looked at Porter.

Porter shoved her back inside. "Kill the lights and head out to the stable with your gun and hide. Take your pack in case you need to run. I am heading up there. Don't follow me; I may be shooting, and I don't want to confuse you with a bad guy. Stay put. Do you understand?"

"I can shoot too."

"Have you been in battle and have you shot anybody?"

"Well, no, but....."

"Don't argue with me; this is what I do. You do exactly what I told you. Don't leave the stable unless you have to run for it."

Porter grabbed his gear and ran out the door. The gun fire continued as he saddled Old Dollar. He soon had him galloping down the road heading to the ranch which was a good three miles away. When he got to a point where he could see the ranch in the distance, he pulled back on the reins and stopped the old mule. He hopped off and lightly tied him to a fence post and proceeded on foot. He pulled his pack off his shoulder and retrieved the suppressor that Charlie's son had made for his Beretta 9mm pistol. He shouldered the AK47 and threaded the suppressor to the pistol as he made his way to the sound of the first shooter. When he was within twenty feet of him, he waited. As soon as another shooter opened fire a hundred or so feet away, Porter placed a round through the back of his target's head. While the man crumpled to the ground, he turned his attention to the next one. Porter heard the crack of the bullet as it passed near his head; then an echoing boom was heard from Indian Joe's house. He thought *that old man almost got me by accident.* He dove for cover and waited until he identified the location of three more shooters. He crept on his hands and knees until he was near two of them that were talking. He waited until there was shooting to creep closer.

He listened as one of them spoke, "I thought I winged the old coot when he was sitting on the porch smoking."

"I told you to let me take the first shot, now unless we get lucky, we won't get him."

The first one rose up and shot toward the house. When he did, Porter popped the one next to the shooter through the head, and then he shot the shooter, as he was ducking back down for cover. As expected, a bullet from the old man's rifle zinged overhead returning fire in the direction of the last shot. That left only the gun fire coming from the far side of the house. Porter eased his way around to that side of the house staying low as he crept toward the sound. The old man fired his rifle from the house, and a man who had been running fell forward and landed in front of Porter. This was a guy that Porter had not seen or heard. *That old man was a heck of a shot.* Gunfire erupted from the house again and was answered by the same person that Porter was trying to intercept. From about thirty feet, Porter spotted the man. He placed three rounds through his upper torso and finished with one to the head once the shooter was on the ground. The final gun was silenced. Porter waited silently hidden behind cover and listened for any others. He could hear no more movement or see any evidence of life. He sat quietly until morning because he didn't want to get shot by accident from the house or stumble on any more enemies waiting for a shot. As the sun came up, he eased around the house looking for any more bad guys. All he found were the ones killed from last night.

Sandy called from the house, "Porter, are you ok?"

"I'm ok," he yelled, "just doing a little clean up. Stay put until I get back."

He verified all the dead men. All of them had red arm bands; two of them appeared to have rashes, although it was hard to tell on dead men. He followed their trail back up the road to where they left a truck with a trailer. Evidently, they were going to kill everyone and clean out the house. He headed back to the ranch where he met Indian Joe followed by Sandy.

Sandy looked over at Indian Joe and smiled. "I told you he would save us."

The old Indian shook his head. "Not bad, kid, not bad at all. Who taught you to shoot and fight like that?"

"Charlie taught me the basics; the rest I had to figure out on my own. Stay clear of the bodies. I think they are infected; just leave the bodies where they are and don't touch their stuff. I would also keep the dogs away from them."

"I have the dogs locked up in their pens. I will take my backhoe and cover them up where they lay."

"Good idea. I spoke with my Grandfather Cooney Jones last night. He said they would let me know what my orders are."

With an ear to ear grin the old Indian blurted out, "You say your grandfather is Cooney Jones? Why I had to help him drag a deer out of a bottomless pit about thirty years ago. I'll never forget that good for nothing scoundrel. One thing I can say about him; he could really shoot. Sandy and Ally said that you could outshoot any man alive."

Sandy was turning red. "I just know what I've seen him do."

Porter replaced the suppressor in his pack and shouldered the AK47 and replaced his pistol in its holster. He followed them back to the house.

"I believe two of them had a rash. If that's so, we should be rid of the red arm banded communists in about three weeks."

Sandy nodded in agreement. "I hope so; I'm tired of feeling like this, and I am tired of waiting to get my arms around you."

Porter could only grin when Indian Joe looked at him and winked.

# CHAPTER 19

Dix was so deep in sleep that it took several nudges from Fox before he woke up. It was night, and the rain had subsided.

"Dix, Butch wants you on the radio."

Dix took the radio from Fox. "What's up, Butch?"

"Just wanted to let you know that Mr. Lester died earlier this evening. Doc said that he provided enough of the live hot virus to infect what's left on Earth. We also heard from Porter Jones. His girlfriends are safe but the rest of his adopted family didn't make it. Cooney said that Porter has not exhibited any symptoms of the plague as of yet and is awaiting orders."

"That kid has been through a lot. Tell Cooney to let him rest up a few days. I want him ready to head to Houston. I've got to get some intelligence on what those bastards are doing down there. Ask Doc if he can put together a portable infection kit that we can take with us. Once we are sure they are infected here, I want to be able to travel to Houston and finish them off there as well. As soon as it's light we are going to head up the river for twenty or thirty miles and hide. Radio us if a boat passes Natchez heading north. Go ahead and get a couple of those mortar tubes aimed so that when one of those boats passes Natchez, we can hit it with a mortar. We only have about a hundred mortar rounds, so don't waste them playing around."

"Will do, Major, I have been sending men over to keep an eye on Rachel and Beagle.

"Keep us posted on what's going on. How's your wound healing? How much longer before I can put you back in the field?"

"I'm already in the field. I just stay in the truck and make the guys come out to meet me."

"Good thinking. Call back if you need me, Jernigan out."

Morgan retrieved a small stove out of his bag of tricks and soon had a pot of coffee boiling. After they drank the strong black coffee, they filled the water filter from the river and let it drain into their canteens and water jugs. Morgan fried up some pancakes in a skillet using the fresh ground whole wheat.

Dix commented, "I hope some of those old farmers we gave diesel to have some wheat and corn in the ground. Otherwise, the only thing we'll be eating is what comes out of the river."

When dawn came, they motored out to the edge of the sunken barges and tugs so they could peer up and down the river. After glassing the river and verifying that there was no boats coming or going, they headed north again. After traveling another forty miles, a Chinese boat was spotted heading downstream. They turned and ran south, and once again took refuge in a small cutoff of the main channel. This time it was near some grain elevators. While their boats were hidden, Dix and Fox took the opportunity to look in the huge structures to see if there was any grain inside. One was half full of corn, another full of wheat and the other three were empty. He radioed Butch and told him the GPS coordinates of the giant silos. After the big boat passed, they headed back north and once again traveled without seeing friend or foe. They were nearing Vicksburg before they decided to sit back and wait for another Chinese boat. A little stream lay on the Louisiana side of the river and was all that was left of a small bayou that at one time fed the river. It was probably cut off by the levee unless it had formed an inland lake on the river side. Either way, it allowed them to watch the river and still be shielded from view. As daylight was fading, Morgan had the little stove fired up and once again he was frying up some pancakes in his skillet. He also produced some greasy sausage from the food stores. They ate well and finished it with some more strong black coffee. The kid was a whiz with supplies! The mosquitoes were tolerable and were only a problem when the river breeze let up. Just before dark, a boat from the south came lumbering by. It was dark enough that Dix and Fox could ease out in the stump thumper and follow it without being seen. As they watched from behind the boat, they noticed that several of the crew members were hanging around outside. Some held their heads over the rail. Others sat in the open and leaned back against the wall of the wheel house. Once a door opened, and from the light they could see that two men were carrying a third wrapped in a sheet. They walked over to the edge and rolled the body into the river and retained the sheet. As they followed, three more bodies were casually dumped in the river. Fearing contamination, they let the stump thumper drift back, and they headed to the cutoff where Morgan waited.

Dix climbed over into his boat and told Morgan, "It has started. There are some of them dying already. Some people must be more susceptible to the virus than others."

Morgan suggested, "They may be putting them down as soon as they determine they have it. It would make sense. Why treat them when you know there's nothing you can do. They don't have the same views on death and dying that we do; they are just more practical."

Fox grinned. "It saves me a bullet; good for them."

Dix poured another cup of coffee and got on the radio to Butch. "It looks like our little presents have taken hold. Get with Doc and seed a few more boats. We should know where the boats are going tomorrow. As soon as it's light, we will be moving north.

We got creeped out following the boat tonight, so we're going to hang out here until daylight."

The radio crackled, "I'll get with Cooney and Doc, and we'll keep delivering our treats to them every night."

"Keep it up. I have a feeling that we'll be on foot by tomorrow night getting a look at their encampments. Jernigan out."

They finished eating and tried to get some rest. They took turns watching and were awake and running as soon as it was light enough to see. They ran flat out heading north on the river. They soon spotted what Dix had suspected. The Chinese were at Vicksburg. There were grain elevators on the Louisiana side of the river, and one of the boats was anchored up nearby. They came under small arms fire as they raced by on the opposite side of the river. They turned back and, once they were out of sight, found a place to hide the boats on the Mississippi side of the river. They waited until dark, geared up and took to the stump thumper because the little outboard was very quiet; the boat rode low in the water, and they could stay close to the shore as they puttered up the river. If Dix's hunch was right, they were getting fuel from a tank farm located on a diversion canal below Vicksburg. Here was food, fuel and the some of the richest farmland on Earth.

Morgan had a backpack with the drone and its controls mounted on it. Fox had his old 30-30 rifle. Dix was carrying Jake's AR15, and Morgan packed his AK47. Fox had acquired a leather bandolier that held a hundred or so rounds of 30-30 cartridges. Dix and Morgan each had a pouch that held one-hundred and eighty rounds of ammo plus a full magazine in their rifles. In a bad firefight they would easily run out of ammo and would be in trouble, but they weren't looking for a fight. This trip was to observe and report. In the moonlight they slowly went up the river. Going dead slow, they easily spotted logs and debris floating in the river. They quickly made it to the canal and were soon puttering by one of the big boats. Just as Dix suspected, the Chinese were taking on fuel at the tank farm. The stump thumper motored past the tank farm, and they found a landing spot below the bluffs. They could see the abandoned casino still moored to the canal bank. After landing the boat, they pulled it up the bank and hid it in a bunch of small willows. A steep road led up the bluff, not far from the casino. They used a leap frog pattern of each one taking the lead until they reached a spot of cover. The man at the rear would overtake the first two and take cover. In this way there were always two men in covered positions able to provide cover fire in the event of ambush. They continued this method until they were well into the city. There were no lights, and if it weren't for the moonlight, they wouldn't have been moving very fast. After a few blocks they found themselves overlooking the fuel tank farm and observed the big boat where the crew was refueling it. A crane at the dock was unloading supplies from the deck. A pile of bodies were burning to one side. A couple of young men came sneaking up, but didn't see Dix, Fox and Morgan hiding in the shadows.

Dix spoke up, "Boys, don't touch your weapons. There are three guns on you. What are you doing out here?"

Without hesitation the first one answered, "Probably the same thing you are doing, watching the Chinese. Every now and then we catch one out that we can kill and rob."

"You need to pass the word to avoid them and their gear. They have the plague, and it doesn't care if you are friend or foe."

"We got word through the shortwave to quarantine ourselves, and everyone has been doing it. We thought it was about over."

"No, it is running rampant with the Chinese. Tell everyone that if they see one just kill him and let him lie there if they can't cover him with dirt. They will be trying to escape the virus and deserting their camp very soon. So just shoot first and ask questions later. Are there any communists left up here?"

"No, sir, they pulled out and went to Jackson when they heard what happened at Natchez. A bunch of us local guys formed a militia to fight 'em."

"Who's your leader, son?"

"We don't really have one. Some of the guys from the academy just met up at the school one day, and we decided to start killing the bastards. We keep a scoreboard of the verified kills. We got tired of them threatening and enslaving people. We started shooting their police, but we never got a shot at the governor. After someone killed the Natchez governor, he panicked and left with a dozen of his men and headed to Jackson."

"Can you pass the word about the plague? We're going to have to keep the Chinese bottled up and let the plague thin them out. We are going to need a bunch of guys making sure that none of them get away. You'll need to round up your men as soon as possible."

Dix proceeded to tell them everything that he knew about the plague. "I am Major Dix Jernigan with the new Constitution army." He then asked, "What are your names, and is there a place I can meet your fellow militiamen?"

The boy answered, "I'm Jack Bradshaw and this is Mark Dunlop. We've been wanting to join up."

"How old are you boys?"

"We both were seniors at the Academy."

"You have any family left?"

"Yes, sir, my folks are hiding out in the country at my Grandpa's farm. I bring back what I can find."

"How about you, Dunlop?"

"My family is dead. I've got a girlfriend, and she's staying with her two sisters near Jack's folks. I do the same thing. I gather what I can find and try to keep them fed."

"Guys, I can swear you into the Constitution army. There isn't any pay and there will be little to no support because we are just as rag tag as you. When you join, you are in for life, and you have to swear allegiance to the original Constitution. If you refuse an order, I'll kill you. Do you still want to join?"

They looked at each other and Bradshaw asked, "What about taking care of our folks?"

"You will take care of your folks first. Just let us know what you're doing and why. I will not fault any man for putting his family first. I need men who can help put an end to this communist and Chinese threat. There won't be any medals; just hard work and ruthless killing. Any questions?"

"Can we join up now?"

"Raise your right hand." They both raised their hands and Dix said, "Do you swear to all that stuff I just talked about?"

In unison they said, "I do."

"Ok, guys, you are both privates. This is Sergeant Fox White and Corporal Hunter Morgan; you will follow their orders. We need a spot to hole up while you gather your troops. If they aren't willing to join, we don't want them. We have to mount a defense, and I can't have a bunch of freelancers running lose. Where can we hide out around here?"

Dunlop spoke up, "There's an old antebellum house that didn't get knocked down during the civil war. It still has a basement and a cave that was here during that war. That's where we've been hiding on this side of town."

"Take us there, and we'll wait until you set up a meeting with your men."

The house was only about a half a mile away. When they went in, they could smell the ancient wood. Using a small green LED light directed at the floor, they made their way down the hall. The wide plank floors beckoned from the days when huge virgin trees were felled for lumber. They went down the stairway into the basement and through a door that opened into a tunnel that was cut into the soil. Ancient heart cypress boards lined the walls and ceiling and old beams sat atop columns of handmade bricks. Dix noted that some of the bricks still had the finger marks from the builders who had made them. The floor was covered in the same bricks and was slick from the mold and mildew that loved the dark and damp conditions. The tunnel opened onto a room about twelve feet wide and about twice as long. A set of brick steps led up to a set of double doors that formed the escape hatch. Fox went up through the hatch and verified that it opened to the side of one of the many gullies that ran throughout the city. Morgan retraced their steps to make sure the house was empty and set up a couple of noise traps to alert them if anyone came in. Dunlop and Bradshaw had set up some army cots and folding chairs in the room. A kerosene lamp and some candles were on an ancient table in the middle of the room. Two benches sat on each side. Small powder post beetle holes covered the table and the benches as testimony to their age. From the looks of the table, it was probably original to the house.

Bradshaw said, "We'll round them up for a meeting in the morning. It will take a while to find everyone. We do all our scavenging at night; there are still some local snipers who try to shoot you during the day. We'll come get you once we have them notified and have a place."

As he closed the door behind them, Dix said, "Good luck, boys; make sure everyone gets word to their people about the infected Chinese before we have the meeting."

Dix looked around to Fox and Morgan. "What do you think, guys?"

Grinning, Fox asked, "Now that I've been promoted, don't I get a hat or some stripes or something?"

Morgan just shook his head, and Dix laughed. "I kinda like giving field promotions. Morgan, get Butch on the radio."

"We'll have to go upstairs. We aren't going to be able to get a signal out of this hole."

They went upstairs and got Butch on the radio.

Dix told him, "We are organizing some resistance up here. Add privates Mark Dunlop and Jack Bradshaw to your roster. I also field promoted Fox White to Sergeant and Hunter Morgan to corporal. I want their next paycheck to reflect their new rank."

Butch laughed out loud. "This is one hell of an army; no pay, no grub, no uniforms, and we steal our gear, bullets and guns from the enemy."

"I'm glad you have a full grasp of the organization. Get word to Cooney and Miller of our situation. It appears that the plague is hitting the Chinese hard. There was a pile of burning corpses near one of the boats. It looks like they are entrenched here in Vicksburg, so they can control the grain elevators and fuel tank farm."

Butch questioned, "Why Vicksburg? Aren't there grain elevators and fuel tank farms down around Baton Rouge and New Orleans?"

"I've thought about it. If you can't go home, and don't have a chain of supply, then you have to go to an area that is rich in resources where everyone is not trying to kill you. We practically eliminated them in that area. The local populations there are hostile to everyone, even each other, and I'm sure the plague was running rampant with the survivors. The river is blocked at Greenville, so Vicksburg was the logical choice with food, fuel, low population and fertile farm land. After I see our new recruits in the morning, we will be going in close so I can verify without a doubt that they have the plague."

"Don't get yourself shot or contaminated."

"How's Rachel and Beagle?"

"They are doing just fine. Beagle has that smoke house almost half full. I think he has another hog and a gator skinned out and hanging."

"Any word on our boy Porter?"

"I'll have to check with Cooney; as far as I know, they are waiting on your orders."

"I would like to meet him near Houston as soon as I get things buttoned up here."

"Shall I tell Cooney to get him started?"

"No, I want the boy to rest and make sure he isn't infected, and then I want him to spend some time with his girlfriend. He is human like the rest of us."

"Major, I think we quit being human a year or two ago."

"I think you might be right, Captain. Jernigan out."

Morgan reached into his coat and came out with a flask. "Hold out your hands, Major. We don't know who's been in this house or when." He poured some bourbon whiskey in his and Dix's hands. They went back downstairs and poured some in Fox's hands also.

Fox said, "I think I need to play it safe and cleanse myself from the inside out." With that Fox reached in his pack and pulled out a fifth of whiskey.

Dix grinned. "Where did you find that?"

"Beagle said that the late Mayor of Natchez had some of his men leave it for y'all."

"I knew that old coot was good for something." They passed the bottle around and each opened a package of the Chinese cookies.

"Morgan, it's almost midnight, and we've had a busy day. You and Fox get some sleep. I'll hang out here in the hallway. Anyone coming in will have to wake me."

They passed the bottle around once more. Fox headed down to the cave, and Morgan headed up the stairs. Dix sat near the bottom of the stairs and waited. The old house was quiet. As all old houses do, this one would creak and pop occasionally as the wood cooled or swelled depending on the humidity. Somewhere in the walls a mouse was cutting on a board. When a rat ran down the stairs next to Dix, he swatted at him and sped him on to his destination. Dix thought about it for a moment *that rat would make a tasty meal for somebody.* Dix leaned back against the wall and was soon asleep.

The old ghosts in the house left him alone, and he slept soundly until almost morning. He dreamed about his parents, his sister and the old home place at Jonesville. He was startled awake by an aluminum can hitting the floor. It was one Morgan had set on top of the back door's knob. Dix was sitting in a dark shadow, so the only move he made was cocking his pistol. In these close quarters he figured the pistol would be the more efficient weapon. He heard a voice and recognized it as Bradshaw.

"Don't shoot, it's me and Dunlop."

Dix relaxed, let the hammer down on his pistol and restored it to its holster.

Bradshaw reported, "We're meeting the guys down at a church about a quarter mile from here. There's a basement where we can all meet out of sight."

"You guys sure put this all together pretty quick."

"We're anxious to get rid of all the Chinese and communists. We're all ready to finish them off and want things to get back to normal."

"Things will never be back the way they used to be, guys. We will get back to where there is a quiet normal life, but it will never get back the way it used to be if I can help it.

Let's get some rest. I assume the meeting is in the morning?"

"We are all meeting over there at 9:00 a.m. in the morning."

They all disappeared into the dark house. Some took the beds upstairs and some went to the cave. Dix stayed put and slept at the bottom of the stairs. All he needed in order to sleep was a quiet spot out of sight and free of gunfire.

The next morning they awoke and passed around some of the Chinese rations.

Dunlop spoke up, "Is it true what they say about you?"

"What are you talking about, Dunlop?"

"Is it true you ran the communists out of Natchez?"

Morgan heard his question as he was walking down the stairs. "It's true, boys. You are looking at what one committed man can accomplish. We are getting ready to take on the remnants of the first army to successfully invade America since the 1700's. If we are successful, the new America will have you in the history books and your role will be no different than that of the founding fathers."

Dix looked up at Morgan and then back at the boys. "Let's get over to that meeting."

Fox came up the basement stairs and whispered to Dix, "Don't let all that crap go to your head; you and I both know that we are lunatics on a murderous rampage."

"We can't tell them that; they need to feel good about getting killed."

Fox winked. "These aren't kids any more. They wouldn't still be alive if they weren't a tough bunch of little bastards."

They spread out with the boys in the lead heading for the church. A shot rang out and almost hit Bradshaw. Fox spotted where the shot came from and placed a round through the wall just beside the window where it had originated. Dix, Morgan and the two boys quickly covered the house from every angle.

Bradshaw said, "Cover me; I'm going in."

Before Dix could speak, Bradshaw was in the back door. A loud boom and then another sounded before Bradshaw came out the back door reloading his 12 gauge pump shotgun.

"That son of a bitch shot at me a week ago from across the street. He used to work for the newspaper and was one of the grunts for the communist party. They didn't take him when they ran off to Jackson. Sergeant White, you winged him when you shot through that wall. I thought you had missed the window; good shot."

Fox grinned. "Just call me Fox like everyone else."

They made it to the church without any more incidents and found themselves looking at a room full of high school age boys, some men and a few women. Dix looked around the room and ordered Fox, Morgan, and Dunlop to get outside and guard the doors. Everyone in the room was armed to the teeth. Dix had them take a seat in the fold up chairs that were being passed around the floor. Dix stood up at the front with Private Jack Bradshaw.

Bradshaw spoke, "Everyone, this is Major Dix Jernigan with the Constitution army, and he has come with some news." He turned and nodded to Dix.

"As Private Bradshaw has said, I am Major Dix Jernigan with the Constitution army. I am stationed near Natchez, and probably like most of you have been fighting almost nonstop for the past year. I fought with the Constitution army against the Chinese and became a Major after the campaign to get them out of Natchez and central Louisiana. I am spearheading operations to finish them off. Most of you have heard about the plague. If there is anyone in this room infected, there is a good chance that every one of us here will be dead in a few weeks. My understanding is that you have been practicing quarantine measures. That's good. I am here to warn you that the Chinese are currently infected and spreading the plague among themselves. That means that they and any of their equipment are contaminated. Whether you join the army or not, you need to kill them on sight. You need to pass the word to everyone you know. You should all wash your hands and bathe after leaving this meeting, and I'm glad you have all the windows and doors open in this room. The immediate problem we are facing is the hundreds of sick Chinese. Virtually all the Chinese will be dead within three to four weeks. In the meantime, they will be trying to desert once they realize what is taking place. I need men in positions to keep them on the river and on those boats. If they try to come up the bluffs, we need to keep them bottled up. I would like to also get some guys across the river where they have a pier by those grain elevators. I do not want you to attack them. Just contain them and let the virus eat them up. It is also my understanding that some of you want to join the Constitution army; we can use all the men we can get. I need you to all understand that there is no pay, no uniforms, no gear, and you are in the army for the rest of your lives. You will swear allegiance to the original Constitution with the provision that every man is a member of the militia at birth and women as well if they so choose. If you want to join, stand and raise your right hand." Everyone in the room stood and raised their hand.

"Do you swear and agree to everything I just said?"

They all said, "We do."

"Congratulations, you are all privates in the Constitution army. How many of you are former military?"

One old man in the back stood up. "I am a retired Marine Sergeant."

Dix grinned. "I am restoring your former rank. Do you know everyone here?"

"I know most of them."

"Great, I want you to stick around while I dismiss everyone."

Dix looked around the room. "I want you to go home and get your families situated and explain to them about the plague. Be back here in the morning. If some of you do not have any family, stick around if you have your gear and enough food to last a few days. If you need food, we located some silos downriver with plenty of corn and wheat; we have the GPS coordinates."

The room cleared out, and the old Sergeant came up. "I'm Odis O'Leary, and I retired from the Marines about twenty-five years ago. I saw a lot of action in Vietnam."

"Well, I'm afraid you're going to see some more. How far inland has the Chinese set up?"

"As far as I have been able to tell, they are sticking close to the river. They are using the casino hotels as barracks. They get killed pretty quickly if they venture out into the city. They have been moving in men, equipment and food for the past month. They have snipers set up on top of the hotel, so it's hard to approach. It looks like they are afraid to leave the river."

"They are afraid of the plague and us. We've pretty much held our ground with the help of some A10 warthogs. Now the warthogs are grounded waiting on parts; they may have to cannibalize a couple to try and get two of them in the air. The Chinese ceased their offensive and retreated to New Orleans and Houston. I don't know what they have on the East and West Coast. My job is to fight them here. We think they are here as a last resort. They have no supply line from China or any forward bases. It looks like the plague is kicking everyone's butt including ours. Has anyone gotten sick up here that you know of?"

"We heard of some cases over in Jackson. So when your guys got word to us, we shut down the city as best we could. We've just started in the last few days getting out."

"Try to keep everyone buttoned up as long as possible; we don't need to lose them to the plague after we finish off the Chinese. Are there any communists around?"

"There is a group operating out of Jackson. Some of them are wearing red armbands. We've just been killing them on sight."

Dix looked around at Bradshaw. "Send Morgan back in here and stand guard, don't get yourself shot."

Morgan came in. "Whatcha need, Major?"

"Do you have an extra radio we can give Sergeant O'Leary?"

"Sure thing." Morgan dug around in his pack and came up with one. "Sergeant O'Leary, all these radios are encrypted so no one can hear what you are saying, but the Major. I can turn this radio off by keying in a code from the major's radio. Try not to lose it; we don't have a lot of them left. Here is a set of charging clips. Just attach them to a car battery to recharge."

Dix looked at Morgan and back at O'Leary. "These single guys hanging around outside need to be positioned at the most probable places that the Chinese may try to escape through. Are you ok to deploy right now, or do you have family to take care of?"

"I don't have a family any longer. It's just me, and I'm ready to make the bastards suffer."

"I'm sorry about your family, but I want you to get your wish. I'm in the same boat. Where do you want to set up headquarters in Vicksburg?"

"Not here. We're too close to the bluff; we could get overrun. There's an old car dealership further in that would be better. It is surrounded by a chain link fence, making it difficult to storm. It wouldn't take much to fortify the building; it's made of concrete block with a brick veneer. Bradshaw can show you where it is. I'll get these guys positioned with instructions on what to do."

Dix nodded. "When you are finished, come back here and draw me a map of the layout on this side of the river and where you have men deployed."

O'Leary left; leaving Dix and Morgan in the basement.

Dix looked at his radio. "You can make these radios do all of that?"

"Sure and more."

Dix stopped him. "Don't tell me. I've got too much to think about. Let's get with Bradshaw and get directions to the new headquarters. Get Butch on the radio."

# CHAPTER 20

Porter got back to the cabin and found Katy napping on the big couch. He didn't wake her but went to the kitchen and ate some cold rice and beans. He quietly refilled his pistol magazine from a box of 9mm bullets he had in his pack. He found himself dozing at the table. He was startled awake when he almost fell out of his chair. He went into the shower and rinsed the red Texas dust off his body and out of his hair. The red dirt formed little lines in the bottom of the shower as the water carried it to the drain. He was soon asleep in his bunk and didn't stir until sometime late in the afternoon. Katy was stirring around in the kitchen and sat down at the table.

"What happened last night? I heard the shooting, and I waited a couple of hours before I poked my head out."

"The guys with the red arm bands showed up again."

"Did they leave?"

"No, they are lying where I found them. Indian Joe is burying them with his backhoe."

"Doesn't it bother you that you've killed somebody?"

"Not so much. I don't like killing anything, but I didn't start the trouble, I just resolved the problem. If the problem means I have put a bullet or knife in somebody, I'm going to do it. Do you think talking to them would have worked? As long as they know we have something they need or want, they are going to come back with help or they are going to sneak around and shoot us from a distance."

"What do we do now?"

"You just need to stay put and don't get out in the open if you can help it. I'm going to take my long gun and set up within sight of the communists' truck and trailer. I have a feeling that some of their friends will come to check on them. Remember, they probably have the plague, so your life depends on not coming into contact with them or their stuff."

"How long do you think their things and places they've been will remain infectious?"

"I don't know. I reckon Doc will figure all that out in time."

Porter dug out his long rifle and partially filled bandolier of .308 cartridges. He opened the boxes of ammo that his grandfather had given him and finished filling it. He saddled Old Dollar and headed out with all his gear. He had to close the gate quickly to keep Ruth from following. When he got to Indian Joe's house, he waved to the girls who were both waving to him from the porch.

Indian Joe came out to the gate and greeted Porter. "Where are you headed all geared up?"

"I figure when our guests don't return, someone is going to come looking for them. Is there a place I can set up with my long gun where I can see their truck and trailer?"

"South of their truck is a rise about two-hundred and fifty yards away. You can set up a blind there. There is plenty of cover, brush and rocks to work with."

"I'll put Old Dollar in the corral and head up there on foot."

## Chapter 20

Sandy followed Porter to the corral. "Six more days, I can't wait."

"Me neither, I have really missed you. I am looking forward to the end of this war so we can all settle down."

"Have you thought about where we can go?"

"We've got a lot to think about. I like the idea of going to the ranch, but I don't know how long the plague virus can live outside a live host."

"What about your grandfather's place back in Louisiana?"

"I'm thinking that we either need to be there or have him come out to the ranch. The trouble with the ranch is the lack of water. When the windmills break, everything dies or goes back and forth to the river. I don't have the knowledge to repair it."

"At least we have options. It looks like most of the killing and fighting will be coming to an end soon."

She blew him a kiss as he headed out to set up the blind. When he arrived, he walked out to the vehicle and made sure that no one was around. As he looked up toward the rise to see the best place to set up, he spotted a natural gap between some rocks and trees. He spent the next half hour arranging brush and rocks. Off to his left he could see the ranch; it was about four-hundred yards away. The communists' vehicles lay about two-hundred yards in front of him. He could see the roadway, leading in, off to his right. Someone driving or walking down the road would come into view as the road meandered across the landscape. He made a quick walk further to the south. There were no roads; only rangeland as far as he could see. It was much like the Cross ranch. He settled in to wait and watch. A light wind was blowing across the range; the light red dust had his teeth gritty and his eyes watering. If the communists held true, they would not be on foot. All of them he had come up against used animals or vehicles. He didn't expect them to change their habits this time. He also knew that they would have to come soon if they were coming at all. Once they started getting sick from the virus, the travel would stop; only those trying to make a run for it would be on the move. As he suspected, he didn't have to wait long. In the distance he could see the dust boiling up behind a vehicle coming down the gravel road. The road he was sitting on led out to the state road that traveled from north to south. He listened as the vehicle slowed and turned off the highway. Since the sun was getting low behind him, if they looked in his direction, they would be blinded. He unfolded his tripod and deployed it so that he was sitting on the edge of the small ridge. Brush was piled up in front of him with an opening to shoot through. There were rocks he could duck behind if they started shooting in his direction. They stopped when they spotted the parked truck and trailer. Three of them were in a black pickup truck. They got out and surveyed the area with binoculars. One of them climbed in the back of the truck and rested his elbows on the cab as he looked around. Porter dialed up the scope and found what he was expecting. All had on the red arm bands; he knew what his task was at this point. He didn't have long to wait as he heard Indian Joe's big rifle boom. One of the men in front of the truck went down. Porter squeezed the trigger on his gun and placed a round through the torso of the man in the back. The man collapsed into the back of the truck. Porter didn't expect him to get up, but saw him trying to roll over the opposite side. The second shot from Porter's gun knocked him over the side. Porter knew that he wouldn't be getting up again. The last man fired wild, ran back to the truck and tried to get in. Indian Joe's gun barked, and steam rolled out from under the hood. The big bullet from the old gun had gone through the radiator. Porter shot through the driver's door as the windshield exploded from the bullets fired from the old Indian's gun. The truck took off in reverse and bounced as the passenger side front wheel passed over the body of the one Porter had knocked out of the truck. It sped out of control down the road until it swerved and turned over in the ditch. Porter watched as Indian Joe casually shot the two on the ground through their heads and walked down to the overturned truck. The engine was smoking and knocking from being upside down. The rear wheels were spinning harmlessly in the air. A loud pop from the exhaust and a loud knock deep within the engine brought it all to an end. He watched as Indian Joe squatted down a bit to get a bead on the dying man still in the cab. The old gun bounced when he pulled the trigger. Porter heard the sound a half a heartbeat later. Porter picked up his hulls, walked down to the road, and waited for Indian Joe to walk back.

"Porter, that was a good idea you had; I think you can hit as good as your granddad with that gun."

"Thanks, this is my granddad's old hunting rifle."

"I'll be damned. That's the rifle he used to shoot that big buck that I had to help drag out. I didn't mean to surprise you by shooting. I was on my way out to see if you wanted some grub when I spotted them driving up. I was shooting from behind the truck and trailer."

"I appreciate the help. It would have been dicey once I shot the first one. I was deciding my firing order when you made the decision for me."

"We got the sons of bitches; we make a good team."

As they walked back toward the house, Indian Joe told him stories about his grandfather and Charlie Cross. Sandy and Ally had a box ready with dinner and desert. Once he was on Old Dollar, they handed it up to him, being careful not to touch him. Both blew him a kiss when he looked over his shoulder at them as he rode away. Once again he was looking down the road between Old Dollar's ears. It was funny how Old Dollar seemed to know the road home.

He called out, "Katy, dinner's ready."

She came out. "Great, I hope it's not beans or lizards or frogs."

"I don't know or care what it is. After all the time on the road, I'll just be happy if it's hot and been cooked recently." He handed her the box of food and put Old Dollar in the corral. Ruth came walking over. The old mules looked as though they were glad to see one another.

When they broke open the box, they were surprised to see fried quail, corn bread, beans, potatoes and gravy, and sugar cookies for desert. There was even a jug of sweet ice tea to wash it down. Compared to what they had been living on this was a banquet. Porter saved two sugar cookies for Old Dollar and Ruth. When he came out, he whistled; but they didn't budge until he waved the cookies.

Katy came out and joined him at the corral. "I didn't want to ask, but I heard some shooting, what happened?"

"Three more red arm banded corpses are drawing flies."

"You aren't the least bit fazed about this are you?"

"I haven't had time to think about it, I haven't murdered a single person; everyone was killing or trying to kill me and mine. I would rather it be me doing the killing than them, and none of them will be hurting anyone ever again."

The two mules didn't stray far; they were hoping for another sugar cookie. Katy wrinkled her nose, "Do they always smell this bad?"

"You get used to it. I need to give them a good brushing and file their hooves; that will be a good project for in the morning."

Katy looked at him. "You are right in killing those men. I wish I could kill the people who killed my family."

Porter went in, fired up the shortwave and contacted his grandfather.

Cooney asked, "Any symptoms yet?"

Porter grinned. "None as of yet. We had some run-ins last night and this afternoon from some red arm banded communists. They won't be bothering folks anymore."

"Just don't get yourself killed. Major Jernigan is planning a run to Houston. We need to get some intelligence on their operation there. He is going to want you to head down there and find out what's going on and radio back your findings. We will probably want to deliver the plague directly to them. We don't have enough men to make an assault. How long do you think it would take you to get there?"

Porter thought about it. "At least two weeks by mule. If I can find gas, I can get there in a few days on my Rokon; it's stored back at the ranch."

"Give it some thought; I want you to sit tight and relax if possible until you hear from me."

"I've been fighting more since I got here where I can relax than when I was on the trail. Do you think all of this will ever come to an end?"

"Sure it will. We are almost at the point where we are running out of people to fight. With a little luck we'll either wipe the Chinese and communists out or they'll have to put to sea to save their skins. At that point we'll start acting and living like civilized human beings again. It'll never be normal. All the cars and machines are wearing out pretty quick so those of us who survive will be living a much simpler life."

"I hope so, I'm ready to start worrying about hunting and fishing and not fighting."

"Porter, as long as there have been men on this Earth there's been fighting and killing. That'll never change; that's the nature of man. How are all the girls, are they ok?"

"They are all fine, and I will be out of quarantine in five more days."

"Be careful, son, I haven't had a chance to talk to you about boys and girls."

"Don't worry. Charlie Cross took care of that before I left."

"Good, I'll sign off, try not to get yourself killed."

"I love you, Grandpa."

"I love you too, son. Jones out."

## CHAPTER 21

Butch answered the radio, "What's up, Chief, are there any left that we can shoot?"

"I see piles of dead bodies being burned. I would say something is killing them. We have them confined to their boats on the river. We're putting men in place to kill any that try to get off the river and up the bluff. We're stretched pretty thin; we only have about thirty men and several ladies to do the job." About that time, they heard someone open up several hundred yards away.

Fox poked his head in. "I'm on it. I'll radio back what's going on."

Dix looked around. "Make sure the boys are not taking potshots at them. I don't want the bastards shot unless they are trying to leave the river. They need to stay put and spread the plague among themselves."

Putting the headset back on, Dix asked, "Butch, what are you hearing from Cooney and Porter?"

"I just got off the radio with Cooney. Porter is ready to move when we give the order; how long before we try to go look at Houston?"

"If I can get this operation going, I say we head that way in a week to ten days. How long will it take Porter to get there and report?"

"If he can get gasoline, two days. If he has to go on horseback, it's going to take a couple of weeks."

"Have Cooney radio him and find out his mode of transportation and time frame. Don't forget, I want him to have some time with his girlfriend. I know we have managed to fight for months and live through it. The odds are unbelievable that we're still alive, but that doesn't mean the kid won't get himself killed. He needs to have the opportunity to be human for just a little while. I am having second thoughts about even sending him."

Butch piped in, "There isn't any one of us still alive that hasn't wondered, why me. But let's face facts; he has survived because he has the instinct to survive. If you send someone else, what do you figure their odds of survival are? I've had a chance to talk with some of the men who rode with him from Texas. He isn't a boy in any sense of the word. He's just young, and let's face it, Chief; he's there and knows what he's doing."

"I suppose you're right, let him stay put for a week; he needs a little down time. Also, have Doc get me a traveling gift basket for Houston."

"Will do, Chief. Erwin out."

The radio crackled and Fox came on, "Sergeant O'Leary's men just dropped a couple trying to break out; they both had a rash."

"Stay away from the bodies and warn everyone about them."

"Sergeant O'Leary knows what to do; he hasn't lost his touch. They are covering them with dirt and gravel."

"Tell everyone to stay alert and do not be tempted to go through their pockets. We need a fifty-five gallon open top drum and some rubber gloves so we can salvage their rifles and ammo. We must sterilize them before we try to use any of them."

Dix looked around at Morgan who was fiddling with the drone he had been packing since they landed. "Do you think we can get a good look at the Chinese camp?"

Morgan looked up. "Sure, but we will probably lose it if they start shooting at it. It would be better to fly it at night; its cameras have low light settings."

"Good, we'll see what we can see tonight. How can we charge it up?"

"The same way I keep the radios hot. I've got a roll up solar panel that I can use."

Fox radioed. "I think we are going to have a problem after dark. I figure they'll try to do most of their escaping under the cover of darkness. Sure wish we had some night vision equipment."

Dix looked thoughtful for a moment. "Do you think we could find a bunch of barbed wire? Morgan, call O'Leary and find out if there is a hardware store around where we can find barbed wire. There has got to be an animal supply house. We should be able to roll out barbwire in the areas we are short of men. That would slow them up long enough for us to get a shot at them."

Morgan pointed out, "We can also use the wire to funnel them into fire zones."

Dix agreed. "Just remember, all we have to do is hold them where they are for two or three weeks. The plague will do the work for us. The goal now is to keep them from fanning out across the country spreading death to the few of us that are left."

Fox returned with O'Leary.

Dix looked up when they came in. "O'Leary, do you think we can round up some barbed wire to slow them down in the areas where we are thin? I'm afraid they'll be trying to slip out at night."

"I'll get some men on it right away. They won't be in a mood to challenge us now that they are dying."

"O'Leary, we are going to fly this drone into their midst tonight and look around. If they are as bad off as I think, this will be a containment operation. No one is to go down off the bluff into their camp or onto those boats until we find out how long that virus can live outside of a living host."

Fox pointed out, "If that virus is bad enough, that could be a no man's land for centuries."

Dix frowned. "If that's so, we may have to start burning houses and cities, but for now let's concentrate on what we know and what we can control. O'Leary, get started on the barbwire, and set up our headquarters at the car dealership. Our job is to guard this bluff and keep them on the river."

Dix, Fox and Morgan took up their posts to bolster the defenses until night fall. Suddenly, a Chinese army sniper had them ducking. He was shooting from somewhere near the top of the casino hotel. Dix wished he had the Springfield rifle. Since the sniper was about four-hundred yards away, Dix could observe his position from where he was hidden. After one shot, he saw the muzzle blast puff the curtains. The sniper was sitting back inside one of the hotel rooms on the top floor. It was the fourth window from the left. Three shots and three puffs later, Dix radioed Fox and Morgan and told them where to look.

After everyone spotted the location, Dix radioed, "Any ideas? He is going to fool around and hit somebody sooner or later. I'm pretty sure I can put a round through that window, but we need to kill him when we shoot, or he'll just move. Morgan, I wish that drone of yours could carry a hand grenade."

"Sorry, Chief, a hand grenade is too heavy for it. It's doing good to carry the cameras and its battery pack."

Fox speculated, "He has to be sitting up on a table or something about six feet back into the room for that curtain to be puffing that much. He isn't a real sniper, or he wouldn't be shooting so often. My 30-30 is not going to have the range to make an accurate shot, but your AR15 can easily put one through that window from here. Morgan's AK47 is like my 30-30, it might hit the window, and it might not."

Dix's eyes gleamed as he agreed with Fox's assessment. "You're right. He has got to be about center of the window and about six feet back in the room. He is probably elevated a bit to see over the window ledge. He may even be standing and using a tripod. If I were to aim about head high on a man standing in the room, the bullet should drop five or six inches. If I wait until those curtains puff out again, I can fire four or five shots at him before he realizes it."

Dix slowly slid back out of sight and using his Kbar knife, cut three sticks and tied them together to form a tripod. He eased back into position and rested Jake's AR15 across the fork they created. At that distance the orange dot created by the Trijicon sight covered about half the window. He tried to imagine the exact center of the dot and held that imaginary point about where he thought the man's head would be. The curtains puffed out and at that instant he squeezed the trigger. In quick order Dix fired five more times.

Morgan, who had been watching with his binoculars, radioed, "All six rounds went through the window. One was a little wild and dusted the window frame going in."

"If I didn't hit him, I probably made him mess his pants. I am sure it was very exciting in that room for a few minutes."

Fox laughed. "I'm glad I wasn't betting. I didn't think you could hit that close with one of those rifles."

"This one has a heavy barrel; it's a lot more accurate than the light barrel ones, but it's heavy to pack."

There was no more sniping coming from the hotel, but to play it safe, everyone kept their heads down when they were within sight of it.

As it has done for countless days, the sun went down across the river offering a spectacular sunset. Dix sat watching and remembered happy days of fishing in the South Louisiana marsh and watching the sun set from the deck of the old fish camp. Then he came back to the present when some gunfire erupted down the road.

He called Morgan. "Let's get that drone fired up so we can see what's going on. Fox, get over here. O'Leary, try to cover the gaps we're creating by leaving. We're going to fly the drone in to see what we can see."

Fox and Morgan converged on Dix's location next to a civil war mortar canon that was displayed along the road on the bluff. Morgan soon had the drone in the air. The suitcase was open and revealed a computer screen. Morgan was looking at the screen with the control box around his neck and resting on his chest. The drone was hovering about twelve feet in the air. Morgan flipped a switch and the camera came to life, and although it was dark, it plainly displayed Dix, Fox and Morgan hovering over the control panel.

Dix looked at Fox. "Stand guard, I'm sure Morgan is recording all of this."

Morgan nodded in agreement and concentrated on his task. With a twitch of his fingers the drone took off straight up; the numbers indicated its height from the ground. It rose vertically to about two-hundred and fifty feet and leveled off. Morgan deftly toggled the joysticks, and it took off east over the edge of the bluff and over the Chinese encampment. Morgan hovered over the pile of burning corpses and zoomed in. The grisly remains were emitting an oily smoke and skulls and bones were accumulating at the base. He moved the drone down over the boats, keeping it well out of sight. There were guards scattered about, but none seemed to hear the little drone high in the sky.

Morgan watched the battery meter as the little drone darted from building to building and from boat to boat. There were some men around one building, lounging in chairs and leaning against the building. Most were sitting with their heads resting in their hands. Others were leaning listlessly against the building. A number were stretched out and appeared unconscious. Morgan turned the drone and ran back across to the window where the sniper had been. He positioned the drone in a hover about twenty feet out and zoomed in with the camera to look into the room. In the twilight, a face stared back with a gaping eye socket where there once had been an eye looking through a scope. The rifle lay on the table where it had fallen. The sniper never knew what had hit him. Morgan quickly killed the camera and recalled the drone which landed about twenty feet away. He replaced the battery with one that came from the drone Dix had shot down some weeks earlier. This time they ran the drone above the bluff with its infrared camera looking down. All of their new troops stood out like light bulbs at their positions. The drone spotted a dozen or so men making their way up a trail out of the river bottom.

Dix got on the radio to O'Leary. "We've got about a dozen trying to slip out; they are coming up a road on the south end."

O'Leary answered, "We got 'em."

They watched as several of the Chinese troops converged at the top of the ridge. Gunfire erupted, and the drone watched as they retreated back into the river bottom. Two of them fell behind and collapsed, but the others went back down in the bottom.

Morgan recalled the drone and said, "It looks like Doc's cigarettes are doing the trick. I hope they all die out before any of us get infected."

Fox said, "I wonder if we'll be able to get back to the stump thumper. It's hid mighty close to all those sick men."

"We'll worry about it in a couple of days. We've got to keep them pinned up here or heading south in those boats. We'll have more guns showing up in a few days as more of those from the school start joining the fight."

Morgan, who had been concentrating on flying the drone, piped up, "Once they realize they are trapped, we can expect some kickback. I don't know what kind of ordinance they have, but I expect we will see some of it if they decide to stay and fight."

Dix watched the video as the feed from the drone came in. "Bring it on back. Can you charge it again?"

Morgan concentrated on retrieving the drone while he answered, "If we can find a car or truck that will crank, we can charge it off the car battery."

Dix called O'Leary, "O'Leary, can you get us a small boat or canoe that we can use to come in from up river? Our boat is hidden down there in a willow thicket. I want to slip down there in a night or two and head back to Natchez, but I want to stick around here long enough to make sure you don't need any backup."

"Thanks, Major, I have a little boat and some guys who can take you and drop you off. What are your plans?"

"I'm heading to Houston. I want to take the attack to the Chinese base there. I also need to confer with my superiors on hitting these big boats here if they try to escape south in them. I hope we can get some air support, but if we have to, we'll attack them from the banks. I'd really like to sink them in the river with all hands on board. The last thing we need are dozens of plague infested troops escaping into the countryside. Have your guys dig in or set up something to hide behind. I am sure they have mortars, and I'm afraid they'll try to take us out since they know we are up here."

O'Leary came back on. "They may think we are getting ready to mount an attack. I'll get my guys started right way. Major, since you are quarterbacking this game, I'd feel better if you weren't so close to the line."

"Thanks for your concern, O'Leary. I don't feel like myself unless I am in the thick of it. We'll dig in and help you hold the line until you get the rest of your men in place."

It turned out to be a long night. Several times men got tangled up in the wire and set off the cans full of rocks that were tied every so often. Each time the enemy was dispatched or chased back into the river bottom. Dix pulled up some construction rubble and soon had a nest where he could lie if they were bombarded. It wouldn't stop a direct hit or an airburst but would shield him from small arms fire or shrapnel if he could duck in time.

Fox crawled over and whispered from the darkness, "Dix, you asleep?"

"Hell, no, how can I sleep with you sneaking up on me in the middle of the night? I could've shot you. What the hell are you doing over here?"

"I couldn't sleep, and that Zizzy Witch of yours is keeping me awake again."

"Me too, I'm calling Morgan."

Dix keyed the mic and Morgan answered, "What's up, Major?"

"Call O'Leary. I want everyone on high alert. The hair on the back of my neck is standing on end; something is fixing to take place."

No sooner than O'Leary had alerted his men, they heard a wail come from the river bottom below. Everyone dove for their holes as the mortar rounds came thumping in across the bluff. Trees fell and limbs came down when the rounds detonated as they hit the trees. After several hundred rounds had been expended, the first wave of Chinese soldiers started up the roads. Their cry was not unlike that of the Southern Rebel soldiers who fought from these very bluffs. Dix, Fox and Morgan fired at the muzzle flashes of the Chinese rifles. At their current rate of fire, they would soon exhaust their supply of ammo. They stopped the first wave just as the sun was starting to break. O'Leary reported that almost half of their men and boys were dead or wounded, but the line held.

Dix cursed and looked over at Fox. "We might be winning, but at what cost? I only have two more full magazines. I don't know if we can stop another attack. We are about out of men and bullets."

"What's your Zizzy Witch telling you now?"

"I think my Zizzy Witch messed his pants."

Morgan called from his hole, "I see movement." Single shots rang out and slowly got closer as they sat at the ready.

Dix got on the radio. "Get ready guys; we've got some movement."

Suddenly, a lone man came walking up. Dix started to drop him but realized he was shooting the troops who were down, but not dead. He weaved in and out as he walked up the road around the bodies of the dead and dying, finishing them off as he walked. He was an American in a black uniform; he emptied his rifle and dropped it. He stopped about forty feet away, put his hands on top of his head and slowly turned to show that he wasn't armed.

Dix called out, "One step closer, and we'll kill you."

The man answered, "I'm already dead. Every one of us is infected. The remaining men just want to die in peace. I shot the officer who was ordering the attacks. He was delirious from the infection and convinced the men that the disease was coming from the river water. I am sorry for my part in this war. There are only about one-hundred of us left. We are all exhibiting symptoms, and I have explained to them that they will be dead in a couple of weeks or less. I don't expect any of them to try to get away. They at least have food and shelter for now. A group of several hundred have taken one of the big boats and are heading south."

Dix asked, "Is there anything I can do for you?"

"Yes, shoot me; I'm not brave enough to do it myself."

"Do you still have forces in New Orleans and in Houston?"

The man nodded. "Yes, there were several thousand in New Orleans, but they are infected so they will be gone soon. Houston still has itself quarantined."

"How many are in Houston?"

"Seventy-five hundred at last count, and they are dug in like Texas ticks."

"Is there anything else you would like to tell us?"

"I think that's about it; for what it's worth, I'm sorry for my part in all of this."

"We all have regrets." Dix nodded at Fox. A shot rang out from Fox's 30-30 rifle, and the man fell backwards dead in the road.

Dix radioed O'Leary. "Good news, O'Leary. I think they are licked. I need to make sure that this disease doesn't get out of the river bottom. Do we have any backup coming?"

"Yes, Major, I have our last fifteen men on the way. We'll hold the lines until the rest of the devils are dead."

"Keep track of our dead. One day there will be a memorial for them. Do you think it would be possible to get me that boat? I'm heading to Houston. I want to finish off the rest of them."

Dix looked at Fox. "Did it feel good?"

"Yes, sir, I watched those black uniformed bastards advising the communists in Florida. I saw them on boats, and I hear they helped with the interrogations. He probably helped beat that man from Natchez to death and probably raped his daughter. My poor old mama and daddy were killed in their kitchen by bastards like him and the communist soldiers. It feels good every time. I should have made him suffer a little by gut shooting him."

"Fox, I know how you feel. I usually try for a center of mass body shot, most of them won't live long, and I don't miss. I've left a few gut shot ones to die the hard way. I don't like wasting bullets on them. They aren't making any more."

"Dix, why do you think that fellow came up here and told us what he told us?"

"I guess he was seeking redemption. I figure he is explaining things to his maker about now."

# CHAPTER 22

Porter took his file and straddled Old Dollar's front leg with his hoof between his knees. He took his time cleaning it and rubbed some axle grease on it. Over the next three hours he dressed up the rest of Dollar's hooves and Ruth's as well. He then brushed them down and trimmed their tails and manes to get out all the burrs and briars. He rubbed some of the grease on the ticks that were trying to reside on the rear of the mules. Soon they were dropping off and disappearing in the dust. Porter washed up using a bucket of water next to the trough and watched as Dollar tried to poke his head through the rails to get to the green grass just out of his reach. He hobbled them and opened the gate; they soon made their way out to the grass and ate to their heart's content. He pulled off his shirt and dumped the cool water over his head and let the sun shine on his shoulders. He hoped that things would be quiet for a few days, but he knew that he would be called on to meet the Major at Houston soon.

Indian Joe rode up in his golf cart with the solar panel on top. "How's it going, Porter? It looks like you got your mules dolled up like show horses."

"They've needed some attention. I have worked them half to death over the last few months."

"Nonsense, boy; they look as good as I've seen them. I've got some worm medicine we can give them. There is also a sack of DE powder you can dust them down with, and you can put some in their feed. It helps kill ticks, flies and worms."

"What's DE powder?"

"It's earth or dirt that is comprised of the skeletal remains of diatons, microscopic shell fish. The tiny shells cut into the joints of bugs and kill them. It really slows up the parasites on you and your animals."

Indian Joe disappeared in a cloud of dust and came back about an hour later. They wormed and dusted the mules.

Porter asked, "I need to run over to the Cross ranch and look around. I'm going to have to go to Houston soon. I had a motorcycle stored in one of the outbuildings. If there's any gasoline left, I think I can use it to make my run to Houston. Do you have any way of getting me over there? If I take the mules, I'll have to leave them, and I don't want to abandon them. They have been my constant companions for so long, I feel like they're family."

Indian Joe looked over at Porter. "I sprayed down the truck those damned communists were in with chlorine this morning. I sprayed every square inch of it and the trailer behind it. There is enough gas in it to drive over, put the motorcycle and what gas you can scrounge up in the trailer and come back. Can you drive?"

"My dad was teaching me, and my Grandpa let me drive his truck around the farm."

"Hell, boy, you are good to go; besides anyone who can spend months with two old hunting mules and get them to cooperate should be able to handle a Dodge truck. How did you get them two critters to mind?"

"It was easy. They love the Chinese cookies and biscuits. I try to give them a treat when they come. I've started trying to get them to come like your horse when I whistle, but most of the time they come over just in case I have a treat in my pocket."

"How many days before you know if you are infected?"

"I figure about three more days."

"You have some young ladies who shore think a lot of you. You need to be careful or you're going to find yourself with a baby on the way."

Porter blushed. "I don't know what to do. I've got Sandy who is my girlfriend. I have Ally who is bound and determined to marry me too; and there's Katy who has let me know she's available. She is even hinting that since there is a shortage of men maybe I should consider them all; I know that's what Ally has come up with."

Indian Joe grinned. "I can think of a lot worse problems for a young man to have."

Porter was still blushing. "Life was a whole lot simpler when all I had to do was kill communists."

"Porter, do you know what communism is?"

"My dad told me that it was when you had a group of people, led by a dictator, that control every aspect of your life. They tell you what to do, how to do it, what to think, what to eat, and if you don't cooperate, they kill you or chain you to a work bench until you die. If you even mention, out loud, anything that does not agree with their beliefs you will be exterminated."

"You have a good understanding of what it is. It started in this country with big city liberals. In this case it backfired on them, and all it did was get almost everybody killed. Those red banded fools we've been killing are communist government and union workers. Those guys are just a bunch of thieves who are in league with the communist Chinese. They think that by being in league with them they will be spared, but that's never the case. They're useful idiots that would've been dealt with by the Chinese in time. The plague saved us. As hard as we are fighting, there are more Chinese being born every day than we are killing. All they have to do is get them here. With heavy lift cargo planes and transport ships they can haul them over here quicker than we can kill them. The only thing we did was kick back their first wave. If we can survive the plague, we'll win. Just remember, the liberals, progressives and communists destroyed America and your family, not those childish Chinese. Those Chinese troops are innocent victims just like us. If they didn't land and fight, they would have been shot by their own officers. Why do you think they didn't fight very well?"

"I kinda wondered about that. They sure didn't act like they wanted to fight."

"They weren't as aggressive as us because they weren't fighting for their very existence; our guys are fighting for survival. A lot of our guys are fighting out of vengeance. How many Indians spent their entire lives killing the white men who had killed their families? The same goes for white people, how many killed every Indian they laid eyes on after having their families killed and their homes burned? Vengeance is a powerful motivation."

Porter looked at the old man and wondered at the wisdom that stood before him. "I started out killing for vengeance too. I killed all but one of the men who murdered my family. I don't know about the one who got away, but I am certain he was packing lead. After that, I just start killing bad guys and defending my new family the Cross's, Sandy, Ally and now Katy and you guys. I only killed people who have been attacking me and mine."

"How many men have you killed, Porter?"

"I'm not sure. I just tend to business and make sure none of them can get up and walk away."

"What do you want to do, Porter?"

"I haven't had the chance to think past the next battle or fight. I figure I will help polish off the Chinese, those red banded bastards, and then I'll come back for my girls."

"What if you get killed, have you thought about that?"

"I'll never have a life so long as there are any of them left. They'll just keep coming for us unless we finish what we started."

"You're right, son."

"Tomorrow, I'll make a run over to the ranch and load up the Rokon and some gas. I'll also load up some food. Can I borrow your chlorine sprayer so I can disinfect everything before I bring it back?"

"Sure, son, I'll have it ready in the morning when you come get the truck; I'll have you a map drawn so you won't get lost."

"Thanks, I'll see you early."

Once again, Indian Joe, heading home, disappeared in a cloud of dust. Porter walked back to the cabin where Katy was cooking a pot of beans.

She smiled across the room. "Have you decided what you are going to do?"

He frowned at her. "Yes, I have."

"Well?"

"I'm going over to the ranch in the morning and bring back my motorcycle. I'm heading to Houston in a few days to meet the major. I hope there's still some gasoline left. If not, I'll have to make the trip with Dollar and Ruth."

"I wasn't talking about your next mission. What about Sandy, Ally and me?"

"I keep hoping that I can keep changing the subject and the problem will go away."

"Well, the problem isn't going away; most of the young men are dead. What are you going to do?"

"When I get back from this next battle, I'm going to have a talk with my Grandfather and decide if I'm heading back to Louisiana or to the ranch. Both are places that we can live and feed ourselves. Louisiana has the better soil and water but doesn't have as much wild game. My Grandfather will welcome us with open arms. If we wind up at the ranch, we will have the safety of isolation, but we'll be pretty much on our own. When the tools and machines wear out, we'll be in trouble. You'll notice I said we. I'm not going to abandon the three of you because other than my grandfather, y'all are all I've got. I don't know how we are going to work out the details, but the way I figure it, we all need each other."

She walked across the room, put her arms around his neck and cried.

## CHAPTER 23

O'Leary delivered as expected. They hiked about five miles upriver and met an old man with a green aluminum skiff. It had what appeared to be a new four stroke Yamaha on it. The engine was quiet. The only indication that it was running was the little stream of water pouring out the back. The sun was down when they shoved off, and they quietly headed down to the willow thicket where they had the stump thumper stashed. It was just as they left it. As the old man disappeared into the night, they shoved the boat out into the current and let it drift in the darkness toward the river. They floated past the remaining boats, where the aroma of rotting corpses permeated the air.

Fox said, "We've managed to kill more of them than we could have ever killed with rifles."

Morgan tilted back a bottle of bourbon. "I've got to get that smell out of my throat; I can never get used to it."

Dix grabbed the bottle and took a swig before passing it to Fox. "Good idea, kid." After they found Dix's fishing boat where they left it, they called Butch on the radio.

"Erwin here, how's the battle going?"

Dix pressed the mic button, "Battle's about over. They were pretty much whipped when we got there. We had to shoot a few that tried to break out. What's going on back on the lake?"

"We had one boat pass by here heading south. We let it pass. I figure it was full of plague, and it could take it to the ones in New Orleans."

"The boat traffic should dry up pretty quick. How's my gift basket for Houston coming?"

"Doc says it's ready when you are."

"I want to head that way as soon as I get a report from Porter. Any word from Cooney on the boy?"

"Cooney said they have been hit a couple of times by those idiots with the red arm bands, and the boy is still symptom free. Two more days and he can smooch with his girlfriend."

"Let's let him smooch for a week, and then I'll head out. We found out that there are or were several thousand Chinese and communists in New Orleans and most are infected. We also found out that there are seventy-five hundred hunkered down and uninfected in Houston. What's our diesel situation looking like? Do you think we can scrounge up enough diesel for me to take my catamaran to the Gulf and back?"

"Most of the diesel is in fuel tanks on farms, but we've got plenty of jet fuel."

"Can you get me some used motor oil?"

"Sure, every abandoned vehicle in the country has used motor oil in it."

"Get some of the guys to get me several drums of jet fuel. Put in one quart of motor oil to eleven gallons of the jet fuel. The jet fuel is just very clean kerosene; that's what old timers used to do when kerosene was real cheap. Run that oil through a paint filter if you can find one. That will take out any large trash; otherwise, the fuel filter in the boat will catch it. I don't want to stop up the boat filter. I only have a couple of spares. After they're used, I'll have to scrounge up a filter and spares off something else."

"You're right, Dix, we won't be buying any more. Once all these machines and parts are gone, we're going to be back in the Stone Age."

"We're going to need to start making sure that we have some cattle, horses, sheep and goats. I hope we have some garden seeds that aren't hybrids. I'm going to get tired of eating catfish and acorns."

Butch shook his head. "I'm afraid the difficult part will be living day to day after we kill off all the bad guys."

"Butch, it might not be that bad. There should be plenty of fish and game. In a couple of years, people will settle down and start gardening and trading. I think most of the bad guys will have been dispatched, and then it will be a matter of getting on with life. You're going to have to find some tobacco seed or go cold turkey."

"I just want you to know; I am now tobacco free for the last three days, and I haven't shot anyone yet."

"We are also going to be caffeine free in a few days if we can't round up any coffee or tea."

Morgan chimed in, "Well, Major, at least we can make whiskey as long as we have corn, potatoes and rice. We won't be seeing any ships laden with coffee beans, tea leaves, bananas or chocolate in our lifetimes."

Thinking about the future, Dix suggested, "We need to set up a library somewhere while books still exist. Find someone willing to take on the project and see if the existing libraries have a set of the Foxfire Books. I have a set of them in Gulfport at my old home, if I ever get back there one day. It is a collection of old stories and methods of the way people lived in Appalachia. We'll be living like that in the next few years. There aren't enough people left to maintain what we have. I think we can at least live a medieval lifestyle. We've done a good job of cleaning out the rats among us. I'll radio when we get back to the fish camp, so someone can pick us up."

They rode in silence as they made their way down the big river. The boat was tiny in comparison to it. Before the levee system was built, the Mississippi River was thirty miles wide at Natchez in the spring. The Indians who lived there built mounds throughout the Louisiana delta and would retreat to them in the spring when the floods came. It would be just a matter of time before the levees failed, and the floods would come once again. All would be just as it had been in the past. Dix's mind wandered back to his home on the coast; he visualized the shot out windows, the skeletons in the yard and the graves of his family and friends around the oak tree. He wondered if the house was still there and if he would ever see it again. It didn't matter. That life was gone and would never return. He thought about the Chinese at Houston and the man in the black uniform. Fatigue was setting in, the weight of the world was back on his shoulders and the vengeance that drove him festered in his guts. Fox and Morgan saw the look in Dix's eyes as he focused on the river ahead.

Fox broke the silence. "You planning on taking me to Houston with you?"

Dix took a deep breath and turned. "Yep, we've got some more dirty to work to do; we're going to have to run the gauntlet on the river at New Orleans. I don't know how it is now, but in the past I had a fight on my hands every time I went by there. I expect it to be a little quieter now that the plague went through."

Morgan spoke up, "You taking me with you guys?"

Dix looked over his shoulder. "I'm afraid so; Fox and I will never figure out the radios and the drone."

Morgan grinned. "I rode with Fox in an old Chevy pickup he found that would still run; it had a manual shift on the column. I couldn't figure that out."

Dix laughed at the thought of someone not being able to use a column shift on a vehicle.

"That's what we grew up with watching our fathers shift. Before too many years all that will be a forgotten technology. We'll be using car bodies as chicken coops and dog houses."

It was late in the afternoon when they reached the entrance to the old river. The boat was running smoothly. They stopped when they spotted Beagle paddling back toward the boat launch. They tied his boat to the stump thumper, and Dix's boat pulled all three up the lake and back to the launch. Beagle unloaded his fish into his fish cage. Since Beagle was in Dix's jeep, they piled their gear behind the seat, and the four of them headed to Dix's camp. They dropped Morgan at his camp up the lake and pulled into Dix's yard. Ben and Frank came bounding out barking and greeted Dix by almost taking him off his feet.

Rachel stepped out onto the porch. "I told you that you would make it. Did you lose any body parts this trip?"

"No, I've got everything I left with."

She grinned and gave him a big kiss. "Get some of that river washed off and relax."

Dix looked at Beagle and Fox. "In the morning I want to pull the catamaran up to the dock and make it seaworthy. I'm not planning on walking all the way to Houston, and I don't imagine we can get there in a vehicle."

The next morning, Dix awoke to the smell of bacon and rolled out of his bunk. Butch was in the kitchen finishing off a plate of bacon and eggs. A hot whole wheat biscuit sat steaming on his plate.

Dix grumbled, "Why didn't you wake me up?"

Rachel handed Dix a plate. "I told them you needed your rest, so unless they needed you to lead an attack to let you sleep."

Butch just nodded. "You ain't a spring chicken any more. You need your rest. Besides you ain't been looking too good lately. You've been steadily going downhill since you started getting shot and blown up."

"You aren't exactly a James Bond yourself. What's brings you by so early?"

"I've got you three barrels of diesel made up and waiting in the trailer. That should be enough for you to get up and down the river and have plenty left over for sightseeing."

They finished eating and headed out. Dix grabbed Jake's rifle and a pack with six full magazines for the AR15. His Browning High Power was resting in its shoulder holster and his Kbar was on his belt. Fox and Beagle met them at the truck. Dix and Fox followed in Dix's jeep while Butch and Beagle led the way in the truck. The catamaran was still resting where Beagle had tied it to the other house boats after the mortar attack. Beagle went about his task of running his nets and lines. His fish trading was keeping them supplied with items they would otherwise have to live without. A steady supply of eggs and milk came from a man who had a small farm up and running. Beagle's fish supplied him with meat while his flock grew and his animals reproduced. Other people swapped things like sugar, salt, pepper and other trade goods. The barter system was alive and well.

The catamaran was none the worse for wear. They towed it over to the boat launch where they siphoned the diesel into five gallon cans to carry on board the catamaran. They topped off the water tanks from Rachel's boat that Beagle had towed back near the landing several days earlier. Dix cranked the little diesel engine, and it fired right up. A quick once over of the boat showed that it had survived after the mortar attack. Other than a few shrapnel holes in the cabin, all was well. A square of duct tape over the holes would take care of things until he could affect a permanent repair. He deployed the sails and checked the riggings, all were sound. A hole in the canvas was repaired with a patch and a little needle work. His plans were to spend the next week stocking it with food, ammo and supplies for three men for two weeks in the field.

Morgan arrived in his 4X4 diesel suburban. In the back he had extra radio gear, a bigger solar panel for the top and tools to install more equipment on the catamaran and on Dix's fishing boat.

He pointed to the catamaran. "If we are going to work out of it for two weeks, I need to upgrade the electrical and put an antenna on the mast. That will boost our range. We are going to be pushing the limit of these radios. I can run the shortwave at night, but we need to be able to communicate back here and with Porter. Don't worry, Chief. I'll have us up and running in less than a week. Butch also sent over that .50 caliber Barrett rifle in case we need to engage some big targets from a distance."

Dix pointed to the port hull. "There's a long dry compartment that it will slide into under the bunk in there."

Cooney called on the radio, "Dix, Doc wants to come over to see you and plan the attack. He has our package ready to go and has it stored in a freezer. He wants to send one of his men, is that going to be a problem?"

"It will be a little crowded, so long as it's not raining one or two guys can sleep on deck; otherwise, the cabin's going to feel real small."

"We'll be over within the hour."

## CHAPTER 24

Porter was awake before the sun was up and was busy cooking breakfast when Katy stirred.

She hopped out of bed, quickly dressed and joined him in the kitchen. "I want to go with you over to the ranch. I want to help you get what you need, do you mind?"

Porter thought for a minute. "No, I think it's a good idea. I want you to see the place. I'm afraid it's going to be a sad trip, because one of the Cross boys is still lying dead in the house. We can't go in, and we have to be careful and spray everything before we go into any of the outbuildings. I want you armed as well as me. I have no idea what we will be driving into. I hate traveling down the road, but I don't see that we have a choice."

Indian Joe arrived in his golf cart just as Porter and Katy were coming out. He called out, "I thought I would save you the time and energy of saddling up Dollar and Ruth."

Porter waved. "Thanks a bunch. That'll save me an hour of saddling and unsaddling them."

They hopped on the back of the golf cart. They both had their AK47's and a pack of loaded magazines. Porter had his pistol and

Kbar; Katy also had a hunting knife she found in the cabin. They had packs with extra clothes, food, canteens and supplies should they become stranded and have to walk in. The ride to Indian Joe's was bumpy, but so would a ride be on the mules. At least the golf cart was clean. The mules would smell bad and be dusty from rolling in the dirt. They stopped at the house where Sandy and Ally came out on the porch.

Sandy called out, "Two more days." Porter grinned and gave her the thumbs up. Ally was waving for all she was worth.

They loaded their gear in the back seat of the truck and climbed in. The smell of chlorine was still strong in the truck. A large pump up sprayer was in the back seat already full of water and bleach. Another bottle of bleach was behind the seat in case he needed to make a refill. It took Porter several attempts to back the trailer, but he caught on quickly once he thought about the geometry. He pulled down the road and drove over a couple of humps where Indian Joe had covered up the dead bodies. He passed the upside down truck that was now shoved off the road and had a layer of dirt around the doors and windshield to encapsulate the dead communist. Following the map, they turned out of the driveway and headed up the road. They met no one and only passed an abandoned car on the left side of the road. It had been there a while and was noted on Indian Joe's map. A thick layer of red Texas dust covered its body and windshield. About seven miles later they came to an overturned truck. At that point they had to start looking for a break in the low trees and brush where an ancient wagon road came out. Porter flipped the 4 X 4 switch on the dash and turned off the highway and pulled up the road out of sight. He hopped out of the truck, snapped off a branch and ran back to the highway to wipe out the tire tracks in the dust. He didn't want to advertise that anyone had left the highway. The trek down the old wagon road was rough as it was rutted and in terrible condition. Several times it switched back and forth as it went up to ridge tops and back down into the bottoms. They stopped at the ancient remains of a cabin where he walked around the truck to make sure it wasn't damaged. Other than some scratches on the paint and trailer, it all looked ok. The old cabin had a windmill and a water tank. The cold well water tasted good. This cabin was on the far south side of the ranch. Porter had been told about it, but had never had the opportunity to venture this far south. This was the trail the Cross ancestors used to get to the ranch in the days before highways, and this was the first cabin they lived in when they arrived.

They climbed back in the truck and drove up onto the range. After a couple of miles they could see the ranch house off in the distance. Porter stopped the truck, took out his binoculars and surveyed the country. He could see the graveyard under the old oak tree. The backhoe was still parked, where it had been turned off. One mound of dirt sat next to an open empty grave. The house was still; the windmill was still spinning. Several cows and horses were hanging around it. There was no smoke coming from the chimney. A piece of tin was loose and banging on the roof of the barn. There were no chickens, or dogs or anything. He climbed back in the truck and drove over to the trail he had first traveled when he rode up on the ranch. He remembered Charlie Cross standing on the porch with his AR10 rifle slung on his back and the curl of smoke from his pipe as he called out to them. He thought of killing the Chinese soldiers in the snow around the house. He instinctively reached to his shoulder and felt the knotted scar where the Chinese bullet had punched through. His cracked and broken ribs still hurt when he turned just right.

Katy asked, "Is this where it all happened? Is this where you fought the Chinese?"

"Yep, this is where it happened. It is all a blur now."

"How many?"

"I'm not sure. I quit counting after I killed the ones out here in the yard. I just knew what needed to be done and did it. I don't think about it. I just tend to business, and I don't look back or worry about it."

They drove around to the shed where the Rokon was stored. Porter sprayed down the door handles and opened the doors. The Rokon was where he had parked it. A layer of dust had it coated; it had not been touched in months. He opened the gas tank and peered in. It was dry just as they had left it. Charlie had insisted on draining the tank and running the carburetor dry. They had cranked and run it until there was no more gas in the carburetor to go bad. In the front corner of the shed a large metal tank stood on a stand. Charlie Cross had gasoline stored in the tank with added stabilizer to keep it from going bad. Porter took the butt of his knife, tapped on the side and by the sound determined that it was half full.

Katy looked puzzled. "How did you know to do that?"

"I watched Charlie Cross check it one time. I learned a lot from him and his boys. My dad didn't know much about mechanical or farm stuff. He was a CPA. My mother and grandmother wouldn't even let him keep a tool box in the garage. If it weren't for my Grandfather Cooney, I would be just as helpless."

"What about your mother's parents?"

"They were retired rich people. As far as I know, they always lived in one of their condos scattered around the country. My grandfather knew how to drink and go to the golf course. That was all I ever knew him to do. I don't think he could even drive unless it was a golf cart."

"That's a shame. Doesn't sound like they had much of a life. Do you know what happened to them?"

"No, but I can guess. I only saw them every other Christmas. They had a pretty active social life; they weren't much of a family."

Porter bumped the bike out of gear, rolled it over next to the tank of gas, opened the valve, took the nozzle and filled the tank. He turned the gas valve on the bike and waited a moment. He turned on the key and gave the starter cord a pull. He flipped on the choke and tried it again. The motor roared to life, so he killed it and turned it on its side. Both wheels were designed to hold gas so he opened the caps and filled them also. He found the Rokon's trailer standing in the corner and brought it over and hooked it up to the Rokon. Soon they had it loaded in the other trailer and twenty 5 gallon cans of gasoline loaded in the bed of the truck. He left about a hundred gallons in the tank in case he came back this way. Next he took the pump up sprayer, disinfected and opened the other buildings and brought out cans of wheat, beans and dehydrated food. He took an hour and ground up enough wheat to fill five 5 gallon buckets. He rolled a couple of blocks of salt into the trailer and ten sacks of horse feed for the mules. From another building he opened another storage box and pulled out two Chinese AK47s that were stored along with ammo and magazines. He needed a backup since Katy was now carrying his former backup rifle. Charlie Cross had them packed away for just such an emergency. Once he had the trailer loaded, he made sure that everything was sealed up tight, and he asked Katy to wait at the truck.

The walk up to the front door was long and dreadful. He walked up to where he could see in the doors. Indian Joe had written **PLAGUE** across the doors to the home as a warning. Porter peered in and looked over to the bunk by the wood stove. Just as Indian Joe had said, what he assumed to be one of the Cross boys was lying face up dead in the bed. The body was almost reduced to a skeleton; there was nothing Porter could do. He thought about torching the house, but he felt it would be wrong. He would wait to see what Doc said about the disease before he did anything to the house. After all, he and the girls may have to live here one day. He made the long walk across the yard to the truck. Katy didn't ask anything, because the look on Porter's face said everything. He drove the truck up to the cemetery by the oak tree and parked. He walked over to the graves and counted. They were all there and the ground was open for the last one. Maybe the Cross son had planned to crawl out here to die. They would never know. None of the graves were marked. Porter decided to get a marker one day and simply label it: the Cross family lived here and died. The year would be placed under the statement.

He was as profoundly sad as he was when he found his parents and little brother dead.

He disinfected the backhoe before he cranked it up and put it back under the shed. There was no sense in letting it rot in the weather.

When they got back in the truck, the sun was getting low in the sky. Katy slid across the seat and put her arms around Porter, and they sat for a while until he was composed. He cranked the truck and headed back across the range to the old wagon road that led them back to the highway. They didn't stop until they were back at Indian Joe's ranch.

They sprayed everything down with bleach again and unloaded it all. Porter told Sandy and Ally what they found and what they did. Everyone was sad, but the next battle was coming, and it was anyone's guess what the outcome would be. Porter had been lucky so far. The question was would his luck hold out? He strapped gas cans on the bike and on the trailer along with a sack of sweet feed for the mules.

Sandy called from behind the gate, "I can't wait to see you tomorrow afternoon, since the quarantine will officially be over."

Porter grinned and gave her the thumbs up. Katy climbed on behind him, and they motored down to the cabin. Old Dollar and Ruth whinnied as he approached because they could smell the sweet feed. They pulled up to the gate of the corral and hopped off the Rokon. Porter soon had the sweet feed in the feed trough with a hand full of DE split between the two mules. The two mules wasted no time emptying the trough. The sun was below the horizon, and in the growing twilight, the cabin beckoned. The crickets were singing and filled the night with noise. Porter cranked the Rokon, drove it around to the ATV shed behind the stables and parked in underneath. He heard Katy walking around in the cabin, saw the lights come on and heard the pump connected to the water tank come to life when she turned on the kitchen sink. Now was a time for rest and reflection. As soon as the order came, he would be heading to Houston for a battle. Hopefully, this would be one of the last.

He walked through the back door of the cabin carrying his rifle and pack. He stripped down the AK47 and cleaned it. He reassembled it and reloaded. He repeated the process with his Beretta 9mm pistol. Katy put a pone of corn bread in the oven to go with the reheated beans and sausage left over from previous meals. Porter called her over to the table and spent the next hour showing her how to disassemble, clean and reassemble her rifle. After eating, he got on the radio, and they soon had his grandfather on the other end.

"Porter, what's been going on? Did you make it over to Charlie's ranch?"

"We left early this morning, got there and picked up my motorcycle, fuel and some extra supplies."

"Did you run into any trouble?"

"No, but it was just like Indian Joe said. They're all dead. I sprayed everything down with bleach before I touched anything. As soon as Doc finds out about how long the virus lives, let me know. I need to bury the last of the Cross's."

"Have you exhibited any symptoms as of yet."

"Not yet, if I don't have a rash by tomorrow, I will have dodged a bullet."

"Call back tomorrow night if you start having symptoms so we can notify the Major. He'll be leaving later in the week. Once you leave, how long do you think it will take for you to get there?"

"If I travel at night like before, I should be able to make it in a couple of days. I don't want to ride the highways during the day. I would be a sitting duck for snipers or someone in a vehicle. This motorcycle will go almost anywhere; it just won't do it fast."

"I want you sit tight and spend time with your girlfriends, relax and get all your gear together. Plan on being in the field for weeks if necessary. We'll talk in a few days, and I'll let you know when to head out."

"I'll radio tomorrow night, and let you know if I have a rash."

"Good night, son, I love you."

"I love you too, Grandpa. Porter out."

# CHAPTER 25

Cooney came over the levee in his ATV with Doc hanging on in the front passenger's seat. Louie, the deployment technician, was sitting in the back and hopped out as they came to a halt. Dix was sitting under the Bimini top out of the sun while Morgan was busy running wires and making connections. An old barbecue pit was smoking away. Pork from the smokehouse covered the grill. Fox was tending to the meat; his 30-30 Marlin was within arm's length. He had it hanging from a nail on a tree.

Dix motioned them over to some lawn chairs on the bank. "Your timing is perfect. That meat will be coming off soon. What do you have worked up for me?"

Doc said, "The reason I wanted to have this meeting is to explain how you are going to have to carry out the mission."

"What's the problem, Doc? All we have to do is get some of those cigarettes over the fence so they can find them."

"Up until now all we had to do was get the virus out of the refrigerator, inject the cigarette filters and drop the packs onto the boats. The problem we have is that the virus has to remain refrigerated until just a short time before we deploy. We don't know how much time we have before the virus starts to die. I don't think there needs to be more than two or three days between inserting them in the filters until someone puts them in their mouth. After that I believe the virus will start to die. We can't load up a case of cigarettes and send you on the mission. They need to be prepared just before you deliver them, so Louie needs to be with you, and you need to have a refrigerator to keep the virus in."

Dix turned and pointed. "The catamaran has a small diesel generator that I have not run as of yet. The refrigerator will run on AC or propane. I don't know if it even works."

Morgan spoke up, "We'll check out the generator and the fridge. If we have to, I'll pull the generator off the houseboat and mount it on the front deck."

Cooney, trying to not burn his lips and tongue, speared a piece of pork off the grill with his knife and nibbled on the hot meat. "Porter has fuel and his off road motorcycle ready to roll. He's coming off quarantine today, and there are some young ladies ready to attack him."

Before Dix could respond, Fox piped up, "Dix knows just how he feels."

Dix shook his head and looked back at Fox. "Now don't you start; we're talking about poor little ole Porter here. Cooney, I hope you've had a talk with him."

"My dead friend Charlie Cross gave him the talk, and I'm sure it was a good one."

Fox swooshed his hands at the smoke that was blowing over him and looked over his shoulder at Cooney. "Do you think you could have that talk with the Major; I'm afraid he's going to get himself in trouble too."

Everyone laughed and heard the diesel generator in the bowels of the catamaran come to life. A little blue haze rose in the air from its exhaust and cleared as the engine got hot. A stream of steaming water was soon pouring into lake from the generator's heat exchanger.

Morgan came out wiping his hands. "I have the refrigerator on and will know in a little while if it is working. I changed the oil, oil filter and the fuel filter on the generator. There's some extra filters stowed in the compartment along with some extra motor oil. It feeds off the main fuel tank so we are good to go."

Doc replied, "It just needs to run for about a week. After that you won't need it."

Butch walked over to the truck and got on the radio. When he came back, he said, "I ordered two more barrels of diesel and several more bottles of propane. If you're going to be running the generator, you're going to need it. Five full bottles of propane should run the refrigerator for a long time if you see you're getting low on diesel for the generator."

Dix agreed. "I still have some hose and a small pump stowed in a box on the back deck. If we find a tug with some fuel still onboard, we can always pump their tanks. Make sure we have several five gallon fuel cans that we can hand carry fuel in if necessary."

Fox poked around in the coals under the meat and came out with a dozen or so sweet potatoes that had been roasting in the fire. They, along with some honey for sweetening, created a great dish to go with the smoked pork. After lunch they retreated to Rachel's former breakfast bar and rolled out the atlas showing the Texas's and Louisiana's Gulf Coast. This was an immense area with dozens of places for the seventy-five hundred man army and ships to set up and hide.

Cooney pointed out, "We don't know how many ships they have, but if they have more than a half dozen or so, they are going to need fuel and a lot of it. It's hot down there, and they will have to have generators and a way to keep the boats running twenty-four hours a day. I know there were a couple of huge oil refineries on the water and several tank farms. I bid on a couple of pipeline construction projects within those facilities. I have some blueprints you can carry with you. I'm sure they have them well guarded. You will have plenty of opportunity for a guard to find a pack of cigarettes dropped by an intruder."

Dix took a magnifying glass and looked at all the waterways in the area. "I am going to want Porter to come in from the southwest. I want him to take his time and make his way toward Texas City. That seems to be the least populated area. Although we don't know what the plague has done and how much of the local population is still alive, I venture to say they are pretty desperate with the communists dug in. I need him to see what the boat traffic looks like in Galveston Bay. My bet is its only patrol boats. I don't want him engaging the enemy unless he has to."

Cooney shoved his cap back on his head. "That's a lot of ground to cover. How long before you want him to hit the trail?"

They all looked at Dix. "How long before the cat is ready?"

Morgan answered, "I need five more days. I want to finish getting it wired and tested. I also want some systems in your fishing boat as backup. I found another refrigerator we can use as a backup in case the one in the boat fails. It is cooling just fine so far, but let's face it, if we lose the virus then we have to come back here to reload."

Butch shook his head. "Do you think that four men and all that equipment will fit on the catamaran?"

Morgan grinned. "What won't fit on or in the catamaran will fit in the fishing boat."

"Morgan, can you raise Colonel Miller on the radio from here? I want to see if they still have Satellite control."

"Sure, just turn to his frequency on your hand radio. I have a repeater set up on the catamaran with its antenna at the top of the mast. We can hit the tower in Jonesville at Captain Cooney's headquarters, and from that repeater we can hit the Colonel's radio."

Morgan took the radio from Dix, set the frequency and called Colonel Miller's radio. After a few minutes of back and forth with the radio operator at headquarters, Miller came on the air.

"Major, congratulations on the mission in Vicksburg. The word we're getting is that they are dying like fleas in New Orleans. What's next on your agenda?"

"They have about seventy-five hundred at the port in Houston. That's a huge area and our understanding is they are bottled up tight. I have Porter ready to head south and to reach a point where he can monitor boat traffic in Galveston Bay. We're planning on heading out of the mouth of the Mississippi, cross the Gulf and hide somewhere near Port Arthur. From there we'll rendezvous with Porter and plan the attack. I'm calling to find out if you still have access to any satellite recognizance that we can get our hands on."

"We lost all that about a month ago. The entire East and West Coast have gone dark. I am in radio contact with some of the Constitution forces in Texas, Arkansas, Tennessee, West Virginia and, of course, some out West. We hear nothing from the West or East Coasts; nothing out of Florida or Georgia. We have communication with ham radio operators in remote areas only. Our assumption is that the plague has cleaned the areas out. We have no operational aircraft at this time. We are maintaining control of our areas because of your quarantine. I have about five-hundred men scattered out over three states. We are all well armed and equipped for ground operations only."

Dix stretched his neck. "So we are basically outnumbered fifteen to one by a better equipped army that is dug in with plenty of fuel and grub."

"Major, I think you have a firm grasp of the situation. Once they decide to come out, and they will, there will be nothing on this Earth to stop them from killing all the men and rounding up all the women. The only thing holding them in is the fear of getting the plague. They also know that the plague is the only thing keeping us from coming for them. Major, it is all riding on what you can pull off."

"I can't speak for the rest of these guys," Dix replied, "but I can't wait to hit them again. What you're telling me is if I can take out the base in Houston, we will be close to total victory."

"That's correct, Major, and then the real battle begins, putting it all back together."

"We'll be hitting them in about ten days if everything goes on schedule."

"Good luck, Major. God speed. Miller out."

They all sat quietly for a minute before Dix spoke up, "I guess we have our marching orders. Cooney, I want Porter to have the best week of his life up to now. I don't care if he's almost fifteen years old; he is a man, start treating him like one. I am afraid I am sending him to his death. Hell, I may be sending all of us to our deaths! Here are my orders: eight days from now I want Porter rolling. I want Butch and Cooney to put together another boat with a generator and a refrigerator for the virus. If for some reason we fail, I want the second mission launched. Hopefully, we will have radioed enough information that your mission will be more successful than ours. I don't care if you have to use volunteers to take the virus and crawl into camp with them. Any questions?"

Cooney spoke up, "I hope you are successful, and I wind up with more grandkids than we can feed. We'll start rounding up another boat and equipment right away."

Butch nodded. "I know where there's a boat; we can have it running and over here in a day or so."

Dix looked at Morgan. "Do you need any help?"

Morgan pointed to Louie who was cinching down loose wires and waterproofing connections. "Doc, can you spare Louie for the rest of the week?"

"He's yours as long as you need him."

Everyone saluted and headed out as Dix grumbled, "I hate all this army crap."

They all burst out laughing and headed to their vehicles. Dix took a plastic bag and filled it with a good helping of the smoked pig and several of the baked sweet potatoes. He hopped in the jeep, headed up and over the levee and down the road to the camp house. Ben and Frank came running out, and as usual, he had to take the time to give them a good greeting. Rachel met him at the door with a big kiss.

In her sultry voice, she asked, "Have a big day, Major?"

"Yep, we'll be pulling out heading down the river in a week. They'll have the catamaran outfitted and the boats geared up for our trip to Houston. I brought you some pork and some sweet potatoes for supper."

"Great, I've got some squash and peas that the family across the way brought over. I gave them some of Beagle's catfish. All this horse trading is working out pretty good."

"I think I'm going to grab a shower, eat early and hit the sack." She gave him a big kiss, and he disappeared into his room and hit the shower where he surveyed all of the scars from bullets, shrapnel, gravel and briars.

He couldn't believe the changes that had taken place in the country over the last five years. During the last year alone events had taken him from one fight to the next. He didn't know if this would be the last battle or not. His gut feeling told him that it wouldn't be the last, but he was ready; he would always be ready. He closed his eyes and let the hot water do its job. He felt a cool draft and opened his eyes to see Rachel slip into the shower with him. Before he could speak, she simply said, "Shut up, not a word, not this time................."

## CHAPTER 26

Porter didn't sleep well that night. For one, he was wondering if he would have a rash when he got up; and two, he knew he would be spending some major one on one time with Sandy. He rose early, went into the bathroom, stripped down and looked in the mirror. There was no sign of a rash; just an ugly scar between his shoulder and neck, another rubbery looking scar on his side and a scab on his head near the hairline. His hands were calloused, and he needed a haircut. He took a hot shower and slicked his hair back with a brush. He found an old stick of deodorant left in the medicine cabinet. He used a bar of soap to lather up his face and one of his dad's disposable razors he had been packing since he left home a lifetime ago. He was developing a good growth of whiskers; at the rate they were multiplying, in another six or eight months, he might have a full beard. An old bottle of aftershave killed the sting. He had quit sprouting pimples after spending all the months in the sun. Soon he was neat and trimmed. He put on his one pair of clean blue jeans and his one canvas shirt that wasn't full of holes or patched. Luckily, previous inhabitants of the cabin had left socks and other items he could use. When he came out of the bathroom, Katy took one look at him and whistled.

"Wow, you sure clean up good."

Porter's neck turned red. "'Thanks, you look pretty good yourself. Get cleaned up and we'll head up to Indian Joe's and see everybody. Check yourself for a rash when you're in there just in case."

She grinned slyly. "I think you ought to check me for a rash."

"I'm not about to. I have one heck of a situation on my hands as it is."

Katy laughed and closed the bathroom door behind her.

Porter slipped the holster containing his Beretta over his head and fastened it to his belt so it wouldn't flop. He strapped the Kbar on his belt and fastened the British Commando knife to his leg under his pants. When he slipped on his boot, it rode just on the outside of it but was hidden by the pants leg. He placed the .38 into a back pocket because it was now too hot to wear a jacket. He went outside and walked around to the shed where the Rokon was parked. He unhooked the trailer, bumped it out of gear and pushed it around so that it was pointing in the right direction and pulled the starter cord. Three yanks on the starter cord brought the engine to life, so he climbed aboard with his rifle across his back and his ammo pack hanging to his left side. He bumped it into gear and headed around to the front of the house. Katy came out wearing her knife, the AK47 slung on her back and a pouch of loaded magazines. Porter was proud that he did not have to remind her to stay armed at all times. She hopped on the back and hung on to Porter's waist as he gave it gas and pulled away. The little bike rode well, and he kept it in second gear as he wasn't in a rush and the road was rough and rutted. The red Texas dust boiled up behind them as they ran down the road. They soon arrived at the ranch house where Sandy and Ally came running out. He climbed off the bike and was quickly smothered in kisses by the two girls who practically took him off his feet. Tears flowed down Porter's face as he embraced them. Katy stood back watching.

Ally looked up at Katy. "Don't you want to hug Porter too?"

"As a matter of fact I do." With that she joined the group hug.

Indian Joe's wife Josie called from the porch, "Y'all gonna stand out there in the sun all day or get in here and eat some breakfast? I've cooked up some pancakes, bacon and eggs, and I opened a can of cane syrup.

When Porter walked through the front door, the screen door springs sang out as he pulled it open. The old ranch house was very old. There was a gas stove in the kitchen, and next to it, was a door that opened onto a screened porch where a long table with benches on each side sat. The porch also had a big gas stove that backed up to the brick wall of the house. In the summertime they used this stove because the one in the house would quickly overheat the kitchen. In addition, there was a wood stove in the kitchen that had been used in the early 1900's. Josie and her two daughters Lucinda and Juanita had a platter of pancakes, bacon and scrambled eggs in the middle of the table. Lucinda and Juanita were in their early thirties and each had two kids. Two of the children were infants and two were crawling. Their husbands had been killed in battles with thieves and communists.

Indian Joe came up the back steps with a jug of milk from their milk cow. The fresh milk was stored about twenty feet in the earth in an old water cistern that held rainwater. It kept the milk cool as the earth was many degrees colder than the air at the surface. The milk was kept in a wire basket that was secured to a rope tied at the top. Lowering the milk jug into the well allowed the milk to last several days longer. Cheese and butter were stored in the cistern as well.

Indian Joe explained, "That's the way we kept it back when I was a boy. We didn't have any electricity back then. So the cistern was the only place we could keep things cool."

Sandy piped up, "I'm glad you remembered what to do."

Indian Joe carefully poured the milk from the jug into each of the glasses before they were passed around.

"All the old skills will come back. I don't think there are enough people left to operate the electric power lines again.

Maybe someone will be able to in eight or ten generations from now after the plague is over. We all have the basic knowledge of what once was. I'm pretty sure that we can rebuild it again."

After eating a hearty breakfast, Porter spent the rest of the day just hanging out at the ranch house.

Indian Joe asked, "Porter, do you want to move up to the ranch house?"

"No, sir, if you can take Katy in, that would be great. I've got all my gear at the lodge house, and I will be heading out in a few days. I've got to meet the major, and I am waiting for my orders."

Ally came up to Porter and slipped into his lap. "Porter, haven't you fought enough? Why can't you just stay here and protect us?"

Porter took his time and tried to choose his words so she would understand. "Ally, do you remember when all those soldiers came to Charlie's ranch, and y'all had to run?"

She nodded her head.

"Well, there are thousands of them still left, and they aren't going to stay put for long. They will be leaving their forts and spreading all over the place. They won't be trying to make friends. They will be attacking people, killing the men, capturing the women and animals; there will be nothing left. I am meeting the major to attack them, and with a little luck we will wipe them out."

Ally looked puzzled. "Porter, I don't think you have enough bullets. Shouldn't we go along and help? I still have your rifle to shoot."

Porter smiled and gave her a hug. "I want you to stay here safe with Sandy, Katy, Indian Joe and his family. I am used to fighting by myself. I can't do what I have to do and worry about you."

She raised her head off his shoulder and patted his check. "Don't worry, Porter. We'll wait just like we did last time."

Porter and Katy took the golf cart back to the lodge, loaded up Katy's things and took her back to the ranch house. Indian Joe drove Porter to the lodge where he saddled up Old Dollar and Ruth. Soon he had them in the corral at Indian Joe's where they seemed right at home. Porter was certain they knew where they were because it was likely that they had stayed there before. It was a quick ride back to the lodge on the Rokon.

That night alone in the cabin, he pulled out the radio, called Cooney and soon had him on the line.

Cooney asked, "Any sign of a rash or the plague?"

"It looks like I dodged the bullet one more time. There is no sign at all; in fact, I am feeling pretty good."

"Boy, I would be in a good mood too if I were the center of attention of a couple of healthy young women. By the way, do I have to keep reminding you of what can happen?"

"No, I think about it all the time; I mean all the time."

"You're supposed to. I'm not going to give you any advice. Just remember, you can get killed. That would leave me coming over to try to fend for my great grandbabies."

"I'm trying to hold off on anything like that until I know where we are going to end up. When am I getting my orders to head out?"

"It will probably be by the weekend. The Major is retrofitting his boat. As soon as he is ready to leave, he will let you know. They are studying maps and getting ready. He will inform you when and where he wants you to proceed. So start checking in with me every morning and every night until we get the orders."

"I'll call back in the morning. Goodnight, Grandpa, I love you."

"I love you too, son, stay alert."

Porter walked out on the porch; the evening was cool and a soft breeze was blowing. He sat in the old rocking chair with his rifle leaning against the rail so that it would be within easy reach. From where he sat, the full moon lit the landscape. The last year had taken him from being a helpless child to being a grown man. He had killed countless men and traveled many miles. He remembered the lessons taught to him by Charlie Cross and his boys. He thought about killing the men getting ready to rape Sandy and his little brother clinging to his dead mother's body. He nodded off sitting in the chair and was awaken by Indian Joe's golf cart coming down the road. He grabbed his rifle and sat quietly until it stopped near the gate.

Indian Joe called out, "Porter, don't shoot, it's just me and Sandy."

Porter was surprised to see Sandy climb out with her pack and rifle. She was wearing her pistol.

"What are you doing here? I thought you were going to stay at the ranch?"

"Sorry, Porter, you're going to have company until you leave on your mission."

Looking back over her shoulder, she called to Indian Joe, "Thanks for the lift."

"Sorry, Porter, it was either bring her or let her walk."

Porter gave him the thumbs up as the old Indian headed home in the golf cart. Sandy reached around his neck and pulled his lips to hers for a breath stealing kiss.

"Get used to it. You're stuck with me. So unless you are off fighting, I am going to be by your side. And from the looks of things we are going to have Ally and Katy by our sides too. It's a new world; you're going to have to get used to it."

"All of this is a little overwhelming; don't I have a say in any of this?"

"Nope, unless you get yourself killed; you're stuck, sorry." She grabbed his hand and led him through the door and to his bed.

The next morning he awoke with the sun. His rifle hung on the bed post and his pistol was under his pillow. Sandy lay snuggled up against him, and she stirred long enough to plant a good morning kiss on him. She got up, put on one of his tee shirts which hung almost to her knees, headed across the room and laid a broom on the floor.

"Get over here, sleepy."

Porter slipped on his shorts, and came across the room.

"Hold my hand while we jump the broom."

"Why are we doing this?"

"Simple, there aren't any preachers, and there aren't any Justices of the Peace. This is the way people used to get married in olden days."

"Don't you think we're a little young for marriage?"

"If you're old enough to do what you did last night, you're old enough to get married. You love me don't you, and want to spend the rest of your life with me don't you?"

"Well yes, but...."

"I feel the same way, now JUMP." They jumped, laughed and kissed.

She grinned. "How does it feel to be an old married man?"

"It feels good. I'm just afraid I might get you pregnant, and I have no idea how to deliver a baby."

"It's ok. One of Indian Joe's daughters is a PA who worked as a midwife. She can deliver a baby, and she has enough medical supplies and surgical equipment to supply a small hospital. When she saw the collapse unfolding, she commandeered several years of supplies and antibiotics. She implanted me with a Norplant when we got here after I told her you would be coming back for us. We all had a talk last night, and Katy got hers. We won't be getting pregnant until we are all older. I didn't want you going back to war without, well you know."

"Dang, y'all have my life all figured and planned out."

"We have everything figured out but how to keep you from getting killed."

"I pretty much have that figured out. The trick is to get off the first shot and hit what you're shooting at. Once people have holes in them, they panic."

She grinned at him. "I can see where they might. Let's get some breakfast in you, big guy."

They cooked up biscuits, chicken fried venison, white gravy and eggs. They sat down, and Porter almost choked when Sandy said, "Eat plenty; you're going to need the energy. Katy is coming by after supper."

# CHAPTER 27

Dix woke up the next morning with a naked leg lying across his body. He looked over into a pair of green eyes. Her smiling face was framed by lush red hair.

"What are we going to do now?"

She grinned even bigger. "I'm going to spend another couple of hours right here with you, and then I'm going to take a shower and cook breakfast."

"Good answer."

Later that morning after finishing breakfast, Dix came out of the house and found Beagle and Fox working on Beagle's nets. They were strung out across the yard and tied to the front porch so that they were hanging in the same fashion as they did in the water. Fox and Beagle were looking for holes and tears to repair.

Fox called out, "I see you decided to sleep in this morning, Major, have a late night?"

"Don't start, and that's an order. And quit grinning like possums."

He got on his radio with Butch. "How are you coming on our backup boat?"

"Well, you finally decided to get up. Fox and Beagle said you and the missus were sleeping in."

"I guess Cooney should have had that little talk with me yesterday. I have a question, 'Do we have any preachers still alive?'"

"As a matter of fact we do; you've had three of them in your command the whole time and the only preaching they've done lately is at funerals."

"I'm probably going to need one before I head off."

"Major, you need someone to preach your funeral?"

"No, but if you keep it up, we're going to need one of them to preach at yours."

Dix hopped in his jeep and headed over to the catamaran. Morgan and Louie were busy working on the electronics. The diesel generator was purring away and everything was running on the catamaran and the fishing boat. Dix walked up the plank and dug around in the compartment under his bunk. He found the bag that contained the gold, silver and jewelry that he had accumulated since the collapse. He looked until he found a suitable diamond ring and a couple of wedding bands. He had never recovered the wedding band and engagement ring taken from his murdered wife. This bag contained everything he had brought with him from the Mississippi Gulf Coast a lifetime ago. There was a bigger cache hidden there, along with his family photos, in the PVC pipe that he had buried with his family and friends under Gretchen Oak. Gold held little value in this new world: food, knowledge and ammunition were the new wealth.

"Morgan, how long before we can launch the mission?"

Morgan backed out from under the console at the helm. "Today is Wednesday; I say we can roll by Saturday or Sunday. I want to triple test everything, and get the boats full of food and gear. There won't be any marinas, grocery stores or boat mechanics where we're going."

"Make sure we have enough gas and diesel to last us. If the catamaran gets sunk, we're going to have to have enough gas to get back somewhere close with the fishing boat."

Morgan pointed to all the fishing rods in the rod holders around the boat's console.

"It will be a good idea for us to try and do some fishing when we have down time; that will stretch our food in case the mission lasts longer than three weeks."

"Good idea, kid, that's why we pay you the big bucks. Can you get O'Leary up in Vicksburg on the radio?"

"Yes, sir, it will just take a second."

Morgan ducked into the catamaran and soon came out with a radio and handed it to Dix.

"O'Leary, how are you holding up in Vicksburg? Any trouble with Chinese troops?"

"They are all pretty quiet; they haven't tried to get away. The funeral pyre is still burning, but there seem to be less and less of them. We took a tractor with a front end loader and covered all the bodies in the road with dirt. We dunked all their weapons in a tank of chlorine water, dismantled, cleaned, oiled and stored them. We spread all the ammo out in tanning beds and kept stirring it for about eight hours. We then wiped it all down with alcohol and quickly dried it off under fans. We test fired random rounds, and it all seems ok. I have a number of the men outfitted with AK47's, magazines and ammo."

"Good job, O'Leary. Keep us posted and call if you need help. Remember; keep the people away from those boats and men after they are dead. You will have to decontaminate anything you are planning to use."

"I understand, Major. O'Leary out."

"Morgan, get Cooney on the radio."

Morgan fiddled with the radio and soon had Cooney on the line.

"Here you go, Major."

"Cooney, it looks like we are going to be leaving here on Monday. Any word on our boy?"

Cooney laughed. "I think he has more than he can handle with those young ladies. What does the schedule look like?"

"We are going to launch Monday morning. Tell Doc that we need to have the bugs here early. It's going to take us several days to get into position. I want Porter rolling on Tuesday. Tell him that I want him on the west side of Galveston Bay looking around. See if he can locate where they are without getting into a fight. We don't want them to suspect that we are even there. I want to get in, deliver the bait and be out without firing a shot."

"Dix, I've never known you to go anywhere without firing a shot. It's a full time job keeping you in ammo."

"I like shooting the bastards. I won't lie to you, but I want to deliver a knockout blow, and this is our chance."

"I'll have Doc there and ready to load you up first thing Monday."

"Tell Porter to get in there from the west. He'll probably need to set up camp in a secluded spot and quietly poke around until he can see where they're hold up. All he has to do is locate a place where we can plant our bait. Once he locates them, I want him to hightail it back to camp and radio us. We'll arrange to meet him. Does he have a map?"

"He has a map."

"Ask him to locate a spot on the water where we can meet him in my fishing boat.

Cooney, we got work to do over here, so I'll let you get back to what you were doing."

"Major, do you still need me to have that little talk with you?"

"Captain, you're too damned late. Jernigan out."

Dix was still shaking his head when he handed the radio back to Morgan.

He barked at Morgan, "I want you to give me, Fox and Louie a crash course in these radios and what you have set up before we launch. Also, write it down and put it all in a binder and stow it in the catamaran. If you fool around and get yourself killed, we'll never figure all this crap out."

Puzzled at Dix's foul mood, he simply said, "Yes, sir, let's plan on doing it Sunday afternoon. Everything will be in place by then."

Dix scrambled across the gang plank just as Fox and Beagle came driving over the levee to the landing. They both just looked at him as he stormed past them and got in his jeep. He headed over the levee cursing under his breath as he headed back to the camp. The ride in the jeep relaxed him as the cool wind blew through the open windows, and he accepted the fact that his life was going to continue for now. He took a moment to apprise himself of his situation. Victory was within his grasp as he contemplated the defeat of the enemy. Although he was heading into battle again, he felt good. Other than the ribbing he was enduring from his friends, his relationship with Rachel was good. He felt guilty about having these feelings, and he regretting yielding to temptation. But the more he thought about it, the more he realized that now he was not only fighting out of revenge, but to protect his loved ones again. He had a family, whether he wanted one or not. By the time he got back to the camp, he had calmed down, and his plans were in order. First, he would make love to a beautiful woman. Then he would clean his guns, put together what he needed from an offensive standpoint and assemble his pack for the battle ahead. If he got killed, he would just be dead and that would be that. If he didn't fight them now, it would just a matter of time before they would be coming down the road to his home. The plague would not keep them bottled up forever. Some might want to return home, but they would more likely stay and eventually move out into the countryside. Only rape and pillage would result from seventy-five hundred men roaming the country of a strange land.

Rachel saw him coming and had on nothing but a smile when he walked in the door.

Dix spent the next three days honeymooning, cleaning his guns, and organizing his pack. It was actually two packs in one. He could drop the big one and just carry the small one if he had to travel fast. These would only be used if he had to abandon the catamaran and the fishing boat and return on foot. If his radios were intact, he could arrange for Butch or Cooney to meet them with transportation; if not, he would be on foot. Both the Springfield 30-06 and Jake's AR15 would make this trip.

Sunday rolled around, and Dix found himself, along with Louie and Fox, listening to Morgan explain the radio systems. They had pretty much quit ribbing Dix about Rachel as none of them wanted to get accidentally shot. Once they all had a complete understanding of the radio system, they pulled out the maps, went over the route and made decisions on where they wanted to leave the catamaran so they could use it as a base of operations. Once they started, they would have to avoid all contact with people.

Dix reminded them, "I want no personal contact with anyone, especially once we leave. The plague is still going wide open, and we are just going to make it worse. Hopefully, there will be enough of us left to start over. We're going to win this war! I'm not planning on having to worry about gangs of Chinese soldiers breathing down our throats in the future." They all nodded in agreement. Dix looked around at the group.

"Any questions? Morgan, I just had an idea, do you think you can rig up the drone to carry a pack of cigarettes and a mechanism to drop them?"

Morgan smiled. "I can do that. All I have to do is remove one of the cameras and rig up a basket so that when I push the pan button it will open a side instead of moving the camera. It'll take me a day."

"You got it. Then we leave Tuesday morning after breakfast. Morgan, get Cooney on the radio."

Morgan pulled the radio from its pouch on his belt and called Cooney. Cooney answered, and Morgan handed the radio to Dix.

"Cooney, we're leaving Tuesday morning heading down the river. Porter should be able to travel a little faster unless he gets into trouble. Have him head out Tuesday also. I don't want him getting in a hurry and getting careless. That should give him a couple of days down there to figure out what's going on and where we can set up."

"Sure thing, Major. If anyone can slip in, I'm sure Porter is the man."

"Explain to him that even though it is tempting, I don't want him in there with guns a blazing. Tell him to take his time, find out where they are and where they're patrolling."

"I'll let him know."

"How is the boy's girl problem?"

"Major, I'm afraid to ask. I assure you, I didn't have that problem when I was his age."

"I hope his problem leads to a dozen great grandchildren for you. We'll plan on seeing you and Doc early Tuesday with the bugs."

"We'll be there. Jones out."

# CHAPTER 28

The Rokon was running steady as Porter ran down the rutted gravel road heading out to the highway. He was pulling the trailer, and it was loaded with enough fuel to get him to Houston and back with a little extra for exploring. His pack was strapped to the back rack, and his other provisions were strapped to the front rack. He wore his AK47 on his back and his Beretta 9mm in his shoulder holster. As usual he wore his Kbar commando knife on his leg and the small .38 revolver in his back pocket. He turned his cap around so that it wouldn't blow off as he opened the throttle. He reached the road and turned south heading toward Houston. The sun was setting, and the moon was peeking out. As long as the nights were cloudless, he could make good time and minimize his exposure. His orders were to leave on Tuesday, but he wanted to travel at night; so it was Monday night, and he was leaving the last place on Earth he wanted to leave. The past week was one week he would never forget. He thought *if I die tonight, I could never top the past few days.* He kept the motorcycle slow letting it run in second gear. He didn't want to get surprised by a roadblock, and the engine was reasonably quiet at that speed. He rode through the night with the only light coming from the moon and stars. He stopped to stretch, killed the motor and listened. Only the sounds of insects and night animals could be heard. Coyotes howled in the distance. Behind him lay his family; before him waited the enemy. The cloudless sky let him look into the heavens. There were no flashing lights from aircraft. A single star slowly crossed the sky--a satellite making its way from south to north. It would continue its journey for possibly thousands of years until its orbit deteriorated and it burned up in a spectacular display.

He cranked the bike and continued until the sun started streaking the sky on the horizon. He found a side trail and ran up it until he came to a tank where he could camp. An old barn sat near the tank; its big doors sat open. There were lots of animal tracks in the mud around the tank. He drove the Rokon up into the barn out of the sun and turned it around so that it was heading out, but not where it could be spotted if someone were glancing in. The tire tracks were wiped out with a tree limb. He broke out his last package of Chinese cookies and his water bottle. He had a five gallon can of water and a water filter from Indian Joe when he needed a refill. Finding some hay in the loft, he piled it up in the deep shadows in a corner. He was careful not to close the doors as he didn't want anyone to notice from a distance that the barn had been disturbed. He estimated that he had covered about a hundred and fifty miles his first night on the road. He rolled out his wire, fired up the radio and gave his progress to his grandfather. The spot he selected was well back in the shadows, and the exterior wall had some large loose boards where he could push his way through to escape should he get hemmed in. He lay back into the straw with his rifle in his lap. The tank was visible from where he lay; deer, cows, wild hogs and birds came to the tank as he lay watching. Soon he dozed off and was lost in his dreams. He awoke with a start when a large rattlesnake crawled across his legs. He could feel the snake as it pushed with its belly against his leg. The natural revulsion common to most humans kicked in, and he felt the urge to panic; but he didn't, just as in dozens of other situations where he didn't panic. The big snake paused a moment, its tongue flicked and tasted his jeans before continuing. He had no interest in Porter; he was looking for rats and mice. Porter eased the Kbar from his belt and with one quick throw pinned the snake to the barn's dirt floor. The big blade practically severed the snake's head from its body. It twisted its head around in an attempt to bite the blade. Porter pinned the head to the ground with a stick and finished cutting it off. The rattles' buzz set his neck hair on end. A flip of the stick sent the big head flying off into one of the abandoned stalls. He made short work of skinning and gutting the snake and quickly had a small hot fire burning with the snake cooking over it. The big snake made a good meal along with some biscuits and a sugar cookie for desert. His Dad's watch still worked, and it read 3:00 p.m. The sun would be going down soon, and he was ready to roll. The map showed that he had about four-hundred and fifty miles to go. If he were going to get there in time to meet the Major and do some recon, he would need to make better time, so throwing caution to the wind he would head out early. The plague was probably doing a job on the communists with the red arm bands, so if he ran into trouble, it would probably be just some opportunistic locals. Since the two lane highway was smooth, he could run a little faster. While it was light he topped off the fuel tank from a can on the trailer. He fired up the Rokon and ran in third gear down the highway. The Rokon, an off road two-wheel drive motorcycle, had a top speed around thirty-five mph. It was slow going on the highway, but it could navigate off road because it was designed as an all-terrain vehicle. It wasn't as nimble as a mule, but he didn't need to let it rest. He ran the bike flat out, and other than some abandoned vehicles from time to time the country seemed desolate. Even though he passed gates leading to homes and side roads, he saw no one nor did he run up on any barricades.

It was nearing dark when he came to a barricade on a bridge at the end of a long straight section of the highway. He was more than a fourth of a mile away when he realized that the road was blocked. He quickly spun the Rokon around in the road and ran back in the direction he had come. Half expecting bullets to be bouncing around him, he ran back a mile or so and found an abandoned driveway leading off the road. He quickly took it and turned off in a pasture that was somewhat overgrown. He killed the bike and headed back to the road with his binoculars. There was no way of knowing if it were manned or just an abandoned blockade. He was well aware that he could be killed by a sniper. He didn't have his long gun, but he knew that there were people who could make long range shots; if a sniper was manning the barricade, he wouldn't know. The map showed that there was a route around, but it would take him many hours out of his way. He eased up to the road where he could get a good view through his binoculars.

He watched the road until his arms were tired. He looked back down the road from the direction he had come and saw nothing. He returned to the Rokon and followed the driveway up to a burned out house. The gates to all the pastures were open, a stable sat empty out back, and a skeleton lay scattered in the yard. He took a moment to slake his thirst from the canteen and munch on one of the cookies that Ally had made for him. He wished he was back at the ranch with his beautiful girls and the good food. It was a lot easier when they were just some girls he wished were his. It was a different thing all together when they were his family. Time was wasting, so he steeled himself to the task before him. He headed toward the barricade by walking through the scrub and brush and by keeping the road in sight as he made his way. The sun was below the horizon when he stopped to listen and to let his eyes adjust to the waning light. Every so often, he paused and listened. He took a full hour to work his way to within a hundred yards of the barricade. From there, he crawled the rest of the way on his belly. Voices were coming from behind the barricade.

"Be patient, guys, this is the only way south; they aren't going to waste gas going around. They'll be back, and we'll take them. We'll do it just like we have a hundred times before."

Porter thought about what he heard. He couldn't wait all night, and they were dug in like ticks. He crawled closer until he could make them out. They had a small fire, but it was shielded so that there was no light to be seen from road. Based on how it was laid out, there had to be another barricade further down the road snagging any traffic heading north. Continuing his crawl, he eased off into the dry creek bottom and found they were camping under the bridge. Not wanting to be exposed to the plague, he avoided the camp and instead eased up the bank on the opposite side of the bridge and was almost behind them when he made it to the road. They were still focusing their attention down the road. That they were still trying to rob and steal from people made no sense. Either they were stupid or weren't aware of the plague. Maybe they were red armed communists who hadn't caught the plague or were in the process of dying. He sat quietly on his knees with his rifle at the ready. One of them walked back to the fire to get some coffee.

When he got to the fire, the man said, "This rash is driving me crazy, do you have any of that lotion you've been using?" A course looking woman walked up with a bottle of lotion.

"Here's the lotion; it don't help much. I hope that guy on the motorcycle comes back soon. I really don't feel good, and I want to go to bed."

There were three of them: two men and the woman. Porter fired three quick shots from his rifle. All three crumpled where they stood. Three more shots insured they wouldn't get up again. Double timing it back to the Rokon, he once again topped off the fuel, reloaded his rifles magazine and headed down the road and around the barricade not even looking at the carnage he left. He slowed back down to second gear for the night. It was early morning before he reached the second barricade at another bridge. Fortunately, this one was abandoned as he almost ran into it before he spotted it. He veered around it and ducked low as he sped past. No gunfire erupted, and he didn't see anyone, even though they could have been lying dead or were dying in their beds under the bridge. He ran flat out in third gear for another four or five miles. He stopped, topped off the gas and ate several more of the biscuits. Because his adrenaline was still high, he wasn't sleepy, so he traveled on.

Mid morning found him well down the road when fatigue started to set in. This time he turned the Rokon down into an almost dry creek bottom where he ran for a couple of hundred yards. After brushing out his tracks near the road, he turned the bike up the creek bank where a cow trail came down to the creek. The creek was not flowing, but there were pools of water in the creek bottom separated by sand and gravel bars. The Rokon was designed for this type of terrain. The cow trail led up to a pasture with a windmill in the distance. Thunder rumbled across the land as storm clouds gathered. The wind picked up, and over the course of the morning it grew so strong that it was difficult to stand up in. The rain came, and it became apparent that he could not go back the way he came. The creek was now full of water so he sat in the edge of the pasture with the Rokon turned sideways to the wind. He tied a tarp over the Rokon and his gear and made a makeshift tent on the downwind side. It provided a shelter out of the wind and rain. The wind continued to increase, and it almost blew the bike over on him. He leaned hard into it as the storm raged. Hail the size of golf balls came raining down, and he could hear the pings on the metal of the Rokon's racks. If it hadn't been for the shelter of the Rokon and the tarp thrown over it, Porter could have been killed. It was dark before the storms ended so he sat tight for the night. Although it was early summer, the knee deep hail stones brought the temperature down. He shivered through the night and found a different scene before him when the dawn arrived. The windmill that he had seen in the distance was now lying about twenty feet in front of the Rokon where the wind had deposited it. Most of the trees and brush were gone; even the grass in the pasture was beaten into the ground. The Rokon was still in workable condition along with most of his gear. In his pack he found that several of his rifle's magazines had been dented beyond repair. He pulled the ammo out and discarded the magazines. The tarp had softened some of the blows from the hail, as well as, a pile of brush and debris that had blown up to and over the bike. It was a miracle that he had not been hurt or his bike and gear destroyed. He fired up the Rokon and worked his way across the pasture to a fence where he stopped long enough to cut an opening with his bolt cutters. Other than having to move some small trees and limbs from across the gravel road, he didn't have much difficulty reaching the highway and continuing his run.

He ran the Rokon at top speed heading to Houston. He needed rest, and he needed it badly. He soon found what he was looking for: another barn up a hill off the highway. He cut another fence and headed up the rise and around the barn. As he expected, it was empty so he went in and settled down. He found a corner next to a window where he could rest on a pile of empty grain sacks. He used a pitchfork to make sure a rattler wasn't hiding in his new bed. After drinking some water, he went to bed and slept. Many hours later he woke. His father's watch showed 4:00 a.m. He unrolled his antenna and radioed his grandfather. It took a few minutes to get him on the radio.

Cooney asked, "How are you making it, son, any problems?"

"Nothing I couldn't handle. The weather got pretty bad last night. I was almost beaten to death by hail."

"Porter, are you seeing any people? Any word on the red arm banded communists?"

"I ran across three people with the plague; I don't know if they were affiliated with the Red's."

"Did you warn them about spreading it?"

"No, sir, I didn't have time to discuss it with them; they were preparing to waylay me. We don't have to worry about them spreading the plague."

"Dang, be careful, son. Let me know when you reach the coast."

"I should be there by dark or sometimes in the morning. I am going to have to slow down because I am starting to run into a lot of houses and businesses along this highway. I am bound to start running into people and trouble soon."

"Porter, don't get careless. Don't go in with guns blazing. You simply need to find a place to set up camp and locate a guard shack or a trail where they are walking every day. Remember, hide and observe."

"Will do, Grandpa. I love you. Porter out."

"Love you too, son."

# CHAPTER 29

The diesel motor in the catamaran ran smoothly and deliberately. The sail boat cruised down the lake with the fishing boat in tow. The stump thumper was tied to the deck of the fishing boat and could be deployed when necessary. It was low to the water and could go where the fishing boat and catamaran couldn't. In a pinch it could hold all four men and with its little motor could go a long way on a gallon of gas. Dix looked over his shoulder and waved at his new bride, Cooney, Doc, Butch and Beagle. Fox stretched back in a cloth folding chair while Louie and Morgan double checked the gear. The virus had been loaded into a small chest freezer on the deck and in the freezer section of the catamaran's refrigerator. The diesel generator was purring along almost silent; its smooth vibrations could be felt from the depths of the boat. He hoped that this would be the last major battle of the war. They were soon at the outlet into the river, where huge trees, casualties of a great flood somewhere upstream, could be seen out in the current of the river. The catamaran, dwarfed by the huge river, powered its way downstream. Dix ran the engine just fast enough to maintain directional control in the current. By letting the current carry them, they could conserve fuel for the battle ahead and the trip back. As they passed under the two bridges at Natchez, they saw a partially sunk barge lying wedged against the west bound pier of the first bridge. It disappeared toward the bank where it was wedged into the bottom. The next spring flood would probably dislodge it and deposit it further down the river or on top of a sandbar. They should be free from attack until they neared Baton Rouge, and by Dix's estimation they would be in New Orleans within two days. Large Asian carp jumped from the water around the boat as the gyrations from the prop upset them. A couple landed in the boat where they were scooped up by Morgan.

Dix asked, "What are you going to do with those things?"

"I'm going to see if I can clean one. I hear they have lots of bones, but there has got to be a way to clean and cook them. I bet I can clean and fry them."

Fox piped up, "I tried to eat one after he almost knocked me out of the stump thumper. I had to spend a lot of time picking out bones, but I was really hungry, and he tasted good."

Morgan grinned. "Worst case, we can boil him and add the meat to a pot of beans and rice."

Dix frowned. "I would hate to ruin a pot of beans; try to fry him first. That bacon grease should make him taste good. I believe we could fry up a flip flop in that stuff, and it would be tasty."

They soon passed through the school of fish, and the excitement of running through them subsided.

Louie pointed out, "With no one left catching fish and killing game, the populations should rebound rapidly. We'll be living in a real hunter's paradise."

Dix agreed and added, "When we finish this battle, we have got to start gathering stuff, particularly books and encyclopedias if there are any left. If not, all this knowledge will be lost as we descend into the Stone Age. There aren't enough people left to make things like electricity. As soon as the electronics and batteries wear out, we will be back in the dark ages. I believe we are going to be living a medieval lifestyle within the next five years."

Morgan was listening as he quickly cleaned the fish and had them ready for the fryer.

"When we get back we need to start looking in the antique stores, flea markets and museums so we can find and preserve all the hand operated tools."

Dix nodded in agreement. "I think we'll make the transition. There is enough of the modern stuff that can be cobbled together to work. We can cannibalize other equipment for a few years before we have to rely totally on man and animal power. People are already starting to use horses, and there are a few old guys who remember how to forge metal. There should be plenty of scrap metal to scrounge for years to come."

Fox looked up at the levee they were passing. "Food is going to be the issue. I think we need to think about moving over to the Mississippi side of the river. Those levees aren't going to last long, and it will be just a matter of time before they are washed out by a good spring flood."

Morgan soon had four fillets fried in bacon grease. Although there were a lot of bones, the fish was delicious. The bacon grease had saved the day. They made it almost to Baton Rouge before the sun started to set. They found a cutoff from the river channel, near St. Francisville, LA, and anchored for the night. They took turns standing guard. Clouds were starting to blow in, and it looked as if they would have some bad weather soon. During Dix's turn at guard duty, he sat on the rear deck underneath the Bimini top. A small fan blowing on him kept the mosquitoes at bay, but with the moisture from the river, it was cool enough for him to bundle up in a quilt from his bunk. He didn't like sitting in the dark with a generator running. Although it was quiet, the sound of a running engine would travel a long way, particularly when they were in a world that was virtually devoid of motor sounds. From where he sat, he could see almost nothing. The weather was building, and although it was pitch black dark, lightning lit up the sky. Over the course of the next few hours, the lightning grew stronger and stronger. Soon the lightning strikes were coming so fast that the entire river and the bluffs beyond were lit up. Morgan and Louie came to him.

"We need to drop the mast; if it gets hit, all our radio equipment will be fried."

Dix replied, "Drop it; unplug the radios and other equipment."

They quickly unplugged the equipment and lowered the mast. The crack of lightning was deafening as it struck nearby. The hair on their heads was standing on end when they dove for the protection of the catamaran's cabin. Lightning hit a tree on the bank about ten feet away. The thunder was so loud that its concussion cracked one of the windshield panes in the catamaran. They were practically deaf from the force of the concussion.

Dix said, "I don't think we have to worry about being attacked tonight. I suggest we try to sack out and get some rest."

The lightning didn't subside, and when the fierce rain and wind arrived, rest eluded them. From where they were anchored, they were shielded from the worst of the wind, but the trees on the bank were not spared. They could hear trees snapping and feel the waves from the trunks hitting the water. Torrential rains pounded the catamaran. Soon hail pounded the vessels as the storm intensified. The only thing that saved the windshields of the catamaran was the wind that angled the hail away from the windows. The anchor held even though the wind pushed the fishing boat up against the catamaran. The bilge pumps in the fishing boat came on over and over again as the storm dumped the rain down upon them. All at once the wind and rain became so intense that it felt as though the catamaran was being pulled from the water. The stump thumper rose about five feet in the air before it settled back onto the fishing boat. All aboard were silently praying as the storm raged. With the dawn came a pause in the hellish weather. The wind and lightning had subsided, and the rain had slowed to a drizzle. When they ventured out to raise the mast and redeploy the Bimini top, they could see what had taken place. As far as they could see in every direction, the trees and camps along the cut they were in were gone. The only thing that saved them was the fact that they were down below the banks so that the tornado passed over their heads. Morgan and Louie went over the vessels repairing damage and getting them up and running. Fox checked out the stump thumper and pronounced it seaworthy. The fishing boat's windshield had a large limb through it but was otherwise functional. Every exposed metal surface had a dimple where the hail had pounded it. They were thankful to be alive. The freezer sitting on the rear deck was still sealed and running although the top was well dimpled from the hail stone's impacts. Had the storm upset the contents, they could have all been exposed to a horrible death.

They radioed Cooney. "How bad was the weather up your way?" Dix inquired.

"We had one heck of a night; it stormed and rained like you wouldn't believe."

"We'd believe it. We were in the middle of a tornado; everything is blown to hell around here. We are still fully operational other than the terrified look on Fox's face. What about our boy, any word?"

"He weathered out a storm in South Texas. Hail almost beat him to death, but he is back on the road and should be close to the coast by tonight or in the morning."

"Has he run into any trouble?"

"Only the storm and some plague victims who were trying to waylay him. He made it through the storm, and the plague victims aren't a problem any longer."

"I don't want anything to happen to that young man. When you talk to him, I want you to stress that I want him to observe and report. At this point we don't want to kill any Chinese."

"Understood, Major; y'all be careful too."

"We will. I'll radio back later. With the way Morgan has this boat equipped, you should be able to call anytime."

"Will do, Major. Jones out."

The cut was littered with debris and fallen trees. Dix ran the catamaran at dead slow as he idled back into the river. The river was churning towards the Gulf just as it always had and always would. It would continue long after Dix and the guys were gone, and this entire war was long forgotten. The bridge at St. Francisville was still intact with the exception of the roadway on the east side. The concrete road bed was gone in about a hundred foot section. A rope bridge spanned the chasm and allowed one person at a time to cross. There was no one to be seen as they silently passed under it. Several hours later they passed under the bridges at Baton Rouge. Large sections of these bridges were in the water. They came under sniper fire as they passed but could never locate the shooter, no boats put in to follow and other than a new hole in the cabin, no one was hurt. Dix couldn't help but wonder *why would someone be wasting ammo? Even if they disabled the boat, how did they expect to capture it out in the middle of the river?*

Dix called all the guys around. "We are going to get to New Orleans before dark. We need to be on high alert; I have no idea what to expect. The Chinese there should be dead or too sick to care to fight. We have no way of knowing who or what is left. I want to make sure that the bilge pumps are working. If we come under fire, I don't want to lose the boats. I know the ones on the fishing boat are running fine; I heard them cycling on and off last night in the rain. Check the ones in this boat to just make sure."

"I checked them after last night's storm; this boat is in good shape."

"Thanks, Morgan. If anyone needs to rest, now is the time. I don't want to stop for any reason until we are past the city and well on our way to the Gulf."

As they approached the city, there were more and more derelict vessels along the bank. Many were sitting on bottom with just the tops sticking out. There was a large column of black smoke coming from one of the warehouses on shore. Occasionally, they spotted people sitting on the banks fishing. Some waved, others ran and hid, and some just defiantly watched them go by. Several young ladies mooned and flashed them as they passed. They all hooted and laughed at the spectacle; after all, this was New Orleans. It was late evening when they came to the point where Dix sunk the tug boat and dredge in the channel. The river was still blocked to large ships. The top of the dredge's pilot house was still sitting out of the water. It had to have been difficult for the large boats the Chinese were using to navigate past this point. If the river were any lower, it would have probably blocked their access. As Dix negotiated the turn in the river, everyone on board kept their eyes peeled for danger. Louie had his binoculars trained on the large dock on the opposite shore. One lone man was standing on the rail outside of the pilot house of one of the big boats tied to the dock. He was looking back through binoculars, but did nothing other than watch. They were soon past the blocked channel and were back in the middle of the river heading south. They passed the Luling Bridge; the approach ramp on the west side was down, but the superstructure over the river was intact. There weren't enough people left alive to ever repair it again. It would stand there with the rust and weather eating away at it and would one day fall in the river. Before then this portion of the river would probably be one of the many oxbow lakes along the mighty Mississippi River. It would just be a matter of time before the Mississippi River in its rush to the Gulf punched through the Old River Control Structure and diverted its course down the Atchafalaya River Basin.

The river was much more treacherous than Dix remembered when he traveled up it almost a year ago. New sandbars had formed, and there were dozens of derelict vessels sunk or sitting on sandbars. A few tugs still sat moored and anchored, but there were hundreds of sunk and semi-submerged barges in the river. It was difficult to know if they would run up on one and damage the catamaran. They pulled Louie up the mast so that he could see further ahead. It would be difficult to see anything in the muddy water, but even a moment's notice could be the difference in hitting a submerged object or missing it. After several close calls, they found another canal off the river where they could take refuge for the night. The voyage had been hair-raising so far, but it was probably nothing compared to what they could face in the Gulf and around Galveston Bay. That night they ate a pot of beans Morgan had cooked in a crock pot. The beans along with some rice made a hearty meal. They were forced to stay in the cabin because the salt water mosquitoes were vicious; they couldn't wait to get back out in the middle of the river to get some relief. One thing for sure, no one in their right mind would pick this night to do anything, but take shelter in a building or inside a screened enclosure.

After two more days of slow traveling to run the gauntlet of vessels, trees and debris, they reached the mouth of the Mississippi River and entered the Gulf of Mexico. Once there, they put up the main sail and headed out to sea. The GPS satellites were still working, but for how long would be anyone's guess. They went far enough out to avoid any coastal sandbars, but they had to be careful to avoid running into offshore oil platforms. Running in the daylight was okay because they could see where they were going. They could run radar at night, but were afraid there could be enemy vessels that would pick up their radar signals. They decided to tie up to a nearby oil platform that night and take the time to fish. Morgan rigged a light pointing down into the water. Plankton swarmed around the light, and soon after, small fish came to eat the plankton and then larger fish came to eat the small fish. They caught several mangrove snapper and a couple of large speckled trout. Fox made up some hush puppies using powdered milk, corn meal and some onions that he had brought from his garden back on the levee. They ate until they were about to burst and went to bed. It was unlikely they would have company tonight. The little generator was still purring away in the belly of the catamaran. Before he retired, Dix walked out on deck and looked across the water. The moon was peeking through the clouds, and other than the boats and oil platform there was nothing in sight. Dix thought about his family buried in the yard, and he thought about his bride waiting for him on the lake. So much had happened. So many friends and family were dead and missing, and all of it was so unnecessary. He was angry thinking how the preposterous politicians had brought about the economic collapse with their crazy spending and the idiotic printing of money. Now, he was going to fight the remnants of the Chinese invading army. They were innocent victims of the war just as much as he and his family. They were probably drafted and forced to come, but like all conquering armies, they would be ruthless in their conquest once they decided the plague was over, and they ventured out. As any group of single men, there were some specific things on the menu: nubile women, food supplies, land and property. Dix wasn't prepared to part with his nubile woman or anything else. The Chinese should be figuring out how to get back to China, but he wasn't going to try and convince them. It was time to send them to their ancestors. He just hoped the politicians and their handlers could join theirs also. He went into the cabin and climbed into his bunk. Tomorrow would be a busy day. He heard the radio crackle, and Morgan handed it to him.

## CHAPTER 30

Porter consulted his map and turned south. He saw people from time to time, but no one tried to stop him and no one wanted him to stop and talk. The plague had instilled a healthy respect for strangers. He continued in a southeasterly direction and traveled well south of Austin. He was soon traveling along the coast. He found a spot where he could actually run the Rokon along the beach. He spotted a couple with their children running nets out into the water. A rack of bamboo was covered in fish waiting to be smoked.

The man shouted, "Don't come any closer; I don't want to kill you."

Porter stopped. "I don't want to get killed either."

"There's a rifle on you right now, so don't get off the bike."

"Don't worry. I'm not making a move. This is my first time here, and I was wondering what I will run into if I keep heading in this direction."

"If you keep going east, you are going to run into Galveston Island."

"I know where I'm at on the map. I was wondering what I could expect in the form of other people."

The man looked at him closely. "You are doing a lot of hinting around without saying much. If you are looking for the Reds, they, or what's left of them, are up around Austin. The plague has pretty much taken them out. There are still a few Reds operating around here. If you are looking for Constitution forces, they're mostly dead. You have to get up north of Houston and Beaumont to find them. They have isolated themselves since the plague started. If you are looking for the communist Chinese, just keep going east. Once you hit the bay, you will get shot. They have set up shop at one of the refineries. Now my next question will decide if you are going to live or die, 'which side are you on?'"

Porter grinned. "Just like me, you are wondering if I am on the communist side or your side. I am on your side. I haven't seen a communist yet that wasn't trying to steal what other people have. You can tell that lady who has that rifle aimed at me she can relax. I would have shot her when I drove up if I were out to get y'all."

"How did you know it was a lady and where she was located?"

"She is sitting in the only cover around here which is that sand dune, and she lowers the rifle because her arms keep getting tired. Take three pieces of that bamboo and tie it near the end and make a tripod to rest the barrel of the gun on."

The man looked toward the sand dune and called, "Ma, relax, he's on our side."

"Let me introduce myself, I'm Porter Jones. I am a Sergeant in the Constitution army, and all I am doing is looking around and reporting what I find. You are obviously familiar with the plague. Do you have any questions about it?"

"All we know is that it has killed a lot of people, and the only way to avoid it is to have no contact with anyone."

Porter took a few minutes to explain what he knew about it and then he asked, "I need to get close enough to the Chinese to observe them. Do you know if any of them have the plague?"

"I don't think so. No one goes in or comes out. They run patrol boats around Galveston Bay, and they don't hesitate to shoot. The refinery is fenced in, and they stay behind it or on their ships. We come down here to spend a few days catching and smoking fish. Then we head home, and hope we don't get killed."

Porter replied, "People have to eat. I am seeing a lot less people. Things should settle down pretty quickly now that most of the Reds have the plague. The Chinese in New Orleans and up the river have been taken out by the plague. I would avoid them over here in case they have been exposed. Without getting too close, can you point out on my map where the refinery is located?"

The man grinned. "Is the Constitution army planning on making an assault?"

Lying, Porter said, "No, I am strictly here to observe and report. There aren't enough Constitution troops left to mount an assault. If they decide to come out, we will be hard pressed to stop them. The only reason they are staying put is because they are afraid of the plague."

"Porter, my name is Roy Guidry. That's my wife Mary and our two boys Bill and Jack. My mama Penny is our guard. She can hit pretty good with Dad's old Winchester 30-30."

Porter rolled out his map. Roy came over with a stick and pointed out the locations on the map.

Porter asked, "How do you know about these locations?"

"We have all come up against them, and we all share information. We keep tabs on them too. I hope you figure out their weak points. We know what's going to take place if they get out."

Porter warned him. "Don't get near them or touch any of their equipment. If they have the plague, nothing they have will be safe unless you can sterilize it. I recommend chlorine or high heat."

"You act like they have the plague now."

"The Reds think that the Chinese have a cure and will be trying to get into their camp to get it."

"We heard they have a cure, and that all the Chinese medics have a treatment in their med kits."

"There is no cure. I know the foremost authority on the plague, and the only cure is death."

"Are you certain? We heard it from one of the Reds. That's how we know all about their locations and defenses."

Porter grinned. "I am telling you the truth. I personally know the foremost authority on the plague, and I am telling you the only cure is death. It takes no more than three weeks for symptoms to appear. You will die in two to five weeks after exposure. You can spread the infection after ten days to two weeks depending on how strong your immune system is. We don't know how long the virus can remain deadly outside of a human body. If the Chinese had a cure, don't you think they would be out gathering up the remaining girls and young women? There would be more men coming to relieve or reinforce them. You had better believe me--**there is no cure**."

Roy looked concerned. "One of the Reds comes by here every day to get some of the fish. He calls it tax collecting."

Porter glanced around. "What time? There's a good chance he's infected. You haven't had any close contact with him have you?"

"No, we put the fish in plastic bags. He just grabs them and goes. He and his driver just drive up; his driver puts a gun on us and collects the tax. In fact here they come now. They'll be collecting from you now that they see you."

Porter looked over his shoulder. He couldn't outrun them, since they were in a Jeep Wrangler 4X4.

"You and your family need to get over behind that dune." Roy started to say something, but Porter gave him a serious look. "Get over there now, if you want to live."

Porter didn't wait for them to respond, but turned to the rapidly approaching jeep. He calculated the distance and flipped his AK to full automatic. He put the Rokon on its kick stand, swung his leg over and sighted on them when he estimated that they were about two-hundred and fifty yards away. He squeezed the trigger and traced a mental figure eight over and over again on the jeep. It took just a moment to empty the 30 round clip. He dumped it on the ground, replaced it with a fresh one and opened up again. The left front tire of the Jeep blew out and steam boiled out of the radiator. The blown tire dug into the sand and flipped the jeep. Its occupants were thrown out, but Porter continued his firing at the prone bodies. He dropped the clip, reloaded and headed in their direction rapidly. He flipped the AK back to select fire and shot both of them through the head when he was within fifty yards. He checked the Jeep to make sure there was no one left inside. Since it was empty, he walked back to his Rokon. Roy ventured out from behind the dune.

"My God, oh my God, I've never seen anything like that, what possessed you to do that?"

Porter, who was busy knocking the sand out of his empty magazines, quickly replaced the empty ones with full ones from his pack, and looked at Roy.

"It's simple, Roy; they have the plague. If you hurry you can still see the rash on the last one I shot. I only had one choice. Do you think for one minute they would have let me keep all this gear once they saw it? I couldn't let anything interfere with what I'm doing. Now, they won't be spreading the plague, I still have my stuff, and I fought them on my terms. If I had let them get closer, they would have run over me or been able to get off a shot. If they had started shooting over here, you and your family could have been hit. Leave everything they've got alone, unless you have some rubber gloves and chlorine. I would cover the bodies with sand or dirt. I've got a question, 'Roy, how have you lived this long, surely you have had to kill bad guys?'"

"Actually, I haven't. I lost my dad and brothers when it started; we've got by since then with bluffing and giving people what they wanted."

Porter pointed at the dead bodies. "Until the rest of those bastards are dead, we will all live in fear. People just like them killed my mama, daddy and little brother. I killed three of them and got a bullet or two in the one who got away. I've been fighting for the past year, and I'm not stopping until the job is done. Then I'm heading back to my ranch."

Roy called his boys, "Bring me a shovel; stay away from those bodies. They have the plague. Porter, what if someone comes looking for them?"

"I doubt you are going to see any more of them. They're busy dying right now. If they show up, you have two choices: kill them, or tell them what happened and hope they believe you. I wouldn't get that close to them if I were you. They have the plague. I appreciate your information. I hope to see you again after the war. Remember, there is no cure."

"Porter, does trouble follow you?"

"It seems to find me pretty often, but up to now, I've climbed out on top."

Porter cranked the Rokon and drove in first gear down the beach until he was well away from the Guidry family. He then pulled off the beach and back onto the roadway. Taking out his map and using a small lead pencil, he circled the locations he wanted to locate. There were a lot of abandoned businesses along the highway. He felt vulnerable here, so he put the bike in third gear and went down the highway at full speed until he reached a road that would take him into one of the Wildlife Management areas. Using his bolt cutters, he cut the lock on the gate, closed it behind him and disappeared down the road heading toward the bay through the woods. Because the road was overgrown, there was no indication that there had been any traffic on it; therefore, he rode slowly until it was too dark to see. He stopped and set up camp. The mosquitoes were wicked, so he dug out a bottle of the insect repellant and applied it on his body. He then built a fire, strung up his hammock between two trees and set up his radio. Cooney had given him the frequency of the catamaran, and he called the Major.

"Major Jernigan, this is Porter Jones, come in."

Morgan handed Dix the radio. "Porter's on the line."

"Porter, how are you making it?"

"I'm almost in position. I received some Intel from a local; I just have to verify what I was told."

"Have you run into any of those communists with the red arm bands?"

"I ran into a couple of Reds several hours back. They both had the plague; however, they didn't survive the encounter. I am set up to the west of Galveston Bay; the Chinese are embedded at one of the oil refineries located at Texas City and are staying behind the refinery's security fences. The Reds have been trying to get in. They think the Chinese medics have a cure for the plague. It is my understanding that the Chinese are shooting at anything that moves in the Bay or around the fences."

"Porter, we are still several days away. Don't get yourself shot, and stay low. I don't want them to know we are there or that we've left."

"I understand, Major. As soon as I verify the Intel, I'll set up a spot where we can meet."

"Porter, keep up the good work, and don't get killed."

"Yes, sir, Porter out."

# CHAPTER 31

As the morning dawned, the men quickly polished off the remaining fish and hushpuppies. After Morgan brewed a pot of coffee, they untied from the oil platform and raised the sail. Since the wind from the southwest was brisk, they were soon making good time tacking across the Gulf. Using the GPS satellites, they set their heading toward Galveston Bay and let the wind do its work in order to save their fuel for the generator and the return trip. Fox put a large silver spoon bait on a line and cast it behind the boat. The boat pulled the shiny lure along as they sailed, and soon a dozen Spanish mackerel fillets were cooking on a small grill on the back of the catamaran.

Dix commented, "If we weren't on a mission and fixing to die, I would say this is one heck of a trip."

Fox grinned. "Dix, how are you going to make it once everything settles down, and you have to give up fighting and just start living?"

"I will be pretty busy trying to figure out how to keep from starving to death and how to make it without coffee."

Louie looked over his cup of coffee. "When what we have squirreled away gets used up, we are going to be in a fix. I am going to miss chocolate and bananas too."

Dix thought a moment. "There may be some bananas we can get to in South Florida. Who knows, I may see if this boat will sail to South America one day. There is bound to be someplace where bananas will still be growing. The only trouble is they would be spoiled by the time I got back; I would have to dry them and put them in jars."

Louie said, "Put me down for a jar full."

"Sure thing, kid. Morgan, how long before we get close to Galveston?"

Morgan did the calculations. "If we can keep our present speed and don't stop, we can be there in fifteen hours. We will have to stop when it gets dark, and decide where we are going to hide the boat. I say we will be there by tomorrow afternoon. If we can hide somewhere close, we will be about two hours away from Galveston Bay with the fishing boat. It can run about thirty miles per hour if the waves aren't bad. If the waves are bad, it will take a lot longer. It's a bay boat; it won't handle five foot waves easily."

Dix grimaced. "Let's hope the weather holds out."

Morgan pointed to the barometer. "It's been holding steady. There shouldn't be much change in the next twelve hours, but you never know out here in the Gulf. An afternoon storm is always possible this time of year."

Dix held up his crossed fingers. "Keep your fingers crossed, boys. After that storm the other night, I don't want to ride out another one any time soon."

The weather held as they made their way across the Gulf. Fox caught some more fish, and they were able to once again eat without digging into their supplies. Every day they could eat off the sea was one more day in the field.

With Louie at the helm, Dix, Morgan and Fox looked at the map Dix had rolled out on the dining table.

Dix pointed at the map. "Here is Texas City. It is down on the lower end of Galveston Bay close to the Gulf. It won't be easy to sneak up on them especially if they are on the alert."

Morgan scrutinized the map. "Major, I bet we can find something over around Port Arthur. It wouldn't be a long run over to Galveston. We should be able to pick up Porter just about anywhere along the coast. We'll just need to do it in the fishing boat at night. If we go real slow about ten miles out and then go straight in, we should be able to reduce our radar signature."

Fox suggested, "Or we can use the stump thumper and not have a radar signature at all. With about fifteen gallons of gas I can skirt the coast all the way, pick him up and come back with gas to spare. It'll take about two hours in and two hours back; it'll be easy as pie."

Dix stroked his whiskered covered chin. "You know, we could take you half way in the fishing boat and that would shave an hour or two off your trip. I think it'll work. Let's head to Port Arthur and find a place to hide. I'm sure there are some islands or sunken ships we can hide among. I just hope Porter can sneak in and out without getting himself killed."

Fox shrugged. "If he can fight as good as they say, I think they are in more danger than he is. Back when I was in the army, I was in a special unit that operated in some out of the way places. We had a guy like Porter. He was quiet and pretty much left everybody alone, but when the Jihadist hit us, he didn't panic and didn't miss. When we were in the field, he just seemed to have a gut feeling and always knew when to dive for cover and never lost his cool. I only saw him cry once when we came up on a Christian village where the Islamists killed everyone, including the small children and babies."

Morgan asked, "What happened next?"

"We trailed the bastards back into the bush for two days. His name was Hank, and he stayed on point after that. He was raised up in the Arkansas Ozarks and spent his entire life hunting and fishing. The bush was thick, and we felt like we were surrounded. Hank motioned for us to stop and whispered something to the Lieutenant. The Sergeant came down the line and ordered us to spread out and be absolutely silent. I found a big rock, dug me a hole under it and got in. Even though nothing was happening, my heart was beating out of my chest. We stayed put until dark. That was when Hank slipped out and disappeared into the bush. He was gone three hours when we heard him start shooting; he was only firing his rifle in select fire. In my mind's eye, I knew what he was doing. I had seen him take deliberate time to aim and fire in battles before. He didn't shoot rapid fire like the rest of us. At twenty or thirty feet, he never raised the gun to eye level; he just pulled the trigger. He always knew where the bullet was going to go. When it was light enough to see, we went up the ridge and saw what had taken place. Three of them had their throats slashed; they were the posted guards. The rest were shot. They made the mistake of having a fire, because they didn't expect us to be so deep into their territory."

Once again Morgan spoke, "Don't stop now, what did y'all do next?"

Fox continued, "First we took any weapons we thought we could use and destroyed the rest. We dragged their bodies out to the main trail and piled them up for anyone who came by to see. We wrote on a canvas tarp they had in their gear the words in their language: Brave Baby Killers. We went back to the village, called for helicopter pickup and went back to the firebase. We were part of a broader mission to knock out a terrorist training camp and knock the Jihadists off their feet. We were pulled out about a week later, and I never saw Hank again. I mustered out about a month after that."

Dix exclaimed, "Wow, what a story. I bet Hank has kicked some tail since all this started. He's probably up in those Ozarks fat and happy."

Fox agreed. "Dix, where did you get your military training?"

"Hell, Fox, I've been winging it every since all this started. I just started killing bad guys; it wasn't because I knew what I was doing. It's an absolute miracle that I haven't been killed and gotten all of you killed. I managed to get my family killed because I didn't listen to my Zizzy Witch. I was drafted into the Constitution army, and my rank was forced on me by Colonel Miller, Cooney and Butch. All I did was give them my opinion on how to take on the Chinese and communists. I have never had any desire to be doing anything other than killing bad guys. In order to keep killing bad guys, I had to figure out how to keep from getting killed. At first all I wanted to do was die, but I had to kill the bad guys who were responsible. Then I wanted to kill a thousand of them for every one of my family that had been murdered. I was very good at culling the bad guys. At that point I wanted to kill them all. I read a book one time about a civil war sniper. I can't recall his name, but when he returned home, he found that the Union soldiers had decapitated his sons and left their heads on his fence. He spent the rest of his days killing Union troops and officers. He was one of the most successful snipers in his day. He was motivated; so you might say, I have been and am motivated."

Fox nodded in agreement. "That's how I feel. I have no idea what has happened to my son, but I know what they did to my parents. I tracked the unit down, and I killed them with my dad's old Marlin 30-30 deer rifle that he gave me many years ago when we used to go deer hunting. I will continue killing them until I can't find any more. I understand what you are doing and why. Vengeance is a strong motivator."

Morgan and Louie both told their stories, and they were much the same. Morgan lost his entire family including his young pregnant bride. Louie was left for dead in the back of a car with the rest of his family robbed by the Ferriday police about a week before Dix cleaned out the town. He woke up at Doc's house where some friends had taken him.

Dix looked at them. "Guys, that is why we have prevailed with the odds stacked against us one-hundred to one. We're not afraid to die. Our only fear is that we will let them get away with what they've done. Morgan, how much further?"

Morgan consulted the GPS and maps. "We are making excellent time, so we need to start looking for a place to spend the night. I don't want to anchor out here in the middle of the ocean. We need to find an island, oil platform or a sunken ship sticking out of the water to anchor next to. I don't want to stand out on a radar screen somewhere. Some guy sitting alone at night with nothing to do might spot us and wonder why we just showed up on his radar screen."

Louie and Fox took the binoculars and searched the horizon in every direction. They soon spotted what they were looking for. On the horizon, due south of their location, sat the top stacks and bridge of a cruise ship sticking out of the water. It was resting on bottom, but due to its extreme height and size it came to rest sitting upright. It would a great place to tie up for the night. They covered the distance in about forty-five minutes and soon had their sails down and the diesel engine running as they idled up to the ship. Morgan scrambled aboard with his rifle on his back and his pistol in a shoulder holster.

After a quick inspection he called down, "It's all clear. Nobody has been here for a while. The cabins and windows are all water tight, and there is a crew's lounge up here that still has coffee and snacks."

Dix hollered back, "Is there anything we can use besides the food?"

Morgan poked his head back out the door. "I'll let you know when I finish looking."

Fox called to Dix, "Shut off the engine. I have the boat tied to the rail."

The water was clear, and he could see down toward the deck below. Dix thought he could see where the swimming pool was located on the deck. Barnacles had built up on the hull and on the rails where they disappeared into the water. There was no way of knowing if it went down with passengers and crew. Chances were it broke loose from its mooring during a storm and floated around until it sank here. Dix went into his small cabin, looked under the bunk, pulled out the case with the Barrett .50 caliber rifle, one of the boxes of ammo and carried it out on the deck.

"Morgan, is there any rope? I want to send up the Barrett. If we have any unexpected company, I want to be able to shoot back. Do you remember that Zizzy Witch I told you about?"

Morgan nodded.

"Well, it's all fired up. I don't know if it's this place that's got me spooked or if we have some trouble brewing. I've never been this far along on a mission without trouble showing up."

"Sure thing, Major. There's some rope on the flag mast. I'll shoot you the end down in a minute."

Several minutes later the end of the rope came down with a flashlight tied to it as ballast. Dix tied the Barrett and ammo can to it, and Morgan had it pulled aboard. Dix rode the wave up, caught onto the rail and stepped on the ladder leading up. He was soon on the bridge looking out across the ocean. They flipped open the windows and let the Gulf breezes blow through the hot bridge. It didn't take long before it had cooled off.

Dix called out to Morgan below, "I want two people on the catamaran at all times. When one of us comes down, one of you can come up."

Fox looked up and shouted, "Sure thing, boss, we'll keep our eyes peeled from down here."

On the bridge there were four telescopes mounted on posts. Two were on the port side and two were mounted on the starboard side. Two others were situated where they looked fore and aft. If they were powered, each of them would have been gyroscopically stabilized, but since the ship was firmly anchored to the bottom, the gyros were not needed. Dix looked into the starboard telescope which was now on the north side of the ship. He scanned the horizon and was surprised that he could see the shore line. He cranked up the magnification and saw the entrance to a dock and some ships sitting on bottom. He saw a small vessel slowly making its way along the coast heading west. It was a good thing they decided to tie up here for the night. Dix and Morgan went to each telescope and searched the surrounding waters for other vessels. They saw nothing. When he went back to the starboard telescope, he watched a larger vessel come out of the harbor and head in their direction.

"Fox, get up here with my Springfield; Morgan break out that Barrett now." He leaned out the window as Fox grabbed onto the rail wearing the Springfield across his back and carrying a full bandolier of cartridges.

"What do you see?"

"If they don't turn, we're going to have a good sized vessel here in about forty-five minutes; look see."

Fox buried his eye in the telescope. "How soon before we can start shooting?"

"I want to make sure they saw us; they probably picked us up on radar. There's one thing for sure, we can't outrun them in the catamaran. Morgan, I want you and Louie to take the fishing boat with some radios and gear and haul ass south. Can y'all load that little freezer, the drone and some cigarettes and take them with you?"

"Sure thing, Major."

In the span of five minutes, they had the fishing boat loaded and a portable radio in Dix's hand. Soon, they were hauling tail south and out of danger. Dix had the Barrett set up across a console and aimed so it would shoot out a window. Fox went back down to the catamaran and retrieved shooting muffs for their ears.

"Major, if you pull the trigger on that in here without these muffs, the concussion and back pressure will burst our ear drums and possibly knock us unconscious."

"Good thinking, Fox. I should have thought of that; I must be slipping."

"Maybe Cooney should have that little talk with you. I think all that love making has knocked you for a loop."

They both broke out laughing and were able to get back to business.

"Fox, I want you to take that Springfield and pick off any of them that you can see. I'm going to try and put these 50's through the engine. The Springfield is zeroed at three-hundred yards. If they are dead in the water, the only thing they can do is try and knock us off with their guns. I'm not sure what they have, but I bet it is better than what we have."

The approaching boat was soon close enough that they could see it without the aid of the telescope.

"Fox, see if that telescope has some sort of range finder. This .50 cal can engage targets about as far away as we can see them. With you spotting, I can probably hit that boat at better than half a mile."

Fox squinted and rolled a small dial. "Yes, I think they are at ten-thousand plus yards, and I can see them looking back. They have a guy on a big ass gun on the front deck. It looks more like a cannon than a machine gun."

"That's what I am afraid of. Let me know when they reach the one mile mark. That will be my maximum shot distance. The scope on this rifle has aim points out to two-thousand yards. It will be very important that you tell me where the bullet hits. Look for the splash. The wind is going to throw it off to the right, so I am going to have to aim down the left side of the boat. If I get hit, you take over this gun; otherwise, keep running those 30-06 through any of them you can see."

"Don't worry, Major. I won't be bashful about it." Fox still had his eye buried in the telescope.

Dix had the Barrett's telescope cranked up to fifteen power and had a good view. They could both see the instant the deck gun fired. It dropped a round off what would have been the bow of the ship. "How far, Fox?"

"One mile, Major; fire when ready."

Dix slowly squeezed the trigger, and the big rifle bounced.

Fox called out, "You hit the water just to the right; the water from it splashed the boat."

"Just keep calling them out as I fire."

Dix then put the cross hair dot, immediately to the right, on the boat and fired again. The boat disappeared from the rifle scope as the concussion bounced the front of the gun in the air.

Fox called out, "Hit, I didn't see a splash."

Dix fired eight more times in quick succession.

Fox called out again, "Two hit just in front of the boat. I think they ricocheted off the water and hit it anyway."

The deck gun fired at them again. This time it struck the deck just below them. The concussion took them off their feet. Dix replaced the Barrett's magazine with another ten rounder from the ammo box and got back on target. He raised the cross hairs to the head of the man behind the gun and pulled the trigger. It appeared as though he disappeared from the bullet's impact. A wisp of his clothes floated off in the wind to the right of the boat. The boat was much closer now, so Dix just aimed at the center of the boat and ran nine more rounds into it. By this time, Fox was firing the Springfield. The range was five-hundred yards and closing. Another ten round magazine was inserted, and the charging handle pulled back and released. A machine gun opened up on them and riddled the cabin. Fox went down. Dix once again ran a magazine through the boat. This time the boat and the machine gun fire came to a stop, and the boat was drifting. Dix looked around at Fox who had a horrible gaping wound through his right shoulder. Dix stopped long enough to take off his shirt and stuff it into the hole to stem the flow of blood. He used the sleeves to tie it into place. Fox was unconscious and wasn't feeling anything. Dix took the final magazine and replaced the empty one in the Barrett. The boat had drifted sideways a bit which enabled Dix to concentrate his fire at one particular spot at the water line. Dix knew that with the engine down, there may not be a working bilge. He also knew that the bullets were going through the boat and out the bottom. He took up the Springfield and shot at anyone who picked their head up. The boat drifted by about three-hundred yards away, and it was visibly taking on water. Dix watched as the men on board tried to deploy a life raft. He quickly shot holes in it rendering it useless. He continued to fire at them until every target was well out of range.

He got on the radio to Morgan, "Get back here. Fox is hit real bad, and he might not make it. That Chinese boat is sinking fast. I don't need a bunch of them trying to swim over here."

Morgan answered, "We'll be there in five minutes."

Although Dix fired as the sailors tried to leave the sinking boat, he watched orange life vests bobbing in the water as the current carried the survivors to the northeast.

When Morgan arrived, Dix called him on the radio. "We've got to finish them off."

"Don't worry, Major. We'll clean up." Morgan gunned the boat with Louie shooting from the bow. They soon had them all double tapped and headed back.

Dix went over to the telescope and verified that there weren't any more vessels heading their way before turning back to Fox. He located a blanket in one of the storage compartments and draped it over Fox to keep him warm. Fox was pale and breathing shallowly. Dix didn't try to move him further. He found an extensive first aid kit and was about to remove the shirt when Morgan came up the ladder.

"What do you want me to do?"

"Get that other box of ammo for the Barrett up here and another bandolier of ammo for the Springfield. Make sure the catamaran isn't hit; we can't afford to lose it. Get everything secured and get that little freezer back on power. "When everything is secure, get back up here so you can help me get him cleaned up and moved to the catamaran. I don't know if he will live; he has lost a lot of blood."

Morgan disappeared, and Louie appeared a few moments later with the ammo.

"Major, Morgan sent me up while he is going over the catamaran. I need to look at Fox. I worked with the Doc for the past year, so I know what to do." Louie opened his bag, pulled out some plastic gloves and put them on. He told Dix, "You are going to assist me. We have to stop the bleeding. I am going to lay everything out, and you will have to hand me stuff when I ask." It took him a few minutes to get the big kit unpacked and the items he needed to use lain out within reach. Dix opened the door so that the sunlight could stream in. Louie looked at Dix. "When we pull out the shirt, he will probably start bleeding. I am going to need you to soak up the blood so I can see the bleeder." Dix pulled on a pair of gloves.

"I am going to have to clamp the bleeder off and then sew it shut. He has almost bled out. I don't have any way to do a transfusion, so we have to be quick."

Thirty minutes later, Louie was ready to close the wound. He reached in his bag and produced a jar of honey. He filled the wound with the honey and pulled the skin closed over the hole. He put a small piece of tubing in the wound so it would drain, finished closing it up and bandaged it. Fox never woke up. They bundled him into a canvas tarp and cinched it tight. Then together they lowered him to the deck of the catamaran where Morgan caught him and laid him on the deck. Louie and Dix returned to the catamaran with the Barrett, ammo and the Springfield. They moved Fox into his bunk and covered him up.

Dix asked, "Why honey in the wound?"

"My kit has several different types of antibiotics that you can take by mouth, but Fox won't be swallowing any pills right away. Honey is a natural antibiotic and antifungal agent. Hopefully, it will stop any infection until we can start him on oral antibiotics."

Dix nodded and refocused on their situation. "Let's flip on the radar. I don't think it's a secret that we are out here. They don't know who we are, but they know we can fight back. Now that it's dark, we can't take a chance heading off into the night without knowing what we might run into. Morgan, how far are we from Port Arthur?"

Morgan consulted the maps and GPS. "We are about twenty miles from there. We should be able to spot another oil rig that we can tie up to nearby. I suggest we use the engine."

"Cast off and let's get started. Louie, what's the word on Fox?"

"He's breathing stronger, but I need to get some fluids in him."

"Is there anything in that fancy first aid kit we can use?"

"Yes, sir, there are some large syringes that we can fill with water, but I'm just not sure how to get it in him."

Dix thought a minute. "I had a puppy once that was dehydrated and just about dead. The vet injected water under her skin where it was absorbed. If we boiled some water, added a tiny bit of salt, and injected it under his skin; do you think it will work?"

Louie pondered the idea. "It's not ideal, but it will work. I am going to try and rouse him with some smelling salts. If that doesn't work, we'll inject him like a Thanksgiving turkey."

Dix cranked up the catamaran and backed away from the derelict cruise ship. Once they were clear, he bumped the transmission into forward and idled away from the wreck. Morgan came in and soon spotted what looked like an oil platform on the radar. He took over the helm while Dix turned on the gas stove and started a pot of water to boil. He added salt to the water until it was barely salty to his taste. Louie tried to bring Fox around with the smelling salts, but he was still out like a light. They let the water boil to kill any microbes and let it sit until it cooled. The syringe and needle were sealed in sterile packages, so when they were ready, they opened one and drew it full of the water. They found skin on the bottom of his arm that was loose enough to push the needle in. They filled the syringe four times, and Fox soon had a bubble of fluid under the skin of his arm. If he failed to wake, they would give him more in his other arm. They couldn't stop the mission to try and get Fox back to Doc. Fox knew the rules and would have done the same thing in Dix's place. They found the oil platform, tied off for the night, killed the radar and waited.

Fox opened his eyes and groaned, "I don't know what happened to me, but I am hurting like I have never hurt before. Can someone loan me a pistol?"

Dix pulled up a stool beside his bunk. "Louie, do you have some pain killers?"

"Yes, sir, I've got some strong stuff in this new kit."

"Light him up, Louie."

"You got it, Major."

Dix turned back to Fox. "You got hit by a slug from a machine gun several hours ago."

Fox grimaced. "I don't remember any of it, did we get them?"

"We always get them. Louie is going to give you something that will help with the pain. We need you to swallow something with some sugar in it. Think you can get a little tea or coffee down?"

Fox nodded his head.

Louie said, "After I get this morphine in him, he should feel better, and I'm going to get him started on an antibiotic right away."

Dix looked at Fox. "I'm going to put you on light duty for a couple of days. You stay put and get some rest. You don't have to worry about catching any more fish until after lunch tomorrow."

Fox looked up, and could only grin.

Dix took his right hand. "Fox, move your fingers."

Fox gave his hand a weak squeeze. At least the nerves were still intact. Dix shook his hand and turned away. Morgan gave him thumbs up.

"Morgan, that's why I don't like getting in gunfights; I like to shoot and run. I want nothing to do with a fair fight."

Morgan agreed. "I'm right there with you, Chief."

# CHAPTER 32

Porter got up before dawn, packed his gear and broke camp. His goal today was to get within sight of the refinery. He continued down the trail through the Wildlife Refuge. There were plenty of snakes and alligators in the bayous that the road skirted. He slowed as he approached a road. While still in the shadows of the woods, he pulled out his map and looked at his options. Directly ahead was a bayou he could cross with the Rokon. From the number of alligators that he had seen so far, he was reluctant to try and cross it by attempting to wade or swim. The road went north to where it intersected with another one that would take him across the bayou. Using the bolt cutters, he opened the gate, walked to the road and looked in both directions. All was quiet. He was very reluctant to use the road, but there was no choice. A huge alligator surfaced in the bayou and eyed him. Porter thought about popping him with his rifle, but he didn't want to alert anyone to his presence. He walked back to the Rokon, fired it up and ran it in low gear to the wide paved road. Once on level ground, he put it in third gear and ran down the road wide open. He kept an eye out for wires across the road. There were sections where trees and limbs lay in the road, and several times it was necessary to drive around and over debris. The trip was uneventful. Other than a few abandoned vehicles and left over litter, there was no sign of a living human being. The absence of men and machines was a bit unnerving. Either the plague had cleaned everyone out or the Chinese had done a thorough job of killing and running off all the locals. He thought it was probably a combination of both. He stopped short of an intersection, dismounted the Rokon and eased up to the intersection on foot. Peering though his binoculars, he couldn't see any indication of trouble in either direction. It would have been easy for a sniper to set up on this long road. It seemed to go out of sight in a straight line, just like the Roman roads he read about in England where the Roman engineers constructed perfectly straight roads for miles on end.

Peering again through his binoculars, he selected a tree about a mile down the road as a stopping point. His plans were to drive a mile or so, then stop and observe. All went well until late morning when he stopped and saw vehicles off the side of the road in the distance. Not only were they off the road, but some were in ditches. This was probably an ambush point. Remembering his orders not to attack, he turned the bike and ran back a mile until he reached a short road that led to a boat landing. He carefully hid the Rokon and decided to kill some time in case someone had spotted him when he turned around. This was a good opportunity to relax and eat. He thought about the girls waiting for him back at the ranch. He was in no hurry to get himself killed.

He had to be ever mindful that there could be alarms, land mines or booby traps along the road. A sniper or people at a checkpoint would be looking for someone to be on foot or in a vehicle. The more he thought about it, the more he came to realize that it would be suicide to try and approach from the road.

He pulled out his map and reviewed his options. They would not be expecting someone to approach them from the rear. With bayous and canals on both sides of the road, it would be difficult to travel. He had read that alligators did not view humans as a food source, so there was no need to fear them. His dilemma lay in the fact that he saw a huge gator that could easily kill and swallow him in one bite. He went in his pack and pulled out the suppressor for his Beretta pistol. It readily screwed onto the threaded portion of his barrel. This was a wonderful gift from Charlie Cross and his boys. He knew where to shoot an alligator for a quick kill from watching the swamp shows on TV. His mother didn't like him watching red neck shows, but she couldn't monitor him twenty-four hours a day. It was just like he and his dad sneaking off to the waffle place down the highway where the truckers ate, what she didn't know didn't hurt her. Any hole in an alligator would probably discourage them from trying to eat him so he decided to walk in the shallow water with one eye open at all times. He took his time, taking care not to splash; the pistol was cocked and in his hand ready for action. As he walked, he looked up and down the bank and in the trees. When he was within sight of the cars, the stench of death overtook him. A crater in the dirt alongside the road confirmed what he suspected. The remains of a body lay scattered, and blow flies were everywhere. It appeared as though a land mine had killed someone. When he got to the cars and trucks, he realized that human remains were in most of them. He carefully looked at the vehicles. They all had bullet holes in the windshields, while others were riddled from machine gun fire. Porter didn't dare leave the water. The water was covered with small green floating plants called duck weed. There were also large patches of floating water hyacinth encroaching on the waterway. The going was really slow in the water and mud. He got down on his hands and knees and immersed himself so that he was soon covered with the small green duck weed. Each plant was only one or two leaves that were no larger than a drop of water with several roots that grew under them into the water. What they lacked in size they made up in numbers as there were billions and billions of them growing all over the bayou. They made the surface of the bayou look like a vast green lawn, and they completely hid everything beneath, including alligators. As he eased along past the cars, he had to be especially alert. The shooters were near and so were the alligators. Out of the corner of his eye, he detected movement in the water hyacinth. The beautiful blue flowers waved in the air as the movement beneath them gently pushed them up and aside. A snout and two eyes set atop a head that was more than twelve inches wide soon emerged from the water hyacinths and pushed the green carpet of duck weed apart as it ever so slowly came in his direction. Only the dragon like scales at the end of his tail showed any movement as it gently pushed the huge reptile in his direction. Even though his pistol was suppressed it would still make a little noise, and he had no way of knowing how near the guards of the checkpoint were. About half way across the bayou, the big gator slipped under the surface. Porter knew what to expect next. He carefully watched as a few bubbles came to the surface as the creature disturbed the bottom of the bayou. He waited until he could see the duck weed start to move about three feet from where he was standing in the knee deep water before he fired three quick shots into the water. The huge lizard went crazy splashing and turning in the water. It quickly reversed direction. Porter had missed the sweet spot, but he had instead put three full metal jacket 9mm bullets in the beast. Porter immediately turned his attention back to the roadway. He half expected a hand grenade or a bullet from a sniper's rifle to cut through his body. Nothing happened. Instead he heard a vehicle in the distance. He soon realized that the sound was getting closer and was not coming from the direction in which he had come.

His first fear was that he had tripped a sensor, and that the bad guys were on the way. He made his way down the bayou and noticed where there was an animal trail leading up to the road. This must have been a deer or wild hog trail crossing the road. There would be no land mines on this trail. He immediately got on his belly and slithered up the trail between the tall grasses on either side. When he reached the road, he carefully peered in both directions. To his right were the shot up vehicles, to his left was a van off-loading two Chinese soldiers. One was packing a scoped rifle, and the other had an AK47. Two other soldiers climbed down a ladder from a raised platform off the south side of the road. The platform was not unlike a large deer stand, but it was extremely well camouflaged. It would have been unlikely that he would have spotted it in time. The stand was about one-hundred yards down the road, so they would not have heard his encounter with the gator. He looked at his father's watch. The time was 3:00 p.m.--shift change. He stayed put as the two came down. One of the ones coming down also had a scoped rifle; the other carried an AK47. There were three more in the van including a driver.

The van turned around and headed back after swapping out the guards. While the replacement guards climbed the ladder, Porter crawled back to the water, retraced his steps through the shallows and made it back to the Rokon. He was well hidden so he decided to stay put and camp for the night. He hung up his wet clothes and cleaned his weapons as everything was wet including his knives. The wind was coming out of the south, so he built a small fire to dry his boots and cook his dinner. He kept the fire very low, and after the boots were dry, he put them back on and unrolled his radio wire. He soon had Cooney and Dix on the radio.

Dix asked, "How are you coming on your recon?"

"They seem to be taking no chances. I found a checkpoint about four miles from the refinery. It appears that my information is correct. Nobody is going to go past the checkpoint without a fight. The shift change was at three o'clock this afternoon. I have an idea. There were five of them in a van that came up and swapped out the guards. If I had some way to deliver the virus, I think I could figure out a way to expose the guards. They stay in an elevated camouflaged stand about fifteen feet in the air."

"Porter, are you aware of how we have been spreading the virus over in Mississippi?"

Cooney chimed in, "Major, I didn't go into much detail with Porter. I didn't want to tell him too much, in the unlikely event he were captured. I didn't want him to be able to give up any of our plans or actions."

"That was a sensible precaution, Cooney. Porter, I know you remember the old man that you helped helicopter out?"

"Yes, how is Mr. Lester?"

"Porter, Mr. Lester is dead. He volunteered for a suicide mission. He was dying of lung cancer so he only had a month or two left. He volunteered to get infected with the plague virus so that we could create a huge supply of it. We placed the virus in the filter tips of cigarettes and arranged for the Chinese soldiers to find packs of them. When the soldiers put the filter tips in their mouths to smoke the cigarettes, they were exposed to the virus and as a result most of them are dead or dying right now."

"Major, I hate to hear that Mr. Lester is dead, but we talked before he left, he wanted to kill the bad guys."

"Porter, he was wildly successful in taking out the bad guys. In fact we are carrying virus from Mr. Lester and the cigarettes. We need to find a way to get a pack into the hands of one or more of the soldiers."

Porter thought a moment. "There is only one way I can think of getting a pack to them. I am going to need to get some of the baited cigarettes. I can't sneak up and deposit the cigarettes the way they are set up. I don't know how I can trick them into picking up the cigarettes, but I can slip up and shoot them without much trouble."

Cooney chimed in, "What if you kill them, and we tuck a pack into one of their pockets for their comrades to find. You can leave a crumpled up pack and a bunch of cigarette butts on the ground like they thumped them out from smoking them all day."

Porter jumped in, "Great idea. Major, can you give me some of the cigarettes so I can do it?"

"Porter, it's not that easy. Louie is our virus technician. You are going to have to meet us on the beach, pick Louie up and deliver him to the location. How soon can you pick him up?"

"I can meet you guys where I left the beach a couple of days ago. Meet me on the beach just south of the intersection of Hwy 332 and Bluewater Hwy. I can be there tomorrow afternoon if I don't run into any trouble."

Dix thought a moment. "Porter, I want you to meet us there just after dark. Do you have enough room for a rider and his gear?"

"Yes, sir. If you have some extra rope or paracord bring it along. Once we deliver the virus, I am going to need to load Louie, his gear and mine when I come back. I am at a dead end on this end. I've got to figure out how to slip in from the other direction or even by water."

"Porter, I'll see you tomorrow night. Be careful. I'll get off now, so you can talk to Cooney."

"Porter, please be careful. I very much need you to survive and live to load me up with a slew of grandkids."

"Believe me, Grandpa. I completely agree with you."

"If you can pull this off we will have achieved a great victory. It probably won't be remembered very long, but it will enable us to rebuild our civilization from scratch. Keep up the good work. I love you, Cooney out."

"Love you too, Grandpa."

## CHAPTER 33

Dix handed the radio back to Morgan. "I guess you guys heard all that over the speaker. Louie, looks like you'll be hitting the field. Morgan, locate our rendezvous point on the map. Tomorrow is going to be a busy day." He walked over and looked at Fox asleep in the bunk.

"Louie, I want you to write down a treatment protocol for me and Morgan. We need to know how much morphine, antibiotics and anything else we need to do in your absence."

"Will do, Major. The main thing is to make sure he gets three of those antibiotic pills a day in him for a week. After you give him a shot of morphine, give it a chance to kick in. Once it kicks in, you need to help him use his arm. He will lose the range of motion in his shoulder and arm if we don't manipulate it several times a day. You have to force liquids in him and get him to eat. We'll need to get him up and walking when he wakes up; if not, he could develop blood clots."

"Morgan, how long a boat ride is it to our rendezvous point?"

"Major, I've already got it figured out. We are about twenty-five miles out. It will take an hour in the fishing boat to get there, or about two hours in the stump thumper."

Dix thought a moment. "I don't think it's a good idea to take the stump thumper across the open ocean. Here are my plans: we are going to take the big boat with the stump thumper on it to the rendezvous point. Morgan, you'll drive the big boat, and we'll get Louie and Porter off on their mission. I'll take the stump thumper, slowly skirt the coast and see if I can get into Galveston Bay. You'll take the big boat back to the catamaran. Fox will be up and moving by tomorrow afternoon. He'll have his .45 where he can get his hands on it. We'll have radios. Do you have an extra handheld we can give to Porter?"

Morgan grinned. "I anticipated him needing one so I brought a couple of extras."

Fox stirred. "I've been listening with my eyes closed. I'm ready to get up now."

Louie walked over. "I'll help you up. It's the loss of blood that has you so weak. Your wound is bad, but not bad enough to keep you down."

Louie grabbed Fox's good arm and pulled him to a sitting position. Fox sat wobbling on the side of his bunk until he was steady.

"Louie, hang on to me while I walk to the head." Louie grabbed his left arm and eased him to his feet, and the two of them walked to the head. Once they reached the door, Fox went in.

"I've got it from here, Louie."

A few minutes later he came out and Louie asked, "Did everything come out ok?"

Fox looked up from concentrating on his feet and the floor. "The old kidneys are still working."

"That's good news. I'll hit you with some morphine and then get that arm moving."

"I am not wild about taking morphine; it kind of makes my skin crawl, but it beats being in agony."

Dix asked, "You feel like you can guard the boat by yourself?"

"Hell, yes, I can shoot my .45 with my left hand. There shouldn't be anything happening but the wind and waves."

"We'll all stay in touch by radio. Morgan will drop everyone off and get back here while Louie and Porter deploy the first weapon, and I will try to find another place we can deploy another one. For now, let's crash for the night. I'll take the first watch. Morgan, flip on those lights you had rigged under the boat. I want to catch some fish."

It was quiet; the radar was off, and they were radio silent so unless someone was coming out to this particular platform they could sit undetected. Soon schools of plankton were swarming in the water under the lights at the end of the catamaran. A few small fish started darting in and around the plankton storm. Suddenly, a dark shadow flashed through the light, and one of the small fish was neatly cut into two. Its head and tail drifted in the plankton swarm where other small fish quickly consumed the remnants. Dix took Fox's rod and dropped a line overboard with an artificial plastic jig on the hook. He dropped it through the plankton school and let it sink for a few seconds before pulling it back toward the fish. Dix soon had the live well filled with a mess of fish. The pump hummed as it circulated fresh water from the Gulf into the live well. The fish sat suspended in the water awaiting their date with the frying pan in the morning. Dix worried about his men heading into danger. He had no problem going on the hunt for the enemy by himself, but it was a different matter all together ordering men into battle. Getting himself killed was one thing; getting his men killed was another. It was a miracle that Fox wasn't dead. If he hadn't disabled the engine and silenced the guns on the attack boat, Fox would be.

At two a.m. he kicked Morgan's foot and whispered, "It's your turn, buddy. Wake me for the next watch. I'm going to let Louie get all the rest tonight. I don't want him slipping up while handling the bugs because he's exhausted. By the time he stays up all night with Porter on the bike, he won't be worth killing."

"I understand, Major. I'll let him sleep. See you in the morning." Dix disappeared into his small cabin. Morgan walked out on the fantail and clicked off the fishing lights. The generator was humming away keeping their precious cargo cold.

Dix awoke to the smell of frying trout and pancakes. Pancakes seemed to be one of Morgan's basic food groups. They were hearty, hot and easy to make. They spent the day putting their gear together for the mission. Dix elected to take Jake's AR15 and a pack of 30 round magazines. As always he wore his Browning 9mm in a shoulder holster and a Kbar knife. Louie was armed with a Remington 12 gauge pump shotgun with an eighteen inch barrel, a Colt Python .357 revolver and a bandolier of 12 gauge buckshot and slugs. Morgan packed an AK47 and usually did not carry a pistol, but today he had a Beretta 9mm on his hip. They cooked up more fish and hushpuppies. They put two days of food in plastic bags for Dix, Louie and Porter. They would have to live off the land if they ran out of food before they got back to the catamaran. Late in the afternoon, they topped off the fuel in the fishing boat and loaded all their gear. They all lit untampered cigarettes and puffed away until they had a pack of cigarette butts to scatter around the base of the guard house. Dix crumpled up the package and put it in a separate bag. Louie put on a respirator and long gloves and carefully loaded a vial of the virus into the well-padded ice chest. He completely sealed it with duct tape. In another pack he loaded a carton of cigarettes, the cigarette butts, crumpled package, syringe, and a jar of moonshine.

Fox was getting up and moving on his own. He was able to move his arm a little and refused to take more pain meds. He grimaced.

"I can't stand guard if I am on the pain meds. I'll take some plain aspirin and a sip of bourbon if I need anything." He stuck his .45 in his waistband and a couple of magazines in the pocket on his pants leg. His rifle was leaning in the corner next to his bunk. He could hold it in his right hand and shoot it from the waist with his left hand if needed.

Dix just watched in amusement. "Do you have everything situated where you can fight?"

"I'm ready."

"Fox, once we launch, we won't come back until Louie is on his way with Porter. If you get in trouble, call. Morgan and I can come back fast. Once I am launched, it will be up to Morgan in the big boat to assist you. I'll be in the thumper trying to slip into Galveston Bay. Does anyone have any questions? All of this sounds easy, but we haven't been on a mission yet that has gone as expected. It's getting late; let's launch."

They loaded everything and headed out. The seas were calm, and they were able to make good time heading to the rendezvous point. All three of them kept their eyes peeled for any boats or aircraft. They didn't expect any aircraft as the supply chain of parts had been broken. There was, however, the danger of drones.

Dix told Morgan, "I am going to try to locate a place where we can use the drone to deliver the cigarettes. I am starting to get a little skittish about getting shot at."

"You know, Major, I have never grown accustomed to that either." They both laughed and concentrated on the ride in. The boat was running a little slow to lessen the impact of the hull on the water. It was also trying to bounce on the water; the speed and trim on the motor had to be constantly adjusted to smooth out the ride.

As the boat approached the beach, they reduced the speed to dead slow. When the motor started hitting bottom, they killed it and raised it out of the water. A push pole with a foot on it was used to push the boat up to shore.

Right on schedule, Porter appeared out of nowhere. "Good to see you guys again. I hope you are ready to roll; I don't think we need to waste any time out here in the open."

Dix agreed, "Let's get Louie and Porter on their way." They quickly had Louie and his gear hauled up the beach where the Rokon was parked.

Dix looked at Louie. "If you get shot or blown up, try to crawl back here, because you might not make it if you let Porter doctor on you."

Porter grinned. "I learned a lot about first aid from the Major. I won't feed you if you get gut shot."

Laughing, they finished tying Louie's gear on the Rokon trailer. Porter climbed on, cranked it and motioned for Louie to climb on behind him.

Louie swung his leg over and settled in behind Porter. "Do you know how to run this thing?"

"Sure, it's easier to run than a pair of mules."

Dix shook their hands. "Good luck, boys; don't get yourselves hurt. Your job is very simple--deliver the virus to the bad guys."

Morgan came running up. "Wait, guys, here are your radios for communicating with us and each other. You can charge them with the solar charger you use for your regular radio. Try not to lose them; we don't have many left."

Porter and Louie waved and disappeared into the darkness.

Dix turned to Morgan. "Radio Fox and make sure he is still alive."

"Sure thing, Major." Morgan got on the radio and reached Fox. "We are getting ready to launch the stump thumper, is everything ok out there?"

"Everything's quiet out here. I'll call if I get in trouble. Fox out."

Morgan and Dix moved the fishing boat out into deeper water where they heaved the stump thumper into the water and loaded Dix's gear. The little Mercury outboard cranked on the second pull. Morgan handed him two five gallon cans of fuel and pushed him off.

"Good luck, Major; radio me if you need me to come pick you up."

"Thanks, Morgan, get back to the catamaran and put Fox back to bed. I'll keep you posted."

Dix stuck around long enough to watch Morgan turn the boat and disappear into the night.

The moonlight was strong enough that he could see quite well in the twilight. The little motor ran flawlessly as he crept along the coast. He traveled several miles within sight of the beach before he could see the opening to the Bay in the distance. He would be in extreme danger as he neared the Bay's entrance. If anyone were watching with thermal imaging equipment, he would look like a light bulb sitting in the water with the hot engine on the outboard shining even brighter, so he dropped the anchor over the side and waited. Because he needed the engine to cool off, he poured some water from the ocean over it. Fox practically had lived in the little boat for a year. He had some willow poles in the bottom, along with a large tarp. With poles set in pipes bolted to the gunnels, Fox could create a full shelter for the boat. The camo canvas fit completely over the boat and hung to the water. It could be rolled up on the sides, front and back as needed. Dix set the tarp and soaked it with water so that it was the same temperature as the water. He draped it over the motor in the back and rolled it up on the ocean side and front. He left it partially down on the land side so that his body was shielded from view. He left a spot where he could paddle between the tarp and the side of the boat. Over the next couple of hours, he paddled the boat toward the opening to the Bay. Ever so quietly, he entered the Bay staying as close to the middle of it as possible. As he entered the Bay, he lowered both sides and just left the front open so he could see straight ahead. In the distance, he spotted a sunken tug still attached to a string of barges that were half submerged. Upon reaching the derelict, he paddled the boat so that it rested between the exposed bridge and over the partially sunken string of barges. He tied up to the tug and rolled up the tarp high enough that he could see in every direction. The tug still felt warm from the residual heat from having been sitting in the sun all day. That heat would mask his thermal image for the time being. He listened quietly to water gently lapping against the boat. He took his binoculars and peered into the darkness. The moonlight allowed him to make out piers and facilities along the coast line in both directions. The binoculars magnified the light making things much more visible than with his naked eyes. All at once he saw what he had been looking for: a cigarette flared as its owner took a draw from it. Cupping his ears, he could hear men talking, and they weren't speaking English or Spanish. He took out his compass and looked at the luminous arrow and determined that they were almost exactly due west from where he sat. He spent another hour searching the edges of the Bay with the binoculars. He found another guard post on the opposite side of the Bay entrance. From a distance the stump thumper looked like a big piece of driftwood. It was painted brown and all the wear and tear on it left it mottled and smeared with mud. Dix couldn't see the men well enough to determine if they had night vision equipment. All he knew was that if he were the enemy commander, this would be one of the places it would be deployed. He checked the time on his watch; it was two a.m. He would need to either go further up the Bay, head back out or hide where he was. He could see a small piece of drift wood floating about ten feet from the barge out in the Bay. It was not floating in any particular direction. There was no current, and that could only mean one thing: the tide was turning. He had evidently paddled in at low tide; otherwise, the outgoing tide would have made it impossible to paddle into the Bay. With the tide turning, all he would need to do was ride it in, and that would put him northeast of Texas City. Galveston Island lay to his left and Bolivar Peninsula lay to his right. Due north was the Texas City Dike where there would, no doubt, be another post for the guards to fire from. From those three points, men with cannons or .50 caliber weapons could stop anything moving in or out of the Bay. With Hwy 45 shut off, they could cut off all marine traffic other than their own. With the refinery behind extensive security fences, it would be difficult for anyone or anything to get in or out. Galveston Island was probably a no man's land with mines and snipers placed around it. Dix noticed that the wind had picked up. Off to the west, he saw the distant flash of lightning. He didn't relish being out in the big Bay in a storm with the waves and lightning. If he could survive the storm, it would provide excellent cover to get into the Bay and close to the refinery. No matter what, he would have to find a place to hide or risk running the motor and making a run for the ocean.

He dug out his radio. "Morgan, are you at the catamaran?"

"Yes, sir, everything is fine. I've got Fox fed, gave him his antibiotic and put him to bed. How's it going?"

"I've made it into Galveston Bay, and I'm hid out in the middle of the Bay on a sunken tug and string of barges. What kind of range does that drone of yours have?"

"I can get about five miles out of it before I have to return and put in new batteries."

"How much hover time do you have once you are out that far?"

"None. If it's windy like it is now, it has less time and distance."

"From where I'm sitting, I am about one mile from two guard posts and about a mile and a half from another one. I can probably get within a mile or two of Texas City at night, but I am going to have to find a place to hide and to time the tides. The tide is getting ready to run into the Bay; unless I run the motor, I won't be paddling out for another ten or twelve hours. Have you heard anything from Porter and Louie?"

"They are camping in the woods and are planning on planting the bugs before lunch tomorrow. They are going to call once they verify the bugs have been delivered and if they are able to verify that they were picked up."

"There's a storm coming in. Do you think you can handle the boat by yourself?"

"I think so. I may have to untie from the platform and ride it out under power from out at sea. I'm sure it won't be fun, but the boat is very seaworthy and plenty big enough to ride out anything short of a hurricane."

"If something happens to Louie, do you think you can help me deploy the bugs via the drone?"

"It'll be no problem, Major. We'll just have to have someone on the catamaran that can run it. Fox won't be in any shape to do anything much more than shoot his pistol for several weeks or longer."

"As soon as this storm gets here, I am going to take the thumper up into the harbor and find a spot where I can hide until it passes. I'm not going to try and run this little boat in the surf. I will be doing good to keep it from sinking in the rain. I'll let you know if I want you to attempt to pick me up at the rendezvous point. I have an idea. Jernigan out."

The rain was starting to come down as Dix paddled the thumper around, and just as he hoped, he found an open doorway on the back of the bridge. He shined his flashlight in and found what he was looking for. The high water mark showed how high the tides had been getting inside the vessel. There was enough room to float the thumper inside the area without sinking it at high tide. The door opening was just barely wide enough to get the little boat in. He paddled in and secured the boat to a ladder. He was protected from the wind, lightning, waves and rain. His small aluminum flashlight illuminated the room. When lightning struck outside, it put a quick shaft of light down through the opening to the stair well. Taking the flashlight in his teeth and with his rifle on his back, he ascended the ladder up into a hallway behind the bridge. One direction led to the galley and a bunk area; the other to the bridge. He made a quick pass through the floor to make certain he was alone. He was pleasantly surprised to find a case of unopened coffee and some canned goods. This was an absolute miracle. He had to be very careful where he shined the flashlight. A light, even a small one, out in the middle of the Bay could be seen for miles in the pitch black dark. The flashes of lightning were a big help in keeping him hidden. In what appeared to be a TV room for the crew, he found some recliners covered with imitation leather. He sprayed one down with some spray cleaner from the galley and turned it around so that the base on one side rested on the floor and the base on the other side on the tilted wall. He could then recline in it without turning it over and falling out. He was asleep in an instant. No one would be out in this weather. So unless the storm broke the tow boat and barges loose from the bottom, he would be safe tonight.

When he awoke the next morning, the sun was already up. He climbed out of the recliner and made a quick daylight inspection of the wreck. The floor was at a 30 degree slant making walking a little awkward. He climbed onto the bridge where he could see in all directions. There was a spot where they could launch the drone just outside the doors. All he would need to do was make a level surface out of some of the cabinet doors off of the consoles on the bridge. He pulled out his binoculars and observed the enemy in their guard houses on either side. Both posts had cannons and heavy machine guns in place. He looked northwest towards the Texas City Dyke and soon located another guard house with guns in place just as he expected. Nothing was going in or out of the harbor unless they passed these points. There was no way of knowing if they had night vision capability; therefore, he would have to assume that they did. He dug around in the can goods he had found and selected a can of stew for breakfast. Today would be a day of watching and waiting. He could only leave under the cover of darkness, and only if it weren't storming.

After several hours of observing the activities, he determined that the guard changes took place at 7:00 a.m. and 3:00 p.m., so the third change would be at 11:00 p.m. With a little luck, they could make the bug drop near those times. He called Morgan on the radio.

"How did you guys weather the storm last night?"

"I had to untie from the rig and head out into open water until the waves subsided. Other than a little puking, we are ok. Fox looks a lot better this morning."

"That's saying a lot. He didn't look too good to begin with. I'm glad we had to cut that pony tail off a few weeks back when they tried to cut his head off."

"You've got a point there, Major. He is doing a lot better considering what he's been through. When do you want me to retrieve you?"

"As soon as you hear from Louie and Porter, radio me back. We'll coordinate you picking us all up at the same time. Have you heard anything out of them as of yet?"

"Not a word. I'm sure we'll hear from them as soon as they get to a safe location. Don't worry. I expect the only way they could catch Porter is with a trap baited with a young lady."

"That seems to catch him every time. I'm hidden in a half sunken tugboat attached to a string of half sunken barges in the middle of the entrance to Galveston Bay."

Dix proceeded to explain to Morgan where the three gun emplacements were located so they could find them in case he was killed or captured. Dix sat back, watched and waited.

## CHAPTER 34

With Louie behind him, Porter drove away from the beach and onto the road he had driven on his first day there. He wasn't running his lights, so he ran slowly. The last thing he wanted to do was wreck and upset the load he was carrying. He didn't want a broken vial of the plague in their laps. They ran on until they were back on the trail through the Wildlife Refuge. Porter had to run with his lights on here so that he could see the trail, and when they reached the road on the opposite side, they stopped, turned off the light and waited for their eyes to adjust to the darkness. As soon as they stopped, the hordes of mosquitoes found them. Porter fished the bug repellant out of his pack, and they had some relief from the biting swarm. The buzzing from their wings was nonstop as the vile creatures searched in vain for a spot that wasn't coated with Deet.

Once their eyes adjusted to the darkness, they headed down the road, turned at the intersection and proceeded east toward the guard house.

Porter called back to Louie, "Keep your eyes peeled. I left a broken beer bottle on the right hand side of the road next to the pavement; that's where we turn and make camp."

"I'll keep an eye out."

After about five miles they found the bottle, turned into the old boat launch and found the spot where Porter had camped before. Once again it was basically a cold camp. Louie broke out the sacks of fish and hushpuppies.

"The Major sent you some fish."

Porter answered in a whisper, "Thanks for the supper. Keep your voice low. We're only about a mile from the guard shack. I hope they didn't hear our motor. It isn't very loud, and I was going slow, but you never know."

"Do you think they'll come looking?"

"I doubt it. I just don't want them on alert expecting trouble. Also be careful around the water. There are some huge gators around here. I had to kill one trying to get me the last time I was here. I think they are losing their fear of man since they aren't seeing any more of us. I need you to also understand what we are up against here. Both sides of the road are mined. The only place you can walk is on the pavement or in the water. If you get within sight of the elevated guard house and you are on the pavement, they will shoot you. One of the guards has a scoped rifle."

"If the water is full of gators and the road is out, how do we get in?"

"I will go in by water. Hopefully, I can kill any gators with my suppressed pistol. I will engage the guards, and if I prevail, I'll call you to come down the paved road with the bugs. We'll set the scene and see if we can find a tree I can climb where I can see if they have taken the bait. If we can't be certain they took the bait, we will rendezvous with the Major. We won't be able to approach this guard house again, because they'll quickly realize I came in by water."

"What time do we start in the morning?"

"I figure to shoot them before lunch. I'll call you to deploy the bugs and be out by lunch. If I can't find a tree, we'll come back here, get on the Rokon and head back to the woods. Then we'll radio the Major and wait for orders."

"Dude, that sounds like a plan. Do you want me to help you kill the guards?"

"Louie, you do what you do best, and I'll do what I do best. I am simply going to slip in, and as soon as I can see both of them at the same time, I will shoot them. If I can't get a shot, I'll wait until the guard change, and I will kill them while they are climbing down and while I can hem most of them up inside the van. If I survive, we will deploy the bugs as planned."

"Damn, Porter, do you think you can shoot that many of them at once?"

"So long as my gun doesn't jam, it should be doable."

"Can you hit that good?"

"Yes, the only problem would be if the van windows and metal cause the bullets to be deflected. I will be pouring a lot of lead through the vehicle. I doubt anyone will walk away. Only a lucky shot from one of them is going to stop me. Most people can't shoot straight when they are being shot at or hit, but I can shoot straight while being shot at. Luckily, I have only taken one good hit, but I overcame the pain and shock and kept fighting."

Louie lamented, "I've never shot anybody; I'm pretty sure I can though."

"Have you lost anyone yet?"

"My whole family was killed, and I was left for dead."

"Just keep them in your mind's eye and remember that the bad guys are no different from the people who murdered your family; vengeance is a great source of strength."

"Porter, that's why I'm here instead of hiding in the woods somewhere."

They unrolled a tarp and strung it between two trees. A storm was rolling in. It would be a miserable night with the wind and lightning. It suddenly occurred to Porter that if he were to attack during the storm he could probably slip in during the distraction of the storm and make his kill. Porter took out his pistol and screwed the suppressor onto the barrel. He slipped on a poncho, and carefully taped anything that clinked or made noise.

"Louie, I'm going while it's storming and kill the two that are there now. They won't see me if I am wearing a poncho covered in cold rain water. Once I get under the guard house, I'll simply climb the ladder, kill them and come back and get you. I'll be shooting my suppressed pistol. If you hear shooting, it will probably be them."

"You sure make me nervous, Porter. Be careful, dude."

The lightning flashed and revealed a grin on Porter's face. "Remember, don't walk off the pavement and get blown up."

With that, Porter turned and disappeared into the darkness. He found the edge of the road and followed it in the dark. The only time they could see him was if they were looking out at the instant the lightning struck. Porter thought *I bet they are shaking in their pants sitting in an elevated structure during a lightning storm.*

He took his time not wanting to fall. He held his arm over his face so that it would not shine out from under the poncho. It was not likely they would be using the night vision. The lightning flashes would likely white out the display, and if they were smart, they would have it off. He was soon under the structure. He took off his poncho and leaned his AK47 against the nearest support post and bracing board. He could see light coming through the cracks in the floor and hear the nervous chatter of the men. The elevated hut was no more than eight feet by twelve feet. There was no door, and there were broad windows with an extended porch roof over them. Camo netting was hanging down from the eaves making the structure almost invisible. To his delight the wind was moving the trees, and their limbs were brushing the structure. The rain hitting the tin roof further blocked any sound Porter could make. He turned his cap backwards and carefully ascended the stairs and stopped just as he reached the floor where he could peer in. Both guys were sitting looking out at the storm and talking, and both of their weapons were stowed on nails out of their way. To his delight both men were smoking. Porter reached into his belt, retrieved his pistol and in one quick motion shot the far one through the side of his head and hit the other one three times through the upper back. He pitched forward and landed on the first one. Porter climbed on in and popped each one through the head once again. He stamped out their cigarettes. There was no need to burn down the house and ruin their trap. Porter double timed it back to where Louie and the Rokon waited.

Louie jumped when Porter showed up. "Damn, you scared the crap out of me!"

"Get yourself cleaned up; you're up to bat."

"That didn't take long; are they dead?"

"It doesn't take long when everything goes as planned. Let's roll. Pack up; we won't be coming back here."

In a few short minutes, they broke camp and were at the guard house. Louie put on his gloves and mask and sat under the shed where it was dry. He soon had three packs of cigarettes loaded. Porter scattered the cigarettes butts and crumpled pack on the ground in front of the main window. Porter pointed up the ladder.

"The guards are up there." They climbed up, and Louie planted the contaminated packs in the pockets of the dead guards. One pack was left in the backpack of one of the men. Porter checked the time; it was 4:00 a.m. The shift would probably change soon, so he and Louie hopped on the Rokon and headed back.

Porter called out, "We will never find a tree in the dark I can climb and watch from. We are just going to have to act on faith that nicotine addicts will not let the cigarettes go to waste."

"We'll know in a few weeks. It won't be long before they catch and start spreading the plague."

"I'll feel better after we get back to the woods where we can hide. Anytime we are in the open we are in danger. This will be my third trip to the rendezvous point using the same trails and road. A patient man will be waiting for me to come back.

As they reached the road turning back south, they realized that the storm had been worse in this direction. There were more trees and limbs on the road. These obstacles slowed them to a crawl. It was after noon before they made it to the trail through the Wildlife Management area. As expected, there were even more limbs and trees down here than in the road they had just traveled.

Porter stopped. "This road isn't long, but we are going to have a hard haul getting through this. Call Morgan so we can report." Louie pulled out the radio and reached Morgan.

"Morgan, this is Louie. We delivered the bugs."

"Great news, Louie. When do you want to arrange for pickup?"

"Let me put Porter on." Louie handed Porter the radio.

"Morgan, this is Porter. If we can make it off this trail, I would like to meet y'all at the same spot after dark. It's going to take us several hours to cut our way down this road after the storm. If I see we are going to be delayed, I'll radio you in time to call it off."

"Great, I'll let the Major know. Morgan out."

Porter handed the radio back to Louie. "Now, we have to work our way though this mess so we can meet them back at the rendezvous point after dark."

It took them all afternoon to make their way through the tangle of fallen limbs and trees. The sun was setting when they popped out on the road. Before they could continue, they were surrounded by a half dozen Reds with weapons trained on them.

The leader said, "I was hoping you would come back through here again, what are you boys up too?"

Porter quickly spoke up, "We just swapped the Chinese a carton of cigarettes for a vial of the plague vaccine, and we are on our way back to our families and to trade some for food."

"We've heard they have a vaccine. Tell you what I'll do. You guys give me the vaccine, and we'll let you live."

"We went to a lot of trouble to get it. It's not easy finding cigarettes to swap for it."

"How much of the vaccine do you have?"

Louie quickly caught on to what Porter was doing. "There are about fifty doses. All you do is put one drop under your tongue."

"I told you if you give us the vaccine, we'll let you live."

Porter left Louie sitting on the Rokon, walked back and untied the little ice chest that held the virus and a syringe.

"Here you go. Can we leave now? It's the least you can do for us saving your lives." Louie cringed as the man opened the ice chest and pulled out the vial of virus.

He spoke up, "One drop under the tongue is all you need." Porter cranked the Rokon.

"Can we go now? I've got to locate some more cigarettes so we can get some more vaccine for our families, and can I count on being able to come back through here in a couple of days?"

"Ok, boy, we'll pass the word to our guys to leave you alone and will let you know if we need any more."

As they pulled away Porter looked over his shoulder. The Reds had the vial open and were drawing up the virus in a syringe.

Louie said, "Thank God, we were heading away before they opened it. It's not safe being near it without a respirator and gloves. He was probably infected just handling the vial. I've got another ice chest stowed in the catamaran.

Porter asked, "How much virus do we have left?"

"We have three more vials, that's enough virus to take out several million people."

They ran flat out toward the beach.

# CHAPTER 35

Dix spent the day watching the guard houses and verifying the eleven, seven and three guard rotation times. He also constructed the landing platform for the drone to land on. They could install it when they returned.

Morgan came on the radio. "The boys delivered their bugs and are on their way to the rendezvous."

"I knew Porter could pull it off. That kid is seasoned and tough. I'll head out with the tide and meet you guys. Fox still improving?"

"Yep, he's getting around good. I'm sure glad I don't have to change his diaper."

Fox could be heard in the background. "That'll be the day."

The sun was getting low in the sky, and the tide was heading out to sea. He wet down the tarp over the stump thumper and prepared it for the ride. He loaded the case of coffee and the can goods into the bottom of the boat and shoved off. He left the sides down and the front open. He paddled out into the Bay and let the current carry him toward the Gulf. When he was well out from the Bay, he took down the tarp and willow sticks and stowed everything back in the bottom of the boat, before pulling on the starter cord. It started on the second pull, and once again he was heading down the coast just on the seaside of the surf. After several miles, he ran up on Morgan with the fishing boat floating in the shallows with the surf trying to beach it. Porter, Morgan and Louie had the Rokon, trailer and gear loaded in the boat. It took all of them to get the thumper back on the fishing boat. They were soon heading across the open water back to the catamaran. Because they were all exhausted, there was little talk. When they reached the catamaran, Fox was waiting on the rear deck.

"How did it go, boys; did you pull it off?"

Dix grinned. "We delivered three packs."

Porter spoke up, "Major, Louie and I have some more news. We were cornered by the Reds and were able to bargain for our freedom with the plague 'vaccine' we had gotten from the Chinese."

Louie was laughing. "They think they have 50 doses of vaccine. I told them that one drop under the tongue was the cure and preventative."

Dix looked in disbelief. "Quick thinking, guys; good work. Morgan, get on the horn with all our people and tell them to call all their contacts and stress that there is no vaccine. Also notify Cooney that Porter is alive and well and on board the catamaran."

Morgan got on the radio, and the warning went out.

Dix looked around at Louie. "You need to check your body parts. You're liable to be missing a few that you might not have missed yet." Everyone laughed as Louie pretended to count his fingers and toes.

Dix clapped Porter on the shoulder. "It's sure good to see you again, Sergeant. Can you stick around until we're sure the virus has taken hold? We should know in three weeks."

"Major, I'm here till you tell me to go."

"Tomorrow, Morgan, Louie and I are going to take the thumper back into the Bay to a half sunken tugboat, and we are going to launch the drone and deliver cigarettes to three guard posts. We will go back in after dark and set up in the tug. We'll then radio for pickup. Congratulations, Porter, you're our new boat operator."

Morgan was busy putting radios back in charging cradles, and Louie was disinfecting gloves, mask and clothes.

Dix looked around at the crew. "It is getting a little stout in here. I want everyone, but Fox, to take a shower or go for a swim in the Gulf, and I want your clothes washed. Flip on the lights under the boat, and I'll catch us some fish."

The next morning they were all up early cooking the fish. Their clothes were drying on a line they had run the night before. Porter and Louie were refreshed after catching up on their sleep. Dix pulled out the maps and showed the men the location of the tug, and where the three guard houses and gun emplacements were located. They all agreed that the tug was the ideal platform from which to launch the drone. Dix got on the radio with Butch and told him to hold off on starting the second mission unless they went silent. It appeared as though the first bugs were delivered. Once a pack of cigarettes was delivered to each of the remaining guard houses, the fate of the remaining Chinese army would be sealed. Dix got on the radio with Colonel Miller.

"Colonel, this is Jernigan; I just wanted to give you an update. The first bugs have been delivered. If all goes as planned, we'll deploy the final bait tonight. We'll then sit back and see what happens."

"That's great news, Jernigan. How's our boy Porter?"

"He's alive and well. How goes the rest of the army and the country?" Dix flipped on the external speaker so the men could hear what the Colonel was saying.

"Jernigan, we are back in radio contact with the West Coast and the East Coast. We have about a thousand men in our command scattered out from Texas to Georgia. We have a few isolated pockets of people not infected. From what I can tell, we have eight or ten women for every man left alive. The women couldn't fight and take care of their kids, so we now have quite an imbalance. I figure that will level out pretty quick in a couple of generations. We hear almost nothing out of the Northeast. Between the winter and the plague, they are wiped out. The West Coast is almost silent. The plague cleaned out the Americans as well as the communists. The water pumps quit pumping, and all of that is now turning back into desert. We have a good population base in the South and in the states on either side of the Mississippi River up into the middle of Missouri. When I say a good population base, I am saying we have a five to ten percent survival rate. Not enough to resume life as we once knew, but plenty of good breeding stock. I am afraid we will be living a medieval lifestyle until we get the population built back up a bit."

Dix glanced around the room. "Colonel, what's the word from around the world?"

"We have picked up some shortwave broadcast from Australia and New Zealand. They have people living out in the middle of nowhere in those countries. We also picked up some broadcast out of Russia from wilderness areas. Everything else is totally silent. We are following up on some Intel that our former leaders are located in an underground bunker in the Ozarks. I have three teams looking for the bastards now. It seems there is a huge facility located in giant mines that were fronting as food warehouses and distribution centers. If they are there, we'll find them. I've got men following Porter's lead and traveling on horseback." Porter grinned at the prospect.

Dix replied, "If you find the hole they are hiding in, call Cooney; I mean Captain Jones, and arrange to pick up some bugs for them."

"Don't worry. We will come running."

"Colonel, we've got some work to do, so we'll give you an update in a few days. Jernigan out."

They waited until almost dark before heading out. Morgan taught Porter how to run the GPS on the boat as well as how to use the compass. If he got lost heading back to the catamaran, he would call Fox who could turn on a light at the top of the mast for a few moments.

Fox called out as they were leaving, "I wish I was going with you. I hate sitting around the boat wondering what's going on."

Dix looked over his shoulder. "You did your part Fox, relax for once, keep exercising that shoulder. I'm sure you've still got some fighting to do before all of this is over."

Porter figured out the fishing boat operations quickly, and they soon had the stump thumper in the water and loaded. They pulled one of the auxiliary batteries out of the back of the fishing boat, and set it over in the thumper. It would be used to recharge the drone batteries as needed. Their goal was to deposit cigarettes at all three of the guard posts. They would consider the mission a success if they made successful drops in at least two locations. After installing the willow poles and the tarp, Dix hosed it off with the hose that was used to wash down the boat deck after fishing. As usual the little motor on the thumper cranked on the second pull, and they were off. The boat was loaded heavily with three men and gear so they elected to run dead slow with the little motor. With the wind blowing, it would have been impossible for anyone to hear the little motor running more than a hundred feet or so away. They soon found the sunken tug and barges, and eased through the open hatch and tied up to the ladder. Morgan took a head lamp and his pistol and made sure the decks were clear. Everything was just as Dix left it. Dix showed them the launch platform. They soon had it set up, and the drone was sitting on top of it. Dix pulled out his compass and showed them the headings where they needed to look in order to see the guard houses.

Morgan soon had them spotted. "Major, I think with the night vision on this drone we can fly over there and get low enough to make a drop. This wind is going to hurt us, but we have no way of knowing if it will let up any time soon."

"Let's do it. If you see the battery getting low, retrieve it; otherwise, we are going to have to use the Porter method of delivery. Which one of y'all wants to slip up there and shoot them through the head?"

"Major, I'll do my dead level best to not lose the drone."

Without a word, Louie took the ice chest into the TV room and with a headlamp donned his mask and gloves. He carefully drew some of the virus from the vile and secured the top. He inserted the needle tip just under the paper and on top of the filter tips. He set the cigarettes down and laid the syringe next to the vial in the ice chest. The vial was sitting on top of a towel, and below the towel were plastic bags full of ice from the freezer. Louie secured the lid and returned to the bridge carrying the cigarettes. As he and Morgan had rehearsed earlier, he opened the basket under the drone, inserted the pack and then closed it. He turned to Dix.

"Pour some of that moonshine over my gloves."

Dix did as he was asked; whereupon, Louie rubbed his hands together to make sure the gloves were coated. With his wet gloved hands, he took off the face mask and proceeded to disinfect it as well. He then closed the basket side and looked at Morgan.

"She's ready to go."

Morgan looked at Dix. "Let the battle begin."

With that, Morgan fired up the drone, and it was soon flying at a thousand feet above the Bay heading to the first guard post off to their west. Once over the house, Morgan placed the drone in a hovering mode. He zoomed in the camera, and in its infrared mode, they could see everything. He allowed the drone to reduce altitude until it was a mere fifty feet above the guard house. Allowing for the wind, he moved it in a slight southeasterly direction. He tapped the release button, and they watched as the white pack of cigarettes fell to the sidewalk just outside the door. He tapped the home button, and the drone headed back and was soon sitting on its platform. Louie used the spray bottle with soap from the kitchen, and gently sprayed off the basket and wiped it dry with some paper towels. He looked around at Morgan.

"It's safe to change the battery now."

Morgan pulled the battery pack off and set it on a charger hooked to the battery from the fishing boat. He then replaced the battery with a fresh one, and they repeated the process at the second target. The wind grabbed the pack and blew it out into the driveway in front of the guard shack. It was not ideal, but well within view where it could be found. This battery was almost exhausted when the drone returned to the platform, because it had been bucking a headwind the entire way back. Louie repeated the process; and they now had two batteries being recharged. Dix looked at Morgan.

"How long before the batteries are hot?"

"At least two hours, Major."

"Get the drone and the platform in here out of sight. I'm going to bed. You guys can do what you want. Get me up when you are ready to try again."

Dix was dead asleep and was dreaming about Rachel when Morgan woke him up.

"Major, we're ready for the next one."

"Make it happen, boys."

The drone buzzed to life and headed east to the last guard house. This one hit the sidewalk and wouldn't be missed. The drone returned again, and they waited for morning.

Dix pointed at the guard post. "Can you run the drone over in the morning, so we can see if any of the packs were picked up?"

Morgan cautioned, "I'll have to leave it pretty high or they may see it, but we can zoom in. Unless the wind is very bad, we should be able to see the pack just fine if it's still there."

"Make sure the drone and platform are pulled in before daylight, I don't want one of them to be bird watching and catch sight of it."

"We'll put the platform out just long enough to launch and retrieve once it is daylight."

The next morning the wind had calmed; they loaded another pack of cigarettes in the drone, flew it over the first guard house and hovered at five-hundred feet. Morgan zoomed in on the side-walk and found the pack was missing. He retrieved the drone, and replaced the battery while wearing his gloves and mask. It was soon on its way. The second pack had been flattened by a vehicle. They noticed that there was an area where some of the soldiers were fishing. Morgan released a pack where it would silently fall behind them. He raced the drone back, and once again it almost didn't make the trip. After disinfecting it, they carried it and the platform inside and waited for the batteries to recharge.

It was after lunch by the time the batteries were ready for use, and they were able to verify that the remaining two packs had disappeared. They waited until after dark, repeated the process of wetting down the canvas tarp and headed back to the Gulf. Porter picked them up as planned. Soon, they were all aboard the catamaran. Fox broke out a bottle of bourbon, and they passed it around until it was empty.

Dix took the last swig. "Fellows, y'all have done a good job. None of us have gotten killed yet, and all we have to do is sit around for another three weeks to see if they start disappearing. Do we have enough diesel to keep the generator running to keep the remaining virus alive?"

Morgan nodded. "That little generator doesn't pull much. It is using about half what I anticipated. We can run it for several months if we never use the main engine."

"That's good news. We'll just sit out here and fish for the next two or three weeks. Once we see that the plague is killing them, we'll put Porter out so he can go home, and we'll head back to the camp to decide what we're going to do."

# CHAPTER 36

Porter came walking down the long drive to Indian Joe's house. He was wearing a new pair of boots he found in an abandoned store about fifty miles back. The boots that Charlie Cross had given him a long time ago finally wore out. He stopped at an abandoned ranch about ten miles up the road and bathed in the water tank under the windmill that was dutifully pumping away. His rifle was still on his back and his pistol was still in his shoulder holster. His radio and what food he had left were in his backpack. Everything else was still on the Rokon hidden in a barn a hundred or so miles back down the road. He walked around the overturned truck with the dead Red in it and was greeted by Indian Joe's two old dogs who were barking while running down the driveway toward him. They were soon wagging their tails and greeting him. Indian Joe walked out on the porch cradling his rifle in his arm. Old Dollar and Ruth came walking over to the corral gate hoping for a cookie.

Indian Joe asked, "What happened to your motorcycle, Porter?"

"It ran out of gas about a hundred miles down the road. I guess I underestimated how much traveling I had to do.

Indian Joe turned around and called through the door, "You girls can quit fretting; Porter's back."

All three came running out and buried him in kisses and tears. Ally proudly said, "I told y'all he'd come back."

Hundreds of miles away back in Louisiana, Dix was standing outside his camp with his arms around Rachel. His two white eyed Catahoula Curs were sitting nearby. Old man Beagle was mending his nets next door. Fox was sitting next door with Butch's baby sister trimming his hair and beard. A barbecue grill had a trail of smoke curling from around the lid and out of the little smoke stack. Dix and Fox were wearing their pistols, but their rifles were on racks in the house.

Rachel gave him a big kiss. "There's something I need to tell you."

# CHAPTER 37

The speaker sat back in her chair and closed the old journal. The class clamored.

"What happened after that?"

"Well, let's see, Major Dix Jernigan lived another forty years. He and Rachel had two daughters and one son and moved to an abandoned plantation south of Natchez, MS, where he farmed and raised a few cattle. He was nominated, against his will, as a candidate for Governor and won by a landslide. He served two terms then returned to the life of a quiet farmer. He had a number of grandchildren. Rachel lived another fifteen years after his death. They are both buried on the grounds, and his descendants live there to this day.

One of the boys raised his hand. "What about Porter?"

"I think you all know what happened to Porter." They all gave a puzzled look. "Has anyone ever heard of James Jones?"

The class erupted. "He was the fifth New Constitution President. He was the one who insisted on having mules pull his carriage."

"That's right; his name was James Porter Jones. Can you guess why he was fond of mules?" A little girl giggled. "He went back to the Cross ranch after they determined that the virus couldn't survive outside of a living host very long. They buried the dead son and cleaned up the house. His grandfather Cooney moved over to the ranch after the Mississippi River levees failed in Louisiana. Porter had nine children with his girls and dozens of grandchildren and great grandchildren.

My great grandmother five generations ago was Ally Jones. It was her journal and the journal of Dix Jernigan's youngest daughter Rebecca that I used to create this history of what took place. Porter lived to be eighty-nine years old. He outlived Sandy and Katy; Ally survived him and lived to be ninety-seven years old. They are all buried under the Cross Oak along with Cooney Jones, the Cross family and two mules. I still live in the old ranch house and travel around to give these lectures on what it took to save our country. That is why my buggy is pulled by a mule and why my name is Ally Jones Jernigan. I am married to one of Dix Jernigan's great grandsons several times removed.

As a side note, both of the men wore their pistols until the day they died. If you will notice, President Jones is depicted in a painting wearing his pistol when he was sworn in as President.

Dix Jernigan's headstone reads:

**Dix Jernigan**

**Born 1964 -- Died 2059**

The words under it simply read:

**We Lived, We Fought and We Survived.**

Read on for an exciting sneak peak of

**Mitch's Mountain**

**By**

**Ken Gallender**

They were well absorbed in the meeting when the lights went out; a loud boom from an electrical transformer located outside shook the building.

The boss said, "Great, it looks like the transformer has blown; we may get the day off. Let's try to conference by speaker on my cell phone." He fiddled with his phone. "That's strange, my phone is dead."

Tony asked, "Can't get a signal?"

"No, it's dead as a door knob."

Tony looked down at his phone, and it too was dead. Everyone in the room pulled out their phones and found them completely dead. One of the guys dropped his phone; the battery was overloading. Smoking, the phone sparked and died.

One of the inspectors removed his hearing aids and started checking the batteries. "That's strange; the batteries seldom go out at the same time."

It was at that moment; Tony realized that an EMP (electromagnetic pulse) event had taken place. Tony started to mention to the group that he thought that an EMP had taken place, but decided against the idea. He figured that everyone would think him a nut. He went back to his office, tried to fire up his laptop, and just as he feared, it was dead. The portable radio that he carried in his computer bag wasn't working either. None of the emergency lights had come on.

42872367R00209

Made in the USA
Lexington, KY
11 July 2015